AF805310

Praise for HOPELESSLY *Teavoted*

"A witchy romance with cozy vibes, a cursed heroine, and just the right amount of spice. What more could you ask for?"

—Kami Garcia, #1 *New York Times* bestselling coauthor of *Beautiful Creatures*

"The perfect magical read, *Hopelessly Teavoted* is full of charm and yearning and so much witchy fun! Audrey Goldberg Ruoff's debut belongs on everyone's TBR!"

—Brigid Kemmerer, *New York Times* bestselling author of *Warrior Princess Assassin*

"*Hopelessly Teavoted* is a romantic, devilish delight. With wit, flair, and a quirky friends-to-lovers couple, this book is just the right mix of sweet, steamy, and swoony."

—Gwenda Bond, *New York Times* bestselling author of *The Frame-Up*

"*Hopelessly Teavoted* is a colorful, sweet, and swoony debut that makes you feel like it's spooky season all year round! This tender friends-to-lovers romance scorches with yearning and sexual tension, with a unique, paranormal twist. Audrey Goldberg Ruoff writes with all the whimsy, sparkles, and heart to create a magical world readers will want to sink into with a warm cup of tea of their own. I can't wait for everyone to fall under its spell!"

—Mallory Marlowe, *USA Today* bestselling author of *Love and Other Conspiracies*

"If you're looking for *Pushing Daisies* vibes, a cozy Stars Hollow-esque setting, and the weird, loving family dynamics of the Addams Family, *Hopelessly Teavoted* is the perfect romance for you. It gave me things I didn't even know to want—like you've heard of a they take the gloves off scene, but have you ever heard of one where they leave the gloves on? With her warm, assured voice, Audrey Goldberg Ruoff is an absolute star."

—Alicia Thompson, *USA Today* bestselling author of *Never Been Shipped*

"*Hopelessly Teavoted* is a flirty and supernaturally charged romance filled with serious yearning and bite. Readers eager for a tenderhearted and tantalizing read decked out with Gothic goodness and sensual banter will definitely add *Hopelessly Teavoted* to their TBR pile. Goldberg Ruoff, through her whimsical prose, shows that grief can make way for hope and the best love can feel like a never-ending enchantment."

—Celestine Martin, author of *Witchful Thinking*, *Kiss and Spell*, and *Deja Brew*

"Whimsical, horny, and—despite its macabre premise—heartwarmingly optimistic, *Hopelessly Teavoted* is a thoroughly charming debut. Audrey Goldberg Ruoff is an exciting new voice in romance, and I can't wait to see what magical world she cooks up next."

—Rachel Runya Katz, author of *Whenever You're Ready* and *Isn't It Obvious?*

"A delightfully funny romance filled with heartwarming humor and heartfelt charm, *Hopelessly Teavoted* delivers a perfect love story with a side of tender, heart-wrenching thoughtfulness about grief, healing, and how to make the most of second chances."

—Laura R. Samotin, author of *The Sins on Their Bones*

"*Hopelessly Teavoted* is a steamy, gothy, whimsical small-town romance full of heart!"

—Jen Comfort, author of *What Is Love?*

VENGEFULLY *Matched*

VENGEFULLY *Matched*

AUDREY GOLDBERG RUOFF

ATRIA PAPERBACK

New York Amsterdam/Antwerp London
Toronto Sydney/Melbourne New Delhi

ATRIA
PAPERBACK

An Imprint of Simon & Schuster, LLC
1230 Avenue of the Americas
New York, NY 10020

For more than 100 years, Simon & Schuster has championed authors and the stories they create. By respecting the copyright of an author's intellectual property, you enable Simon & Schuster and the author to continue publishing exceptional books for years to come. We thank you for supporting the author's copyright by purchasing an authorized edition of this book.

No amount of this book may be reproduced or stored in any format, nor may it be uploaded to any website, database, large language model, or other repository, retrieval, or artificial intelligence system without express permission. All rights reserved. Inquiries may be directed to Simon & Schuster, 1230 Avenue of the Americas, New York, NY 10020 or permissions@simonandschuster.com.

This book is a work of fiction. Any references to historical events, real people, or real places are used fictitiously. Other names, characters, places, and events are products of the author's imagination, and any resemblance to actual events or places or persons, living or dead, is entirely coincidental.

Copyright © 2026 by Audrey J. Ruoff

All rights reserved, including the right to reproduce this book or portions thereof in any form whatsoever. For information, address Atria Books Subsidiary Rights Department, 1230 Avenue of the Americas, New York, NY 10020.

The authorized representative in the EEA is Simon & Schuster Nederland B.V., Herculesplein 96, 3584 AA Utrecht, Netherlands. info@simonandschuster.nl

First Atria trade paperback edition October 2026

ATRIA PAPERBACK and colophon are registered trademarks of Simon & Schuster, LLC

Simon & Schuster strongly believes in freedom of expression and stands against censorship in all its forms. For more information, visit BooksBelong.com.

For information about special discounts for bulk purchases, please contact Simon & Schuster Special Sales at 1-866-506-1949 or business@simonandschuster.com.

The Simon & Schuster Speakers Bureau can bring authors to your live event. For more information or to book an event, contact the Simon & Schuster Speakers Bureau at 1-866-248-3049 or visit our website at www.simonspeakers.com.

Manufactured in the United States of America

1 3 5 7 9 10 8 6 4 2

Library of Congress Control Number: 2026938962

ISBN 978-1-6682-2674-2
ISBN 978-1-6682-2675-9 (ebook)

Scan here to get book recommendations, exclusive offers, and more delivered to your inbox.

For leatherback turtles, which have survived every mass extinction and swim the ocean still, after millions of years. What a good reminder to appreciate and care for nature. Life goes on and tides roll in and out, and so we beat on with the current, towards the future instead of the past.

And for olive ridley turtles, and for Alison, champion of turtle facts.

Content Warning

This book contains off-page loss of a digit; on-page, brief description of a nongory dismemberment of an immortal body; and on-page kidnapping. This book contains on-page sex, all of which centers clear consent. If you are sensitive to any of these things, please take care while reading.

CHAPTER 1

Priscilla

It was possible that Priscilla Hart should not have waited until this precise moment to change her mind. For a minute, she willed herself to go through with it—she was Priscilla Guinevere *fucking* Hart, mistress of darkness, prankster extraordinaire—and she wasn't about to be brought to her knees by a wedding, of all things.

Least of all, her own.

Snapping her fingers and thinking of her mother's spell for strength, she stared down the aisle in front of her. The magic would work better if she had garlic. Or rue. She really ought to have replenished the emergency herbs in the back of the car, but she'd put it off, telling herself she wouldn't need magic to marry the woman she loved. On any other occasion, she'd have kept vials and packets in her pockets. But in addition to being not quite her taste, the designer white pantsuit was too tight for pockets. Even if she could find a spare sprig or clove to summon into her possession, she'd have nowhere to hide it.

Really, that alone should have been her first clue that this particular union was doomed.

Tugging at the neck of the suit for a moment, she frowned. The crowd murmured, and she shifted her weight from foot to foot on the black heels they had argued about. Evelyn thought the red underside was overstated for a wedding. Priscilla thought they were her lucky pair, and absolutely necessary. Left, right. She weighed it. What were another few moments? She was already ten minutes behind her bride's fastidiously planned schedule, and, right on cue, sparks shimmered and magical fireworks began to pop behind the chuppah. At the end of the aisle, Evie frowned, a disappointed queen in an elegant lace-sleeved ball gown.

Priscilla cursed under her breath but did not make any forward movement. For the first time in months, grief knocked hard against her rib cage, making its memory inescapable.

Her parents weren't alive to see her do this. She had done such a thorough job of shutting away this particular emotion, but now the familiar sting of it squeezed in her chest. Whether it was the biggest mistake of her life or not, they would never know. All she could do was piece together the bits of what she remembered and stand here in an uncomfortable suit that she didn't even like, her shoes the only bit of her ensemble selected with her own agency. She might never have control over her own life again. With one hand, she pulled at the high-fashion collar strangling her, and with the other, she dropped the bouquet of stupidly expensive orchids—Evie's choice.

It shouldn't have been loud, but the thing was, when there were a few hundred of her closest friends and family, including, of course, those who were not close to her at all, everything seemed more serious, amplified by the audience. The string quartet stopped, the crowd paused. Down the aisle, Evelyn glowered. Priscilla stole a glance at the onlookers.

People were judging her, based on the gape-jawed expression from Uncle Larry, who was here as part of a throuple from his senior living community. If even freewheeling Uncle Larry was appalled at her behavior, it had to be bad.

Judgment or not, she turned for the door and considered how much running might be possible in three-inch heels. If she ran, her dreams of continuing the legacy of her father's politicking and one day becoming Council president went with her.

If she stayed, well, she might only ever be the Council president's wife.

"She's making a break for it! Outrageous," shouted one of the elderly Council members from behind her. She didn't know which one, and she decided not to care. "What would Benedict and Persephone say? Dishonor on the Hart family. Shame!"

The familiar squeezing was back at the sound of her parents' names. Prissy stopped in her tracks and scanned the crowd. She pressed her hand against her chest, as though firm fingers could still the panic and grief roiling within. Her eyes darted over person after person, desperate to find the offending speaker and snap ants into his pants or curse him to start each day of the rest of his life by stepping on the smallest, sharpest LEGO. But she couldn't focus enough to guess at the culprit. The snug white pantsuit was a claw, clutching her in its claustrophobic tightness.

The suffocation was too much like the promises she had made to the would-be wife waiting at the altar.

And the impending threat of her decisions wasn't the only thing turning her dreams to ash—it had been her job to stop the fireworks display, but of course she hadn't made it that far. An errant burst lit the delicate tulle draped around the top of the square canopy *she* had insisted on. If she'd been the crying sort, this could have brought her to her knees, but she'd learned to bury her emotions deep, and to bottle them up to explode out later. It was a defense mechanism against a universe that had taken the people she needed most from her. A universe that had left her to marry her first love even though they weren't on the same page for significant things.

What *would* Benedict and Persephone say? She paused at the door, and turned to look at Uncle Larry, who was now gesturing toward the flaming chuppah, his girlfriend at one side and his boyfriend at the other. Was this showering dishonor on her ancestors now? She'd created her very own proverbial burning bush, except it wasn't a miracle; it was a fucking disaster. No one moved to get up, no one moved to come closer. They were looking at her like she was some sort of prey, hunted and liable to bolt if anyone went too close.

She preferred to be the hunter, but in this instance, flight was the only reasonable approach. And her parents, if they were alive, or if she had been brave enough to speak with their ghosts last fall, would have probably told her long ago not to let the beautiful woman she loved think that she might change her mind and *want* kids one day. A better person would have realized this before staring down said beloved at the end of an aisle, under a now-flaming wedding canopy.

"Oi! Someone ought to handle that!" Uncle Larry, bless his heart and his shiny bald head, wolf whistled, pointing again, standing up, and creating enough of a scene to distract a chunk of the crowd from looking at her. One of the bridesmaids hurried to magic the blaze out, demurely tapping the fingers of her right hand against the bottom of her left palm, like she was Clarisse fucking Renaldi or something. Her decorum, even in something as simple as how she accessed her magic, was an annoying reminder that the entire British delegation was here, and she had *definitely* offended them. Uncle Larry was her favorite for a reason. He was buying her time. A better not-a-wedding-anymore gift than anything she could think of.

You'll change your mind. How could you not? Evie had insisted.

Swallowing, she made the mistake of stopping to glance at the guests closest to her. The back section had been tacitly designated for people who didn't very much know or like the wedding party.

"Oh, shit, she's going to run," a blond man with a square jaw and a look on his face like he had been told one too many times how handsome he was whispered loudly to Agatha Vanderbilt Voisin. The woman had only worked on the Council with Priscilla for six months, but that was long enough to know that Agatha was a grade-A, planner-carrying, spreadsheet-wielding pain in the ass. For antichrist's sake, Agatha had once reprimanded Priscilla for using the wrong format for an office supply order spreadsheet. She absolutely would have opinions about this.

One more point toward beelining out of here before any sort of ceremony or reception. At least there would be no awkward conversations with people she barely knew.

"No fucking way," the blond man slurred, not bothering to pretend it was a whisper this time. He was loud enough that someone—possibly Uncle Larry—cleared their throat. Agatha blushed a furious pink, rubbing her palms on her pink sheath dress as though the action could calm her date. This sort of thing was anathema to everything that golden-coiffed, ramrod-straight-postured Agatha loved. This was *definitely* the wrong form for Priscilla to be proverbially filling out.

Priscilla smirked, relishing the discomfort of her most irritating coworker, until she caught the eye of Evelyn's personal assistant. Kevin was wide-eyed, in a smart tuxedo with a bow tie, glancing from her and back up to Evelyn. Priscilla fixed her face into what she hoped was contrite consideration. It was bad form to smirk while actively abandoning a fiancée at the altar.

You'll change your mind, Evie had insisted, over and over again, not hearing or not wanting to hear the response. *Maybe*, Prissy had grown accustomed to saying.

The thing was, though, she hadn't. Or, awkwardly, the thing she had changed her mind about was the wedding, and the time she had changed it at happened to be the absolute worst possible, short of after the vows. She supposed that would have been worse.

"Priscilla Hart." Evelyn's voice boomed down the aisle, and for a moment, Prissy looked away, and out the doorway in front of her. The safety of the outside hallway beckoned her. Evelyn had either grabbed a mic or magicked one, and if Priscilla turned now, she might do something inconceivable and marry the woman just to avoid the agony of awkwardness. "You can trust never to see my face again if you don't turn right back around and at least do me the courtesy of talking to me before running."

Nibbling her lip for a moment, Prissy considered it. She could turn around. Have Evie convince her, again, with those big, limpid eyes, that love was enough to change her life.

Behind her, drunk guy was getting louder, Agatha was blushing harder, and two seats down, Kevin was muttering frantically about how he'd rescheduled an entire delegation from Monaco for this wedding, and how inconceivable it was that he was wasting his life keeping a scheduling calendar if entitled councilwomen were just going to change plans last minute.

"Aggie, really, thanks for bringing me," slurred drunk guy. "This is the best fucking wedding I have ever been to—better than reality television."

"Will you be quiet," Agatha hissed at him. And looming behind them like Mount Doom, wearing a couture princess ball gown and an expression thunderous enough to smite the magical and nonmagical alike, was Priscilla's would-be bride, still at the altar, in front of a now-smoking chuppah that leaned dangerously to the left.

Squaring her shoulders, Prissy reminded herself that she did not have to settle for love that would not take her exactly as she was. And as she wasn't. Selfish or not, it would be *more* selfish to stay, knowing as she did that Evelyn would eventually wear her down.

Evie's words from that tired old exchange echoed in her head as she power walked out the door as elegantly as could be managed, given the circumstances. She picked up her pace down the hall, her snug pantsuit with the matching white jacket making her feel like a gentleman rapper from the late nineties. She could claim she was making a feminist statement, fleeing in suffragette white, but of course, the impact was dulled by the fact that she was actively abandoning another woman at the altar.

She wasn't going to face her would-be partner.

"Don't you dare run away from me," Evelyn boomed, loud enough to reach down the hallway, the slight crack in the last word almost breaking Prissy's resolve.

Someone grabbed her hand, and she turned, ready for the defensive, and then heaved a sigh of relief when she saw that it was only her brother. She waited for him to argue. To try to convince her to go back down the hall and through the door and up the aisle and into a lifetime of sensible decisions that wouldn't jeopardize the future of her career in the witching community.

But Azrael's face looked grim. Not surprised. He took her elbow gently, and sped up to match her pace until they were both at the end of the hall.

Az steered her down a side staircase, the one she had memorized just in case, and yet forgotten in the moment. It led to the parking lot, where the cherry-red Packard was sitting, in the prearranged spot it was supposed to keep until he drove her, with her wife—her ex-girlfriend, she reminded herself, because there was definitely no salvaging this—to the airport to leave for Europe and a luxurious honeymoon cruise.

That part had been Priscilla's idea, and it should probably say something about the state of her relationship that she had been more jazzed about a European river cruise than she had about committing to a life that would force one of them to give up their dreams. She'd realized the moment she stepped on that runner to start up the aisle which one of them it would be. It wasn't Evelyn, standing gorgeous in a fairy-tale gown. Evelyn would have gotten what she wanted. The perfect wedding, the perfect wife, the perfect *family*.

Not what Priscilla wanted.

"Where to?" He waited for her answer as she slid in the passenger seat, staring straight ahead at the trees, still lined in golden hues of orange and red despite the chill of the November air. They were past peak foliage season, but only just, and she'd thought, for a moment, that this could be a sign that the universe had held space for her wedding.

Maybe, though, it was just a sign that the leaves, too, had waited a bit too long to fall away.

Prissy rubbed the throbbing spot between her eyebrows.

"What about Vickie?" The last thing she needed was for her sorrows to spread like poison to her friend. She could obviously live with inconveniencing her brother, but not his girlfriend. *She* didn't deserve that.

"She has the house keys. She'll be fine. She's probably calmly talking people through a graceful exit strategy for the wedding party right now."

He wasn't wrong. Vickie was nothing if not coolheaded in a hot situation. The Starnbergers had lived next to her family growing up, or at least in a close approximation of next, since both houses were set atop rolling acres of manicured lawn (on their side) and wild woods (on hers) that meant proximity was a relative thing. Vickie and Az had been childhood sweethearts, then estranged, and then, last year, had fallen annoyingly and adorably in love again, only to be cursed so they couldn't touch without dying. They had solved the curse and were in the process of living happily ever after. It was a whole thing. The point was, Victoria understood. The Witchery Council, the drama. All of it. And Azrael, especially. That made her chest hurt a little. Not because she begrudged her brother that he'd found the perfect partner, but because she remembered exactly how much trouble she had gotten herself into, thinking she could change someone's mind about their life plans. Letting someone else think that they could maybe change hers.

Her brother slid the key into the ignition and snapped his fingers twice. The temperature dropped, and she exhaled as the windows tinted a shade darker than legal. Azrael had always known how to make people feel better.

How was it possible that her wayward, morose brother had managed to become the one with his life together and she had ended up the runaway bride bringing shame on the Hart family name?

"The airport," she announced.

"Your honeymoon?" Azrael, to his credit, did not bat an eye.

"Yes. Shit. I meant to stop by the parlor. It's in the parlor. My suitcase—"

He snapped again. "Is in the trunk now."

"Thanks, Az," she mumbled, dropping her head into her hand and propping her elbow against the window for one deflated moment before shaking it off and straightening back up.

Wordlessly, he pulled out of the parking lot, a few stray leaves fluttering under the wheels of the car.

Priscilla could see Evelyn in the rearview, storming out the door and down the concrete stairs, magic crackling around her angrily, rubbing her hands together. A bolt of lightning hit dangerously close to the car before Azrael jammed his foot down on the accelerator, rounding a corner and leaving the storm to flicker dimly in the background.

Priscilla sighed, leaning back against the seat, and snapped once to change the pantsuit to black, and the fabric blend to flexible. For good measure, she snapped again, and the horrible restrictive collar met an unfortunate end far, far away from her neck.

A normal person would feel grief, a hole where the love had once been, or some sort of regret or wistfulness about leaving their long-term partner at the altar.

But the only grief she felt was the knowledge that, two years later, her parents were still dead. And when she looked in the mirror, the localized turbulent weather of her almost-wife now a dim flashing glow in the distance, there was another feeling that outweighed all the brewing sorrow and heartache.

Relief. She felt relief.

CHAPTER 2

Agatha

Six Months Later

"President Voisin, your mother is on line two." Kevin paused, the intercom crackling. "Again," he added, voice gentle through the plastic speaker of her desk phone. "She said it's urgent."

"Thanks—I'll grab the call and then we can go over the agenda for tonight's meeting."

"Perf," chirped Kevin. He paused, and then continued, "I'm willing to invent an emergency dentist appointment. Just say the word."

"No." Agatha rubbed her forehead. "Much better to get it over with. Put her through."

"If you're certain," he said sympathetically.

In the privacy of her office, shrouded by frosted glass windows that separated her suite from the rest of the Council, Agatha threw up her hands in frustration, contorted her mouth into a silent scream, and banged her head against her palm. Her silver pothos shifted, glowing slightly at the accidental magic of excessive frustration. One frond wove up the edge of a bookshelf and down the other before she managed to get it under control.

Agatha Vanderbilt Voisin could handle her own mother. After all, she was one of the most powerful witches of the century, particularly gifted with plant craft, and elected Council president. She'd defeated Priscilla Hart, that irritatingly attractive witch with a long family legacy to back her campaign, even after the absolute carnage of Hart's election strategy, which had attempted to paint her as a bumbling airhead. "Galinda," Priscilla had called her, as though she were the culpable, conforming sort, just because she, too, favored pink. Agatha was anything but bumbling, though, and after winning the close race, albeit with a responding slogan she wasn't exactly proud of, she'd instituted order. Yes, she had referenced Priscilla's romantic bad luck in a way that made her a bit queasy, but it was for the good of the whole. After all, it was Agatha who had smoothed an awkward transition following an emergency election and the abrupt departure of the North American Council of Witchery's former president in the wake of Priscilla's horrifying behavior at the altar last fall. It was Agatha who had been proper and composed, never batted an eye, even though she had been internally aghast to find that Priscilla was willing to jilt her bride, and then run for her old job when said jilted bride unceremoniously quit. Heaven, it was even Agatha who had sweet-talked the vice president of the UK Witchery Council into agreeing to a junior exchange program next year. That had been tricky now that the British expat and former NACoW president had, well, repatriated, on account of her fiancée bolting.

It was Agatha all along who was the right person for the presidency. She *could* handle her mother. But that didn't mean that at this precise moment in time she *wanted* to handle her.

". . . Agatha?" Kevin's voice was gentle, buzzing through again. "Your mom's still on line two. Should I tell her you've been called into an important meeting?"

"No," she said. "She'll just keep calling. Put her through."

"Good luck." Kevin was worth his weight in gold, really, which was saying something, because Kevin Cross was six-foot-four of pure muscle, an Adonis in person, so handsome that the interns in the mail room sometimes joked that if man-dough were a thing, they'd sculpt him from clay just exactly as he was, no modifications needed. He was thoughtful, and he had an uncanny knack for securing her honeycomb lattes at precisely the right flavor and temperature.

She shook her head, hoping to clear the cobwebs.

"Hi, Mom," she said, voice pitching a fraction of an octave higher.

"How is the youngest Council president in the history of the North American Council of Witchery?"

She rubbed her temple. Her mom's pride in this victory still going strong, then. "Fine. Busy, but glad to be busy."

Her mother clucked. "Are you taking time for water and a facial routine? You should never be too busy for self-care, hon."

The sobriquet, and the drawling *war-ter* pronunciation of the hydration reminder made her smile. Her mother never had lost the speech patterns of Baltimore, not even after high school, college, and med school up north.

"I never skip skin care. I plan to be young and beautiful forever. How are you?"

Tiffany let out a dramatic sigh. "Your father just finished the new deck, and we have been having cocktails and watching the leaves fall on the weekends. You should come."

"Sure. Maybe this weekend." Agatha was most certainly not going to come this weekend, but it was almost a four-hour drive, so her mother would understand. In fact, when Agatha inevitably made excuses about having too much work to do, which wouldn't even be a lie, her mother would bubble with pride and fawn over her again for winning the Council election.

"Fantastic. You know, Louise down the street has her son visiting from Burlington. You remember little Adam Bumper? A few years older than you in school, and so successful. Owns his own graphic design company, and you wouldn't believe what he has been up to."

"I'm sure he's great." She twirled a pen between her fingers to stop the agitated magic from seeping out. The fronds of the plant behind her swayed.

Her mother was a meddler, particularly when it came to Agatha's love life.

"Agatha, go on. Guess what little Adam Bumper does in his spare time?"

"Runs an OnlyFans for people with foot fetishes?"

"Agatha Marie Vanderbilt Voisin, I raised you better than to shame sex work."

"I wasn't shaming, I was guessing. Maybe Adam has really big feet and does numbers in pictures of them next to coffee cups for size reference."

"All right, Agatha Ann, you're very funny. Guess again."

Agatha had no middle name—her parents had opted to make them all Vanderbilt Voisins on paper when she was born—and one of her mother's favorite pastimes was filling in increasingly creative fake ones in random conversation.

"Uhhh . . . Is he into amateur photography?"

She was thinking of her ex, the horrible one who had embarrassed her at Evelyn's failed wedding. She simply refused to even think of Councilwoman Priscilla Hart in that context, not to absolve her of her sins in bolting, but rather because her rage at the thought of her nemesis was too consuming. Hart jilting her bride had rippled into Agatha's own life, prompting Jonathan to do likewise to her.

That bitch.

"Agatha Chrysanthemum, I would never bore you like that. I had quite enough of your young Jonathan, with the god-awful series he made us sit through last Christmas. What did he call it?"

"'Selfie-Exploration: A New Transcendental American Moment.'"

"Absolute trash—pictures of himself blocking views of beautiful places. He can get wrecked."

"Some of it was decent," she protested, but a genuine smile crept up her face at her mother's shared anger, nonetheless. She glanced at the pile of paperwork she absolutely had to review before the end of the day.

"He fosters husky puppies!" Tiffany exclaimed, as though little Adam had won a Nobel Peace Prize. And sure, she had to admit, Adam had never been terrible-looking, and husky puppies sounded *definitely* cute enough to be tempting.

"That is adorable," she conceded. And much more aligned with her interests than foot pics, but she didn't want to encourage her mother.

"So you'll come around for brunch? I'll make my famous mimosas and invite Louise and Adam to stop by."

Her mom's mimosas were delightful. The obvious ploy to set her up was not. Her love life was the absolute last thing she wanted her mom involved in. She'd take fashion recommendations and health-care suggestions. All good advice. She'd take the majority of it.

Just not dating tips.

"I'm really behind on work, Mom." She hesitated, weighing the consequences of a little bit more honesty. "And I'm not looking to jump into anything new right now."

"Now listen, Agatha Peach. That's exactly what your father said when I first met him."

The Drs. Vanderbilt Voisin had met in med school, and the words of that initial exchange had been lost to history, subject to Tiffany's modification and tweaking in the retelling.

The facts were these: Vincent Voisin and Tiffany Vanderbilt were an unlikely pair. He was a wealthy and standoffish French witch who had visited through NACoW's foreign exchange program in college, fallen in love with New England, and returned for further postsecondary studies. She was a bubbling, effervescent, first-generation witch daughter of a human waitress who left her preacher husband when they somehow produced a magical child. Grandma Vanderbilt was scrappy and rough around the edges, and one of Agatha's absolute favorite people. She would never offer advice about dating. Though, had she done so, Agatha would have taken it in a heartbeat. If there was anyone a clinically anxious thirty-seven-year-old semi-closeted bisexual could trust, it was a woman willing to start from scratch rather than suffer a bigoted fool who was cruel to their daughter.

And so Tiffany Vanderbilt came to be a confident, audacious product of watching her mother pull her through childhood using sheer force of will and luck, and that drive had landed her a spot in a top school, and thus brought her to the fateful night in a diner when she had been waiting tables, like Agatha's Granny Vanderbilt before her, to pay rent. The future love of her life had been crying into a plate of apple pie over his latest heartbreak.

Tiffany gave him extra pie, pulled over a chair, and doled out her absolute favorite thing in the world to give: dating advice. She had even gone so far as to suggest he lose the bow tie he was wearing; her mother never was above blending the sartorial with the emotional. They had just celebrated their fortieth anniversary.

"I tell you what, Agatha May. You visit and I'll make that peach pie you love so much."

No one, absolutely no one, not even Granny Vanderbilt, made peach pie like her mother.

"I'll check my schedule. But leave it alone with Adam. I don't want you hanging mistletoe or shoving us into a dark corner or anything."

"Agatha Marine." Her mother sounded scandalized. "I would *never* hang mistletoe in May. It's far too early. And an affront to the summer solstice."

She smiled, wondering what the metaphorical stand-in for mistletoe would be.

"I have to go, but I'll see you soon."

"Can I expect to hear from you about specifics promptly?"

"Yes, Mom. Love you. Give Dad my love too."

"Love you too, Agatha Dorothy."

She hung up and noticed the three additional blinking lights on the phone.

She pressed the intercom button for the front desk. "Kevin?"

"President Voisin?"

"I see I have several calls. I also still have the permits to get to, and then after I wrap on the phone we can talk agenda."

"Line one is Valerie from Ferndale; I'll tell her you've been pulled into an essential meeting. Line three is the mundane mayor; that one you should take first—it's not even his secretary on the phone. Line four is one of the representatives from the historical society. I can have them give me information about the event they're proposing, and you can call them back later."

"What would I do without you, Kevin?" She thought darkly to the time when Priscilla Hart had tried to hire Kevin out from under her for a presidential campaign.

She could remember the Hart for Honor campaign posters he had sent her, the ones with a picture of her smiling dopily and holding several shopping bags—her mother's entire bridge club, for whom she'd been holding the bags, cropped delicately out of the frame—with the tagline about how a vote for Vanderbilt Voisin was one for style over substance.

"Good thing you'll never have to know!" His voice was chipper, as always.

She put down the phone, and when it lit up again, pressed the button for speaker mode.

"Mayor Khalil?" Goddess, she hoped Kevin had got it right and it wasn't the historical society again.

"President Vanderbilt Voisin." The mayor's voice was gruff, but not unkind.

Her first call with the mayor had been quick but painful; his knowledge of magic in Hallowcross, a secret to all other nonmagical beings in town, was decades old. She'd met with him twice since, and though his frosty demeanor had shifted into polite distance, she was absolutely certain that he would have preferred to work with Priscilla Hart.

Mainly because when she had called on him, that first time, he had been so aghast at her electoral victory that it took him a solid three minutes to convince him that she was, in fact, the new president of the North American Council of Witchery.

"I'd love to talk to you about setting up a routine meeting to discuss magical and mundane interface and prioritize issues on our end," she began.

She could practically see him cross his arms through the phone line, though she'd never violate his privacy by casting any sort of spell that would literally let her do so.

"I can't commit to all that with the current state of my schedule," he said. "But I'd be happy to meet in person next month if you're available."

"Absolutely," she said, laying on every bit of charm she could. "I was hoping that you and I would get a chance to brainstorm. Maybe over a shared document?"

He coughed. "I'll have my assistant call yours to schedule that meeting, and you can share documents face-to-face, the good old-fashioned way." He cleared his throat. "And please have Councilwoman Hart call me about the Constance Witherspoon incidents."

Agatha held back a groan of frustration.

"Of course," she said. "Take care." She hung up the phone and sat back, sighing as the pothos twitched restlessly on its shelf.

Every new mayor was trusted with the highly privileged knowledge of magic in Hallowcross, something that had been kept from the nonmagical humans for hundreds of years to avoid public outcry. Mayor Khalil was a bristling, grumpy old man known for his mittens and his sour expressions, but he was a fierce advocate for diversity, equity, and inclusion, and had kept Hallowcross welcoming for decades. There was no way he would lose an election, and he shouldn't. He *was* an amazing mayor. He just also happened to be committed to print copies over electronic documents and tied to the oldest witch family in Hallowcross.

And the problem with that was the Harts. The mundane mayor had been in office long enough to have worked with Benedict Hart, and his mother before him. Which meant that he insisted his Council liaison be the Council member who absolutely made her the most uncomfortable.

Fucking Priscilla Hart.

Agatha sighed and hit the intercom button. "Kevin, can you come in with the agenda?"

The door swung open, and Kevin gestured with his tablet. "Ready."

She sighed. At least she could count on Kevin.

"The community garden is first." Kevin slid into the chair across from her desk.

"Perfect. Can you make sure it's clear in the item description when the memo goes out that we would like this to be a pilot program for use by the Council nationwide?"

"Noted," he said, tapping furiously. "What's our next high-priority item?"

"Safe storage of magical objects and oddities." She cleared her throat. She didn't like to mention the Fountain of Youth elixir, and fortunately, Kevin didn't press the issue. She rubbed her temple just thinking about the late night she'd pulled last week reading all the footnotes in the compendium documenting the properties of immortality magic and why it was forbidden. Nasty stuff, really, and awfully dry writing to boot.

"And after that?" He tapped away at his device.

"Enforcement of Council decrees on psychic activity and divination regulations."

"Ah," said Kevin, nodding. "Connie."

"Yes." Connie Witherspoon had been a fake roadside psychic known affectionately as Madam Cleopatra until a dustup with a soul eater last year had left her in a magically induced coma, which she awoke from with actual powers. It was ironic that now, Connie could not entirely control her prophesizing. If she didn't figure out how to use her power effectively, it would explode out of her at inopportune times, like at the Shaw's, when a burst of pent-up divination turned into prognostication in the vegetable aisle that had been an absolute nightmare to cover up.

"Do we have an up-to-date report from the witch handling the case?"

She knew perfectly well who that witch was, but she didn't have to say it.

Kevin smiled sympathetically. "No. I will call Councilwoman Hart and tell her that the report is overdue and that you'll have to note it as such on the Council meeting agenda if she doesn't have it over in the next hour." He frowned. "There's a reason people didn't buy her family history shtick for the election. You were the better candidate by far."

She smiled, but maybe it wasn't convincing enough, because he continued.

"Imagine her nerve, driving the old president out and then coming for her job." This was not the first time Kevin had fixated on that. His loyalty was inspiring.

Agatha sighed. "You're a devilsend, Kevin, you know that?"

He winked and nodded. "Anything else? The rest of the agenda is standard, a reprisal of the last meeting's items. I listed the mundane mayoral project. I don't think we have time for anything on the high-speed rail concept."

She sighed. "It will have to wait until next season, which is a shame. That's all for now. Send in the report as soon as it comes."

"You want me to include a little figure of Priscilla to burn in effigy? Nothing serious, just a light prank—maybe dye her hair, or set her washer to turn all of her clothing pink?"

"Tempting, but no. Just the report."

"You got it," he said, sweeping out of the room with surprising grace for a man of his stature.

Kevin's offer wasn't a terrible one. Maybe she *did* need to take matters into magical methods to get the most opprobrious thorn in her side under control.

The idea of pranking impenetrable prankster Priscilla Hart made her smile. She didn't have time today, but she could think of something after the Council meeting.

Plotting took the sting out of the imposing memory of Priscilla—no, it was better to think of her more formally, as Hart—standing there, smirking while abandoning her bride at an altar in that way that made something funny happen in Agatha's stomach. Dark eyeliner had caged her gold-rimmed eyes, as always, and in Agatha's memory, it was both shockingly hot and inappropriate for a wedding. She'd dreamed of those deep brown eyes, their shimmering gold rim and specks, more than she wanted to admit. And then there was that debacle with Jonathan, his drunken blurting, and Hart running out on Evelyn, who stormed out in pursuit, leaving a stunned crowd, frozen and poised, waiting for someone to do *something*.

It was that very same captive audience that set Jonathan up to make someone else's botched wedding the most humiliating moment of her life. But if she thought about it, really, the fault lay with Hart. She frowned and turned back to her notes from the mayor. She really needed to review these now. Revenge would have to wait a few hours.

Fucking Priscilla Hart.

CHAPTER 3

Priscilla

Across from Priscilla, Agatha Vanderbilt Voisin crossed her arms, staring daggers for every Council member present to see.

"The mundane mayor is not happy," she said. "And you are supposed to be monitoring Constance Witherspoon." Priscilla rubbed the bridge of her nose with her thumb, trying not to squirm in her seat. The Connie situation was not necessarily her fault, but it most definitely was her responsibility.

"Outrageous!" Otho Ashbrooke pounded his hand on the beechwood table, his voice just past polite volume. "I gave Mayor Khalil my word that there wouldn't be a repeat of the Shaw's incident."

"Well," Priscilla drawled, forcing her face to remain impassive, "in my defense, it wasn't a Shaw's. And the Ben & Jerry's factory tour participants just assumed it was part of the experience. Ice cream sampling and fortune-telling."

Prissy turned at the sound of a throat clearing from the head of the table. "Councilwoman Hart." The president's voice was dripping with disappointment, as though Prissy had just been caught graffitiing "fuck the patriarchy" in shiny pink spray paint all over the boys' bathroom walls at Hallowcross High.

Not that she would ever admit to having done such a thing,

obviously. The principal hadn't proven it was her then, and Agatha Vanderbilt Voisin, who was not even a native of Hallowcross, absolutely couldn't pin it on her more than ten years later. Her uncanny knack for wiggling out of trouble using her powers of rhetoric and distraction had only been further honed since then.

The trick was to remain unflappable. Casual, but not in the fun, knee-deep-in-the-passenger-seat way. Pretend she hadn't sort of dozed off when Agatha had been blathering on about the Hildebrand von Auden estate and the proper procedure for storing dangerous magical artifacts.

"There weren't even any prophesized deaths this time!" Priscilla held a hand in front of her, inspecting her pristine black nail polish, spelled to remain perfectly matte. She studied each nail as though making sure they were intact, refusing to make eye contact with Agatha. "And in Connie's defense, predicting the demise of Wyatt Vance in a drunk-driving accident wasn't exactly stating anything a normie at that Shaw's couldn't figure out. Knowing that a man banned from just about every bar in Hallowcross was cruising for a reckless end would be as easy as guessing where Wyatt was on January sixth. And besides, he didn't actually *die*. I heard he was so spooked that he checked right into rehab."

Otho Ashbrooke muttered something under his breath and settled back in his chair. Otho had been a friend of Priscilla's father, and though he was a stickler for the rules, he was also a stickler for the swift and effective shutdown of fascists. Most of Hallowcross, Vermont, was willing to drive a jackass right out of town, but every now and then someone clung to cruelty.

"Councilwoman Hart," said the president, again, this time laced with just an edge of irritation. Pricilla resisted the urge to smirk. She loved getting this particular rise out of this particular woman. It's why she had so enjoyed a campaign full of calling her as empty-headed and high-pitched as a pink, fluffy rendition of witch stereotypes. "Regardless of Wyatt's upsetting politics, we cannot have a legitimate psychic walking around town with uncontrollable precognitive outbursts." She cleared her throat. "What do you have to say for yourself?"

Priscilla had planned to remain cool and unperturbed—which clearly ground Agatha's gears the most—but the Council president got to her with her need for rules and order. Prissy had tried to help Connie get it under control, but it had not gone well. "What exactly are you asking, President Vanderbilt Voisin?" Agatha was dressed so colorfully today, in a blue striped peplum top and a snug, coral-colored pencil skirt that matched her blazer and her lipstick. Priscilla couldn't imagine wearing that much pastel.

But soft hues notwithstanding, the president gave her a steely look, not unsimilar to the one she had worn when the election results were announced six months ago.

"I am asking, Councilwoman Hart, for a report on your progress with the Madam Cleopatra fiasco. I'm asking if you're up to the task of helping Connie Witherspoon master her new powers. I am asking if you're too busy gallivanting about to be bothered to do your job."

Otho frowned, but several other Council members chuckled. There was no way that Priscilla could admit her lack of success after that pointed barb.

Priscilla cocked her head lazily. She opened her mouth, prepared to distract her colleagues from her stalled progress. "Perhaps it's too difficult for you to understand the art of waiting patiently so we don't interfere with mundane events more than is appropriate."

Agatha's cheeks flushed bright pink. "Being a Witchery Council nepo baby doesn't mean you know what you're doing, Hart. Age counts for something here."

The titters of discontent from the rest of the Council were louder this time. Priscilla frowned, thinking of how during the election, Agatha had finally snapped and stooped to her level of campaign insults, piling her age on top of her family name as reasons she wasn't truly fit to run the Council.

"It's my experience, not my parentage, that makes me qualified for this position on the Council," she fired back. "And there's not that much difference between twenties and thirties."

Priscilla cursed herself for taking the bait. Most of the other Council members were far older.

Otho banged his fist on the table, managing to make even that action seem genteel.

"I move to call a ten-minute recess. My *old* bones could benefit from a constitutional." Otho nodded at Ben Smith, the only council member who occasionally joined him for a smoking break.

"Agreed," said Agatha. "Please meet back at 8:07."

Priscilla rolled her eyes at her precision; the woman couldn't have given them until 8:10? She held her tongue, though. She was the youngest member, and it wouldn't do to remind them all again. Not that she was ashamed of that; she had worked with the Council since she'd volunteered as a page when she was a teenager. Altogether, she had almost a decade of Council experience. Most of the people here respected her, even if her game had been a little off since the regrettable leaving-her-fiancée-at-the-altar-and-causing-an-international-incident-when-said-fiancée-immediately-resigned-as-Council-president fiasco. She'd tried to fix it by running for the position herself, but just as it had in this meeting, the tide had turned against her.

Everyone else had adjourned to the restroom or the vending machine; the muffins and coffee Agatha's assistant had put out earlier were long gone. By the time the thirteenth member returned—Otho, straggling in from an inadvisable balcony cigar that made the whole room smell rather painfully like her dead father—it was 8:25, and Agatha had been checking her watch, primly at first and then more and more aggressively, the corners of her mouth turning down as the minutes ticked by.

The frustrated blush blooming on Agatha's cheeks and her almost-maniacal watch checking was the highlight of Priscilla's evening. Behind Agatha, the monstera plant against the wall shuddered, shooting up at least an inch taller with the plant witch's irritation.

"Council members," Xiomara Cohen began. "Let's return to the agenda."

Priscilla sat back. Across from her, Agatha adjusted the lapels of her coral blazer.

"Very well. We need Councilman Ashbrooke's decision on the mundane mayoral project, and we need a verbal report on Connie Witherspoon, formerly known as Madam Cleopatra, the charlatan-turned-actual-practitioner-of-divination."

Xiomara nodded.

"And then we can finalize items one, three, and four and hold the Hildebrand von Auden estate and the other carryover items from last time until the next meeting."

Priscilla fought the urge to rub her forehead. As though reacting to her frustration, Agatha smiled and brushed a lock of long blond hair over her shoulder.

Agatha had insulted her dignity, brought shame upon her family name, and worst of all, beat her in the presidential race. The woman was a giant pain in the ass. So it didn't matter that she was hot in that chip-on-her-shoulder-hidden-by-extreme-politeness way. It mattered that Agatha was staring at Priscilla, her perfectly lined lips curving into a slight frown.

"Councilwoman Hart, your report?"

"Right," said Priscilla, definitely *not* noticing how pretty the other woman's mouth was when contorted into a stern little pout. Not one bit. Priscilla shut her eyes tight for a moment before opening them and reminding herself that Agatha was the enemy. "You ought to be pleased to know," she said icily, "that I have been making progress with the mayor. And if he told you he wanted me to call him, I will, of course, be happy to do so."

"The mayor is Councilman Ashbrooke's responsibility." The monstera loomed again, betraying Agatha's anger, and Prissy wondered if Agatha even noticed when she did that.

"Of course," said Otho smoothly. "Priscilla just has such a

rapport with him, on account of Benedict Hart." The mention of her father still twisted her heart in pain a little, even now.

If Agatha had been pink before, she was beet red now.

"I wasn't aware you were handing off that project." The president's mouth pursed.

"It's not handed off," said Otho breezily. He brushed an invisible speck of dust off his suit, a cloud-blue, three-piece affair. "We are collaborators. Priscilla and I have been working together with the mayor since before Benedict Hart passed." He fixed Agatha with an imperious stare that Priscilla wouldn't want to be on the receiving end of. "You do recall, Madam President, what an institution he was." His stare dared her to say anything to contradict him.

"Fine. The two of you should have the project finalized before the fall solstice. And I'll reserve the right to tag along as needed."

"With pleasure," said Otho, bowing his head. "Councilwoman Hart and I are on it."

"That takes us to discussion of item three." Agatha narrowed her eyes. "At our last meeting, the Council made it absolutely clear that Constance Witherspoon requires weekly meetings. Have you been able to visit her following the agreed-upon schedule?"

Priscilla squirmed.

"I thought monthly was more appropriate." She hated the whiny undertone in her words.

"Councilwoman Hart!" It was Xiomara Cohen who reacted this time, and next to her, Gemma Hexley frowned too. "That wasn't your call."

"I move to censure the councilwoman for failing to remember she is not the president," said Albert Thistleworth, narrowing his eyes and adjusting the actual monocle tucked into his breast pocket. She'd always hated him.

"I remember that perfectly," Priscilla bit out. If anything, she remembered it too well.

"I second that," added Mathilda Alvarez, and that was a bit

shocking; she and Mathilda were friends. She shot the woman a withering stare, but Mathilda shrugged. "I'm sorry, Councilwoman," she said, spreading her hands before her, and nibbling her lip, "but it really is inappropriate to forgo part of your assigned duties. In addition to being elected, we get paid to be here."

Priscilla sighed. She and Azrael split property tax and other household costs, and it wouldn't do to put it all on him with a teacher's salary. She was willing to play jokes on her brother, but not to actually put him in harm's way, economically or physically.

"I don't suppose anyone is willing to object?"

Priscilla looked around the table. Hester Grimsby shook her head, Florian Akinde gave her a rather apologetic smile, and on the other side of Xiomara, Eleanor Willoughby looked scandalized. That left only Devin Cumberbund, who obviously wasn't going to help. He was more beauty than brains, and while friendly, he was not going to stick his neck out for her. Ben Smith shook his head. And Mei Nakayama hadn't got to her sixty-fifth year in the council by breaking rules.

"Motion accepted," said Agatha, smiling wickedly. "Councilwoman Hart, consider yourself on probation. Any further violation of Council directive will result in a full investigation as to your ability to do your duties as prescribed."

"This is unfair prejudice because I ran against you," Priscilla snapped, regretting the words almost as soon as they were out.

"It most certainty is not," said Agatha, her face a thunderstorm. "You were given specific guidelines for supervision of a volatile mortal with no grasp of magic and no clear limit to how much she now possesses, and you deliberately disregarded those guidelines, putting the secrecy of our existence and the entire Council at risk." The plant behind her grew wider, entire new fronds popping out.

Priscilla's jaw dropped, just a little. She'd never seen Agatha this angry, this untethered.

Unfortunately, it was extremely hot.

"Fine," she said. She didn't have to like it, and she had ways of making the other woman pay for this. Agatha could have slapped Priscilla on the wrist with a warning instead of jumping right to a full probation.

But as she looked around the room at the other members, Priscilla remembered that even the ones who were, in theory, on her side, also still blamed her for Evelyn's departure.

Which was fair, she supposed.

It was fine. She would get Agatha back. Censure or not, that woman had it coming. And Priscilla knew exactly what to do to leave an impression.

CHAPTER 4

Priscilla

Priscilla stood on her toes, as though inching closer to five-foot-seven would help her discern more about the empty fortune-telling shop. She cursed herself for choosing combat boots over heels today.

Crystal Balls to the Wall was closed, the interior dim, and Constance Witherspoon was nowhere to be found. Priscilla reached into her pocket for the shadow-craft carving she kept for emergencies, and pressed the wood into her palm, snapping gently and closing her eyes. The shadows roiled and then calmed.

Wherever Connie was, she was definitely not here.

Priscilla could see the outline of a curtain, and behind it the dim shadow of the partition that separated the shop window from the small area in the back where Madam Cleopatra kept her crystal ball and tarot cards.

Biting her lip, Prissy looked around. There wasn't much foot traffic here, especially not at dinnertime, when vacationers and locals alike would either be eating at home or on their way to somewhere with more culinary choices.

Priscilla snapped her fingers, and the bottom lock slid, then the middle, then the top.

She slipped inside, the aroma of sandalwood overwhelming. She left the lights off as she made her way through the shop and ducked behind the curtains. Priscilla crept around the room, past the giant ball in the center of a low oval table, something mysterious swirling inside it. She ran her fingers across the deck resting on the altar behind the chair, and then rummaged through the drawers, finding nothing other than the intricacies of a charlatan who had traded in bells and whistles until being stricken with the psychic abilities she had spent so long pretending to have.

Ah. There it was. Her hand landed on something paper, something that felt *right*.

She opened the drawer. Across a folded page, in curling, careful script, was her name.

Dammit. Connie knew they were supposed to check in today. Prissy sighed, pressing the heel of her palm into her eye for a moment and taking a deep breath.

She slid the letter open, careful to avoid paper cuts. Who knew what kind of magic mixing that might lead to.

The note was brief and to the point.

Dear Priscilla,
I'm out of town this week, and I'm afraid I'll miss you. In my absence you will rifle through my things and find this. Psychic privileges and all. I'll be at an off-the-grid family cabin in the woods nearby, just for a break from the hullabaloo. I supposed if you absolutely had to, you could find my location. However, I do hope you'll leave me be.

I'll see you next check-in. Until then, I have the strongest sensation you should pay attention to the other orders of business at the Council meetings you attend. Call it a hunch.

Cheers,
C. Witherspoon

Priscilla scowled. There was no way that she wanted to admit to the Council that she was about to miss yet another check-in.

She looked down at her watch. There was nothing to be

done but slip out of the shop and make her way to the hearse she'd detailed earlier for the express purpose of humoring Uncle Larry when she picked him up.

Now that his funeral home was long closed, there was no need for the behemoth, but Larry insisted, and so she and Azrael kept it in the depths of the garage, bringing it out only when one of them had the Packard and the other needed to go somewhere with a distance too far to travel by bicycle or on foot.

At least this way, people tended to give her a wide berth while driving. So long as it didn't break down, she could pick Larry up with a few minutes to spare, park the hearse in the extra spot behind Hopelessly Teavoted, and walk with him over to the bar.

If the night went as such nights usually did, she'd call him a cab home and make her own way back to Hart Manor through the woods on foot after.

She'd let Connie Witherspoon have her peace and quiet tonight, Council be damned.

"I don't think you can ever have too much Rick Astley, if I'm honest." Uncle Larry drummed his fingers on the top of his cocktail glass. "It's perfectly torturous to subject people to. I love it."

It was one thing to prank someone else with endless synth pop on loop; it was another to listen to it in a bar. Which is why she was grateful that Kessel Run favored the kind of upbeat, slightly weird jazz one might expect in a space cantina in a galaxy far, far away.

She'd tried to convince Larry to join her at Free Spirits for their monthly bust-Larry-out-of-Sunnyhallow-Senior-Living day, but he had grumbled about how it was too hoity-toity for an old dodger like him until she'd finally caved and agreed on the Star Wars–themed bar she'd reluctantly come to love. Besides, it was impossible to take him anyplace with tapas unless she wanted a lecture on how in *his* day, food came in full-sized servings.

The Less Than Twelve Parsecs Nachos here, on the other hand, were extravagant in size and worth it, even if the waiter, Daniel, was her nemesis for trying to persuade her to say the names of the Star Wars–themed drinks and food out loud.

Nemesis was too strong a word, and one she ought to save for Agatha, even if Daniel's T-shirt featured a disappointed Porg with the text "Only you can prevent Galactic Empires."

"Another G—" Daniel swallowed. "I mean, just plain old mojito?"

Uncle Larry howled with laughter. "Don't let her scare you. You can call it a Greedo Mojito."

Daniel smiled. "Another Imperial IPA for you?"

"Make it two, kid." He winked as Daniel moved to the other side of the bar to talk to a group of college kids cosplaying droids in capes. "Look at that dedication," said Larry, pointing. "The fellow has even got a little embroidered rebel logo on his jeans."

"Uncle Larry, that's a decorative pocket button in the shape of a shovel. I think it's got the brand on it. This is why Dr. Finkelstein is always getting on you to wear those glasses."

"They ruin my aesthetic," said Larry, shaking his head and then running a hand over the smooth, bald expanse of it. She had never once in her life, not even in childhood, seen a single hair on his head.

"I'll drink to an aesthetic." Priscilla brushed a crumb of chip off the lapel of her blazer, and raised her not-a-Greedo Mojito to clink against her uncle's glass.

"So tell me about the Council meeting. Was it just the work stuff, or do you think your dream girl was mad at you for something else?" Larry peered at her from over his IPA.

Priscilla groaned. "I knew I would regret telling you she's frustratingly attractive when I piss her off." She shook her head. "Uncle Larry, we've been over this. You're getting senile. She's *not* my dream girl; she's also deeply heterosexual."

Larry waggled his nonexistent eyebrows. "You and I both know I'm as sharp as I ever was."

"That's not saying much," she said, but she could feel a smile tugging at her cheeks. Uncle Larry had always been her favorite, and Priscilla much suspected she was his.

"Don't worry, Priss, I have a sense for these things. Straight is boring. Most of us aren't."

"Statistically, that's just not true."

"You would dare question an old man who feels something in his bones? Your elder? Your favorite uncle, with impeccable gaydar, and a sartorial sense for the ages?" He flourished his dark wool coat, which was not exactly the paragon of fashion. Not for this century, anyway.

She stared at him for a moment.

"Absolutely," she deadpanned.

It was Uncle Larry's turn to smile. "That's my girl."

He raised a hand in the air, and Daniel came scurrying over with the beers and a cocktail.

"It's time for the switch to tequila. Let's have two tequila sunrises and two shots."

"Right, two Tatooine Sunrises and a pair of Blasters."

"Thanks, Daniel," said Larry.

"Good. I'm feeling cross enough to switch to plain old alcohol." After a beat, Priscilla added, "So, I do think it's about more than Council business. Just not the way you think. The pranking probably doesn't help, but it's just so fun to mess with her. I have a history question for you, though. Spell work logistics, really." If anyone could help with the note from Constance that was nagging at her, it would be Larry. He'd taken up amateur magical history in his retirement, and this sort of thing was his Roman Empire.

"Ah," said Uncle Larry shrewdly. "Go on."

"There's something on the Council agenda I feel I should have paid more attention to. Magic I don't quite understand. I have a hunch about it. When I close my eyes, it's shrouded in shadow, the thought of it."

"You're growing paranoid." His eyebrows raised. "I couldn't be prouder, pumpkin."

Priscilla took a long drink of her mojito, ignoring the green alien on the side of the glass.

"What do you know about forbidden magic?"

"Far too much." Larry cackled and took a deep drink, snapping his fingers to covertly refill their ice waters and staring her down in that way he always did. "There are only four types that are entirely forbidden, no exceptions. Immortality, raising the dead for misappropriation of corpses, forcing a love spell, and what I like to call *Gremlins* magic."

"Gremlins?"

"Yes, that's a new one, coined in the nineties. No mass-producing magical creatures that might cause an infestation if something simple causes them to multiply."

"I don't think it's that," she said. She wished she had paid more attention to the discussion points on the von Auden estate.

"Well," said Larry, "then you had better read up on raising the dead, love, and living forever."

"What a time to be alive." She tapped at her glass thoughtfully. Priscilla wasn't sure that she needed to be so worried about a Council item that was not her jurisdiction, but Constance was her problem, and she had left that note.

But Priscilla was not president. And that made it not really her problem.

Besides, hadn't Agatha said that Priscilla was not mature and experienced enough to be a strong leader? If the Council was going to treat her like a child, she was within her rights to occasionally act like one.

"Well, good luck with the most carefully guarded concepts known to witchkind. You'll probably have to override some security spells for the information you need there." Uncle Larry laughed, slapping his knee with a glee that let her know that he didn't actually give a bat's ass about her rule breaking. "How's the other thing, that secret project with the mayor, going?"

"It's good." Sure, it wasn't great to keep it from Agatha. But in the end, the project was in the best interest of the witching community. And she had given the mayor her word.

Larry smiled. "Your secret's safe with me, viper."

Daniel dropped off their drinks and shots.

"Let me know if you two need anything else," he said.

Priscilla resisted the urge to say something salty to Daniel about his shirt, along the lines of how people who lean too deeply into fandoms risk not getting laid. It wasn't true. And besides, he was a nice guy.

"Bottoms up."

She checked the time on her phone. It was early enough that she could still get pleasantly drunk, call Larry a cab, and then walk over to the Council office. She would set a new trap for Agatha and still be home in time to sleep off the tequila. If she alternated with water, well, she might even feel just fine in the morning.

Clinking her glass with Larry's, she took a shot and gestured for Daniel to pour another.

"Your focus really does determine your reality, doesn't it?" Daniel waggled his eyebrows and looked at her expectantly, like she was missing an inside joke that he wanted her to get. A joke Azrael certainly would have understood, but Priscilla had never followed her brother into his galactic fandom.

"Shut up and pour, Daniel." He looked a little hurt. She sighed. "Please?"

CHAPTER 5

Agatha

Agatha slept like the dead after effectively chastising her Council nemesis in front of everyone. This morning, strolling in early, a honeycomb latte in hand, she felt good.

It was the deep sleep of satisfaction after besting one's enemies, second only, maybe, to extremely good sex. The last time she'd felt like this, she'd woken up as the president of the North American Council of Witchery. As for the sated, exhausted rest of the thoroughly fucked, well, she couldn't remember the last time that had happened.

Certainly not with Jonathan. The idea of letting her mom set her up with Adam Bumper was looking better every day. She shook her head briefly, biting the inside of her cheek and pausing in front of the door to the Council offices to finish her drink and recycle the cup.

This was a serious low point. She was *not* at the level of desperate where she could consider being set up with her neighbor, who used to be known as little Adam Booger for, well, obvious and deeply unsexy reasons. She shut her eyes and forced herself to do mental math.

People brushed their teeth for two minutes, twice a day, 365 days a year. That meant that the average person who made it to eighty spent about eighty-one days of their life brushing their teeth.

She breathed a relaxed sigh and opened her eyes. Calculating random shit always made her feel better.

And victory was better than getting laid.

She pushed open the door, ready to gloat—with class, obviously, nothing indecorous—all day about how it had felt to take Hart down a peg.

"Good morning, Councilwoman Hart," she cooed in her most professional voice.

The other woman's head was bowed over her keyboard, a large take-out cup from Hopelessly Teavoted precariously close to the edge of the filing cabinet next to her desk.

Hart groaned. "There's nothing good about it." She picked her head up, and it was unfair, really, how hot she was, even with smudged eyeliner and hair sticking up a bit on the left. Her eyes opened wider, as though she realized she was talking to, technically, her boss.

"Agatha. President Vanderbilt Voisin. It's, um, nice to see you." She managed a smile, and Agatha swallowed the gloating she had been ready to pencil into her agenda. The suppressed emotion made the orchids on Otho's desk sway, but only a little bit.

Hart's lips and nails were stained a bright Barbie pink that she had never seen the resident queen of goth wear. Agatha's gloating had just been promoted to pure smugness. She rocked back on her heels, smirking. The orchids bloomed.

"Well, well, well," she said, smoothing her hot pink pantsuit and looking around. It was early, too early for anyone else to be here or arrive soon, except for her loyal assistant.

And Kevin had emailed that he would be unexpectedly out today—something about a backfiring spell and a stomach bug, which she sincerely hoped wasn't literal—so she'd have to brag about the success of her newest security measure later.

"It's so cute of you to match my suit today, Councilwoman."

Hart looked up, puzzled, and, if the scent of tequila told the truth, which it almost always did, maybe a little too hungover to put it together right away.

A flicker of emotion darted across her face—surprise, and then confusion.

She didn't know she'd been busted yet. Oh, this was too good. Her enemy, caught hungover after a public shaming. It was almost enough to make her feel bad for the woman.

Almost.

Agatha flexed her fingers, inspecting her perfect pink manicure. Waiting.

Finally, Priscilla Hart looked down at her own nails, jumping so hard that the rolling chair rocked backward.

"What the fuck?" She steadied herself, looking worse for wear and a bit green from the almost tumble.

"Nice lipstick too," said Agatha coolly. "You know, I set my private office lock to alter the appearance of anyone messing around where they shouldn't to match my outfit. Think of it as being caught with your hand in a cookie jar. A hot-pink cookie jar."

Hart said nothing, her fingers snapping a compact into her hand.

"No, no, no," she whined, rubbing her lips with the back of her hand.

"It's permanent. Unless you want to tell me what you were looking for, in exchange for a reprieve from the shades of Barbie?"

"Shades of what?" Hart swallowed. "I wasn't looking for anything special. Just some pens. I know you have the good ones in there." She held up one of Agatha's favorite Pilot G-2 07s.

That bitch. Still, her face was too sincere. Like a cat that had gotten into a saucer of cream, feline in the smile, too pleased for someone who had traded a pen for a preppy makeover. She tossed the pen down, crossing her arms. There was something else, and Agatha was going to make it her mission to find out what.

"And you wouldn't dare permanently change my appearance. That wouldn't be very presidential." She sounded out the last word like a slap in the face, and not a reminder that Agatha had beaten her for this very job.

Agatha sighed. She'd find out what Hart was up to, she was sure. This sort of skulduggery had a way of coming out eventually. "Relax. It's permanent in that it won't come off for twenty-four hours. It's not forever." She crossed her arms. She was a nice person, but she had the security protocol in place for a reason. She wasn't a pushover, and the councilwoman needed to know it. "But fuck around in my office again and find out if I'll be so generous next time."

Hart looked at her as though she were seeing her for the very first time, eyes widening, mouth dropping open just a quarter inch. Something about that sent sparks zipping down Agatha's spine. It was hard not to look too much at those perfect lips, strangely colored so bright pink in a way that didn't suit her colleague at all, yet also seemed absolutely tempting. Even if they looked much better stained crimson, or wine-colored.

Agatha shut her eyes tightly for a moment. What was wrong with her today, thinking about Priscilla Hart's lips when the woman had obviously been plotting and pranking against her? She was depraved. And had not taken enough time for proper stress-reducing self-care.

Thinking about masturbation in close proximity to Hart did something to her that she did not want to admit. She refused to, even if those damned orchids were now blooming in an *extremely* suggestive manner.

"Damn, Agatha, I didn't think you had it in you," Hart said. Agatha flushed, thinking, for an absurd moment, that Hart could read her dirty mind, before remembering that this was about her threat.

Turning around, Agatha didn't grace her with a response. She didn't want Hart to see the edge of a smile pulling at the corner of her mouth. She went straight to her office to think about how a pretty girl had smiled at her, even if the smile was literally off color.

"Wait," said Hart, and she was aware of the woman's height suddenly behind her. Agatha was precisely five feet five inches, a fact that had always pleased her in its even distribution. But now, looking up at Priscilla Hart's long lashes and smudged eyeliner, she could see how a bit more height could be a boon. On flat feet, Hart probably only had an inch on Agatha, but like this, in heels, she towered over her.

"Listen," Hart began, and Agatha reminded herself not to look too hard at those pink lips. Five-foot-five meant that it would take 2.2 of Agatha to reach the twelve-foot ceilings. That was better. What were pretty women compared to the unfettered satisfaction of winning?

"What?"

Hart smiled wide. "I just want you to remember that whatever happens next, I am the best person to interface with the mundane mayor. I belong here. I worked for this job."

"Fine, it's noted," grumbled Agatha, too polite, even in her gloating, to mention that she was president for a reason. And the crux of that reason was that, as strong as Hart's work was as a councilwoman, she still ran hot and cold with the caprice of youth, and in a pinch, was likely to procrastinate a task if she deemed it unworthy of her immediate attention.

Agatha pushed her office door open, pausing for a moment to give Priscilla a disappointed look before walking through the doorway.

Exactly two things happened next: Agatha frowned as she felt the edges of her hair creep up and grow coarse against her neck. She patted at it, pulling it forward to find a crop of straw-like blond hair cut in a choppy bob. Looking down, she recoiled. Instead of her fitted suit jacket, she was wearing a horrible puffy pink dress and—oh goddess, the horrors, were those Birkenstocks?

"Oh good! It worked. You're giving Weird Barbie," Hart began, her smile impossibly smug, striding toward her to get a better look.

And then the sound of several sharp somethings whirred

through the air as she slammed into the ground. Priscilla Hart had tackled her and pressed her against the floor, the sound of blades thudding loudly into the nearest wooden desk. Hart rolled her to the side, surprisingly gentle, gaze darting up and down Agatha, searching. Her hand rested on Agatha's arm beneath the puffed sleeve.

She was surprised to find herself transfixed not by the flying swords or the ground against her body, but instead by Hart's eyes. The scent of last night's alcohol was overwhelming, but her eyes, brown rimmed by that Geralt of Rivia Witcher gold and flecked with little specks of it here and there, were frantic. Mesmerizing, even as she hauled herself off Agatha, who watched as Priscilla raised herself onto her knees and bent down to press a palm against Agatha's shoulder. Her touch was gentle. Careful.

"Are you all right?"

Confusion and anger warred in Agatha. Surely Hart had been the one to set up the flying swords now lodged in the side of the desk mere feet away from them.

But Agatha was also dressed like a child's plaything, and Hart was marked in pink lipstick and nail polish. They had each gone to a lot of trouble to bathe the other in pink, and Agatha thought she and Hart had an understanding. They competed, sometimes brutally, but they didn't actually want to do bodily harm to each other. Right?

Agatha wanted to believe that Priscilla Hart had not just attempted to kill her, even if she did hate her. It would be strange to set up both a Weird Barbie hex and a deadly one. Why go through all the trouble of one if the other was in place? To shame her completely in death or injury? To pin her to the desk like a bug for examination in this awful outfit?

"I'm fine," Agatha said finally. She was going to be sore tomorrow. That was the downfall of hitting thirty-seven; she still looked and felt twenty-five, except when injured, tired, undercaffeinated, or suffering from the extreme condition of waking up at the wrong angle. Then she was sore for days.

Agatha frowned. Hart would probably walk away without so much as a bruise. "Was that part of your prank?"

"I would never engage in irresponsible swordplay." Those too-captivating eyes widened as she rocked back, pink mouth pulling into a frown. "I only did the Weird Barbie. I swear." Her eyebrows gathered, and she looked pained. Was that contrition? Agatha had never seen Priscilla Hart contrite, not even when the woman literally fled from her fiancée at her own wedding.

It did something to her. Something Agatha didn't want to admit about a woman who had possibly rigged her office to stab her.

Sitting up, Agatha crossed her arms. "Explain."

Hart stood up, reaching out a hand for her. Agatha half expected it to contain a joy buzzer, but she took it anyway, finding only cool, soft skin, and absolutely nothing vibrating. She let Hart guide her over to a comfortable chair and tried to ignore the look on the other woman's face as she checked her over, again, as though looking for injury.

If she had rigged the flying rapiers, she was doing a great job of selling concern now.

"My Uncle Larry can vouch for me. I had a little bit too much to drink at dinner with him, and I did a very unprofessional thing and slept here."

Agatha frowned. "I'm not mad, I'm just disappointed."

"I wanted to get you back. So I snuck into your office, clearly too drunk to notice this"—she gestured at the nail polish—"and I set up the outfit hex, but I *swear* I did not rig any weapons. Damaging priceless heirloom swords is not my style." She gestured to the offending items.

"How would I know that for sure?"

"Ask my Uncle Larry? Or my brother? Either will provide a character reference. I do mischief, pranks to discomfort and shock. But not to hurt. Nothing that would do serious, deadly harm. It's not my brand." Hart crossed her arms, and Agatha stared at her.

She didn't look like a killer. Or rather, she looked *too* much like a killer. It would be a step too far for Priscilla Hart—all black, high-fashion, bloodred goth beauty—to actually commit murder. But to be safe, Agatha would keep a close eye on her from here on out.

"Fine." Agatha narrowed her eyes. "I believe you."

Maybe she looked unconvinced, because Hart went on.

"I'm not proud of having slept here. I prefer my own bed, but I passed out."

There was, in fact, a little damp spot on the paperwork on her desk that suggested it had been recently drooled on.

"You drool in your sleep?" This made Agatha irrationally smug, because of both the silliness of it and the intimate knowledge of her coworker's sleeping habits.

Councilwoman Hart sat up straight, eyebrows furrowing.

"I'm a highly powerful Witchery Council member." She gestured down to her suit. "This is Givenchy. Do I look like I drool?"

The spot on the TPS reports didn't lie, but Agatha let it go.

"So you are suggesting that you somehow slept through a separate, unknown intruder sneaking in here, managing to avoid my hex and your hex—that's the magic of two of the most powerful, talented witches on the Eastern Seaboard—and add their own?"

"Yes," said Hart coolly. "If you'd met my uncle, you'd understand. He can drink anyone under a table. There was tequila involved."

She had seen Larry Hart at the would-be wedding, sporting an extremely obvious flask that he hadn't bothered to hide, not even before the whole day went up in flames. Agatha pointed at the take-out cup, considering.

"You managed to wake up for breakfast and then came back here?"

"Of course not. As soon as I woke up and realized how hungover I was, I DaemonDashed it. When the dasher looked at me funny, I assumed it was my smudged mascara, not the abomination on my face and nails." Hart splayed her fingers out in front of her, scowling.

"OPI's Strawberry Margarita is hardly an abomination," Agatha snapped.

"I don't understand any of those words." Priscilla turned her chin upward.

"You absolutely do." She was a lot of things, but Priscilla Hart certainly wasn't one to not understand the naming of nail polish. Agatha was not going to let Hart pretend she was a witch who hadn't probably spent years perfecting her manicure spell.

The councilwoman shrugged. "Fine. If you'd like to be snobby and name-drop nail polish colors, I prefer Hermès Rouge H."

"Of *course* you do." That was a sixty-dollar bottle of nail polish, which was an absurd spend on a councilwoman's salary. Agatha gritted her teeth and tried to remember that she hadn't always chosen reasonably in her twenties either. There was a whole slew of ex-boyfriends who could attest to that. Agatha pointedly avoided looking at the orchid. The errant sword next to it had only narrowly missed it. She rubbed her thumb across her fingers, and the sword disappeared into the evidence chamber, along with the others.

"You were the one who started it. I can't be held accountable for my disdain at this tacky monstrosity." Hart waved her hands, and that was a bit too much for Agatha.

"You can't even hold off on name-dropping a three-thousand-dollar suit when you're supposed to be convincing me you're not a murderer! You think, what, your Givenchy shoes preclude any sort of homicidal instincts?" It was actually exactly what Agatha had thought earlier: that Hart looked the part too well, but it would be a 110-degree day in Vermont before she'd admit that out loud.

"Good eye," Hart said silkily. "And you're not dead. So it would be *attempted* murderess, but I am not one. I told you. I didn't do it. Give me gravedirt to make me tell the truth and nothing but the truth if your panties are in such a twist about it." She smiled, a vicious, beautiful thing, even in the wrong color. "I bet I have some truths you couldn't even handle, little Agatha. But I'm not unwilling to share."

The thought of any undergarments made Agatha blush with a heat that felt like *they* could be Strawberry Margarita. Or whatever Hart's high-end version of that would be.

"Fine," Agatha said, crossing her arms. "You know Council members are expected not to administer any sort of altering potions, drugs, or concoctions to one another without Council approval or recommendation, per the code. I'll take your word for it for now, but I will be keeping an eye on you."

She stood up and walked away, not sagging to the side, even though her left knee ached in a way she'd half expected after the impact of the blast.

"Clean this up," Agatha said. "I'm going home, and once I've changed, we're going to pay the mundane mayor a visit about Connie Witherspoon."

Hart nodded. "That's fair." She paused, sucking her lower lip in for a moment. Something in Agatha twisted. "Are you sure you're not hurt?"

"Yes," Agatha said, ignoring the ache in her knee and her lower back. She rubbed her fingers together, thumb across all four pads, the way her magic worked best, and a magical anti-inflammatory took immediate effect. "I'll be back in an hour."

She didn't turn around, not to see if Hart watched her, not to see if she was still standing, that black suit hugging every curve of her body, as comfortable on precipitously high heels as Agatha was in her favorite sneakers.

Turning would mean answering for the part of her that pulled, low in her stomach, at something quite different from hate for the younger Hart sibling. And she was almost completely certain that the office orchid, at the least, was threatening to give her most buried desires away.

But she was Agatha Vanderbilt Voisin, and she would not succumb to needs as basic as lust.

She could, instead, calculate how many bottles of Strawberry

Margarita OPI a person could buy for the price of Councilwoman Hart's fancy shoes.

Ninety-nine. By her count, it was ninety-nine.

So she'd stick with hate. Hate was good. Hate was enough to carry her through this.

She hoped.

CHAPTER 6

Priscilla

Hot bitches got things done, even dressed as Weird Barbie, it turned out, and wasn't that just a kick in the ass. Agatha still looked upsettingly fine, even hexed. Priscilla tried not to think too deeply about exactly what it was about Agatha Vanderbilt Voisin in a ridiculous, pattern-splattered, pink floofy doll dress that did it for her. Could it be the Birkenstocks? Surely if she ignored this feeling, it would go away.

They had been sitting across from Mayor Khalil for almost an hour now, each in one of two worn but comfortable chairs in front of his desk. His thick brown eyebrows were peppered with gray now, as was his curly hair, and his face lined in well-earned wrinkles, but he was still very much the man she'd shadowed her father visiting back in his Council days.

"I understand, Madam President, and I have no wish to supersede the protocol of your Council. But you must understand that working as the only mundane human aware of the magical community here in Hallowcross poses logistical problems that really do require the finesse of someone who has also lived here their entire life. Otho Ashbrooke is such a wonderful option, too, but the Hart family has been working side by side with my office for generations now."

Agatha's expression did not change; she held his gaze for an awkward minute, and then she cleared her throat.

"Certainly. I can keep Ms. Hart on as an adviser, and bring her with me to our meetings, but I do insist, given the unusual nature of a mundane mayor requesting such a thing, that I take over for Otho and remain the official liaison to the human government and your office." Her gaze sharpened. "It is *my* responsibility as the duly elected Council president, something I'm sure you can appreciate yourself, as an elected official."

Mayor Khalil sat back, nodding.

"Democracy is very important to witches and humans alike." He nodded. "Very well. You remain the liaison, but Ms. Hart accompanies you. Now, tell me you two have control of this Madam Cleopatra problem."

"We have the situation in hand," Priscilla cut in smoothly, refusing to look at Agatha, though if a Weird Barbie hex didn't break her composure, a slight exaggeration certainly wouldn't. "Constance Witherspoon is dealing with a difficult transition from being a normal, albeit charming, grifter, to an actual practicing oracle, with reading skills and premonitions."

"An oracle?" The mayor looked horrified. "Like in a Greek tragedy?"

"Of course not," said Agatha, glaring at her. "*Oracle* is an antiquated title, and specific to magical people; humans would use *psychic* or *clairvoyant* interchangeably there. Fortune teller, even."

He looked relieved.

"Like a Zoltar machine at the beach." His furrowed brow said that he needed to believe Connie to be closer to a beach novelty than an ancient harbinger of doom.

Priscilla bit her lip. For all their seeming harmlessness, in the early twentieth century, those machines had been the playthings of devils, well-known as conduits for precipitating bargains. Bringing that up would only cause Mayor Khalil more worry.

"Yes," she lied, telling herself it was in his best interest. What mundanes didn't know couldn't hurt them. "Very much like that. Now, the thing is, it will take some time to find balance with her new powers." Prissy was making it up as she went, but even Agatha was nodding, and she realized it actually sounded so confident that her boss believed her fib as much as the mundane mayor did. And it wasn't a terrible idea.

"Naturally," said the mayor. "But could we help her keep things under wraps until she gets to that, ah, proper equilibrium?"

"Absolutely," said Agatha, soothing. She caught Prissy's eye, and her gaze was sharp. She probably didn't love the lying, but surely she knew it was the best course of action. "Priscilla is in charge of it entirely."

The mayor sat back, checking his watch. "Perfect. Thank you both so much for coming. I appreciate your time, and I'm sure we can iron out the details on the phone before our next scheduled meeting."

It was the universal politically correct way to ask them to leave. Agatha stood up, and Priscilla swallowed a laugh at her dress in full view. It really did look like a bright pink potato sack with crinoline layered underneath, and the topsy-turvy spiky hair was so absurd that she was impressed Mayor Khalil didn't laugh either.

And here Priscilla was, thirsting over the woman, absurd attire and all.

"Thank you, Mayor Khalil," said Agatha primly, as though she weren't dressed like a doodle-laden children's plaything.

"Yes, lovely to see you as always," Priscilla added, and they walked out, Agatha's head held high despite the fact that more than one person on Main Street did a double take passing her ensemble.

Priscilla had expected the hex to derail Agatha's confidence, but Agatha had been unflappable, even when Mayor Khalil had grilled her at the start of their meeting.

She replayed that bit in her mind, *not* because of the way Agatha managed to still look lush and inviting even dressed like a Kate McKinnon character—maybe even more so for the comparison to Kate?—but also not *not* because of that. She forced herself to act normal as she left work, by herself, heading home on foot to clear her head.

The walk home from the Council building was pleasant enough, and by the time she cut through the old forest, she was deep in her thoughts.

She made her way past the path; she'd been cutting through these woods for long enough not to need to follow it. There was a patch of low growth here, a spot of clearing there, and then a five-minute brush through thickets that were easy enough to part with magic and walk through, shaving ten minutes off her afternoon commute. She didn't do it every day, but it helped her think, slipping into the woods and snapping her fingers to carve her own secret labyrinth, winding through the bushes that grew taller than her head here.

Priscilla needed a moment to brew the plan for Connie in her head; her previous approach had been mostly avoidance, and if she was honest, the avoidance was born of a frustration with her inability to help Connie as easily as she wanted to. She and Connie had talked about it, and the easiest solution was to ignore it, but all the ignoring seemed to be having the opposite effect.

The outbursts of prognostication simply could not continue.

Sighing, she snapped her fingers, rubbing the shadow-craft ward she kept in her pocket, and the grass grew, thick and soft, in the small, secret space she had wrought for herself in the middle of this magical clearing.

She sat down and set her tote bag to the side, readying herself to cast a protective spell, to stop anyone from coming near the clearing or her until she had worked her way through the problem.

Before she could, though, the scent of bergamot filled her nose, and her eyes flew open.

Glittery purple smoke surrounded her, and she frowned.

She knew exactly which sort of dramatic devil was arrogant enough to invade her thinking maze in a puff of extravagant magic.

"Olexandre," she said, snapping her fingers and tossing up the protective spell anyway. Whatever he wanted with her, she was willing to guess it would be more trouble if an unknowing mundane stumbled across them.

"Priscilla, darling, please call me Lex."

She rolled her eyes, sighing deeply. Unlike her brother and Victoria, the handsome devil had no particular appeal for her. And besides, she was still cross that he'd unseated her in gravedirt pranking last year.

"Lex, if you call me *darling* again, I'll magic your long-gone horns back on and cut them off myself, with relish."

"Now, now, Priscilla Hart, I haven't had horns in centuries, and you know that. Is that any way to greet a friendly visitor simply here to offer advice?"

"Yes," said Priscilla, crossing her arms. "I love threatening people who offer unsolicited advice. In fact, I find that it is the absolute best method for dealing with unsolicited advice."

Lex chuckled. "Fair enough."

He plopped himself down across from her on the grass, running a hand across it.

"Very lovely magic here, as usual." He shook his head, tossing his blue-black waves, an insouciant smile creeping across his face. "Now, do you want my help with the psychic or not?"

Priscilla scowled. "Of course you would be meddling in my affairs." Lex winked, which she did her best to ignore.

"You know I dabble when it suits me. Now would you like help, or not?"

"Fine." She wasn't happy about it, but she'd had so little luck, and he couldn't possibly make it worse.

Well, probably not, anyway. Given what Lex had put her brother through last year, it was possible for him to make things worse. Just not likely.

"Her unexpected outbursts happen when she gets all blocked up," Lex offered.

"Excuse me?" Priscilla had gotten up to some unfortunate things, but never had she ever had to dabble in human bowel movements. “I don’t think this is a physical-ailment-with-magical-consequences situation.” She blanched at what might be necessary if that was the case.

“Not that sort of blockage, Priss.” She frowned at the abbreviation of her name, but somehow, from the devil, she didn’t hate it. They had bothering her brother in common, perhaps more consequentially on his end than hers, but she thought they might be friends.

“A sexual blockage, then? I guess I could help Connie find love,” she mused.

“Hah! You Dirty Bertie, no, not a sexual blockage.” He threw himself on the ground, a pillow appearing beneath his head the second before it hit.

“What,” she said, knowing she would probably regret asking, “is a Dirty Bertie?”

Lex waved his hand. “One of the British royalty some years ago, up to all sorts of dreadful things, but terribly creative in his furniture choices. They called him Bertie, and Dirty Bertie because of his siege d’amour, obviously.” He paused. “His love chair.”

“I speak French, thank you. And that’s more information than I need.” She scowled at him. Even if she had further questions. Those could be solved by an internet search later. Hells knew what this devil had gotten up to in his thousands of years and might recount to her if she asked him about it.

“Now, don’t be like that. Your parents had something quite like it, I believe, at one point.” Lex’s eyes glinted.

“I cleaned out the sex dungeon.” She’d remodeled it after they died. It wasn’t the sort of thing one kept of their parents. Best to disinfect, remodel, and move along with the blessing of Hart Manor, which clearly approved, growing full-length mirrors and extra ceiling fans without even being asked.

Lex’s mouth dropped open a bit. She shrugged. “It’s a lovely home gym now.”

“An affront to love chairs everywhere,” he admonished, as though she’d stuck a fist through the *Mona Lisa* or something.

"I didn't throw *all* the furniture away." She sighed. She'd thrown all of the toys away, for obvious reasons, and all upholstered pieces, for even more obvious reasons, but the frames, and chair, and such, well, she'd simply magicked those into storage. "They're in the back attic room." She rubbed between her eyebrows. "I tell you what," she said, an idea forming. "I'll let you have the chair, and anything else you want from that collection, if you tell me how to solve the Connie problem."

"Really?" Lex sat up, eager. "I don't suppose you'd be willing to draw up a contract?"

She eyed him.

"Absolutely not." She concentrated, closing her eyes and picturing the things she'd moved. She snapped her fingers, and it all landed with a soft thump on the forest floor, neatly inside the protective dome.

"Take as much as you want." She gestured at the pile, which contained the impossible-to-figure-out chair, and several other bits of furniture she tried not to think too hard about in the context of Benedict and Persephone.

Lex grinned as though he were a cat let into a saucer of cream. "All of it," he said, smiling wide, violet eyes sparkling. "I want all of it."

Priscilla gestured toward it. "Help yourself."

"Don't mind if I do," he said, and he winked. The furniture dissolved into his signature purple smoke, gone to wherever it was that the devil made his den.

"Now," he said, "that's just splendid. I've always wanted one of those. I'm so chuffed, in fact, that I'll give you a bit of information. Someone's been sniffing around, looking for an immortality bargain."

She balked. This was bad news. Uncle Larry had warned her, and it seemed her research focus had just been narrowed.

"Who?" Her voice came out sharper than intended, but he nodded, approving. Even careless Lex knew this was trouble.

"I'm not certain, but the rumor mill has been abuzz. I heard that someone from this coast made the trek out west, to Lucifer, but he's been on his best behavior since the censure he's faced from the Syndicate over all that bad business with Chet."

Priscilla shivered. Not even witches knew very much about the Syndicate, that mysterious group that governed devils and demon business, and if they'd formally admonished the very king of devils for the human he'd imbued with powers last year, the one who'd caused such trouble for Vickie and Az—well, she had to imagine that wasn't pleasant.

"Just pass it on to the Council, will you? To be on the lookout for any talk of immortality."

She nodded. "Thank you. Now, you promised. Connie."

"Indeed. What you need is for her to remove the magical blockage."

"And how do you recommend she do that?"

"Excellent question. By using it, of course."

"But we want to prevent her from using it too much."

"Yes, and to do that, she has to have a handle on the thing. You've got to get her to siphon off the excess power. Fresh, new powers like that? She's in a magical adolescence. As time goes on, she may be able to get by just fine without using it, but until then, she's got to use the foresight, the premonitions. Palm reading, candles, tarot cards—anything that suits it; anything that can channel it. You might even try a crystal ball."

"All right. How much should she use it? To prevent any sort of outbursts?"

"I don't know. I'm not a doctor. Though if I were, I'd probably take a look." He winked.

Priscilla rolled her eyes. "I'm not interested in your kind," she reminded him.

"Devils?"

"Men."

He smiled, catlike. "Very often one and the same."

This made her laugh, despite herself. "You're not wrong, and I'm still not interested. Do you think once a day should work? For the magic?"

He cocked his head, thinking.

"Do you know, I would treat it like recommended exercise? Aim each week for two and a half hours of moderate, an hour and a half of intense, yes? That would do the trick."

Priscilla inhaled sharply, feeling, for the first time in ages, like she got it.

"She has to keep running the shop as she did before. To start telling fortunes like she used to, and sprinkle in just enough real magic to work the muscle of it, but not so much as to attract attention. Oh, Lex, that's clever."

"I know," he said smugly. "I'm quite brilliant. You're welcome."

He blew a kiss, and with a puff of smoke, vanished into the dusk.

CHAPTER 7

Priscilla

Priscilla put the final touches on the outline of her planned work with Connie, and hit save. She snapped twice to back it up magically, for good measure. There was no pain like drafting something majestic and forgetting to save. A power outage had once caused her weeks of woe, and today was a good day.

She smiled, which felt weird, to be honest, but maybe this was the product of a successful write-up. She would earn her way back up to the top. She was Priscilla gosh-darned Hart, and she could do whatever she put her mind to.

Something nagged at the back of her mind that this sort of cheerful thinking was not the norm, but she pushed that aside. It was okay to feel good about, well, feeling good.

Goddess, the thought made her want to break out in song, and that did make her frown. Putting a palm to her forehead, she checked for fever; her effervescent joy felt like it should strike her as unsettling.

And yet, all she felt was calm and sunny, like the world was her oyster.

"You all right, there, Councilwoman Hart?" Otho's assistant, Nancy, called over from his desk. Otho was rarely in the office in person these days, but his niece was a decent stand-in, and enthusiastically part of the intern program in the way that Priscilla once had been.

"I think I'm just hungry." She smiled, and it ached a little, like a limb twisted slightly out of place, not enough to break but enough to bend at an odd, uncomfortable angle.

Nancy stared at Priscilla. "Maybe grab lunch. You were smiling so big that I was worried."

It was odd for her to be bubbly; this morning she had actually giggled a little over a typo.

Giggled! Priscilla Hart. The mistress of darkness. She really did need lunch. This had to be low blood pressure or something.

She stood up, smoothing out her skirt, which fell to her ankles, a fact she was certain made up for the slit up the side and the slice of midriff below the matching top.

Before she could stop herself, she walked up to the president's open door, poked her head in, and smiled.

"I'm headed to lunch—want anything?"

What was *wrong* with her? She had never in her life offered to get her nemesis food.

It was fucking disgusting is what it was.

Agatha smiled, eyes glinting. Even that didn't bother her. Maybe she was wrong about Agatha. Maybe people that hot deserved to be happy.

"Do you think a crop top is appropriate for work?"

Maybe not, then.

Agatha wore a lavender three-piece suit with a well-tailored vest. It was egregiously pastel. Still, there was something about Agatha, and Priscilla Hart was determined not to notice, through the power of positive thinking.

"This isn't a crop top. It's a Aya Muse set, and for hell's sake, it's long-sleeved! And floor-length!" She smoothed the sparkling pattern that ran to her wrists.

"Yeah, floor length if you don't measure from that."

Agatha's finger pointed at the slit high on Prissy's thigh, and she tried not to think about the proximity of that long, purple fingernail to her skin.

The length of the nail should be enough of a deterrent. It

looked downright stabby, but Priscilla still had the sudden urge to grab that wrist and pin it up above Agatha's head.

So Agatha's fingernails were a little long to be knuckles deep in anyone. She could be creative. And they were witches, so fingernail length was a snap away from changing.

Priscilla flushed, shoving *that* unbidden thought out of her head, and decidedly not eyeballing the wall behind Agatha Vanderbilt Voisin for the position she could best press her up against into something solid without knocking down anything important.

It was a disturbing impulse. Priscilla rested her hands on her hips instead.

"I can't be held accountable for your lack of fashion knowledge."

There. That felt closer to normal, and less like she wanted to lick the strip of skin exposed by the plunging V-neck of that stupid lavender vest.

A haze. Priscilla was in a haze.

"I'm all set for lunch, but you have fun. Oh, and it's a bit chilly. Don't forget a coat."

Agatha winked, and that was so off-putting that Priscilla spun around and left without further comment. She snapped her fingers, donning her favorite oversized forest-green blazer.

It was only a ten-minute walk from the Council offices to Hopelessly Teavoted, but she was so utterly off-kilter that she took a wrong turn, ended up in front of the diner Don't Go Bacon my Heart instead, and found herself on the other side of Main Street.

The street was closed; must be for some sort of town event she'd forgotten about. Victoria's shop was just a few blocks down, but for some reason, the crowd was thick enough that she would have had to weave down to it.

Music blared from the speakers attached to the streetlights so suddenly that she jumped.

Why, this car is automatic. The music didn't just buzz in her ears, she could feel it under her skin. Filling her. She needed it.

She wanted to be part of it. This was what she had been training for. She recognized the song and she needed everyone here to know that!

For a second she couldn't figure out what was happening; she was in the center of the street, her arms flaring behind her, jacket almost discarded.

The lyrics continued.

It's systematic.

Her jacket was in one hand now.

It's hydromatic.

She spun it around and tossed it, and someone wolf whistled and caught it in the crowd, but she didn't have time to see who before she was surrounded by people, all of whom were dancing the same right-leg-jiggling, arm-pumping "Greased Lightnin'" choreography that she was unfathomably in the middle of.

"Greased Lightnin', go, Greased Lightnin'." She belted the words, gyrating and shaking the way she had practiced, the way that gave her a nagging, one-too-many-drinks feeling that she might regret this later.

Priscilla had never danced on the street a day in her life, and the mere idea of a flash mob was enough to give her chills, and not in a good way.

And yet here she was, hand-jiving and tap-dancing like a goddamn manic pixie normie.

Not that there was anything wrong with that, but it clashed with her goth-queen-of-night aesthetic.

And here she was, dancing with a crowd of strangers, a choreographed dance she couldn't recall ever learning, and somehow loving it.

That is, until the final chord struck, and she stopped, a round of applause pattering out, and the street clearing. She was only mildly out of breath; she did enough kickboxing not to be winded completely, but the dance had been grueling and not in her usual wheelhouse.

A sense of sizzling slid down her spine, and her shoulders relaxed. A hex, she realized.

That explained the effervescence, and the devil-dammed dancing.

Fucking Agatha. She hadn't expected retribution to come so soon.

Standing with her phone up, holding Priscilla's favorite blazer carefully, was her brother's girlfriend. The smile on Vickie Starnberger's face told her everything she needed to know as her old friend jogged over to her.

"Hoisted by your own pranking petard there, Prissy?" Vickie's grin was far too satisfied.

"I don't know what you're talking about."

"Oh, so you willingly joined a flash mob?" Her friend crossed her arms, cocking her head to the side.

Priscilla scowled, reaching for her blazer and then snapping a few times so it wouldn't wrinkle from all the dastardly flinging and swinging it had endured.

"Fine. I may or may not be engaged in a prank war with my colleague."

"This wouldn't happen to be the cheery, lovely president of the North American Council of Witchery, would it? A little shorter than you? Blond? Curvy? Loves a honeycomb latte with an extra shot?" Vickie's tone was downright gleeful now.

Her scowl deepened, and her friend tucked her phone in her pocket and turned, gesturing for Priscilla to follow.

"Come on. I'll get you a donut of the day and you can tell me all about how you don't have a type. Hot for presidential power, and all."

"I don't have a type! Agatha beat me for president; I *should* be president, and besides, we are hex-level enemies." It wasn't a sign of anything other than knowing her enemy that she noticed everything about the woman.

Prissy lowered her voice as they walked into Hopelessly Teavoted, the shop's little skull bells jangling cheerily behind her on the door.

At the counter, she recognized the teenager who was undoubtedly one of her brother's brood of students now. The girl had grown at least an inch, and she was wearing her hair differently from the way she had last year, in micro-braids piled on top of her head, but it was still the same signature pink. Priscilla checked her name tag to make sure she remembered correctly; she wasn't in the business of knowing children's names off the top of her head.

"Hazel!" Priscilla's cheery dancing hex was over, but she smiled, a real thing.

"Ms. Hart! Hi! I have your brother again this year! I just saw him last period."

She was glad to see schools were still being flexible about students leaving early for college courses and work. She remembered Az mentioning Hazel taking an advanced-level literature class on top of his senior lit class at Hallowcross High at the local university twice a week. This must be one of her off days.

"Az says you're doing a university class?" she offered.

Her face brightened. "He remembered! I knew it. I knew I was a favorite. Ooooh, Celeste is going to be jealous to hear this."

"Whatever she has on the house, Hazel," said Vickie, pushing through the double doors to the back, presumably to wash her hands and find an apron.

"I'm absolutely paying. Doing my duty to keep this place afloat." If Vickie hadn't bought Priscilla's late mother's tea shop and café, then devil only knew what sort of terrible chain would have replaced it. She certainly didn't have the time or interest to run it, and it took serious commitment to make a small business profitable.

Hazel nodded, grinning. "What will it be? We have two donut specials today, Summer Bites, which is a honey-glazed dark chocolate donut hole, and You're the Bun That I Want, which is strawberry jelly filled." Priscilla's eyes narrowed. Had Agatha checked the menu schedule to magic a flash mob? That sort of organization was exactly the devious shit that woman would get up to.

"An iced honeycomb latte and the second donut."

"You have to say it. There was a whole themed flash mob and all." Hazel's eyes glinted with mischief. "Which I take it you knew about. Surely you are aware that this store is named for that cover of a *Grease* song from *Pushing Daisies*. So technically this mob is for us, specifically."

Dammit. If the teens knew, everyone would know. Priscilla was going to get a bad reputation. People might think of her as mirthful. Lighthearted, even.

Her stomach recoiled at that.

"Fine," she gritted out. She was dour, but she wasn't a monster about to be cruel to a child over it. "A You're the Bun That I Want, and one of those little yogurt parfaits, if you have any left."

"Coming right up."

She smiled at Hazel again—genuine, as this little mortal had nothing to do with the hate of her life hexing her to dance in public like a plebeian—and scoped out the seats. Her favorite corner table, a round, mahogany thing that reminded her of the dinner table at home in Hart Manor, was free, and she slid into the red velvet high-back chair behind it, letting herself sink into the relaxation of planning her next attempt on Agatha's peace of mind.

She *should* be thinking about the Constance Witherspoon situation. And she would.

She'd just get her revenge first, that was all.

CHAPTER 8

Agatha

That slit in the side of Priscilla's skirt was driving her fucking crazy.

Obviously, she did not give a fuck about a bit of tasteful midriff, but thighs? Thighs were her kryptonite; they always had been. There was something about a firm, curved thigh that she wanted to squeeze a shade tighter than comfortable.

She knew she ought to be listening to Hart, who was seething about the flash mob.

"—total disregard for my bodily autonomy," Priscilla—no, that was wrong, thighs be damned, *Hart*—Hart was saying, chest heaving. Behind her, Agatha's pothos twisted, agitated. Even her plant thought she'd taken it too far.

Goddess, was she the lady version of a dirty old man at work? Hart was annoying enough to have lived a thousand lifetimes, but she knew from the rather ugly campaign of mudslinging back and forth that Hart was twenty-six, which cognitively should have been the point at which the human brain was fully developed. Her face was unlined, or at least it was normally, when she wasn't twisting it into that scowl. The things she would do to those lips, even snarling like that, were depraved.

"Oh, because changing my clothes and hair right before one of my most important meetings of the year was totally respectful of boundaries, wasn't it?" If they were going to talk bodily autonomy, Agatha was certainly not going to let Hart off the hook.

From his desk in front of her office, Kevin looked aghast; he had only just made it back in after a leave of absence. Speaking of toned thighs, she was doing impeccably at ignoring his. It was easy not to ogle Kevin, even though he was the appropriate age. He was her assistant, and at six-foot-four, he was the stuff of romance books, but somehow, and maybe it was a sense of propriety, she had never lusted after the cornflower blue of his eyes, or his blond flip of hair that always landed perfectly.

She was a professional, that was why. And Kevin was kind, which historically was not her type.

Her lack of interest in Kevin was not because of the decidedly licentious thoughts she had about her nemesis, who was currently standing in front of her, fuming. It was not because of gold-tinted brown eyes, raven hair, and a jawline that begged to be licked. It was *definitely* not because of those lips.

"I'd say we are even," she said, and she immediately regretted it, Priscilla blushed, *actually blushed*, and she hadn't seen the woman ever do such a thing, not even when booking it out of her own wedding, and fuck, why was that blush so pretty on the smooth skin at the nape of her neck, the way it crept up toward her face and down her chest?

Agatha wanted to know how far it went. She wanted to trace it with her fingers and her tongue. She was down bad, and the plants on her wall reached toward Hart. Agatha ran her thumb across her fingers, magicking a warning for them to keep their tendrils to themselves.

Agatha rubbed her fingers on her eyes. They were just coworkers, and practically rivals, to boot. There would be no licking here.

"I swear on the name of every single Hart that has graced these halls, all the way back to my great-great-grandmother, to start with, that this indignity will not go unanswered."

Hart's voice was booming, magic unspooling, possibly unbidden, from her. Her fingers twitched; she was one irritation away from snapping something terrible.

"Let's talk about it in my office," Agatha said, looking pointedly around. Kevin was not the only one staring, and that seemed to wake Hart from a trance of outrage; she looked around and blanched.

Right. Hart might not give one single fuck what Agatha thought, but she did care about the Council. She'd tried to lead it herself, after all.

After driving out the previous president. With her thighs, probably.

"Fine," she said, gesturing for Agatha to go first.

Agatha sighed and adjusted her lavender vest. She could hear Hart on her heels, could smell her, all lemony, with a hint of something herbal—mint, maybe—and she'd be kidding herself if she didn't admit that she smelled good, even after dancing her ass off in a flash mob hex that Agatha was quite proud of.

It may have been devious, but the magic was impeccable.

They were only a few feet into the office when everything went white, the force of the explosion tossing them both back into the hall.

From behind the ringing in her ears, she could hear Kevin panicking, and someone else—Nancy, maybe?—shouting for help, but she was too dazed to be sure. Her ankle twisted at an awful angle that would hurt to high heaven once the pain registered, and her back would ache later for this. They had certainly never warned of this sort of prank in any workplace mockumentary sitcom. She should be outraged. She had every right to be outraged; someone was clearly trying to kill her. But for now, all she noticed was Priscilla, limp on the floor, a trickle of blood oozing from her forehead.

Panic spiked through her, blood rushing, and she reached for the other woman, desperate to find a pulse.

Hart's wrist was cool to her touch, the skin impossibly smooth, but she couldn't find one, quite possibly because she absolutely had little medical training beyond the required yearly magical resources sessions on how to magically administer Narcan and an EpiPen, neither of which would help in this particular instance.

She moved two fingers to the space just below Hart's jaw, the way she'd seen people do on medical dramas, and there it was: a fluttering, living pulse.

The tension eased, she rocked back onto her heels, not taking her hand off Hart, but feeling the agony of her ankle—twisted, for sure—beneath her.

Priscilla's hand rose up in a flash, circling her wrist, cool against the warmth of her own.

Her eyes shot open, and there they were, deep brown, only the slightest bit of gold rimming them.

Agatha's breath caught, and not just from the pain in her ankle.

For a moment, Priscilla's long, elegant fingers slid up, cupping the hand touching her pulse point. The edge of her mouth curled into a smirk, and she sat up, a cat about to pounce.

Agatha dropped her hand at the clatter of Kevin setting the first aid box down on the floor and yanking out a magical contraption that could check for broken bones.

BLEEP, it blared—*BLEEP*, a second time, clearing Hart, and then Agatha, but the moment was gone, shattered by the beeping and the incessant chatter of Kevin.

"Well, ladies, that was lucky—that you didn't break anything, I mean, obviously not lucky that the office exploded, assuming *you* didn't mean to be in there when that went off, did you?"

He levied a sharp glare at Hart, whose eyes widened. Either she was an excellent actress, or she truly had not been the perpetrator of this particular trap.

"Why," she began, wincing a little, prodding her wrist, and then snapping her fingers twice until her face relaxed, "why the heavens would I explode myself? If I had anything to do with this, why would I have walked in there with her?"

"Miscalculation," said Kevin, tone still accusatory as he stood up and offered a hand to Agatha, leaving Hart to get up on her own. Kevin's defense of her was noble, and she would be lying if she said that she didn't wonder if the person trying to off her was her fellow councilwoman. Could she have misread their rivalry? Was it of a more deadly nature?

A cluster of interns and Council members had gathered, watching the tense exchange.

"I would *never* do this to my Aya Muse set." She gestured to a gaping hole in the right thigh, opposite from that befuddlingly hot slit up the other side. "This is almost the exact outfit Aubrey Plaza wore to the Gotham Awards. I would never besmirch an homage to my personal style icon like that." Agatha tried pointedly to ignore Hart's thighs. Goddess, her thighs.

Kevin glared, tapping his hands together delicately, each finger meeting its match on the other side. The hole closed, the smoke and charring vanishing.

"You could have fixed it as easy as that," he said primly.

Hart crossed her hands, brow furrowing. "It will never be the same," she hissed, tugging at the fabric as though he had burned her.

"Easy," said Agatha, raising her hands placatingly. "I'm sure we can all agree that something this serious requires a full investigation. Kevin," she said, a tad sharper than she meant to, and his pretty face winced in surprise at her tone. "We don't accuse people without evidence."

"And she did get hurt pretty badly, too," said Nancy. A year out of school at the University of Havenwall, she was already on track for a permanent Council position. Agatha had heard her tell the other interns that she wanted to apply for Kevin's position when he inevitably got promoted one day. She liked Nancy for the job.

"That's right," said Agatha, relaxing into the familiar comfort of protocol. She snapped her fingers, and yellow caution tape covered the perimeter. "The Council has clear procedures for situations like this. Kevin, clear the conference room. I'll be using it as my office while we collect evidence. Give me an hour to contact the International Council, and page all Council members to give them a report. Assume nothing, mark and tag everything, and move forward with an unbiased and thorough investigation."

"But she—" Kevin spluttered. Agatha shook her head. Privately, she did think there was some possibility that Priscilla Hart had tried to impale her, and now to blow her up, but it wouldn't do to express that publicly. And besides, part of her thought that actual deathly antics were past Hart's capabilities.

Or at least, part of her wanted to think that.

"That's my final decision, and I need the conference room to settle things." Kevin tapped his fingers together, and the door swung open, revealing her spare laptop and a fresh set of notebooks and pens on the table. She rubbed her thumb across her fingers, and the emergency snacks she kept in stock in the storage room appeared on Kevin's desk.

"Help yourself to energy bars and water." She took one of each herself. "And no one bother me until this door is open," she said. "I need privacy to talk to the ICoW."

She also needed to magic some Advil and a heating pad for her back, but they didn't need to know that. Least of all her inconveniently beautiful, and potentially murderous, rival.

CHAPTER 9

Priscilla

She couldn't believe that Kevin, of all fucking people, had accused her of attempting to kill Agatha. Kevin, who she'd been so nice to when he was Evelyn's assistant. Kevin, who she'd even tolerated when he'd chosen to work for her rival instead of her.

Fucking Kevin.

"You know, I would never be this obvious in attempted murder," she said, glaring at him. "Fire and explosions are so pedestrian. Admittedly, the swords were my style, but that wasn't me either."

"What swords?" Kevin blinked. Priscilla ignored the little thrill of significance that Agatha must not have logged that particular incident.

"I would have doubled your salary if you had come to work for me instead," she mumbled.

Kevin shook his head, frowning. "I hardly think now is the time."

She looked around. Council members gathered, the buzz of conversation loud enough that no one heard the indecently timed proposal.

"Councilwoman Hart." Agatha's voice boomed, bossy, and damn if that wasn't hot.

"I'll come," said Kevin, eyes narrowing at Priscilla as though she might at any minute start a fire. She was thinking about setting *him* on fire, the insufferable jerk.

"No," said Agatha, mouth set in a firm line, face determined. "Just Hart."

Priscilla nodded, slinking into the makeshift office and shutting the door. Agatha rubbed her thumb across her fingers in a gesture that had always reminded Priscilla of a slower version of the Hart family snap, and the room quieted, the noise outside silenced.

"A privacy spell, huh?" Priscilla slid into the chair to the right of Agatha's computer. "I must be in big trouble."

Sighing, Agatha sat down. "No," she groaned. "But I am. Truly." Was she sweating?

"Go on . . ."

"The International Council insisted that in light of your history, this was two strikes."

Priscilla's cheeks heated. "But I didn't—that's unfair. Evelyn was my fiancée. Leaving her had nothing to do with her role as president."

"Hey." Agatha's voice was firm again. Her blue eyes determined. "I know that. I *know* that. It's fucked up, but the optics aren't good." She swallowed. "And so I may have told them something rash. Accidentally."

Priscilla rubbed her eyes. She wasn't trying to murder Agatha, and she hadn't been trying to run Evelyn out of town. And today's explosion, at least, was totally out of her hands.

"What did you tell them?"

Agatha took a deep breath, eyes darting away and then back, as though she refused not to stare directly into Prissy's soul. She rubbed at the bridge of her nose, and Priscilla would be lying if she said she didn't notice that Agatha's nails were shorter now, her fingers long and nimble.

"I lied to them. I said I was your alibi. It was definitely something I should have asked you before doing. In fact, if you want, I will go back and come clean." Agatha chewed her lip.

"What, did you tell them we were involved in some sort of weird sex ring for dendrophiles? Recording foot videos? Candling ear wax out of strangers while someone was rigging up an explosion?"

Agatha recoiled. "Good grief, why is that list so specific? I told them you couldn't have tried to kill me, because I was with you all night. I didn't think about how it would sound." She paused, looking miserable. "They thought I meant we were—we are—an item."

Priscilla burst out laughing. She couldn't help it; it was the most ridiculous thing she'd ever heard. Her admittedly hot but decidedly straight boss, dating her? How absurd.

"That . . . wasn't the reaction I was expecting," said Agatha, gripping the table and looking slightly green. Priscilla couldn't remember having laughed this hard in days, maybe in months, not even when she got Azrael with the guillotine on his way to school and it sliced off the perfectly coiffed top of his hair—spelled, of course, not to cause bodily harm.

"It's not that funny." Agatha frowned. "Why are you still laughing?"

"Because," Prissy bit out, between peals of laughter, "you're comically into dudes named Jonathan or Conrad. Imagine, the idea of you, a preppy, man-loving heterosexual, in a relationship with me, an eclectic lesbian. I'm certain you only date people who wear boat shoes and neatly pressed polo shirts. Your parade of men who probably have apartments with far too much leather furniture, the kind that sticks to thighs and ass cheeks while wearing any kind of women's shorts or skirts. Man-cave-loving, bro-time bros. They must have laughed you out of the room."

Agatha's face went ashen. "That's very offensive." The plants on the conference room walls shuddered.

"Oh, come off it," Priscilla scoffed. "I'm sure Jonrad will get over the unknown insult. If he weren't impervious to teasing, there would be no way he could don such hideous footwear. I saw the custom Sperrys he used to love."

Agatha shook her head, mouth a thin line. "No. It's offensive to me."

"I'm sorry. You have great taste in pantsuits. But I remember the guy you brought to my wedding. We all do, I'm sure. More than one Council member muttered about what a jackass he was to even have around the office on occasion, the way he would show up too early and act like you were inconveniencing him by not leaving whenever suited his fancy. You do not have great taste in men." She was a bit worried for Agatha, whose face went from unnaturally pale to a shade of scarlet that looked painful.

"His name was Jonathan, not Conrad, or Jonrad. And he *was* an asshole. But . . ." Priscilla shook her head, waiting for Agatha to call him *her* asshole. But Agatha took a deep breath and exhaled audibly. She swallowed. "I'm bisexual, you presumptuous ass."

Priscilla's jaw dropped.

Her hot boss. Her superhot, older, off-limits boss, who she had of course noticed, but not thought about too much, because it wouldn't do to get lightheaded over beautiful straights all the time. Her hot, straight boss with her breasts and her hair and—oh goddess, this complicated things.

It was Prissy's turn to swallow and fear the shade of her own blushing. It hadn't just been a joke, a lark they had laughed at before firming up a more believable story. The International Council of Witchery now believed that they were dating, and would have to continue to believe that, unless Prissy wanted to face the consequences of the Council considering her willing to blow up a president to get to a job.

"Oh goddess. You told them we're together."

"I did."

"Why?" A small part of her, and she wasn't proud of it, wanted the answer to be something . . . hopeful.

"Because once they assumed it, I couldn't see any other way to get them to believe you were innocent, and they wanted to summon you in the Loculus."

Priscilla blanched. She did not want to be locked up in a glass coffin and transported across the sea for interrogation in the International Council of Witchery police bureau.

"Thank you for getting me out of that."

"You're not mad?" Agatha looked relieved. "They won't be so generous again. Even once they thought we were a thing, I still had to beg. A toe out of line and you will know what the inside of that Loculus feels like until they can interrogate you."

"I've faked worse for less," Priscilla said. "Lay it on me. What do we have to do?"

"Well, we investigate. We prove your innocence, and then we have a polite breakup. You help me with the human mayor, and I'll help you with the Connie Witherspoon situation, and we get the town running smoothly while we figure out who's actually behind this."

"What's in it for me?"

"Besides not going to international jail?" Agatha's eyes glinted, steely, and Priscilla remembered that this was a woman clever enough to best her. "You get a rehabilitated image. I'm nice. If I vouch for you, people will believe you're good too. I'm sure you had a reason for breaking things off with Evelyn, but there are a lot of folks who don't seem to think so."

Agatha's smile brought out just the smallest wrinkles around her eyes, and she continued. "People don't leave their fiancées dramatically mid-wedding for no good reason, generally. You're broody, but I don't think you're the sort to mess with someone's heart. It's awfully brave to go that far and still turn back."

It was the first time anyone had ever called her brave for what she did, and that made her think. It *would* help to not be known as a vindictive heartbreaker.

"I have one condition," Priscilla said. It was a nonnegotiable; otherwise she couldn't stomach the idea of this.

"I have many, but go ahead." Agatha raised an eyebrow.

"Can *you* dump me? We stay friends, but I can't break up with two presidents in a row."

"Absolutely," said Agatha. "I'd be honored to break your heart. For pretend. About the other conditions."

Priscilla shrugged. "I'm flexible." She waggled her eyebrows. "As my girlfriend, you'd know that."

Agatha covered her face with her hand. "Am I really doing this?" she muttered.

"Yep," said Priscilla, checking her nails. She was pleased to find that her spell to keep the polish unchipped held up through explosive blasts. "You signed us up for this. Remember that. It was your idea."

"Okay. We stick to an appropriate amount of physical contact in public. Cheek kisses if needed, hand-holding, hand grazes, nothing rated higher than PG." Agatha clasped her hands, squeezing them together in a nervous tic Priscilla recognized from Council meetings.

"Fair enough," said Priscilla. The other woman's fingers were flat on the table now. Agatha did have nice hands, and the cuffs of her blazer looked soft enough to touch. She remembered how that skin had felt when she ran her fingers over Agatha's for a moment as they lay there, muted by the aftershock of explosion.

"We'll need to hammer out the details. A meet-cute, a reasonable series of low-profile dates." Agatha pushed a blond tendril behind her ear as if this was perfectly normal.

Those fingers again.

When Agatha had checked her pulse with them earlier, Priscilla hadn't let herself think about the touch. But now that she knew Agatha wasn't off-limits, the memory shifted into something more. Something delicious, something she wanted to run her tongue over and taste, again and again, until she got a sense of the shape of it.

Priscilla cleared her throat.

"My place, this evening? Say, eight o'clock?"

Agatha stared. "Hart Manor?"

"That is where I live, yes." Priscilla, arms crossed, couldn't help but tighten her grip on her elbows. She told herself that it was to keep from snapping and not at the thought of bringing a pretty girl home for the first time in—well, for the first time since Evelyn.

"Sure." Agatha flexed her fingers again, threading them together and squeezing until it looked like they strained. Her cheeks tinted ever so slightly pink, like she had almost managed to hide whatever embarrassment she felt at the invitation.

Something between them *had* shifted, but she could make this work. She could ignore the whispering kernel of longing in her stomach, and perform for a pretend relationship.

One didn't get to be an expert prankster without a stellar ability to pretend.

By the end of the day, it was past time to move the hearse. Priscilla had left it at the tea shop longer than was socially acceptable, and Vickie had texted to ask if it was going to become a permanent fixture.

She skirted Main Street, slinking down a back road instead of walking past Hopelessly Teavoted. Vickie wasn't above meddling in her life after the events of last fall, and Priscilla wasn't ready to talk to her old friend again about the situation with Agatha, now that there was a situation, however fake, to admit.

The behemoth rumbled home, smoking slightly on the uphill toward the small garage that sat next to the conservatory where her mother's plants still grew. The Packard was parked in the front, its cheery cherry-red paint shining in a way that suggested that Az had washed it recently.

Her brother had been using the car; it made sense during the school year, especially since if she didn't want a long walk, she could take the hearse or a bicycle. Portals were still restricted due to the unstable nature of disease transmission. Witches were COVID cautious, even after safe and scientifically proven vaccine mandates had resulted in the end of the pandemic.

And it was reasonable, she reminded herself, to be cautious about an epidemic that had robbed her of both parents. Illness didn't go away just because a silly man with a microphone and a fear of needles pretended years of scientific research was suddenly false.

The knocker on the door to Hart Manor groaned, and she patted her favorite haunted little thing.

"That's my girl. Let's give Azrael some extra trouble next time he comes home, shall we?" The knocker stilled, as it always did when it listened, and she stroked her hand along the filigree carving. The haunted fixture scared her brother, and that made her love it all the more.

It was an epic door, and her loyal partner in pranking Azrael for all these years.

"Next time he comes in, I think add a little bit of a chill to the air, give him your most ghastly moans, and make him drop his keys a few times. Just until he gets shaky and spooked."

The knocker moaned in agreement, and a satisfied smile crept up her face. Her life might feel like a magical train wreck, but she would always have pranking Az to carry her through.

When she walked in, the door shut gently behind her on its own, and Azrael, who was standing in the middle of the foyer sorting through mail, frowned.

"How come the door is so nice to you?"

She shrugged. "We understand each other. You're too old. You wouldn't get it."

Az shook his head, and ran a hand through his hair. "Sometimes you're worse than the teenagers," he grumbled. "I'm barely two years older than you. That's not old."

Priscilla slid next to him, peering over his shoulder at the letters and plucking out one from a credit card company advertising completely free and absolutely painless debt recovery!

She snapped to give the company's owner an impossible-to-reach wedgie that would plague him all day, intensifying during important meetings.

"What'd you do to that one?" Azrael asked, snapping at his own junk mail.

"Incurable wedgie for a predatory lender. You?" They might fight, but there was always one thing the Hart siblings agreed on. It was fine, fair even, to pester peddlers of capitalism the same way those greedy corporate shills pestered mundanes.

Azrael held one up. "Health-care junk mailer about how a corporation cares while the executive just collected a bonus for cutting coverage, and premiums just went up twenty percent."

"Ew. I hope you hexed him good."

Azrael smiled and lifted his chin. "I gave him a nasty fungal rash somewhere dreadful." His grin deepened. "It won't do permanent damage, but it also won't go away without medical intervention."

"Rash on his junk for junk mailing. Noted. It was far less than he deserved," Priscilla agreed.

"How about you?" Her brother's expression was careful, as though he had been considering this. "How are you doing?"

"I'm not currently plotting the justified murder of predators, but there's always tomorrow."

Az bumped his shoulder into hers. "You know what I mean."

She sighed. "It's a long story."

"I've got time. Vickie's at work, and everyone else besides her who lives here is dead, except Emily Lickinson, and it gets old to only talk to a cat, so . . ."

Priscilla choked out a laugh. "So we're left with each other." It hurt, but they had come to a tacit agreement that joking about it was better than crying, at least sometimes.

"So spill." He walked into the dining room, not bothering to see if she followed. He knew she would, and she sprawled into one of the high-back chairs in the corner, across from where he sat down at the table next to a pile of essays and his laptop. He shoved them to the side and put his head in his hands. "Tell me."

She groaned, throwing an arm over her eyes.

"Can you level with me?"

"Sure." It was easier to ask without looking.

"How bad is it?" She hadn't asked him. If she was honest, she was too afraid of the answer. "I mean, what have people been saying? I know I lost the election and all, but how bad do I come across? Like a bad witch taking names, or like a bad witch, derogatory?"

"Why do you ask?" He looked suspicious, like she might set him up for some sort of prank with this, and that made her feel even worse about her precarious reputation in the witching community.

"Someone has been trying to blow up Agatha."

"Shit." Azrael paused, and she heard the indecision in it. He snapped. The room was bubbled in silence, the sort of protection spell that bound whatever was said in secrecy.

Fuck. That could only mean one thing. She sat up, looking him in the eyes as Azrael leveled his gaze on her. "Was it you?" he asked calmly. "I'm not judging. I think we should talk about it if it was you, and I'm not assuming it was. But if you've taken things too far, and you need help figuring out how to deal with it, I've got your back. Harts stick together."

"What the fuck? Of course it wasn't me! I'm a prankster, not a homicidal maniac."

He let out a sigh of relief, measured, as though maybe he didn't want to heave it in front of her.

"Oh, thank goddess." He snapped, and the privacy spell lifted. His face fell. "That probably doesn't look great for you, though."

"Yeah. My own brother contemplated my murderous intentions, so I guess I shouldn't be shocked if other people do too." She squeezed her eyes shut, trying not to let that thought fill her with unbridled rage.

"They don't know you like I do."

"I don't know if that's supposed to be reassuring."

Azrael shrugged. "Is there more?"

"Yes."

"Go on."

"Don't rush me." He would have opinions about fake dating, but she also didn't see a way around telling him, if Agatha was going to be here and Az was going to hear about everyone thinking they were together anyway.

He flicked his fingers, and a seltzer water materialized in front of her, with a few lemon wedges. She smiled and took a sip. Lime seltzer with lemon garnish—her favorite.

Even if he thought she was capable of killing, at least her brother knew her taste in beverages.

"I may or may not have agreed to fake date the Witchery Council president for reasons."

Azrael stared at her, and then looked around, like he expected to find a hidden camera or bugs or something to pop out. Which was silly, because she hadn't done a shock-him-and-make-insects-rain-from-the-ceiling prank in ages. Though his fear of spiders would be useful in distracting him if he asked too many questions.

But that was a thought for later.

She needed to get this out before Agatha arrived and her presence did the talking for Priscilla.

"It was Agatha's idea." She cleared her throat. "She was trying to give me an alibi when she said we were dating, a little bit."

Dating a little bit, he mouthed, eyes wide.

"Yes, after the explosion, things got complicated."

"And she went with saying that you two are dating?" Az's eyebrows were so high, she almost feared they'd jettison off his forehead.

"Well," said Priscilla. "It wouldn't be the first time I got handsy with a Witchery Council president, so it's not completely outside the realm of possibility."

Her brother stared at her, mouth opening and closing, and then he shook. For a second she thought he might cry, until a laugh burst out of him, and she realized he was silently shaking in laughter, cracking up, and then loudly guffawing.

"You sound like a baboon, Azrael," she said thinly.

"I can't help it," he shot out between laughs, bending over, his face resting on the table. "Devil damn me, it's too fucking funny. You left one Council president at the altar six months ago, and you decided that the best way to repair your reputation was to *date the next one*?"

Priscilla frowned. "Well, when you put it that way, it makes me sound bad. But Agatha was the one who came up with this plan. I just went along with it."

Azrael grinned at her.

"Agatha's pretty, no?" He smiled wider. "Vickie said she's pretty and that she's certain you've noticed just exactly how pretty." He looked up, grinning like a devil. "I heard she's your type."

She felt the frown on her face deepen, too hot for comfort.

"No." It was a lie, sure, but it wasn't entirely her fault. Being around her brother could sometimes bring out her least mature behavior.

"Then why are you blushing? You never blush. I don't think I've seen you this red since before I left for college."

"I'm not blushing, I'm glaring." If only her face would stop feeling so hot, she could sell this.

"Sure." Her brother smirked.

The sound of the door knocker interrupted them. Azrael cocked his head at her, and she pulled a hand over her face. There was no way to avoid telling him what he was about to know.

"She's coming over. To get our stories straight."

"Straight?" He looked like he wanted to laugh again.

"Don't you dare," she bit out.

Az held up his hands. "I'm on your side. No matter what." The corner of his mouth twitched, but he jumped a little when the knocker sounded again, this time groaning miserably. "Are you going to get that? I think it's your girlfriend."

There was no sense telling him to fuck off as he followed her to the door; he lived here too. She opened it to find Agatha standing there.

For a moment, her breath caught. Agatha looked so vulnerable. Soft, even.

Her hair was damp and pulled back, as though she'd just showered, and she wasn't exactly dressed down, but she had on comfortable-looking corduroy pants and a cotton shirt that hugged her curves and tapered to a scoop neck in the front.

She looked casual, and for some reason, Priscilla felt like she could breathe, better than perhaps she had ever breathed before. She inhaled, and her lungs filled with a contentment so complete that she could have forgotten herself entirely, if not for the throat clearing behind her.

"Oh. Come in, Agatha. You know my brother, Az."

Agatha raised a hand in greeting. "Hi," she said, smiling and breezing past them both, looking up in awe at the sweeping two-story ceiling. "Gosh, it's even more beautiful than I imagined," she murmured, looking around.

Priscilla's eyes remained glued to Agatha, to the nape of her neck and the blond tendril that had escaped her high bun. "Right," she said. "You haven't been here before. Sorry, yeah. It's lovely," Prissy said, not looking at the house at all, and not daring to look at Azrael.

"Welcome to Hart Manor," her brother said, "but actually, I was just leaving."

His stack of student papers, half-consumed mug of coffee, and favorite grading pens on the table said otherwise. But before Priscilla could argue, he had grabbed his keys off the hook and was halfway out the door, not even stopping to grab a jacket. "Good to see you, Agatha. Sorry to leave—I promised my girlfriend I would help her close up shop."

It was an unlikely story for a weeknight, but she let it go.

It did, however, present a slight problem.

There was now a beautiful woman standing in her foyer, waiting to hear all the ways they could pretend, casually, to be together. While they were alone in a house with *opinions* about romance.

And that beautiful woman also happened to be her sworn nemesis.

So maybe more than a slight problem, after all.

The door shut behind Prissy, landing softly on her rear and nudging her into the room. She swore the lights dimmed just a little, just enough that she wasn't sure if she was imagining it.

The flickering candles that lit themselves on the mantel, however, were obvious, as was the way a breeze blew out of nothing, wafting the scent of Agatha toward her. The woman smelled like peaches and vanilla, and just a trace of something a little spicy—cardamom, maybe?

She smelled like pie, and Priscilla had never been reserved enough to pretend that she wasn't the sort of bluntly crude person who would think of, well, other sorts of pies when presented with that idea.

Damn meddling manor, she thought to herself.

CHAPTER 10

Agatha

Hart looked so pretty that Agatha had to recite facts in her head to focus.

Like how there were more chickens in the world than humans, by about a three-to-one ratio. Good. That was kind of terrifying, like some sort of avian uprising could damn them all to a fate of beaks and feathers.

"There's something else I wanted to talk to you about," she said, trying not to get lost in Prissy's brown eyes. "I'm not sure I should, but, well, the fact of the matter is, I do think that if the Council calls you in, they'd expect you to know." She squeezed her eyes shut, hoping it would dull the shine of the alluring mistress of darkness before her.

Agatha paused. Hart crossed her arms, staring across the library at her. It was a gorgeous room, with the kind of staircases and ladders that book lovers everywhere dreamed of, like something out of a storybook.

A rather macabre one, if you included the suits of armor and the steepled framing of the mahogany bookshelves. A fluffy white cat sat next to the high-back chair Priscilla had taken by the roaring fire, which seemed to make the temperature of the room perfect, despite its height and ferocity.

"Well?" Priscilla's voice was sharp. Acerbic. And something else, something that twisted in Agatha, that strain of anticipation. Goddess, Agatha shouldn't, but she wanted Prissy Hart, claws and all.

Staring at a wall of large, unsettling oil paintings, Agatha rubbed her temples.

"I've been working on a dangerous project for the International Council." That did help dull the longing. Complicated Council business reminding her that they were colleagues, first and foremost, was an excellent buzzkill.

Hart sat up, interested.

"Oh?"

"It's high clearance." This would have been easier if she had told Priscilla earlier, but she had her reasons. Namely, the suspicion that she could be the attempted murderer. And surely there were things about Hart that she didn't know.

"I am also a Council member." Hart crossed her arms. She frowned, which, unfortunately, was still unsettlingly hot. Those pouty lips made Agatha want to do devious things. And was the wall getting closer? Agatha stepped forward, now an inch away from Priscilla. She looked at the damask-patterned wall, certain that it had moved.

"Yes, technically you are cleared."

Priscilla glowered. "Then why don't I already know?"

Agatha sighed. "I wasn't entirely sure if I could trust you."

"And now you can?" That crimson mouth pursed, an expression that filled Agatha with slight dread and slightly more longing.

"Now I can't afford not to," she bit out, ignoring the hypnotic scent of Priscilla—lemon and mint, clear on the air at such a small distance. She shouldn't be thinking of her as something more intimate than Councilwoman Hart. Priscilla was not just any beautiful temptress. She was a woman who had left the previous Council president at the altar. A woman who had then tried to fight her way to the presidency. So what if the smell of her, the shape of her thighs, the pout of her lips, made Agatha want to throw all of those perfectly good reasons for reservation out a window. Emotional defenestration was stupid, but she wanted to be stupid, for a moment in her one wild, beautiful life. She sighed a little, unable to help herself. Priscilla cocked her head, frowning, and Agatha jolted out of the daydreaming, remembering what needed to be shared.

"It's code-named Elixir," she began. Any witch worth her salt would know immediately what the project was. And Prissy, staring at Agatha with the disbelieving intensity and abject sex appeal of Elvira herself, was worth a whole heap of salt.

Hart's mouth opened. "Your top secret project is immortality?" She shook her head. "Immortality." Realization dawned on her. "That makes sense now. One of the forbidden magics."

"Hush." Agatha jumped a little, though they were alone in the library. Well, presumably alone. She'd heard something clatter beyond the wall that could have been Azrael returning, or whatever else might haunt these surprisingly cheery halls. An interesting description, given that she was in a room with a six-foot painting of an anatomically correct human heart being grasped in a hand. But she found Hart Manor to be . . . oddly comforting. Kooky and strange and wonderful. Even if the walls of the place did seem to be literally contracting, as though conspiring to squeeze her and Priscilla together. At her feet, the cat meowed loudly, and brushed against her leg. She reached down to pet it, and the cat chirped, bobbing its head in satisfaction.

"What's the cat's name again?"

"Emily." Hart paused. "Emily Lickinson."

That made Agatha laugh. "Your brother really leans into that English teacher persona, then?"

"You know those English major types." Hart smiled, slightly crooked, and Agatha had to remind herself that this was someone who had broken Evelyn. Priscilla Hart could break her, too, if she wasn't careful. She needed to think of her as a colleague and a potential criminal. She needed to focus on facts, and to ignore the funny skip her heart did at the sight of that insouciant half smile.

Agatha trained her attention on Hart, telling herself it was for business and not for drowning in the depths of them. There *was* something that bothered her.

"How do you know about Project Elixir?"

Hart shrugged, examining her nails. "I know almost everything about the Council. I started interning for my dad in high school, and by my freshman year, I'd decided that I wanted to be just like my grandmother."

President. Her grandmother had been president, but Agatha thought it best not to bring up the sore subject of the election she had won.

And what the fuck was that instinct about? This woman had insulted her good name in the campaign and then, even after she'd won fair and square, proceeded to prank her mercilessly. Now here she was, being sensitive to her losing opponent? Madness, surely.

"Anyway, my dad always insisted that it was a bad idea. The original Fountain of Youth was destroyed for a reason, and the Council had a contingency plan in the event of disaster, but we never had to use it." She narrowed her eyes. "My Uncle Larry has an amateur magical history hobby, and he's really taken things up a notch in his retirement. He was helping me with research on forbidden magic. Constance mentioned I should pay more attention to Council business."

Agatha snorted. "She's not wrong about that."

She wasn't sure that Priscilla wasn't trying to kill her. But the thing was, if she *was* trying to kill her, and if she was behind the attempted theft, well, then she would already know, but telling her would make it seem as though Agatha trusted her.

And if she wasn't, well then they were both screwed, in the crosshairs of some unknown entity resolved to take at least one of them out.

It was this or nothing, really.

She sighed.

"Hildebrand von Auden died last year. In his collection, the

Council unearthed a six-hundred-sixty-six-year-old bottle believed to contain water from the Fountain of Youth. We have just finished testing it—obviously, to do so without disturbing its contents was laborious, to say the least."

Priscilla frowned, a shadow passing over her face. "Definitely what Uncle Larry was alluding to, then." Her frown deepened, and she went on. "Wait, would that have taken a team of European witch scientists?"

"Yes." Agatha wasn't sure where she was going with this line of questioning, but Hart's brows furrowed, and the corners of her mouth pulled down. "Why?" she asked, almost certain that she would regret probing.

"Nothing," said Prissy, voice tight. "Just you're not the first Council president to withhold the details of that particular work project from me." Agatha wanted to remind her that she was unearthing deep Council secrets here, but years of political training had her swallowing her words.

"Always the councilwoman, never the president," Hart muttered, and Agatha's eyebrows shot up at the edge of bitterness in her voice, especially given the origin of that expression. It was a reminder that she was right to hold Priscilla Hart at a distance. This woman could wreck her, like she had her predecessor.

"Fine," said Agatha, voice silky and more vicious than she meant. "The point is, it's missing."

"It's missing?" Hart blinked rapidly. "You mean to tell me that you discovered an immortality potion and then lost it?"

"I didn't *lose* it. Someone stole it." Agatha leaned against the wall, which attempted to nudge her back toward the other woman.

"Are you sure it didn't blow up in the explosion?" Hart's face was unreadable, and she rapped absentmindedly against the wall until it stopped. "There are factions of people who believe firmly that any objects that can contribute to or grant immortality must be destroyed immediately. If anyone got wind of that—"

"They'd be likely to try to blow it up. That was my first thought, too, but there's no trace of the thing, and the bottle was hexed with a permaspell to leave traces if destroyed. If it had been blown up, the stain would have been palpable."

"We all would have felt that," Hart mused.

"Exactly."

"So someone stole what is probably the last of the Fountain of Youth, the only immortality potion left in existence, and then tried to blow you up for funsies and to cover it?"

"Maybe," said Agatha darkly. "Or maybe someone didn't care if I knew it was stolen." Her stomach twisted. Did someone out there hate her so much as to wish not only that her projects would fail, but also that she actually died?

And, more importantly, was that someone the distractingly beautiful, raven-haired woman sitting in front of her?

"If the thief was at all involved in the magical community, which they would have to be, they'd know that the bottle would be rigged. They would know you knew it was gone."

"Which means the bombing was for me, personally."

"Well, fuck me, Agatha. Who would want to kill a stand-up gal like you?"

Agatha glared daggers at her, her stomach twisting rebelliously at the turn of phrase. She shouldn't want to. She didn't want to. Not really. Not that much, anyway.

"I mean, the International Council suggested I start with the person who tried to beat me for office."

Hart frowned. "No fair. When a man has political aspirations, it's admirable, but goddess forbid a woman does, and now suddenly she's a conniving murderess?"

"I know," said Agatha. "However, it is slightly less feminist of you seeing as how the former Council president is also a woman." At the look on her face, she added, "I know you didn't actually discard her easily. I'm just saying it looks bad."

Hart's face was white as chalk, and something flashed across it. For just a few seconds, Agatha thought perhaps she had gone too far, and that the other woman was going to cry.

Hart's expression set back into its normal indolence, though, and she took a seat.

"Enough. We need a backstory. How did we start dating?"

"You helped me move out of Jonathan's place when we broke up, and we started out just friends, but you kept coming up with excuses to drop by my new condo. To fix a shelf, to bring a plant. Finally, it got to the point where I realized it could not possibly be just to help out."

"That sounds suspiciously nice of me," said Hart dryly. "Are you sure it's believable?"

"Yes," Agatha insisted. "We need people to believe that you, in all your beautiful aloofness, fell hard enough for me to forgive the fact you and I threw so much shade at each other on the campaign trail, smeared each other entirely, and that I beat you."

"You beat me by an extremely narrow margin, thank you very much. But more importantly, you think I'm beautiful?"

"That was your takeaway?" Agatha looked at her, but Hart said nothing, eyebrow raised, smirk written across her face in triumph. "Fine," said Agatha. "Yes, you're stunning and an ice queen. Show me how you'll sell it. That you love me."

"Stand up." Priscilla's voice was lower, and goddess, had Agatha ever felt like this at a command before? She got to her feet, anticipation prickling at her skin. Was she about to be horribly embarrassed? Agatha wasn't sure if that would be better or worse than being unbearably horny.

"We need rules. No kissing," Agatha blurted. She wanted to swallow the words as soon as they were out of her mouth. "No kissing, but touching is allowed."

Priscilla Hart slunk toward her, all lithe limbs and catlike grace. "Where will you allow me to touch you, Agatha?" She raised an eyebrow. "Where do you *want* me to touch you?"

She tensed all over, shutting her eyes for a moment and trying to force herself to regret the low register of Hart's words. She would not think about them; she would not replay them a thousand times starting now. She would not let her mind roll over the curves of that first name; she wouldn't let herself even think of Hart as Priscilla, the way the consonants slid off her tongue and wrapped around her. She shivered. Goddess.

"I . . ." Agatha forgot what words were. Priscilla was close enough to smell—lemon and mint, the sweetness underneath almost unbearable. She wondered if her lips would taste like candy and tea, like that same sweetness. She ached to know the answer.

"Where?" said Priscilla, tracing the outline of Agatha's face, pushing a strand of hair behind her ear, so gently as to not touch her skin.

"Anywhere," she bit out, and Priscilla's eyebrows shot up. "Except, you know."

"I really don't," said Priscilla, leaning in, and Agatha thought maybe she understood that it could be worth it to be left at an altar by this woman.

That thought, however, reminded her of the agony of Jonathan, and worse, the public shame. The ridicule. The painful reminder of her reality.

She straightened her posture. "Arms, hands, head only. Nothing below the neckline."

Priscilla nodded, holding up a hand and waggling her fingers.

"Here?" She traced a line from Agatha's collarbone up to her jaw.

Shivers ran through Agatha, and it was all she could do to pretend composure. She straightened her chin, staring up at Prissy. It was too hot already, that tiny touch.

Sure, she was a lot less experienced at, well, what her therapist called "being honest about her attraction to women." But that didn't mean Priscilla had to know about any of it.

Not the way those big brown eyes shook her to her core. Not the thrill of excitement in her veins that she couldn't ignore, even though she'd trained herself so well to do just that.

Not the way her eyes traced Priscilla's body anytime she was in Agatha's line of sight, and not the way she knew, not just saw, but *knew*, where it was that Priscilla Hart was standing, how far out of her orbit and how tantalizingly, impossibly close all the same, without even looking.

She felt Priscilla Hart without having once touched her, and that was it—had they touched at some prior, unimportant date she'd let slip through her mind? Had they met before, in another lifetime, and now they recognized the gravitational pull of each other like old lovers unable to completely surrender the memories of their history? Surely they must have shaken hands, or brushed shoulders, and she'd forgotten to clock it, to log it in her bank of carefully curated memories of this woman.

She ought to have remembered it, but everything from her time with Jonathan was colored in by the all-consuming desperation of wanting someone, mind, body, and soul, knowing that person would never want her back in the very same way, and then clutching desperately, watching the whole thing unravel.

Until he had stood up, after Hart had unceremoniously abandoned her would-be bride and humiliated Agatha in public, worse than anyone ever had.

Her cheeks flushed. She hated Hart. Or, rather, she *should* hate Hart, for catalyzing a heartbreaking split with her own running. Instead, she felt—she felt intensity, that was it.

But the fact of the matter was that the split with Jonathan had been a long time coming. Her heart had been grieving, mourning, for months, if not years, of that relationship.

Winning president afterward had seemed fair, like the universe acknowledging she was worth something. And feuding with her opponent had felt slightly petty, but so good. Every slight against her stoked the fire; every shot she took at Hart coiled desire in her, tighter, more insistent.

Mainly because it meant spending time thinking about and being near Priscilla.

But never so near as now. Now, Hart touched her gently, but it was enough to catapult her into the fantasy of intimacy. Priscilla's finger lingered on the side of her jaw, just below her ear. Now, she felt at once like she knew exactly what to do and like she knew nothing, absolutely nothing, about anything, ever.

"Show me." She meant for it to come out a command, but out came, instead, a reedy whisper, hoarse and full of longing. "Show me how you'll sell it, following the rules. How will you make sure that people believe you're mine? That I belong to you too?"

Priscilla smirked, and her mouth opened. Her hands dropped to her sides. For a moment, Agatha was certain she would say something cutting. They were, after all, vengefully matched. But she tilted her head, so confident that Agatha suddenly wanted—no, needed—to see her leveled. Wrecked by the same agonizing want that had laid her bare.

She raised her own hand and set it against Priscilla's neck, gently at first.

Priscilla let out a little gasp, and for a moment, her face was open, the careful, clever mask of a woman slipping until Agatha moved her thumb, a featherlight brush up, and then a firmer press against the delicate skin beneath Priscilla's jaw. Agatha saw, for just a sliver of a second, a person as desperate to be loved, to be touched, as she was.

She pulled Priscilla's face toward her, closing the gap between them until they were cheek to cheek, flexing her fingers firmly around the other woman's neck.

"Did you think I wouldn't show you too?" she whispered, entranced, almost hypnotized, by her own boldness. "Did you think I'd miss the opportunity to demonstrate what it would feel like to be mine?" She squeezed her hand, flexing it just a little, and Priscilla let out a soft keen that made Agatha almost lose control, rules be damned.

Hart was still against her, perfectly still, and then she wasn't.

Then she was reaching a hand around, an arm bracing Agatha's back, dipping her, cupping her cheek with the other hand, thumb stroking an insistent, careful pattern against her jawline. She ran her fingers down, skating Agatha's neck, raising every hair on her body, eliciting a gasp that she couldn't have stopped if she'd wanted to.

Prissy's fingers mapped a path across Agatha's collarbone, skimming, flirting with lower, stopping, then brushing back up the other side of Agatha's neck, holding firmly for a moment, pupils shot wide, eye contact unbroken.

Those perfect, wine-red lips opened, and Agatha thought her heart might stop.

"I'll show you." Priscilla's voice was husky. "I don't need to kiss you to show everyone exactly what it would be like if you belonged to me. I don't need much to make the Council, hell, the entire world, believe that you're woven so deeply into my bones that I can't bear to stop myself from touching you."

Agatha's breathing was ragged now, and she would be embarrassed if not for the way that Priscilla's cheeks and breath matched hers.

For a moment, she expected Priscilla to kiss her. For them to drop the act and claw off their clothing, to fuck on the library floor.

For a few exquisitely agonizing, glorious seconds, she let herself picture it, running her hands down, down, lower, touching Priscilla, the scrape of the carpet against her back, the spread of her thighs.

But Hart pulled her upright and then took two steps back, so quickly that Agatha thought she might fall. She reached for a chair, grabbing for the extra support, even if it did show the extent of her distraction.

"Oh," she said, and Hart crossed her arms, snapping her fingers to fix her hair back to straight, unruffled perfection.

"See? If you want me to pretend to be with you, that's easily within my capabilities." Priscilla frowned. "The question is, what else do I get?"

"Oh." Agatha blushed, hand pushed against her chest. Could she really agree to faking a relationship in exchange for sex? She would be lying if she said that sounded bad to her.

Hart's eyes widened. "Not like that. I mean, you get to hunt down the culprit. What do I get, careerwise? I didn't mean personally. I'm not that hard up."

That little nagging voice at the back of her mind said that Agatha also got to find out if Hart was that culprit, but that was out of the question to mention.

"You get the benefit of not being detained, obviously." Agatha's composure was coming back to her, haughty and overcompensating for the moment of agonizingly honest lust she hadn't meant to reveal.

"Yes, but it was your idea," Hart pointed out. "Clearly, you're doing this for a reason."

"Fine." Agatha crossed her arms, mirroring the other woman's disdain. "I also need your help with the mundane mayor. And I need to keep a closer watch on how you're dealing with Connie Witherspoon, because you're still shirking that particular responsibility."

Hart scowled. "Fine. You're keeping tabs on me, winning Mayor Khalil's trust, I get it. But then I should get something from you too."

"As long as it follows the no-kissing rule, and is reasonably appropriate," she responded primly.

Hart rolled her eyes. "If we do this, I want you to actively help me rehab my reputation. Yes, I know I am at fault for leaving someone at a wedding. I should have left her before the wedding. She's lovely, Evelyn, but we—we weren't suited."

There was actual pain there. Perhaps Priscilla Hart wasn't quite the heartless monster people accused her of being.

Maybe there had been more to the bolting than met the eye. But it wasn't her job to pry, just to sort out the details here so that they could both get what they needed and not get caught faking it.

"Fine. You'll be a doting girlfriend, and I promise when it's time, I will publicly, but politely, call things off, leaving you heartbroken and proving once and for all that you're capable of feeling things besides disdain and schadenfreude."

Hart's face fell for a moment. "Who said I feel only disdain and schadenfreude?" Agatha immediately regretted being so specific.

"No one. Some random poster on Dreaddit."

"Fuck me," mumbled Priscilla, and Agatha shut her eyes.

The problem was, she wanted to. She really, really did.

CHAPTER 11

Agatha

Crystal Balls to the Wall was far enough away that she had accepted Hart's offer to drive.

She preferred not to, in general, and though she had a license, she didn't have a car, and with an apartment conveniently walking distance from both her job and most necessities, she hadn't been behind a steering wheel in close to a year. Agatha told herself that a bit of pranking might help her redraw that professional boundary, so her traitorous heart might remember that Priscilla really should be just Councilwoman Hart to her. And anyway, she'd been itching to get Hart back for that dreadful makeover hex. The drive was the perfect opportunity.

Agatha stood just outside the door to her apartment building, tempted to check the time, and wondering briefly if Hart would stand her up. Did fake dating necessitate real consideration?

Just as she was ready to go inside in a huff, the cherry-red Packard pulled up to the curb. Hart wore expensive-looking tortoiseshell sunglasses and a headscarf that reminded Agatha of glamorous old Audrey Hepburn movies, but if Audrey had been a goth girl with a flair for the macabre and dramatic. Audrey by way of Aubrey Plaza.

Her lips were that perfect, lush shade of crimson, and her nails matched, tapering into almond-shaped edges, quite different from the coffin shape she'd worn the previous week. Agatha was noticing because it was her job to pay attention to her colleagues, not for any other reason.

She nodded at Priscilla, hoping her face was giving austere and presidential and not revealing her desperate attempt to ignore those long, graceful fingers gripping the wheel. Goddess, those fingers.

Hart held up a hand and beckoned. Even with the oversized glasses, impatience was written all over the visible parts her face, in the curve of her mouth and the angle of her chin.

Agatha slid into the passenger seat, feeling oddly as though she'd been here in this exact moment before, slipping through anticipation and dread and, yes, a small bit of excitement too.

It was like running for Council president all over again. But this time, instead of campaigning on Hart's inexperience, Agatha wanted the precise opposite. She wanted to *experience* Priscilla Hart. All of her.

She remembered herself, and her manners.

"Morning," Agatha chirped.

"Morning." Hart bit it out, as though she resented the word. "Are you ready to supervise my activities, Madam President?" The title, though accurate, felt loaded coming from her mouth.

She was determined not to let this woman intimidate her, pranks and all. "As ready as anyone ever could be for such a gargantuan task."

Of all the things she'd expected at the dig at Hart's responsibility, she had not planned for the honest laugh that escaped Hart's lips. It was like ringing a bell she hadn't meant to knock into, and the result was devastating for her composure.

She was stunning. Priscilla had a lovely laugh, the kind that made her desperate to forget the barrier she was struggling to raise between them, and Agatha reached for her hand before she could think better of it.

"For the façade," said Priscilla knowingly. "Of course." She squeezed Agatha's fingers, and Agatha felt the sensation of it all the way up her spine.

The fake dating. Right.

"Obviously, we're in broad daylight, and now is as good a time as any to start selling the charade."

"We'll need to see magical resources. I have copies of everything we need. We just fill out the appropriate paperwork and declare a serious relationship."

"You know I love it when you talk dirty, baby."

Agatha stiffened at that. "Do not," she ground out, "call me baby."

"Very well. We'll find a good nickname. Here, lean in. I have a secret." She tipped the sunglasses up, setting them on top of the scarf.

Agatha eyed her warily, but leaned in.

"What's the secret?"

Hart's nails skated across the hair by Agatha's ear.

"The secret is that like this, anyone walking by could think we were up to all sorts of romantic endeavors." She paused. "Also, maybe the secret is that I don't hate pretending very much at all."

"Really," said Agatha, her mouth dry. She hoped Priscilla was not aware of the way her heartbeat sped up, of the rise and fall of her chest, of how she suddenly was aware of every single inch of her exposed skin and its proximity to Priscilla Hart's painted lips.

"We'll brainstorm nicknames," said Hart, lips brushing against the lobe of Agatha's ear.

Agatha shivered.

"Sunshine." She moved her mouth lower, lips catching the delicate skin just below her ear. "No, that's not it," she mused, holding still for a moment. Agatha thought she might die, trying to hold her breath and move as little as possible, whether to make the moment last forever or expire more quickly, she wasn't quite sure. Possibly both. "Dearest?"

"No," Agatha managed. "That sounds like I might stab you through a shower curtain. Or you me."

That was better. She was more composed when she was making light and cracking jokes.

"Precious," Hart asked, moving her lips a little bit lower, so they caught the edge of Agatha's jawline.

"No," she gasped, hating the way her voice caught on the word.

"Bunny?" Prissy's lips were on her neck now, just barely brushing against her skin.

"I'm not your pet," she rasped.

"Honey," Hart purred, moving her mouth to the spot just above Agatha's collarbone that made her forget what her actual name was for a moment.

"Mmm," Agatha mumbled, and the truth was, that one felt right, or maybe it was just the spot of her skin that felt that way under Prissy's lips.

Either way, Hart pulled back, her smile reaching her eyes. "Honey it is." She traced her hand softly across Agatha's ponytail, tugging it gently enough that it wouldn't muss, but with enough force that Agatha's rebellious mind tumbled over the possibility there. She'd put her hair up for precisely the opposite of this reason, to stand on business, and here she was, picturing Priscilla Hart pulling her hair in all sorts of terribly unprofessional circumstances.

Agatha cleared her throat.

"Now that that's squared away, what shall I call you, Mistress of Darkness?"

"I don't mind that." Hart's smirk said she didn't mind it a little *too* much.

"Maybe if we wanted people to think this was purely physical."

Hart raised her eyebrows but said nothing.

"You know," Agatha began, "my father is French, and I am fluent. We do have many lovely terms of endearment. And I think I might have the perfect one."

"Really?" Hart purred it, and Agatha felt that low in her stomach.

"*Chérie*," Agatha blurted out, and when Hart's cheeks colored ever so slightly, she knew she'd gotten it right too. She wouldn't examine it too closely, the way sobriquets had fallen so neatly into place for this little charade.

"Let's get on the road," said Hart. Her voice was casual, but the twin spots of pink on her cheeks betrayed her as she pulled onto the street. It felt so satisfying, knowing she'd never seen Hart blush for anything but her. Something in her melted, just a little.

Agatha briefly considered calling off the prank. It would have been easy enough, to run her thumb across all four fingers and cut the magic she'd set up for when they pulled out onto the highway.

But what would be the fun in that?

No, she sat back, ready to play a role and unsettle the woman who had unsettled her in more ways than one today already. Pranking would help sate the lust. Probably.

The road stretched out in front of them, clear and lovely, the skies blue, and Hart reached for the radio, eyes still on the road, and then jolted the steering wheel sharply onto the shoulder, slamming on the brakes when she saw the enormous creature in the middle of the road.

All four hooves were still for a moment, and then the front right one lifted, the giant antlered head turning toward the now-stopped car.

"Oh, fuck," said Hart, raising her hand and snapping.

When nothing happened, she screamed, "FUCK." She shook her hand in front of her, and snapped again, but the giant moose lumbered toward them nonetheless, its torso higher than the Packard, and Hart turned to her.

"Magic isn't working," she said, eyes dark. Frantic. "And if this is how I go—"

"Wait," Agatha said, because perhaps this was going too far.

"No, if this is how I go, I want to do something before I die." She looked so determined, her face pale against the crimson red of her lipstick.

"I—" Agatha was about to explain, but before she could,

Hart's hands were on her face, and for a moment, she shut her eyes, waiting for their lips to make contact.

She was so eager, in fact, that she forgot the next, and most important, step of her prank. Her reverie, however, was interrupted by Hart's earsplitting scream.

"What the fuck?" Agatha opened her eyes, and Hart was staring, mouth open.

Agatha hadn't magicked the moose out of existence, so the illusion had wandered into the actual car, and she had been too busy closing her eyes and hoping to be kissed to notice.

The moose illusion now greeted them with the visible innards of a phantom moose that didn't exist outside of Agatha's magic, but was anatomically accurate nonetheless.

Holding back the desire to retch, she gestured for the magic to dissipate, and watched Hart slow her breath to normal.

"You," she said, when she had recovered. "You." Realization dawned on her. "I almost . . . Damn, Agatha, that was a nasty prank."

"Sorry," said Agatha, wiping her mouth, and wondering what a normal mouth was even supposed to feel like. "I would have . . ." she added quickly, at the horrified look on Priscilla's face. "In your defense, it's normal to look for one last hurrah if you think you might die."

"I apologize. You said no kissing." They hadn't even kissed, Agatha thought, and goddess, that made her a little bit miserable.

Agatha shook her head. "You didn't even make contact. Call it even. Let's just do this."

Hart nodded, staring straight at the road, and turning back in the direction of their destination. She looked stricken, so as they turned on the road to Havenwall, Agatha forced herself to be honest, for just a minute.

"I bet it would have been a good kiss."

"Yeah?"

Her face softened, and they pulled into the lot.

"Come on," she said, not wanting to overthink anything else between them.

The lettering for Crystal Balls to the Wall was new, in a font that looked like an odd blend of modern and flourishing. Agatha had to admit that the name felt a bit off for the place.

Agatha leaned closer and saw from the sun-dappled boards of the trailer that this was a new sign, and the previous one was not quite so large. Behind the words in the middle were darker patches of wood peeking out from behind one of the *A*s and the *O*, as though this had been a recent adjustment.

"Welcome, ladies," said a raspy but not altogether unpleasant voice, and Agatha jumped. She hadn't heard the door open, a feat given the well-loved exterior of the shop, but perhaps Connie had oiled the hinges well.

"Come in," she said, gesturing.

Through the door, the double-wide trailer was sectioned off with curtains on each side, and then corresponding blinds that matched and gave the illusion of a cozy fortune-telling booth in the middle of what almost definitely was also Connie Witherspoon's home.

"Connie," said Hart, holding up a palm. "Good to see you. This is Agatha Vanderbilt Voisin, Witchery Council president."

"I've been expecting you," said Connie matter-of-factly, turning toward one of the curtains. "Can I offer you some tea?"

"Oh, no thank you," said Agatha, and Hart shook her head.

"Very well," said Connie, gesturing to a comfortable-looking upholstered bench across from a small round table that she must use for all sorts of things. "Have a seat, then."

"Connie, I've figured out how to prevent your episodes."

"You mean my obscenely crazy outbursts in public? Shoot. I'd do about anything."

"Two and a half hours of actual fortune-telling a week should do it."

Connie eyed her with disbelief. "You want me to actually read palms and fortunes?"

Hart nodded. "Cards, too, if that's your bag. Anything that

might let the powers out gradually. How many days is Crystal Balls to the Wall open?"

"I close up on Mondays and Tuesdays, but business has been slow since the whole coma incident."

Agatha raised a finger. "When did you change your name?"

Connie shifted in her seat. "After. When it stopped being, you know, all for show."

"Cut the new name, Connie."

The woman raised her hands, the dark brown shawl she wore flapping outward like she was a giant moth. Her hair was graying blond, frizzing out large enough to reach her shoulders, and long enough to hit her waist. She frowned, pouting. "You'd deny an old woman her jokes?"

"'Balls to the Wall' doesn't exactly inspire trust in real psychic abilities."

"Exactly," said Connie. "I stopped dyeing my hair, and I stopped with that silliness to ward off the tourists."

"We need you to inspire enough trust to do a sold half hour of real prediction every day you're open." Hart crossed her arms. "Letting off psychic steam will help."

Connie looked at Agatha.

"She's correct," said Agatha. "Practice makes perfect."

Connie sighed, sitting down in the chair behind the table.

"I suppose I do still have the Madam Cleopatra's sign."

Agatha nodded in approval.

"Good," said Hart, smiling crookedly. "Go on, then. Shall we start today?"

Connie stared at her for a moment, as though reading her face. A smile pulled across it, the mischief of the thing enough to show that Constance Witherspoon, for all her complaining, couldn't be *that* old.

"Very well," she said, rising and turning the lock of the trailer door. She flipped the little sign so the READING IN PROGRESS side faced outward, and pulled the curtain in the door's window, and then the other two.

The room was dim now, and Connie flipped a light switch.

Hundreds of fairy lights lit the curtains and the ceiling, and the room was suddenly a magical wonderland.

"Constance Witherspoon," said Hart, impressed. "I didn't know you had it in you."

"I didn't," said Connie. "But Madam Cleopatra? She was a showman. The real deal in setting a mood. Now come closer, my pretties, and let Madam Cleopatra read your palms."

It was a show, and an overwrought one, and it shouldn't have affected her so much. And yet a shiver shot down Agatha's spine. She set her hand across the table anyway.

Madam Cleopatra picked her hand up, staring at it for minutes that dragged on, saying nothing. Her eyes seemed unfocused until finally she shut them, humming slightly, and reached to the side for Priscilla's hand, without even looking to see where it was. Her nimble fingers worked over Priscilla's far more quickly, and her eyes shot open.

"Ah," she said, nodding. "Yes. You two are truly made for each other. That's nice, dears."

"I thought you said she was a real psychic," hissed Agatha, blushing.

"She's new to this," said Hart, "and being a real psychic doesn't mean she can't also be really delusional."

She expected Connie to have something to say about that, but the older woman simply smiled, nodding.

"Yes. That will do. Let's move on to scrying, and then tarot."

She pulled out what looked like a bowling bag, unearthing a filigreed metal stand and setting it gently on the table before pulling out a crystal ball that appeared to be made of smoky quartz with some sort of glittering liquid swirling inside of it. Setting the ball gently in the holder, Connie took a deep breath.

"You can't rush the production of scrying," she said quietly. "And I'm willing to bet that it's the same when the scrying is real."

"You've never tried it since?" Agatha frowned.

"It was my passion, pretending to scry. I could put on a show so good, weave a tale so strong, that I myself believed it sometimes. At times, I felt I really could see, you know."

Hart leaned forward. "It's likely, for your powers to have manifested this way, that there was some small kernel of magic in you to begin with, perhaps generations lost. It's quite possible that you could actually see, sometimes."

Connie stared, hands shaking.

"Well," she said. "Well then."

"Would you like to stop here?" Agatha asked, worried, suddenly, about unlicensed and untested magic, and the prospect that Hart was advising this woman to continue on—no, to do more of it.

"Better to do it with help," said Connie, looking determined.

Hart nodded. "Do you need our help for this?"

"Just clear your mind and focus on what you need to know."

Agatha had the strangest urge to reach for Hart's hand, but there was no one here except Connie, and it wouldn't make sense.

Connie sat quietly, breathing deeply, and then held her hands over the ball.

Whatever was in it swirled frantically, buzzing, rushing in the direction of the woman's hands, and then moving furiously around the ball, forming a dense cluster so that whatever Connie saw was hidden from them.

She frowned. "Your Council faces upheaval," she said.

Agatha knew that. Someone, possibly even the woman next to her, she reminded herself, was trying to kill her.

Though if Priscilla Hart's death wish was to kiss Agatha while also trying to kill her, well, that was pretty fucked up. But then again, Harts were known to be strange and dramatic.

"We had a recent election. I won." Agatha heard the pride in her voice, but she felt the way Prissy tensed next to her.

Connie shook her head slowly. "No," she mused. "Not that. It's a person—I can't quite see them—they're attempting to take something. Something powerful. Something that isn't theirs."

Connie's face went sheet white.

"What is it? What is the person taking? Who is it?"

"I don't know," she whispered.

"Then what's the matter?" Hart's insistence was borderline rude, but the older woman didn't notice, she just stared into the ball, eyes wide, jaw clenched.

"They've already taken it. I don't know what, or whom, but they've already taken it." Her voice sounded oddly wooden, and when Agatha looked again, Connie Witherspoon's eyes had gone entirely smoky, filled with the same swirling mist as the crystal ball.

"THEY HAVE ALREADY TAKEN THAT WHICH ALWAYS WAS AND ALWAYS WILL BE," she rasped, voice projecting too loud, grating against Agatha's ears.

"THEY HAVE TAKEN THAT WHICH ISN'T THEIR OWN, AND FOR IT MANY WILL BLEED TO THE BONE."

"Devil damn me," whispered Hart, and Connie slumped to the side for a moment. Agatha reached for her, but her eyes were already opening. The psychic sat up and shook her head.

She did not look at all surprised by the sudden outburst of prognosticated doom.

"That was quite a lot for the day," said Connie, face serious. "I'll try again tomorrow, and be sure to try the thirty minutes of real readings, but I can't promise it won't have consequences."

Agatha swallowed. It was terrifying, to be honest. The prophecy, if that's what she could call it. The risk of Connie practicing real magic on real people.

They said their goodbyes, and made their way to the car, driving back in silence.

When they reached Agatha's house, she turned to Hart.

"Are you sure it's wise to have Connie do that on the regular?"

Hart gave her a long look. "No," she said coolly. "But I am entirely certain that it's my call, not yours, to make about what's the best plan of action in this particular instance."

Agatha could, in theory, overrule her. But she didn't have any other ideas, and somehow, the idea of pushing back in this particular instance felt, well, wrong.

She hoped her gut wasn't leading her into the biggest mistake of her career.

Looking back at the car, her gaze caught again on the profile of Hart's face.

She hoped it wasn't something other than her gut leading her wrong either.

CHAPTER 12

Priscilla

Priscilla arrived at work determined to prove Constance Witherspoon wrong. She and Agatha were *not* meant for each other. Agatha knew nothing of her family and this town, which had been in Priscilla's blood since the day she was born here.

So to make herself feel better, she'd come in early to prank the mini fridge in the break room so that it smelled inexplicably of tuna fish. She lingered under the pretense of making a cup of coffee to see the moment when Agatha opened it and gagged.

She might sort of like Agatha, but the woman had taken *her* job. Squeezing her eyes shut, she did her very best to forget the damning nature of the moose incident. The way she'd thought her magic was broken, hexed by Lex or some other meddling devil. The way she'd thought she was about to die by moose, and her mind had jumped to how at least this would be dying in a way that suited her home state, and then, dangerously, to the notion that it wouldn't be so bad to kiss Agatha Vanderbilt Voisin before dying.

She'd traveled the world, loved every second of it, and she'd always come back home to Hallowcross because it was her place. This, the Witchery Council, Hart Manor, all of it. It was hers. This was Hart country, and Agatha was an outsider.

An obnoxiously cute outsider, but an outsider nonetheless. Agatha was currently perched on the edge of Kevin's desk outside her office, pointing to something on a spreadsheet.

Kevin was all smiles and flexing biceps. Did the man really need to work his arm muscles to move a mouse and click something in Excel? Prissy didn't love spreadsheets, but she'd worked with them long enough to know that this was definitely for show. He might be a nice guy, but he sure was a show-off.

"By the way, that new blouse is lovely," Kevin was saying to Agatha, eyes raking appreciatively as though she weren't his boss.

Priscilla glared at him.

"Oh, thank you, Kev," Agatha cooed, and the indulgent tone of her voice made something in Priscilla recoil. No wonder Kevin refused to work for her; Agatha was offering something that she never would.

She was ashamed of herself a little bit for the suspicion, and the stereotypes associated with it, but it was what it was.

"I hate to interrupt," she said, though she did not hate it, not one bit, "but I need to talk to you about Connie." She paused for a second and then leaned in, letting a hand casually brush the hair back from Agatha's face.

Agatha blushed and stood up. "Of course. My office?"

Kevin shot Priscilla a look, but she ignored it, storming after Agatha into her office. She let the heavy door slam a little too hard in her wake, loudly enough that people would certainly hear.

Let them hear.

Agatha leaned against her desk. Did she really need to lean so much? When she stood that way, she was all curves, and Priscilla hated herself a little too much for wanting things she should not want in earnest. Behind her, the plants the Council president loved so much swayed, recoiling a little.

"What the fuck is wrong with you?" Agatha bit out, mouth turned down, peach-tinted lip gloss scrunched into a disappointed pout.

"What the fuck is wrong with *you*? Are we faking an open relationship that includes your assistant? How very trite of us. Or is it feminist? Making sure the tired trope of a powerful man taking advantage is spread evenly across the sexes?"

Agatha stared at her. "It's friendly flirting, not an invitation to my private boudoir."

"I doubt your bedroom could possibly be seductive enough to deserve that moniker," Priscilla shot off without thinking, and she did feel some remorse at the red tint to Agatha's cheeks. The words were harsh, but then again, so was walking into the office to find her fake girlfriend throwing herself at her fucking assistant.

"That's a bit rude to assume." Agatha crossed her arms. "What's gotten into you?"

"Nothing," snapped Priscilla. "Just that I feel like it might be disrespectful for you to flirt with every good-looking man who comes your way if you're dating me. Even for pretend. It's a stereotype." She swallowed. That was crossing a line, but it was out there now.

Agatha flushed deeper red, and clutched the edge of her desk. "Oh, it's like that?"

Priscilla shrugged.

"You absolute bitch," Agatha bit off.

"Excuse me?"

"You heard me." She stared. "If you need something from me, just ask. Don't go around hurling hurtful accusations."

"I did hear you, but goddess, I can't believe that your response to me being mad about you disrespecting our fake relationship is to hurl names."

"That," said Agatha, slamming a hand on the desk, "is not why I'm angry."

Priscilla threw herself down in the chair in front of the desk, clutching the armrests to stop herself from snapping anything truly unforgivable.

"Pray tell, then, *honey*, why are you so mad?"

"Because you're putting me in a reductive box and being a huge bitch about it." Agatha glowered.

"You're flirting with your assistant."

"I'm sorry that it hurt your feelings, but I fail to see how thanking him for a compliment is flirting. And if you want something from a person in a relationship, you know, you have to actually say so. Just say, 'Hey, Agatha, that made me feel bad.' If I knew something would make you feel bad, I wouldn't do it."

"Fine, he was flirting with you," Priscilla conceded.

"Yes, and? What would you have me do? Be cruel to the best assistant on the East Coast? Possibly in all of North America?"

"A little, yes. I quite like cruelty."

"And I like that about you, because it's your way. My way is politeness. Courtesy. I am in this thing, Priscilla, with you in what you need even for a fake relationship, but I get to stay who I am. And you don't need to act like I'm some sort of a slutty bisexual stereotype because I'm not a gold star or something."

"I didn't mean it like that." And she hadn't, but wasn't it true that people could say a thing one way, and have someone else take it another way?

She hated this. Absolutely hated this. This was why she was better off alone.

"I'm sorry if I made you feel like I thought you weren't a good bisexual."

"You first suggested I was taking advantage of my assistant and then told me you thought my bedroom would be boring? So, which is it? Am I too slutty for you, or not slutty enough? Good grief, I expect this sort of shit from mundanes from time to time. From bad boyfriends in the past, but not from you."

Priscilla swallowed. She hadn't thought of any of that, not at all, only that she was humiliated and unreasonably angry to hear Agatha laugh and talk sweetly to Kevin.

"I'm sorry," she said, softer this time. Agatha sighed and walked to the chair, putting her hands on top of Priscilla's and leaning down. "This was about me being jealous and reacting badly," Priscilla admitted.

"If you're serious about helping me catch our rogue arsonist, about restoring your reputation and building mine, you need to treat me like a serious partner. Not some throwaway rebound." She paused at the look Priscilla felt on her face, the stricken agony. "I'm not saying you threw her away, but you treated our last president in a way that at least appeared disposable."

"What's that supposed to mean?" Priscilla was entirely prepared for people to suggest that she was a huge cunt for leaving Evelyn on their wedding day. She was not prepared for anyone outside of her immediate family to assume that part of that was optics.

Agatha leaned close to her face, staring into her eyes, and Priscilla held back a shudder. Antichrist, did those eyes have to be quite so blue?

"Just that people don't typically run away from someone they clearly love deeply for no reason whatsoever. Jonathan didn't humiliate me in public after you left for no reason, though I admit his reasons were despicable. I don't want to assume yours are too. You know what they say about people who assume things."

Priscilla was shocked. She wanted to deflect, as she always did when the subject of her failed nuptials arose. To change the subject and refuse to discuss it further.

For some unfathomable reason, though, she found herself offering a scrap of truth.

"We had irreconcilable differences. I know we should have talked them out before that. And we did. We spent so much time talking in circles, both of us hoping that loving each other would be enough. But it's not always enough, Agatha, it just isn't. Maybe you know that, from whatever it was you were doing before this."

Agatha blinked, leaning back and shaking her head.

"Jonathan and I never loved each other," she said softly. "Not really. But if you wanted to talk about what happened with Evelyn, I'd listen."

She sat in her chair, propping her head in her hands, a safe distance away now, but her eyes no less piercing.

Priscilla swallowed. She didn't want to talk about it. And yet her lips moved.

"The thing is, she wanted to have a family." Understanding washed over Agatha's face.

"And you didn't?"

Priscilla shook her head. "It's not that I don't like children. I don't mind other people's. I just don't want them myself. And Evelyn said I'd change my mind. I thought maybe I could change my mind, for her. I loved her so much, you know."

Agatha bit her lip, features softening. She opened her mouth, and spoke very slowly.

"Sometimes love isn't enough." She hesitated. "I actually think it sounds like maybe you loved her quite well to have let her go."

Priscilla threw her head back, resting it against the velvet of the high-back chair. She wrenched her eyes shut, but she didn't stop talking. It felt good. Painful, but good, like she was relieving a pressure that had been building and building between her eyes, threatening to pop and explode into unbridled cruelty.

"I should have told her earlier," she whispered. "I wanted to be able to change my mind for her. I wanted for love to be enough, like it was for my parents."

Agatha said nothing, for long enough that Priscilla opened her eyes, and the president just sat there, looking at her, not with pity but with understanding.

"You can say it. I was terribly selfish to leave at that precise moment."

Agatha shook her head. "No." She paused, chewing on her lip for a moment, deep in thought. "It was brave to leave when you knew for sure that it would hurt both of you to stay, even if the timing was bad. It would have been very selfish to have children that you were strong-armed into having. Children aren't stupid, and they don't ask to be born. They deserve grown-ups who want them completely. And once you do have them, there really is no walking away completely. Only abandoning. Breaking up with your fiancée sucks, but it was better than pretending your way into making kids suffer for you."

Priscilla blinked. "Yes. I just wish I would have thought of it before the actual wedding."

"Well, you're young."

"I beg your pardon; I'm a sitting member of the Council."

"You're what, twenty-five?"

"I'm twenty-six," she said indignantly. Agatha's eyes sparkled, as though perhaps she knew exactly how old Priscilla was. "Why, how old are you? Thirtysomething?"

"Thirty-seven," said Agatha, her mouth twisting wryly.

Something about that was thrilling; she'd imagined Agatha a bit older, but not that much older. Eleven years was more than she could count on her fingers.

"You're a cougar, then. A cradle robber."

Agatha blushed. "You're far beyond the age of consent, and if I am in fact a dirty old woman, well, I'm a fake one, then. It's not like we're actually together."

"Dirty Bertie!" Priscilla exclaimed and somehow the thought of Lex and his silly obsession with a dead English king was so funny that she doubled over in laughter, a full minute before she could even meet Agatha's now-confused expression.

"What does this have to do with a promiscuous king and his French prostitutes?" She asked it matter-of-factly, as though quite obviously that's what the moniker brought to mind.

"Does everyone obsess over a depraved monarch except for me?"

Laughing, Agatha shook her head. "No, but he is known for it. I wouldn't go so far as to call myself a Dirty Bertie. I don't think I could handle more than one partner at a time—but I am more creative than you give me credit for, with your low blow about my uninteresting bedroom life." She winked, and

Priscilla was suddenly unable to think of a single clever retort. "You might label me a slutty bisexual, and I mind if you mean it derogatory. But if you wanted to call me a slutty bisexual, complimentary, well, I wouldn't mind that very much at all, Hart."

Oh, shit. Priscilla was in deeper than she realized, watching Agatha fiddle with her neckline, pushing a strand of long blond hair back over her shoulder. She found herself suddenly unable to do anything other than watch the path of those fingers, and she leaned forward, setting her head on her palm.

"Prove it, honey." She let the word drip off her tongue.

"I think I'd rather punish you, *chérie*." Agatha grinned and ran her finger down farther, and Priscilla could feel her pulse low, a heartbeat beneath her belly button. Aching for her to touch that path Agatha traced down her collarbone, her breast.

A knock at the door interrupted, and Priscilla was ready to murder whoever it was. Agatha dropped her hand and straightened up.

Kevin, of course.

"President Vanderbilt Voisin, your mother is on line two."

"Of course. Councilwoman Hart was just complaining about her inability to handle the Connie Witherspoon situation, and asking for my help on it. Would you mind logging that and then shutting the door on your way out so I can take this in private?"

Fuck, Agatha hadn't meant *punish* as in sexual punishment.

She was smirking, and she ran her thumb across her fingers in that signature magic move that Priscilla liked watching a little bit too much.

"Er, Councilwoman Hart?"

Kevin sounded nervous.

"What?"

"You've got something on your teeth."

Priscilla snapped her fingers, and a compact mirror appeared. She opened it, examining her mouth to find a smudge of lipstick on her left incisor. She rubbed.

Nothing.

"I'll just leave you two," said Kevin nervously, shutting the door behind him.

"You," said Priscilla accusatorily.

"Me," said Agatha, smiling. "Did you think I wouldn't notice your tuna fish refrigerator prank? You do realize that we all have to use that fridge, yourself included?"

Priscilla scowled. "It's harmless."

"And smelly. The lipstick hex won't rub off until you fix it."

She had to hand it to Agatha: that was both clever and incredibly impressive magic, tricky to pull off.

"Fine," she sighed, snapping her fingers and returning her gaze to the compact. All sexual tension between them gone, for the moment at least, she wiped the lipstick off her teeth.

"Good," said Agatha sweetly. "Now, if you don't mind, I need to call my mother and tell her about my new girlfriend, and then I have to go down to magical resources and declare it. Do me a favor and close the door on your way out, and then go disclose when you have a moment."

Perhaps pretending with Agatha was going to be more interesting than she had anticipated.

She was still thinking of this as she wandered into the break room, which now smelled very nicely of the lavender cleaner that they used to wipe down counters.

Priscilla pulled out the tea caddy, looking for the approximation of the RMS *Titanic* flavor that she morbidly preferred. She flicked on the electric kettle, and for some reason, it didn't seem to work, so she flicked it a second time and heard the familiar sound of water heating swiftly.

Sitting down at one of the carved wooden chairs across from it, she crossed her arms and tried not to think of Agatha's fingers, her long blond hair, her big blue eyes. She was lost enough in thought that when the kettle spluttered and spat out a dozen tiny daggers, she let out a shriek loud enough that it alone would have sent everyone running.

CHAPTER 13

Agatha

The damage from the kettle full of letter opener–sized daggers was suspiciously contained to a small slice on Priscilla's left arm, a fact that Agatha left out while publicly reassuring her fake girlfriend.

It had been a soft launch. After making sure Hart was fine, the daggers collected and tagged, and the offending kettle sequestered for examination by Otho (or, more likely, by Nancy in his stead), Agatha leaned in and, well, made her affections known.

"Are you truly all right, *chérie*?" She let her fingers trail against Hart's arm. The other woman's eyes widened, brows furrowing over those wickedly gold-speckled brown orbs, and then relaxed.

"I'm fine."

Agatha pulled her close in an embrace that made her want to break out in hives for doing so in a public break room, but it couldn't be helped.

Buzzing whispers surrounded them, but they pretended that this was a consuming love that kept her from noticing everyone noticing them. It wasn't *that* hard, really, if she thought about the way Priscilla smelled like lemons and felt like the sort of home she'd be able to wrap herself around. For a moment, it really was like just the two of them in the room.

"Agatha, are you certain that—oh!" She looked up, and Kevin's mouth was frozen in an almost comical little O. He cleared his throat, adjusting his tie. "I had no idea. Gosh, a guy could live forever and still never be prepared for the curveballs around here. President Vanderbilt Voisin, are you quite all right?"

"I'm fine, Kevin." She braced herself for it. What they had talked about. In her peripheral vision, she could see Priscilla's mouth curve into a satisfied little smile, as though the joy of shocking Kevin was not wasted on her. She was so pleased, in fact, that Agatha had to wonder if she herself had set off the kettle.

A shallow cut on one arm was hardly an inconvenience, especially for a witch. And Hart had been here for all of the near-death incidents, really.

What if this was a clever plot to scare her off? Or worse, what if Hart was trying to kill her? She was certainly getting close enough to do a good job of it.

A runoff election in the event of her untimely death would be easy enough to win. Was she making it even easier by proposing the fake relationship? Setting her beloathed beloved up to have the perfect reason why she couldn't possibly have been the one who'd done it?

No. These doubts made sense, but even if Hart was the perp, it was better to keep her close. And if she wasn't? Well, then the plan might as well work to fix her problems in Hallowcross. Dating the resident golden goth girl had to have some payoff, even if there was a slight possibility that she was a murderous, hot goth girlfriend.

"Kevin," she barked, her voice more commanding than ever. "Make sure my girlfriend goes home early. I'd like to call an emergency Council session to investigate the malfeasance in this office. Set it up for tomorrow morning?"

"Girlfriend?" Kevin echoed faintly, scribbling things down on a notepad. "Malfeasance?"

"We won't have malfeasance for malfeasance's sake around

here. Not in my Council, Kevin." She frowned, crossing her arms and resisting the urge to giggle, hoping her face was as stony as she intended.

"Yes, ma'am," he said, scurrying away. Kevin had absolutely never called her *ma'am* before. But then again, she'd never before been in a serious (albeit fake, in this instance) committed relationship in the duration of his time working for her.

Fuck. Maybe it had been flirting, and here she was thinking that he was just friendly, and she was a cool boss.

Hart grinned widely now.

"I insist," Agatha said, channeling her mother as much as possible in a firm-but-loving tone. "Go home and rest. I'll meet you later."

Priscilla leaned forward, sliding her fingers against the red heel of her shoe, and pulling off one, then the other, before snapping, her tennis shoes crisp and black with little gold detailing on the eyelets.

"Whatever you say," she said, snapping her fingers again so that her tote bag was in her hand, and delicately putting the fancy shoes inside of it, though she very well could snap them right in too. It was like she had to have the feel of them against her skin, had to know, and goddess, something about that set Agatha's blood burning. Her craving for Priscilla Hart knew no boundaries; apparently, not even when she thought that the other woman might be the source of all her problems.

"Don't even think about walking." Agatha could feel the office plants threating along with her.

"I'll walk if I want to." Hart's voice was sulky.

"You're injured," Agatha hissed.

"Yes, well, good thing I don't walk with my forearm. As far as I can tell, most of us use our feet, with the exception of my odd cousin Christopher, who does, in fact, walk on his fingers, owing to a most unfortunate bit of necromancy gone wrong."

Agatha made a mental note to ask about *that* later. Now was not the time. Now she needed to convince this beautiful, obstinate woman to go along with her ruse and to follow directions on the off chance that she was actually hurt.

"I'm perfectly fine," Hart said, the words laced with an edge that wasn't there before.

"Oh, really?" The monstera in the corner rustled, punctuating Agatha's concern.

In the hallway to the break room, Nancy was tapping magic around the offending kettle nervously, performing the spell work to sequester it safely and store it for observation to see if it exhibited any additional homicidal urges.

"Really." Hart stood up, crossing her arms, and Agatha saw red. It was all very well and good to compete, but she had won the presidency, not Priscilla, and she had orchestrated this fake relationship, and she was doing Prissy a fucking favor, and it wouldn't kill her to cooperate in the interest of protecting her own health.

She didn't think about it, she just rubbed that thumb along all four fingers, and suddenly Hart jumped, the sensation of buttons and a collar where they ought not to be startling her visibly.

"You turned my clothes inside out?" Priscilla's voice notched up an octave. "What are we, twelve? I'm supposed to be the younger one, and you're stuck in grade school pranks." She snapped her fingers and, when nothing happened, snapped again.

Agatha smirked.

"A permanent inside out? You know I would never be caught this way."

"Exactly. You refused to agree to find another way home, like a normal injured person, and I was forced to take matters into my own hands. Literally."

Hart glowered, nostrils flaring, and Agatha couldn't help herself. It was incredibly hot to actually bother unflappable Priscilla Hart. To get under her skin.

"Let's talk about this in your office," Priscilla gritted out.

"Of course." Agatha could have gestured for her to go first, but she didn't want to, so she strode off, not even turning to see if the other woman followed, relishing the smug notion of winning. She opened the door, hearing the tapping of Hart's tennis shoes behind her, knowing that if she were to cave and turn around—which she most certainly would not—she'd find Prissy a satisfying four inches shorter than she normally was in those heels.

The door to her office made an odd sort of popping sound when she opened it, and the force of the blow was strong enough, hot enough, to let Agatha know that this was more than simply an errant teakettle.

The blast pushed her back, and the heat was unbearably intense on her cheek and her jaw and her collarbone. Agatha felt the crushing impact of her body against the floor, and something thudding on top of her. Her desk, maybe?

Her ears ringing from the sound of the blast, she felt the burn of fire, actual fire, on the right side of her face, but her body was surprisingly . . . unburned.

And yet it hurt everywhere. She looked up and realized that she was lying on the ground just outside of her office. Nancy was yelling for help, and several people were gathering around her. Kevin was in the background, jumping from foot to foot and talking rapidly into a cell phone, probably procuring whatever help was most necessary.

It didn't make sense. She had personally checked the office for traps since the earlier incident. It was clear. Safe. Untrapped. Her foggy brain said she was not dead, and that the thing on top of her was not her desk.

In fact, it wasn't a thing at all, she realized, as it groaned, and she recognized the inside-out seams of the dress, the black tennis shoes when she looked down.

Priscilla had rolled her partially out of the way, catching some of the burn herself, as evidenced by her singed dress sleeve on one side and the angry-looking burn where the fabric had been, harsh and wet. This was much more serious than the kettle.

This was the real intention. The kettle was a distraction.

Nancy was helping Hart, and even Otho ran over to help Agatha. Priscilla gritted her teeth and swallowed hard while Xiomara snapped magic and muttered softly, summoning an herbal poultice for Priscilla's burns, working powerful emergency spells while Otho summoned a few smaller ones for Agatha and her face.

Despite the heat, her face had sustained only superficial burns, the sort of thing that Otho's bits and bobs dealt with swiftly for her. But Hart's had to be second-, maybe third-degree burns. Xiomara was more than up for the task of healing, but Priscilla had to be in terrible pain.

She had shoved Agatha out of the way and taken the brunt of the magical force.

"If I didn't believe that the cool, collected princess of darkness herself was in love with you before, I would now," whispered Nancy, as she handed Agatha a glass of water and a painkiller. "That was horrible, but, like, heroic, really. What's it like to have someone literally jump in front of a fire for you?"

Agatha could see the young girl's mind working, cogs turning, eyes practically sporting hearts in them. She swallowed.

The rumor mill would know about this and then some. So much for a quiet soft launch.

"I'm fine," Agatha insisted, brushing off Otho's attempt to examine her face again, and turning instead to Xiomara and Prissy.

"Are you all right, *chérie*?" Her breath came out too ragged, fear on the surface, but she was glad for it when Priscilla looked up at her with tears—actual tears—in her eyes.

"What, this?" She smiled, and it was a rickety thing that spoke of the extremity of her pain. "I've had much worse than this. My brother and I had a pranking-with-guillotine phase that required a reattached toe once. This is nothing to a detached digit."

She hadn't realized her hand was pressing to her heart until the weight of it, the pressure, actually started to hurt.

"Steady, now," said Xiomara. "I'm just going to put something on to help the healing so it won't scar."

Magically healing things more serious than small cuts never worked out well; a body had to do the work to heal, or the healing didn't take, and the pain would linger.

Xiomara whispered a few words that Agatha barely recognized and snapped her fingers to affix a bandage on Hart's arm. It stretched the length of her biceps to her elbow and forearm, and the way she moved, gingerly, careful with that side of her body, made Agatha think that it hadn't just been the burn, but also the impact of the dive on the side of her.

"You'll want to keep that burn dry, magic it a protection spell, and maybe try a nice relaxing Epsom salt bath for the bruising. Take it easy." Xiomara looked worried. "Follow up with a doctor tomorrow."

Agatha recalled that Xiomara had been premed before switching to public health, and that for the Council, she had done a fellowship in crossover magical and mundane healing. She made a mental note to reach out to Xiomara for a list of things that Hart absolutely should do.

She had never been an impulsive person; she was well-known for her spreadsheets and her careful planning and her thoughtful approach to, well, all aspects of her life. It was why it had shaken her so hard to be humiliated in that dreadful speech Jonathan had delivered impromptu after Evelyn ran out in pursuit of Priscilla at the wedding, and it was why she had dithered so long on the possibility of Prissy being the attempted murderer.

But now Agatha Vanderbilt Voisin was absolutely certain of two things, impulsively and yet unequivocally.

Number one: Priscilla was most certainly not the person trying to kill her. Which meant that it had to be someone else close, someone else clever and magical enough to get past the Council wards. Likely it was someone else on the Council, but she couldn't, for the life of herself, decide who would hate her enough to try to off her. Nevertheless, it was *not* Priscilla.

The severity of that burn, the tears in her eyes. A killer would never.

Number two: Damn decorum, and protocol, and her desire to fill out the appropriate magical resources–required paperwork. It could wait until Monday. For now, she was leaving, and she was taking Priscilla home. Even if she had to white-knuckle it the whole time, and she definitely would; she *hated* driving, but there was no way that she was letting Priscilla drive.

"I'm driving you home," she said, in her most imperious voice, the one she reserved for difficult Council meetings and family arguments on the rare occasion they popped up.

To her surprise, Hart didn't argue this time; she only nodded, wincing at the motion.

"Does anyone have a car I can borrow?"

"I have a car," said Priscilla.

Agatha breathed a sigh of relief.

"Can you walk out of here? I can bring it around."

Prissy nodded. "I'm sore, but walking is probably good."

Xiomara nodded. "It'll help to move. Just take it easy, take the elevator, and if you need to, rest."

Still, Agatha threaded an arm through her good side, the one without the bandages, and guided her toward the elevator, rubbing her fingers together to make it appear right away, and magic a little bench in it before it opened so that it would just happen to be there if Hart needed it.

To Agatha's surprise, Hart got off on the first floor and walked in the direction of Main Street, and not the parking garage under the Council.

"You didn't park in the garage?"

"No, I left the hearse behind Hopelessly Teavoted again," said Prissy.

"The *hearse*?" She had assumed she would be driving the beautiful old Packard that Hart shared with her brother, but Agatha realized her white-knuckling was about to reach new levels.

Prissy smiled, and it was wan, and tired, and yet still a teeny bit wicked. It was comforting to see that she wasn't too badly injured for that.

"Yes, honey, a hearse. Do you have a problem with places dead bodies have been?"

"No," Agatha muttered. What she had was a fear of driving large vehicles, but it was no matter.

Agatha tried to calm herself with facts. Amaxophobia was the fear of driving a vehicle, and though about one in five people suffer from some sort of phobia, there were no actual statistics on how many people specifically were afraid of driving in cars. Agatha was very careful not to let herself spiral and learn the statistics regarding car crashes; she already knew that tired old reminder that cars were more likely to crash than planes were, and fuck if she didn't think about that every time she got behind a wheel.

Still, fake or not, Priscilla Hart was hers now, and she would take care of this woman, even if it meant overcoming her fear of dying while driving.

In a vehicle literally used to haul the dead.

CHAPTER 14

Priscilla

She could shut her eyes and still see the way Agatha had clutched the steering wheel of Uncle Larry's hearse, shoulders tense at her ears, a muscle working in her jaw.

A week ago, Priscilla had taken what Agatha called "a reasonable recovery period." Despite the Council president's worrying, Priscilla's burns had only been superficial second degree, and she had made every case for returning to work earlier. Agatha banned her anyway.

In Priscilla's opinion, this was a forced temporary expulsion, but Agatha proved unflinching, parking the hearse in the garage, seeing her to the door, and going a bit green in the gills when Azrael offered to let her drive the hearse back.

She'd shuddered and summoned a bicycle and a helmet instead, and taken off at a breakneck speed, as though afraid that if she stuck around, the hearse might be pressed upon her. About a week later, and Priscilla still could not forget how she'd hopped on the back of that purple Schwinn and sped off into the sunset. Azrael had jokes for days about Priscilla driving women to flee the grounds of the manor after that.

Speaking of Azrael, she could hear him knocking at the door to her bedroom.

"Prissy," he yelled, pounding it again.

She turned up the volume on the comfort show she was

streaming, the one about the girl who spent her summers at the beach in love with two different brothers, which of course she would never be caught dead admitting she'd watched several times through at this point.

"I can hear you in there," he yelled.

"Shut up. I'm not home," she yelled back.

"Priscilla, either you come out and talk to me, or, so help me, I will tell everyone what you're watching in there."

She jammed the laptop shut and vaulted off the bed, which she immediately regretted. She felt better than she had the first two days after the explosion, but she was still sore, even with the muscle relaxers the human doctor prescribed and the plant craft that Azrael assembled from their mother's best recipes in the family grimoire.

Snapping her fingers, she unlocked the door. She was at least pleased to see him tumble into the room, the force of one last attempt to barrel through it sending him onto the floor.

He rubbed the hand that he had landed on, standing up. "Ouch, Prissy, that's my grading hand."

She waggled her eyebrows. "I bet grading isn't the only repetitive motion you need it for."

Instead of insulting her back, he just sighed, eyeing her like she was made of porcelain and might break, which was not like him. He didn't offer any sort of retort, not even a little one.

"For the thousandth time, I'm fine."

"Yeah," he said. "I've been there. Telling myself that, over and over and over. If you keep repeating it, maybe it will feel true."

"Honestly, Az. Give me a few days and the bruising will fade, and I'll be in top shape."

He looked at her. "I mean more than just physically fine."

She shook her head. "Let's talk about literally anything else."

"You know Vickie's book club has a handful of your Council interns in it, right?"

Prissy dragged a hand over her face. Her brother's girlfriend ran a magical-readers-of-paranormal-romance-books club every other Thursday night, and since it was open to all manner of supernatural creatures—devil-gifted like Victoria, witches like the Council members, and an errant vampire or two—she should have predicted that gossip would get around.

"I think I know where this is going."

"I heard a very interesting rumor about your new girlfriend."

She blinked, hoping to look innocent. "Didn't I mention that? I'm sure I mentioned it."

Azrael crossed his arms. "Did you fail to mention, when you told your favorite brother you're dating the North American Council of Witchery president, only a little bit more than six months after bolting from your intended marriage to the interim president, that someone was also trying to kill your new girlfriend, and now possibly also you, in proximity?"

"Interim and actual president are quite different," she said, hoping her voice sounded as careless as she intended. It sounded awful when he put it that way. "And you're my only brother. You have to be my favorite."

He rolled his eyes, snapping his fingers so that the pair of comfortable chairs in her corner slid closer. She sighed and sat down in one, unwilling to admit how nice it was to be enveloped by the soft cushions of the thing.

"I'm worried about you. I know you're grown, and you know what you're doing. But you did offer me quite a bit of advice when I was in the thick of magical mayhem, and it seems like my time to reciprocate here."

"Fine," she said, looking at the carpet, which was shifting between a two-toned and rather haunting damask floral sprig pattern and a chevron that made her a bit dizzy. The carpet only did this when she was feeling particularly lost and rudderless. "I am dating Agatha, yes." She hesitated, his greenish-brown eyes boring into hers, the little flecks of gold so reminiscent of her father, but the color all her mother.

It felt shitty to lie, so she sighed and went on.

"Well. You already know I'm fake dating her, and part of that, in addition to clearing my name about the hexes, is to try to find out who has been sabotaging her and to help her gain some traction. But I also want to restore my reputation a bit. You know, because of the whole about six-months-ago incident you so kindly brought up."

He stared. Narrowed his eyes. Shook his head.

"What?" she demanded.

"Nothing. It's nothing." Azrael ran a hand over his curly hair.

She glared.

"It's just—you wanted to restore your shattered reputation from dating and leaving the last Council president by dating the next one? By putting yourself in the line of fire?"

"Evelyn was an *interim* president! That's different."

He stared at her.

"Fine," she whined. "I have a type. I like a strong woman in charge, someone who challenges me and won't just roll over and whimper when I get testy and cruel."

"I thought you were only fake dating," he said, smiling wickedly, and she realized what she had said.

"Fuck." She rubbed her eyes. "We are. It is fake."

"Sounds like you've caught real feelings. Which explains the whole trying-to-sacrifice-yourself-for-her-honor-and-safety thing." Her brother's sing-song voice made it impossible to resist, really. She snapped, and rose-gold bubbles hovered over him.

"What did you do?" He looked up. "Oh, shit." The bubbles exploded, showering him in rose-gold glitter.

"Gotcha," she said, satisfied.

"Priscilla, this will take ages to come off. My students will think—gosh, I don't even want to know what they'll think." He scowled.

She shrugged. "Maybe it will earn you points; maybe it will make you more despicable. Either way, it's something interesting."

He rubbed the bridge of his nose. "You're not distracting me from what I want to say, not even with copious amounts of glitter."

"A girl can dream," she muttered, snapping her fingers and procuring an iced coffee. If she had to be up this early talking to her brother about her feelings, she had better do it caffeinated. For good measure, she snapped and deposited one for him on the end table beside him.

He eyed it suspiciously.

"Prank free, scout's honor."

"You were never a scout," he accused.

"No, but I did have that dalliance with one when I was going through that horrible *Could I be straight?* phase in middle school."

He looked stricken. "I remember that. You've never been grouchier."

"Yeah, well, you try pretending to be interested in penises."

"I . . . have no problem with penises, obviously? Still deeply pansexual while with a woman." He straightened up in his chair. "But I am going to be honest with you. It looks like a pattern—dating the president, running for president, losing, dating the next one—if you break up with her."

"Are you suggesting I'm undatable?" The implication wounded her.

He shook his head. "No, Priss. But people do break up." Az hesitated. "And unless you plan on telling her your real feelings, well, there's only one way fake dating ends."

"We have an agreement."

"To date forever? Tell me you didn't get engaged again." He paled slightly.

"Goddess, no. I'm not a fool. We have an agreement that after an appropriate amount of time, she will be the one to leave me, and I will be the one to pine, forlorn in my loss."

He raised an eyebrow. "You've thought of everything, then." He paused. "What happens if you stop ignoring your real feelings? Your words: you have a type."

Priscilla scowled. "I'm old enough to ignore a crush, and

wise enough not to let myself go any further than thinking she's pretty and doing what I need to do to sell it."

"You know . . ." he began.

"Must you?"

"Yes." He smiled. "Fake dating almost always leads to real feelings in books. I happen to be an expert."

"Oh no, would you look at the time, I actually have to meet Agatha."

"No, you don't."

"I really do." She snapped, straightening her hair so that the wave of it was ironed completely out, and then for good measure, she snapped to iron her clothes too.

"You're going on a date at 11 a.m.?" His eyes sparkled. "Brunch sounds cozy and romantic. Where at? Don't Go Bacon My Heart?" That he would think a diner was romantic was a problem for another day, or for Vickie. Priscilla didn't have time to remind her brother about how to be fancy and dashing like his father before him. Besides, that was really her thing.

"We have a business meeting. I'm picking her up so that we can check on Connie."

"How's that going?"

"Lex gave me some advice about letting her blow off magical steam."

Azrael's cheeks pinkened, and Prissy smirked at him. Her brother had a crush on that devil. She worked hard not to wonder if Lex and Azrael and Vickie had all been a thing at any point.

She gagged a little at the thought. The thought of her brother and Vickie, who was like a sister, doing things like that was not something she wanted to spend any mental space on.

"Did it work? The advice?" Az cocked his head.

"Yes, and also no. She hasn't had any more big blowups like the incident at the grocers, but she did have an episode with a customer where she went into a trance so intense, talking about devils and bargains and wishes and soulmates. It freaked out the couple who went in for the reading so badly that they called the EMTs, who I guess assumed that it was drug-related."

"Shit. That must have been a nightmare. A drug test would show that it's not."

Prissy grinned. "Well, the good news is that the prophecy may not have been drug-related, but Connie Witherspoon had plenty of psilocybin in her system. It turns out that she's a recreational mushroom and marijuana user. It was the perfect cover to explain the fit and the prognostication."

"That's a relief," he mused. "I know she used to deal—just pot—and that she's sworn that off after the whole almost dying after being soul-sucked by that asshat not even worth naming from the Brethren of One Love megachurch, but I didn't realize she used recreationally."

"She swore up and down it's legal, from the dispensary. It's a good thing she does, or we would have a time explaining her outburst to the cops, but we also want to see if we can figure out what tips her over the edge. She's got a reading this afternoon. Agatha and I are going to supervise."

His eyes lit up. "You're going to spy on mundanes while Connie tells their fortune? How scandalous!"

"It's not spying; it's Council oversight." She grinned at him, wanting to see his reaction to this. "And it's actually not going to be a mundane reading, because as it turns out, I have a more-than-willing devilish volunteer."

Azrael's face remained impassive, but the tips of his ears went red. She put her fists on her hips and raised an eyebrow.

"I didn't realize that you and Lex were friendly." He sounded nonchalant, but she saw through it.

"Why?" she asked innocently. "Is that a problem?"

"No," he mumbled.

"You've been blushing since I brought him up, and now your ears are bright red."

"I am not. They are not," Azrael insisted, which of course made them redder.

"Someone's got a crush. Shall I tell Vickie?" Priscilla tapped her fingers together, cackling.

He winked at her. "She's already well aware of *our* crush."

That took Priscilla aback enough to leave her speechless, and having regained his composure, her brother leaned in to pat her shoulder, earnest enough to hide that he was bringing his fingers together.

Snap.

She was coated in some of the residual pink glitter, both of them looking sparkly enough to have just emerged from a faerie strip club.

"Gotcha," he said, ducking out of the room. "You better hurry up. Wouldn't want to be late for your hot appointment!"

He was gone before her second glitter-bomb prank could hit, and Priscilla resented that.

They stood outside the shop, an odd trio of preppy, smoking—literally, shrouded in purple smoke—and formidably goth formal. "You know," mused Lex, "she should advertise on Dreaddit."

"I thought that website was kind of over?"

Lex looked affronted, and even Agatha joined him in glaring.

"What? I thought that was for olds?"

"We can't all be twenty-six and too cool for useful internet forums," said Agatha frostily. "Just wait until one day you need a good homemade solution for a droopy monstera."

"Who are you calling 'old,' pet?" Lex added silkily. "I'm ageless. Timeless as the rocks, the mountains themselves, etcetera, etcetera, etcetera."

"Old enough to say *etcetera*, that's for sure," said Prissy, elbowing him.

"She's got you there." Agatha crossed her arms, staring at the little sign on the door, which was still turned to READING IN PROGRESS. She checked her watch. "She's running over."

"Here. See. She could set up a post for witches and vampires and the like who want an actual psychic reading, and then it would be completely fine if things got kinky. In fact, she could probably charge extra for that. Make a solid living."

Priscilla wasn't sure whether to be grateful or furious. How had a slutty, thousand-year-old devil managed to solve a problem while spending so much of his time fiddling in human affairs and people's pants?

Speaking of pants, he reached into his, which were ungodly in their tightness, because of course they were, and rummaged around. It was not lost on her that Agatha watched his long fingers in there, searching, her cheeks just the slightest shade of pink.

"Like what you see, precious?"

Agatha's nostrils flared. "It's a normal human reaction to a beautiful creature, and one I'm certain you must be used to."

Something twisted in Priscilla, similar to the knifelike sensation of watching Kevin with Agatha. She tamped it down. Agatha was her *fake* girlfriend. It wouldn't do to get really jealous. Again. Besides, Lex claimed to be reformed, but she had seen what his jealousy had wrought upon her brother with that whole temporarily-unable-to-touch-his-beloved-without-dying incident.

Still, she was a little relieved when Agatha turned to her and winked, giving her a shockingly lascivious smile. "Don't worry. He's hot, but he's not quite my type."

"What exactly is your type?" Lex pulled a phone out of his pants, which should have been impossible given their taut-leather appearance, but who was she to question sartorially clever magic?

"I like sulky, brooding grumps, too arrogant for their own good."

She ran a hand along Priscilla's uninjured arm, and Prissy decidedly ignored the hairs that stood up in the wake of her fingers.

"Oh, that's splendid," said Lex, looking between them gleefully. "That's *so* on brand for a Hart, wouldn't you know?"

Ignoring him, she changed the subject. "The Dreaddit idea isn't bad."

He brandished the phone with a flourish, typing in a ridiculously long passcode that she was fairly sure ended in 69, which tracked.

"See?" He gestured to the little red creature, fanged, antennaed, and slightly skull-shaped, that sat on his screen next to a bevy of other apps, human and magical alike.

"Do you have Tinder *and* Splinter?" Agatha was looking curiously over his shoulder at what did indeed appear to be both the mundane and the magical version of the dating app.

"Never you mind that, pets. Stay focused." He clicked on the app, and when it opened, scrolled around. "I just saw something that inspired this, let me see if I can find it." Something inside Lex's other pocket beeped, and he handed her the phone, rummaging around, forearm deep this time.

Priscilla's eye caught on a post.

Dreaddit.com/d/hopelesslyromantic
u/LexManningDay
[AITA] I [M, 3,521] keep falling for the subjects of my bargains, but they never fall for me. First there was a musician's daughter who I was sure would thank me for helping her father finally acknowledge her after years of not, but then she wasn't into devilry even after I helped make sure she had a successful career. I even helped her land a star role in an amazingly accurate portrayal of elven culture, but no, still no love. Then there was a death-kissed human and an angsty, sullen witch and I was sure we would make the most glorious throuple, but alas! It was not to be. Am I coming on too strong with my latest object of affection [F, 32] just because she happens to be human, jaded, and 3,489 years younger than me? I've made a bargain with her, but I'll admit it, I am tampering with it to try to get her to like me. I can't help it—she's splendid, and I've been so unlucky in love for eons. Quite literally.
(25 upvotes, 7 downvotes, 69 comments)

Priscilla pointed to it while Lex rummaged, and watched as Agatha read it, her eyebrows shooting up, shaking in silent laughter.

Finally, Lex procured what looked like an oversized car key fob, pinched a button twice, and put the thing back in his pocket, miraculously again, without another word.

Priscilla wondered if it would be possible for her to obtain a pair of Mary Poppins leather pants, too, with seemingly boundless pockets and a snug, perfect fit.

Lex reached for his phone, jumping a little when he saw the screen.

"Not that! That's nothing." She was shocked to see *his* ears pink; she wasn't aware of ever hearing about a devil blushing. He scrolled furiously and pulled up another post. "This is what I was looking for."

Dreaddit.com/d/deaddit
[LivingQ] In search of a medium
I've been dead for almost two years, haunting an old barn, and I am having the darndest time finding whatever it is I'm tethered to. I don't even recognize this barn, but every time I go to sleep, I wake up there, no matter how far I travel. I've tried several alleged spiritualists, and countless churches that claim to commune with the spiritual world—one particularly bat-shit-crazy one believes live people can marry spirits; they're a breath away from drinking Kool-Aid, that one—but no one can SEE me or hear me. I finally figured out how to manifest physical motion enough to steal a cell phone off a hiker, and then a charger off another one, and then it was easy to haunt the house enough to generate electricity and get online. Where ON EARTH (or any other reasonably close plane of existence) can I find a medium who could *actually* help me? I can't work with a summoner, because I don't know what object I'm attached to. And anytime I find

someone who can see me, it's, like, a kid, or a dog, and people assume it's crazy too. HELP.
(389 upvotes, 2 downvotes, 12 comments)

"See?" Lex said. "Connie would be perfect."

The door swung open, and a pale-faced young woman walked out, looking shaken.

"She's leaning way too hard into her shtick in there," the woman whispered. "It's like some sort of over-the-top haunted house that manages to be so cheesy that it's scary."

"Ah, dearest, a real psychic will do that to you." Lex smiled disarmingly, and the woman quaked a little, hurrying to her parked car.

"Real? No. No. None of that was real. It's not real."

She peeled out of the parking lot before the door swung open again.

"Welcome," said Connie, who was dressed in a long, embroidered shawl and a fringed hat that hung low into her eyes. Her hair was freshly blue-black, an impressively shiny color that made her appear ageless and wise. "Madam Cleopatra will see you now."

"Oh," said Agatha.

"She really is leaning into it," Priscilla added. "Again."

They filed in, and it was a tight squeeze with the three of them, Priscilla and Agatha pressed against the curtain to avoid disturbing anything in the room, Lex sprawled out on the large bench sofa seat as though he hadn't a care in the world that he was taking up almost all of the room, forcing Priscilla to be intimately acquainted with the feel of Agatha pressed against her side.

Connie held a finger to her lips.

"For this to be as realistic as possible, to see what the problem is, I need the two of you to pretend you are not here. It is just Madam Cleopatra and this dashingly handsome stranger."

Lex smiled, a crooked thing, and took her hand, raising it

and pressing it to his lips above the crystal ball that was already set up.

"*Enchanté*, Madam Cleopatra. I'm Olexandre, but you may call me Lex. I'm delighted to be here."

"Olexandre," she cooed, ignoring his advice. "Hold out your hand."

He complied, shooting Priscilla a smile until Madam Cleopatra caught him doing that and made a disappointed clucking sound with her tongue.

"None of that."

She hummed, running a finger up and down his palm, tracing something.

"You have been in love many times, Olexandre."

"Yes," he said lazily. "Well, I'm over three thousand years old, so I should think it would be dreadfully boring were that not the case."

Her eyebrows furrowed, irises widening eerily in a way that Priscilla had never actually seen on any creature. That would certainly alarm a mundane.

She shook her head.

"No," she mused. "There was one heartache—*oh*. A human one. Before you became what you are now."

Lex bristled. Priscilla sat up. She hadn't realized Lex had been human once. Interesting.

"That's easy enough to deduce, innit? Given how most people end up in diabolical arrangements?"

"Hmm," said Connie, and she seemed to slip deeper into a trance. Her pupils widened, the darkness bleeding first into the iris and then in the already smaller sclera, turning entirely black, and then clouding over, gray and misty.

"YOU HAVE FALLEN IN LOVE TOO MANY TIMES TO COUNT, AND YET YOUR GREATEST UNDOING LIES AHEAD OF YOU."

Recoiling, Lex clutched his hand as though he had been burned.

"I beg your pardon," he began, but Connie was not done. Whipping around, she reached for Agatha and Priscilla, her hands snaking out to grab one of each of theirs. Her skin was freezing. Cold enough to hurt.

"This cannot be good if it happens with humans." Priscilla ground her teeth. Dammit. She'd thought she had a handle on this thing, for once.

"It seems the blowing off steam isn't going quite as swimmingly as I had hoped," said Lex, still holding his hand, eyes darting between them.

"TRUST EACH OTHER OR YOU SHALL REST NOT IN PEACE, BUT IN PIECES. BETRAYAL LURKS NEARBY. HARK! THE GARDEN! IT BECKONS!"

And with that final pronouncement, Connie slumped over, snoring lightly.

"This is awkward," said Lex.

Connie sat up, shaking her head. "Who? What? Oh, damn. It's happened again, hasn't it?"

"New plan," said Priscilla, hoping her voice didn't sound as shaky as she felt. "We set you up online to solicit magical clients. That way, the explosions are less alarming, and with any luck, you lean into that so that human clients aren't on the receiving end of all of this." She gestured.

"Sure," said Connie, yawning. "But for now, could you lock the door on your way out and turn my sign to Closed? I need a nap, and the two of you have a garden to save." She winked at Lex. "Good luck with your heartbreak, buddy."

The devil scowled at her before vanishing into a cloud of purple ginger-and-bergamot-scented smoke.

Much to Priscilla's chagrin, they called Kevin on the way back. His irritating baritone boomed through the car, Agatha's phone on speaker.

"How did it go?"

"Priscilla has it well in hand."

"Hah," said Kevin. "I'll believe that when I see it."

"You're on speakerphone," said Priscilla, cutting in ominously. "And let me remind you that I'm at that age where I only have one thing on my mind."

"What, men? Women?"

"Homicide," said Priscilla, and then instantly regretted it when Agatha sucked in a deep breath.

"Are you admitting to being behind the attacks on President Vanderbilt Voisin?" Kevin's voice was slick and silky now.

"Are you suggesting," Agatha interrupted, "that an invested member of the Council and the witchery community is trying to kill me?"

"Well," said Kevin, "if the buckled shoe fits."

"That is an extremely serious accusation to levy without evidence. Consider this an official request. Unless you wish to present evidence, please do not bring this up again." Her voice was firm.

"Fine." Kevin sounded pouty. "But you should know she offered me a raise to come work for her. Maybe that's looking better and better."

Priscilla frowned. Fucking Kevin had to go and bring that up now.

Agatha turned and looked at her, and she pretended to be very busy concentrating on the road, a tall task because it was one of those mountainous Vermont highways that stretched on straight for as far as the eye could see. It would be a bit before it curved and turned, and she was certain Agatha would see through the façade of careful driving.

"Oh, she did, did she?"

"Mm-hmm," said Kevin eagerly.

"Well, that doesn't change the urgency of my request. Can you send me the most up-to-date file on Green Witch Gardens?"

"Consider it done. Anything else?"

"No, but I will keep you up to date if it changes." She paused. "Oh, and Kevin?"

"Yes, boss?"

"If you enjoy your employment, mind your manners and remember what I said." Her voice was flinty.

A small, disreputable bit of Priscilla wanted to seize this as an opportunity to finally sway Kevin to her side, but then again, the promise of Agatha's steely voice laying down the law wasn't unattractive. Perhaps two beautiful women ought not to be fighting over something as insignificant as a man.

They pulled up to the greenhouse to find a frazzled old woman outside of it.

"I'm NACoW president Agatha Vanderbilt Voisin, and this is Councilwoman Priscilla Hart."

"Oh, thank goodness!" she exclaimed. "I'm Dotty Jenkins, the head horticulturist here. It's just terrible. I had to send out a message to the mundane occupants that there was a sewer leak, and to the magical ones that there was a zombie bedbug infestation."

Priscilla recoiled. "There isn't actually a zombie bedbug problem, is there?"

"No," moaned Dotty, covering her face with her hand. "Oh goddess, it's so much worse." A loud thumping and buzzing sound came from inside, and the building shook. "There's a magical force field that prevents anything magical in the greenhouse from getting out without my permission or a pass—a necessity because of some of the plots and what they contain—but no one can get in there, and I can't seem to find anything that shuts them down. No amount of magic will fix it. They're immortal chainsaws, I fear! I managed to drop a statue on one of them, and it split into pieces and STILL kept right on revving and sawing the empty air and anything that it came across."

Agatha's eyebrows shot up. Something nagged at Priscilla, as though she should be putting things together here.

"I really don't want to do this, honey," she grumbled to Agatha. The nickname slipped out, but she couldn't bring herself to regret it, watching the other witch bring her hands up for magic.

With a smooth move of her fingers, and then another, both of them were sheathed in crisp lavender armor.

"Really, Agatha? Pastel?"

"It's my signature blend from the vault. Faerie lilacs boost my witchcraft and protection spells. The only downside is that we'll have to be ungloved, obviously, to be free to use magic."

"I'm going to need a stiff drink after this," said Priscilla, frowning. "Fine. Let's get it over with."

CHAPTER 15

Agatha

When the rogue magical chainsaws' dismemberment rendered one of Hart's pinkies impossible to surgically reattach, Agatha began to feel that she had been wrong to ever suspect the other witch of sabotage. The missing tip of Priscilla's left pinky was, of course, the final nail in the coffin of Agatha's theory that the deliciously macabre councilwoman could be the real perpetrator of the attacks. Priscilla was beautiful, even when bleeding.

Agatha tried not to think about how much of an asshole it made her to have believed she was the would-be murderer, to have put up the walls between them, and to be lusting after someone injured as she muttered under her breath, summoning the various blood-clotting herbs she knew of. What was hemostatic, again? And what was a blood thinner? Goddess, she didn't want to make this worse.

With a slide of her thumb across her other fingertips, she summoned yarrow, and then witch hazel, both of which she could see in the garden.

Come to think of it, it was a good thing Prissy didn't need her pinkies for her particular brand of magic. Agatha ran her thumb across her fingers again, sprinkling some of the herbs directly on the wound and reserving the rest to mix. She was relieved to note that the herbs seemed to slow the bleed somewhat.

She ought to really thank Otho for insisting that she should take that First Aid for Plant Crafters refresher course earlier this year. Maybe she should put magic specific emergency preparation in the required training videos for all Council members. Fuck. She could not for the life of her remember the third hemostatic, and Priscilla was looking pale, slumped against the wall next to the now-useless handle of the final chainsaw. They'd taken it apart and stored the individual pieces in separate magical lockboxes to keep them from knitting themselves back together.

She didn't need three. Two clotting herbs would do, especially if they responded to her magic. She rubbed her thumb across all four fingers again, and the herbs mixed themselves in the air, binding together, pressing against the finger.

Priscilla let out a little shriek, but when Agatha summoned clean cloth bandages and reached for her hand, Priscilla shook her head and pressed the cloth to the bleeding digit.

"Painkiller?" Agatha didn't want to dose her without asking.

"I'd kill for some," said Prissy, the joke falling flat, framed by her too-pale cheeks. "Please," she added, and Agatha rubbed her fingers again, sending the poppy opiate directly to Prissy's bloodstream.

Normally, she did not administer emergency opiates, and she certainly was not in the habit of doling out drugs to her employees, but this was an extreme situation, definitely covered by the Good Samaritan witch codes for emergent magical maladies. Besides, her affinity for plants was strong enough that she doubted she'd be able to stop herself from helping Priscilla with them even if that weren't the case.

Priscilla sat back, her breathing slowing to normal, and Agatha felt the exhale on her cheeks and realized she was kneeling too close. She sat back on her heels, looking around her at the destructive wake the bizarre, enchanted tools had left behind.

"I can't believe they wouldn't stop, even when disassembled," said Priscilla, voice shaky, hand still pressed to the now-bloody bandage.

"Cause for inquiry indeed," she said.

She had never seen anything like this, but she couldn't figure out the seemingly immortal chainsaws until she took care of her bleeding girlfriend.

Clarifying that said bleeding girlfriend was a *fake* girlfriend felt like an unnecessary distinction. She rubbed her hands to make a new poultice of the herbs, and then again to bandage it freshly.

"Keep it over your head. Or maybe just above your heart? That slows bleeding. I think."

"What are you, a doctor?" Priscilla's voice was woozy, from the pain, the drugs, or both. It had to hurt. She had been taking a hell of a beating.

"No, just a woman who is now completely convinced that you are not trying to kill her."

"Glad that my smallest finger's sacrifice was not in vain." Priscilla winked. Or winced? Agatha couldn't be sure.

"You must be making it through if you're cracking jokes, *chérie*."

Priscilla grimaced. "Family problem, really. We joke through the pain. All sorts of pain, to tell the truth."

"Well." She chewed on her lip. "Hit me with your best joke. Or your worst?"

"This is going to seriously put a damper on my fisting game until it heals."

Agatha bit out a nervous laugh, that grew into something real when Prissy laughed too.

The color was returning to her face.

"If only they hadn't ganged up like that on the poor discarded fingertip, maybe we could have reattached it and kept your fist intact." Agatha offered. The chainsaws had, horrifically, pounced on the amputated digit and had their gory way with it. "But I am sorry about the finger."

"I'm not actually much of a fister," said Priscilla. Hart, Agatha reminded herself. It would be easier, in the end, if she could only think of her as Councilwoman Hart. "But I do from time to time enjoy the joke that I'll be the most generously endowed lover a gal has known, if she can just give me a few minutes to strap it on."

Agatha's breath caught in her throat at that. "Priscilla," she breathed, unable to stop herself the informality or the mental picture. And wasn't that out of line, to squeeze her thighs together while kneeling on the cement floor of the greenhouse, trying to make sure her fake girlfriend didn't bleed out from a wound by a flock of horrifyingly indestructible enchanted chainsaws. "How big?" she found herself asking, voice husky. This time, Priscilla winked.

"Let's just say big enough to rearrange your insides."

Agatha squirmed, swallowing back a moan.

One shouldn't get hot while discussing mangled body parts.

She tried to remind herself of the most boring facts. Like how an octopus had three hearts and a beak, and was definitely venomous. But only the blue-ringed octopus was dangerous to humans. It was good to remind herself of the fact that one blue-ringed octopus had enough venom to kill twenty-six people, and that it was a thousand times more deadly than cyanide. Still, only three people had been known to actually die; the big danger was absence of oxygen.

Which, actually, wasn't dissimilar to what she felt at the idea of Priscilla wielding something *big enough to rearrange her insides*.

The problem was, some of her body parts wouldn't mind being rearranged. Especially if Priscilla was doing the rearranging.

"You know what they say," she said primly. Prissy looked up at her from under hooded eyes.

"No, what?"

"It feels wrong to say while you're down a finger."

"This is helping."

She sucked in a breath, letting it out and committing to potential embarrassment.

"It's not the size of the boat; it's the motion in the ocean."

Priscilla met her gaze for a long moment that dragged on and on. Was it just Agatha, or was it hot in this greenhouse?

"Oh, honey," Priscilla said softly. "I can make sure you have both the boat and the motion you need."

"I . . ." Agatha started, fingers scrambling at her throat, blood pounding. "I'm glad to hear it," she finished weakly.

Priscilla wiggled her eyebrows and flashed her an irresistible smile, probably because of the painkillers.

"A secret size queen, then?"

Agatha felt her face go scarlet.

Priscilla winked, and she was definitely a little bit out of it. However high she was, her smile was still dazzling as she leaned closer.

"Don't worry, baby. That would be one benefit of fucking a girl. I can go as big as you want me to. As big as you need."

Fuck. She was firmly aware of the pulse between her thighs, of the tension against the sheer, smooth bra under the white silk blouse that had seemed modest enough, until it was soaked by a stray sprinkler and splattered in Priscilla Hart's blood.

Now she was bloody, wet, and painfully aware of the way her nipples hardened. Priscilla was, too, from the way she looked down, drinking in the sigh of Agatha, pupils blown wide. She was still clutching the finger, applying pressure, but her cheeks had plenty of color now, and her tongue darted out, tracing the outline of her unfairly plump lips.

It was the drugs, she told herself. The drugs that had made Hart horny, that had made her lick those lips.

Agatha wanted to bite them. She tried to distract herself with deadly octopus facts, but she found that she was unable to remember a single one.

How the hell had she gone from suspecting Priscilla Hart of murder to seriously considering an attempt to, for the first time in her life, lick a woman until she lost control. Even down half a digit, Hart was like a tempting glass of wine, like a dark bit of chocolate. Agatha suspected she would be decadent on her tongue, and goddess, did she want to consume her.

"Hellooooo," called a voice, breaking her from a lustful reverie just before she did something stupid, like tried to finger her somewhat fingerless fake girlfriend.

Priscilla stood up, wincing slightly, and reluctantly, Agatha rose.

"I tried to tell him not to," cried Dotty. "The gas leak!"

"There's clearly no gas leak; this is some sort of occult mayhem," said the man. Agatha thought he looked faintly familiar. He was wearing a delightfully loud pair of pin-striped tan-and-maroon pants, a bright yellow cardigan, and a tan jacket that floated around his shoulders like a cape, matching a jaunty little cap perched atop his head.

"Hank," said Priscilla, and was that relief in her voice? "This is my girlfriend, Agatha Vanderbilt Voisin."

"So pleased to meet you," he said, holding up the hand that was not clutching a small cream-colored satchel. "I came as soon as I heard there was something amiss at the Gardens."

"Agatha, this is Hank Dewey. He's a friend of Victoria's."

"Pleased to meet you," she said, and then, out of the corner of her mouth, "Who's Victoria?"

Hank's eyebrows shot up. "Your girlfriend doesn't know your brother's girlfriend?"

Agatha kicked herself. Of course she knew Azrael, and by connection, vaguely, Vickie Starnberger. As Council president she was well aware of all of the magical community members, and Victoria was one of them.

Plus, she made a mean honeycomb latte.

"Vickie, of course," said Agatha, smoothing her shirt. "You'll have to excuse me, Hank. I'm a bit frazzled."

"Dear, I don't know that you'll be able to pat out the blood splatters. You'll want to soak it in cold water and treat it with hydrogen peroxide right away."

Dotty cleared her throat. "Ms. Hart, are you quite all right?"

"I'm so sorry, Priscilla, where are my manners? Obviously, your appendages are more important than the sartorial blunder of blood splatter."

Priscilla snapped, keeping her hand by her side, where it wouldn't draw Hank's attention. She winced and then did it again. "It's been cleaned and bandaged. I'll be fine, if a bit less nimble on my left hand than I was this morning."

"In that case, I'd like to take the lead on cleaning this place up. I am, after all, the chair of aesthetic oversight."

"That's not technically a real position," interjected Dotty.

"Dorothy," said Hank, raising his chin. "Don't start with me today, not in the wake of such traumatic disturbance to my most beloved Green Witch Gardens."

"You—you mean Green Wonder Gardens."

"I meant what I said, Dot."

Priscilla's jaw dropped a little, and Agatha watched Hank, frantically racking her brain for protocol on breached containment of magical activities.

"This is a normal, nonmagical garden!" Dot shrieked at a high pitch that did not do her any favors in selling it, but in her defense, it had been a generally stressful afternoon.

"Oh dear," said Hank, shaking his head. "I am a drag queen, my darlings, which means that I am as close to made of magic as one could possibly *be* without actually being magical. You think I can't spot a lovely family of witches when I see one?"

He turned to Priscilla, gaze softening. "You think I didn't know from the moment that I met Persephone Hart that there was something magical about your lovely mother?"

To Agatha's shock, Priscilla's face crumpled. Maybe this delightfully flamboyant man had struck a nerve, maybe the finger hurt her more than she realized, or perhaps some combination of both, but when he held out his arms, Priscilla Hart, the impenetrable fortress of solitude and sternness, dove in for a hug, and sobbed softly, muffled by his billowing sleeves.

Agatha felt herself watch Priscilla, unsure how to identify the emotion spreading through her chest like ink on water. When she turned to Dotty, the woman was looking at her, gaze knowing and sympathetic.

"Come along, President Vanderbilt Voisin. It seems the cat's out of the bag in more ways than one, and we can get started on some of the bigger cleaning projects."

"Right," said Agatha, tearing her gaze away. "Right, I'll have to arrange to teleport these chainsaw bits back to the Council storage as safely as possible. I just need to make a quick call to my assistant."

"You can use my office, dear," said Dotty, smiling and patting Agatha on the shoulder. "I'll get started with patching up the broken glass."

She made her way into the little office, which was charming and snug, and then for a moment she sat silently before bending over and crying quietly into her hands.

It was possible she'd felt more in one afternoon than she'd ever felt in all her years, which was truly saying something, because the depth of agony at Jonathan's breakup speech was up there in ranking, as was the glory of winning Council president.

Somehow, almost losing Priscilla Hart was more than all of that combined.

CHAPTER 16

Priscilla

"How's your finger?" Kevin asked delicately, eying the offending digit as though it might explode.

They sat at the casket-shaped table near the back of Hopelessly Teavoted, the one with the deep, cozy velvet chairs that Priscilla favored.

"Much better." It had been two weeks since the surgery to close the wound, and her finger was healing nicely, even if it would still be some time before she'd feel comfortable administering a well-timed shocker.

Not that she had any reason to slide fingers into anyone's orifices lately.

Just that, if the need arose, she would definitely use the right hand to be safe.

Across from her, Kevin cleared his throat. "You know, I was determined to hate you after the bad business with Evelyn."

She stiffened. "And?"

He shrugged. "Water under the bridge. Then I was determined to hate you when you tried to steal me from Agatha. Honestly, it's an honor to be the assistant to the president." He smiled, that million-watt thing that seemed to turn people to mush. "But once I saw how badly you were burned, and then the whole finger business, well, I can see now that you're trying to get by, just like the rest of us."

It pissed her off, to be honest. His kindness. His stupid smile. His proximity to Agatha. It was possible she was also grumpy after being sliced and burned and then relieved of half a digit, though.

Still, part of her wanted to steal him away to keep him from being around Agatha too much, just in case.

It wasn't the nicest thing she'd ever done, meeting with Kevin before her appointment with the mundane mayor. She was just checking in; that was normal to do as a Council member.

But part of her? Part of her still toyed with the idea of trying to poach him.

It wasn't a proud part, but surely it couldn't hurt to build a bridge in case he was serious about crossing it. And she definitely would feel better knowing that he wasn't working late nights with Agatha, staring into her pretty blue eyes and cracking jokes.

She wanted to stare into those eyes, and she wanted to crack those jokes, and for fuck's sake, if she had to try to steal Agatha's assistant to make it happen, she wasn't above that.

Though a nagging voice in the back of her head reminded her that losing an assistant would be extremely hard on Agatha.

Was this all a workaround way for her to justify trying to steal back the presidency too? She didn't trust herself not to be an asshole. Almost, but not quite.

"I'm so happy that you made time for little old me." Kevin pressed his hand to his heart, staring at her across the table from their spot in the corner of Hopelessly Teavoted.

"One decaf macchiato with five pumps of hazelnut." Vickie set it in front of Kevin. "And an iced honeycomb latte."

Priscilla picked up her drink, not bothering to hide the relief in her face when she sucked down the first sip.

"Agatha get you hooked on those, did she?" Victoria Starnberger smiled at her, green eyes dancing mischievously.

Priscilla raised her eyebrows at Vickie, who stood with a hand on her hip and an accusatory smile on her lips.

"I didn't realize you were well acquainted." Prissy tapped at the glass, which was patterned with black roses.

"She's been coming around a lot in the past few weeks."

Since Hank had asked her why Priscilla's girlfriend didn't know Victoria, she realized with a flutter of guilt.

Here she was, contemplating stealing her fake girlfriend's assistant, in part to stave off the threat of real feelings, all the while her fake girlfriend was going out of her way to get to know her family.

Vickie watched her, smiling.

"Bring her around the manor soon?"

Kevin scoffed. "I still can't believe that she's dating you. I'm sorry to say it, Priscilla, but Agatha Vanderbilt Voisin is far out of your league. You're an excellent councilwoman, to be sure, but too young to satisfy a woman of that caliber."

Well then. It turns out she was not wrong to be annoyed by his niceness. Kevin was secretly a dick. She hated Kevin.

That was a relief, at least.

Vickie gave him a long look and then walked away, muttering something that sounded a lot like "Sour grapes."

Priscilla stared daggers, the kind she hoped he knew meant business, like maybe she'd wither him into raisins and not just sour grapes.

"I didn't come here to discuss my sex life," she said coolly, and she was pleased when Kevin frowned.

So it was a bit of a fib to suggest that she had one of those beyond a very well-used array of toys and a now–frequently exhausted right hand. He didn't need to know that.

"Fair," he said. "What I wanted to make absolutely clear is, my situation has . . . changed. I want to make sure my finances are squared away."

Ah. It was a shakedown, then.

"I enjoy the proximity to power with Agatha, I'll be honest. It would take a lot to tempt me away from working so closely with the president. But I'd be happy to come work for you if you, say, tripled what Agatha is paying."

"Tripled?" She gripped the edge of the table, nostrils flaring. *"Tripled?"*

Kevin shrugged. "I've met with a financial planner to help with some of my long-term goals for retirement, and it's time to think smart."

Priscilla's eyes narrowed. Kevin did seem to like nice things; she recognized the brand of his watch, and his clothes would not be out of place had they gone to a nice restaurant instead of the local tea shop.

Perhaps he'd grown concerned about his expensive taste.

Something about him bothered her. She couldn't put her finger on it. Maybe just his existence.

"I can't triple anything," she said flatly, still turning his words over in her mind.

"You're a Hart. You live in a literal mansion." He crossed his arms, sipping on his stupid decaf. What even was the point?

"It's a manor. Do you have any idea what the property taxes are like for a two-hundred-year-old Victorian manor on that much land?"

"I'm sure you could figure it out."

She stared at him. "My brother is a public schoolteacher, and I am a public servant. We get by on a two-salary income, but there's no hidden cache of gold beneath the grounds or anything."

Kevin pouted. "Fuck. You're serious?"

"As the dead." She sipped at her latte, angry once again that people made assumptions about her family based on their house. People always wanted the chutes and slides of the Addams family, leading to a treasure trove buried deep below. All that was buried in the basement of the house were a few spare bedroom suites that disappeared and reappeared as they pleased, a storage closet the size of a small apartment, and the home gym that had once been her parents' sex dungeon. The level below that was the burial grounds, but the catacombs held no secret wealth.

Absolutely no treasure room, sadly, though Uncle Larry had at one point, decades before, convinced the house to grow a model train room that he still frequented, in that way paying homage to all things Gomez. He even smoked cigars in there when he visited, from the smell of it.

"Well then, it looks like you don't have yourself an assistant, Priscilla." He smirked.

"Maybe that's for the best," she said. "See you around, Kevin."

He left in a huff, not even bothering to finish his drink. She checked her phone.

There was a message from the mundane mayor. She had her heart set on one of those little banana chocolate chip muffins, but this might be important.

When she checked the message, though, he was canceling. Something had come up—an urgent town Council meeting that he wanted to be at to shut down one of those ridiculous women protesting against children having access to books—and she fired off a quick response that she would be happy to reschedule for the following week.

She almost put her phone away, but then she thought better of it.

What was a fake relationship without fake actual dates? It was practically a business endeavor, leaning into the fraudulent relationship wisely and well.

Priscilla: Are you busy tonight, honey?
Agatha: Free as a bird, *chérie*.

Prissy smiled. It was nice that Agatha played into the nickname thing, even if they were fake nicknames.

Priscilla: Want to have dinner at Free Spirits with me? They have great small plates and an excellent wine selection
Agatha: What time?
Priscilla: 8? Meet there?

Agatha: it's a date
Agatha: *a fake date
Priscilla: I'll be the woman in the back with only 9 and a half fingers.

She smiled, tucking the phone into her pocket.

"Who's got you smiling like that?" She hadn't even heard Vickie approach, and she jumped a little in her seat.

"No one."

"Certainly not that douche canoe with suspiciously perfect hair," said Vickie, winking.

"That's a little mean, don't you think?" Priscilla paused, smiling wide before adding, "To douchebags everywhere. To be compared to him."

"That's the Priscilla Hart I know and love." Vickie laughed.

"Well, almost all of her. I am down half a finger." She held up her hand woefully.

Vickie smiled. "Sorry for your loss, *chérie*, but I think you'll survive it."

"My finger play may never be the same." Priscilla waggled her hand, and Vickie shook her head.

"For a time, your brother and I couldn't even touch each other without dying, and we made do. You'll figure it out."

Priscilla resisted the urge to gag at the implication. "And that's my cue to leave," she said. She was happy for Azrael, she really was, but she had a date to get ready for, and she couldn't think of anything that would put her less in the mood than contemplating the formerly complicated logistics of her brother's sex life.

"Have fun with the no one you're smiling about texting," Vickie called after her.

Priscilla flipped her off without even turning around to look at her, but she could hear Vickie's peals of laughter all the way out of the shop.

CHAPTER 17

Agatha

She showed up at Free Spirits at seven thirty, to make sure she had time to grab a corner table in the back and have a glass of wine and a quick refresher in the bathroom. She'd been going over the documents about the Hildebrand von Auden estate and the Fountain of Youth, trying to decide how a tiny vial of something that had been kept under lock and key, in the heaviest security vault of the lowest level of the Council building, could possibly have been stolen *and* be related to the chainsaw incident.

The chainsaws had behaved exactly according to the warnings she had read about immortality.

The saws had continued to buzz, even when taken apart. Their pieces had to be kept in separate containers. Was there an elixir of immortality for inanimate objects? And if so, how the devil would such a thing even work? Would the elixir work on animate and inanimate objects, organic and inorganic? She had a horrible feeling that the chainsaws were the work of someone sampling the elixir without wanting to take it themselves first. No wonder the original had been destroyed, and the magic forbidden. Immortality really was a pain in the ass.

Agatha resolved to leave the mystery at work, but arriving to the restaurant a full thirty minutes ahead of schedule had not helped with that initiative.

And to make matters worse, when she tried scrolling Dreaddit to check up on Connie and her fortune-telling business—which seemed to be going well; there were already several rave reviews recommending her to creatures posting in subDreadds—she stumbled upon an AITA post that reminded her of Jonathan so much that she thought perhaps it was him.

Until she remembered that he had the emotional range of a lump of coal, and that it would be a hot day in Heaven before he even suspected himself of being an asshole.

The biggest assholes were always the least suspicious of their own buffoonery.

She set the phone down and browsed through the menu, which offered an assortment of tapas, and a culinary tour of Spain at the table. It was perfect, the small plate approach, for nights like this, when she wasn't sure if it was fully a date, or fully a fake date even. If it wasn't going well, they could always treat it as a drink and an appetizer and call it quits; if it was, well, they could fill the table with delicious little snacks until they were both satisfied.

Agatha shifted in her seat, trying not to think of the other sorts of satisfaction she might find at the hands of Priscilla Hart.

And, as though the power of her explicit thoughts had summoned the woman herself, there she stood, clad in a black bodycon dress that left very little to the imagination, a slit up the slide so high that it made Agatha nervous that one wrong move would be enough to disrobe her entirely from the waist down.

Her hair was swept up, slightly wavy, Agatha noted. It was usually down or braided to the side, but this way, goddess, her face was epic.

It was the face of her deepest desires, her darkest, most unapproachable dreams. Her fantasies.

Priscilla's red lipstick was a shade darker than usual, past the bloodred and into something more decadent, something

Agatha longed to swipe her thumb against, to see if it would smudge, if she could make a gorgeous, sloppy mess of the other woman's mouth. Her naturally long lashes stood out against a cat eye, which was drawn sharp enough to kill a man.

Or a woman, in this instance, for Agatha had never been more certain that she was sexually attracted to other women than she was right at this moment, when it felt like her heart was seizing and the entire world slowed down, like the only two people in the universe were her and Priscilla. It had never been like this, not with the college roommate she used to kiss sloppily on the counters, both of them claiming it was something everyone did with their friends. Not the times they watched porn together and both of them got off from separate twin beds, somehow also pretending that was platonic.

She hadn't admitted to herself for years that those sexually charged moments were not indicative of simple friendship, and they'd loomed large in her memory, hot and ragged around the edges when she ran her mind around them.

And yet those moments were nothing, absolutely nothing, compared to just looking at Priscilla approach her, dressed all in black, that deadly deep red in her lips and her nails.

"You changed your lipstick," she said weakly. She had meant to tell Priscilla that she was the sun and everyone else the moon, to quote Shakespeare, to throw herself at her feet and beg for the honor of even so much as being stepped on. Run over with her hearse, even. Or, at the very least, to tell her that she looked lovely tonight. But no, all Agatha managed was a comment on her lipstick.

Hart, she thought, *think of her as Hart*, but her mind rebelled.

Priscilla slid into the chair across from her, and the scent of her, lemony and tinged with mint, nearly gave Agatha a heart attack. She should really check in with a cardiologist; past mid-thirties could be late enough to worry that there was something wrong with her body to necessitate the way her heart was pounding, thudding, and the extra pulse between her legs that seemed to have developed a life of its own.

She clenched, shifting to try to relieve the pressure of being so swollen, so slick with want, and she caught Priscilla's carefully lined eyes tracking her, smugly, as though she knew exactly what this attire did to Agatha.

"It's called Monster," she said.

"Beg pardon?"

"The lipstick. The color is called Monster." She smiled, teeth white against the deep red of it. "Because maybe I am a Monster." Priscilla examined her nails, and Agatha thought something flickered on her face, like this was a mask and the real Prissy—well, did the real Prissy fear that maybe, just maybe, she really was too much of a monster?

That struck a chord in her, that familiar fear of being at once too much and not enough.

"That's okay, *chérie*," Agatha breathed, her voice coming out wrong. Too heavy, too laced with desire. "I happen to like monsters." She caught Priscilla's eyes and something stretched between them, entirely new and yet surprisingly familiar after all.

"Can I get you something to drink?" A short woman with reddish-blond hair and a name tag that read Alison stood next to the table.

Agatha welcomed the server's interruption, and took the moment when Priscilla put in a wine order to scan the menu and remind herself to breathe.

She ordered a second glass of white wine. Prissy asked for a glass of red, and Agatha pointed to a few of the menu items that she had painstakingly selected and thought they might share. Prissy smiled, dazzling once again, and added one, though Agatha was becoming so obsessed with the movement of her mouth that she couldn't have recounted what it was that Priscilla ordered, let alone what she herself had ordered, to save her life.

The server returned with drinks, and Agatha took a deep breath. She had wanted to even the playing field, ever since Prissy had offered that vulnerable admission of the problems in her broken engagement.

"I want to explain something to you. I don't think I have been entirely fair." Agatha nibbled on her lip, trying to calm herself with random facts. Like how dinosaurs roamed the earth for about 180 million years, while humans had only been around for about 300,000, which meant that dinosaurs, though now extinct, existed for far longer than human beings had in history.

That calmed her. Magic and all, they were nothing, blips in time compared to dinosaurs.

"Because you suspected I was trying to murder you up until I literally lost a digit?" Prissy smiled wryly, holding up the still-bandaged, albeit much less bulkily, finger.

Agatha shook her head, taking a deep breath and remembering the dinos. "No. I wanted to say I'm sorry for how much I acted like I hated you these past months."

"And here I was thinking we were bosom buddies," said Priscilla, and her eyes did in fact skate Agatha's neckline.

Fuck it. Not even terrible lizards could distract from this feeling, this tension, that stretched taut between them.

She wanted to play it cooler, but she was incapable, and she found her own hand trailing down one side of her neckline, over the top of the heft of her left breast, and then back up over the right one and up the other side of the V.

Prissy watched her, face impassive, but for her eyes, which gave her away—hooded, with pupils blown wide.

"I never really hated you. Just the idea of you, and your freedom, but also because of what Jonathan did." Agatha's hairs stood up. She felt raw from the honesty of the admission.

At the sound of his name, Priscilla's eyes snapped back up to hers, the moment of longing snapped clean in half.

"What did he do?" Her voice was dangerous. Low.

"It was right after you ran, and then Evelyn went after you. Vickie came back in and was talking to the wedding party, I think strategizing a smooth exit plan, and that's when my—despicable drunk Jonathan stood up." She couldn't even bring herself to call him her boyfriend out loud, not even with *ex* in front of it. He was a bastardly, pigeon-livered, rump-fed runion, too dreadful to even describe with modern insults. She needed finely aged ones to match the level of his repulsion.

Priscilla cracked her knuckles. "I'll kill him if you like." She didn't sound like she was joking.

Agatha shook her head. "He's not worth that kind of effort, all things considered."

Raising her glass, Prissy nodded. "Well, I'll drink to being well rid of an awful man."

"Cheers." Agatha held hers up and gulped down what was left. "He gave this absolutely dreadful speech," she admitted. "After you had gone, he got up and spoke the most embarrassing and horrifying things. I very nearly cast a spell to vanish into a hole in the ground."

"A speech? At my wedding?" Priscilla raised an eyebrow. "Are men okay?"

Agatha shook her head vigorously. "Most of them are not, not at all. And I guess it was your almost wedding, not that this makes it better."

"Ouch. But true." Priscilla gestured to the server, her long, tempting fingers somehow procuring two more drinks in record time, and raising another glass to Agatha.

She drank. "He said he was inspired by you leaving, and that he'd like to leave me, too, because I was boring, and trite in what he called my phases and silliness trying to make up for that boredom." Agatha swallowed, trying not to let the memory of the awkwardness creep up too much.

"He told you it was just a phase while breaking up with you?" Priscilla's nostrils flared now, and her voice was angry.

She nodded, miserable at the memory. "In so many words. He didn't say it directly, but he was absolutely alluding to the conversation we had a year or so earlier, when I came out to him." She ran a hand down her face. It had been stupid of her to think that this specific man could see her for who she really was, could look at her authentic self and not feel threatened and like he needed to run, or crack a bad joke at the very least.

"I take it he did not handle that well." Priscilla's pretty

mouth was set in a frown, and she cracked a knuckle on her good hand.

"No," she said. "I didn't realize it at the time, because I was mid-thirties and admitting for the first time out loud that I'm bisexual, but he did not take it well in the slightest." It was a relief to say that out loud.

"That absolute wanker." Priscilla snorted. "You're far too good for him, Agatha."

"He asked if it was a phase, and then he asked if this meant I wanted to have a threesome. I shut that down, of course, but he only ever saw the admission as either a threat to his sexuality or a way to consider objectifying me."

"Fucking men," Priscilla said from between gritted teeth.

"It's what I've been doing all these years, and I must admit I like it, when they're not total assholes. But . . ." She blushed, taking a long drink.

"But?"

"I wish I spent more time fucking women too."

Priscilla's eyes widened. "You don't have to answer this, honey, and I'm certain I shouldn't ask it," she began. "But I am going to anyway, because I have had many alcohols, I have very little self-control, and frankly, I like talking to you. About everything. Anything."

Agatha shook her head. "I haven't," she said softly. "I haven't fucked a woman before."

The server chose that precise moment to drop off several plates of food, and Agatha had never stared so hard at a well-dressed and -prepared endive.

"You're picking a smashing one to start with," said the server, winking, and Agatha's mouth dropped open, a little horrified, eyes darting from the server to Priscilla and back.

"What?" The woman shrugged, adjusting her bow tie and pulling a few napkins out of her apron to set on the table next to their plates. "I call it like I see it, and you two make a fine couple. Good for the both of you, really."

"We're . . ." Agatha almost said they weren't a couple, they were just friends, they were coworkers, but then she remembered the ruse, and also, she didn't want to sit across from Priscilla, wanting her like this, and deny her anything—not her first name, not even a label. "We're new," she said, smiling shyly, and trying not to think of how honest it felt, how nice it was when Prissy threaded her fingers between hers.

The server smiled and headed back for the bar.

Priscilla turned back to her as though the conversation had never paused. "Not once? Not even before the horrid wanker?" Her voice was demanding, riddled with need.

"No. My college roommate and I would do this thing where we got drunk, and there was grinding and heavy kissing. A few times we watched porn and, you know, masturbated in the same room, or next to each other on the couch."

"That's not nothing," said Priscilla, eyebrows arching. "That's actually very gay, which it seems like you know now."

"I mean, at the time I thought that was typical roommate behavior. I thought maybe all close friends did that."

"You thought all close friends dry humped their friends, and stuck tongues down their throats?"

"Well, when you put it that way."

"It doesn't matter how you put it: it's pretty fucking gay."

"Well." Agatha gestured at herself. "Here I am, pretty fucking gay, I guess. I just thought maybe it was a little too late to be honest about it for a while. And then I decided, fuck it, I get this one beautiful life, and I don't want to waste it letting other people tell me what I am and what I am not."

Prissy smiled. "I misjudged you too. I'm sorry for that. I thought you were a boring, stodgy straight." She paused. "But you should know that you'd be just as queer if you'd never laid a single finger on another woman. You are who you are, regardless of your experiences."

"Now you know the truth." She took a dramatic drink, setting the glass down and reaching for one of the plates. The drinking was making things a bit fuzzy, and the fuzzier they got, the more convinced she was that it would be a fantastic idea to scoot closer to Priscilla, to see what it might feel like to touch her—well, more than she had before.

"And what is the truth?" Prissy trailed a lazy finger up Agatha's arm.

"The truth is, I'm a boring, stodgy bisexual."

Priscilla laughed, the sound of it pealing loudly, and then smiled.

"You could never be boring or stodgy. Truly."

"Wait until you hear my hopes and dreams." Agatha sighed. Too many of them involved color-coded planners and pens for her to be a woman of mystery and intrigue.

Priscilla laughed, and the sound was so charming. "Tell me."

"Tell you what?" Agatha leaned in toward her voice, and the smell of her, that hint of citrus.

"Your hopes and dreams?" Prissy's smile was special. Secret. Agatha got the feeling that she could tell this woman anything, anything at all, and she would hold it close to her heart. She would treasure it.

"Which ones?"

"Hmm." She paused. "How about this. What's your dream vacation?"

"A cozy cabin in the woods. Not the primitive kind, mind you: I want water and electricity, but also a roaring fire. Total hygge and total pampering. A huge bathtub, jetted, preferably. A fireplace. A mantel." The wine made her bold. "A luxurious rug to fuck on in front of said mantel." Goddess, she would give anything to have Priscilla Hart sprawled out on a soft sheepskin rug in front of a warm fire, maybe after a long, cold hike.

Priscilla grinned. "Glamping. Your dream is sexy glamping."

"Why, is that awful? I worry that it's awful." Agatha paused. "I just feel like doing it in front of a fireplace is a bucket list item that I need to get to, but maybe it's cliché. Stupid."

"No," Priscilla said, shaking her head contemplatively. "It actually sounds nice." Her smile was wicked now. "I love a good fireplace romance."

"I do also worry that I don't, like, count. That it's too late." Agatha blurted it, the words falling out of her mouth unbidden. She squeezed her eyes shut for a moment.

"Count according to whom?" Priscilla sounded curious, like she really wanted to know.

"I don't know, whoever is in charge?" She didn't want to say the quiet part out loud, which was that she worried she didn't count enough to herself. She was thirty-seven, and the thing with her roommate had been almost two decades ago. She'd dated many men and no women between, and she hadn't so much as held hands with a pretty girl in that span of time.

"You are who you are," said Priscilla. "And your sexual history is not an indication of your sexuality. Are all people who don't have sex incapable of knowing their own inclinations?"

It was sound logic, and Priscilla was too pretty to disagree with, anyway.

She wished she could take Priscilla home with her, and didn't realize that she had said so out loud until the other woman smiled at her, eyebrows raised.

"I don't think you're in any condition for consent, but I will make sure you get home safely, and I will gladly revisit this conversation the next time we are both sober and so inclined." Priscilla's eyes lingered wistfully on her, like she really was sad to turn down the offer, and it was enough that instead of the burning shame of rejection she had anticipated, all she felt was warm possibility.

The rest of the evening was a blur of small plates, more wine, and Priscilla's unbelievably red lipstick, which had to be tattooing itself onto her heart, among other places. Monster, indeed. It was an apt name. She wanted Priscilla to ravish her. She could shut her eyes and see it, see those lips moving, feel herself hold her own hands down to keep from touching them with the gentle reverence that she would be sure to dream about.

The last thing she remembered was Prissy putting a coat around her shoulders and leading her down the street toward her house. Those sexy, heeled boots clicked against the sidewalk, the crisp, leafy scent of fall filled the air, and the unbelievable sparkle of stars lit the sky, still paling in comparison to the celestial spark in her soul at the knowledge that they walked home together, hand in hand, Priscilla not even seeming to mind Agatha swaying and stumbling from time to time.

CHAPTER 18

Priscilla

Priscilla Hart was not accustomed to waking up on the outside of tightly tucked sheets that did not belong to her. Messy, sex-addled ones, certainly. But outside of them, not at all naked, that was new. She was definitely not accustomed to the soft comforter that wasn't hers, but most startling of all was the warm, gently snoring body she found herself draped around, over the blanket and the sheet, one soft arm wound around hers, anchoring her into the position of big spoon.

And, unfortunately—or fortunately, depending on how she looked at it—the sheet and the blanket, though crisply tucked on her side, had ridden down the front of Agatha Vanderbilt Voisin.

She tried not to breathe, because if she breathed too hard, she feared her hand would slip up the silky pajama top Agatha wore. If it did, it would move from semi-appropriate upper stomach area to definitely sexual underboob area. Goddess, she wanted to slip.

But as hot as Agatha was, as alarmingly seductive as those little pajamas were, she was not in the habit of groping fake girlfriends without a proper conversation while both parties were starkly sober. Even if Agatha's proposition last night had sorely tested her resolve to be chivalrous.

Which sucked, quite frankly, because every bit of her was

aching to move her hand, all the way up or all the way down, to run her thumbs along Agatha's impressive tits, or down, down, skating between her thighs.

Fuck, Priscilla was twisted into knots. But wanting was not the same as deserving, and she would never take advantage, so she settled instead for cautiously extricating herself from the surprisingly strong grip of sleeping Agatha, who stirred a little bit, rolling onto her back.

Priscilla tried and failed to ignore the way the strap of her top fell down her left shoulder, the way her breasts threatened to escape it, the way she wanted to lave her tongue across the tight, hard peak of Agatha's nipples, which she could see straining against the fabric, either from the cool of the morning or a particularly good dream. Maybe both. To be that cool breeze or that dream, Priscilla would have traded almost anything.

Instead, Priscilla got up, left what she hoped was a heartfelt note next to her favorite slender Hydro Flask and some Advil on the nightstand, and quietly slipped out of Agatha's place, borrowing a sweatshirt to throw over her dress, cutting through the back roads and ducking through the forest until she got to the maze and her protective bubble of silence.

This time she had plenty to think about, but there was one score she needed to settle, one call she needed to make here, in the secluded labyrinth of her own design, in the comforting woods she'd grown up in. It was time for closure.

It was 8 a.m. here, which meant that it was the afternoon there, a perfectly fine time to call.

The phone rang for enough beats that she thought perhaps Evelyn would not pick up. It did seem socially acceptable to decline calls from a former fiancée who had not only abandoned her on the day of their planned wedding but also dodged all communication since.

"Hello?" The chirp of Evelyn's voice was so surprising that for a moment, she said nothing. She had expected to feel something—a pain, or an echo of love, or intense regret. But what she felt, in reality, was certainty.

She had done the right thing. At the wrong time perhaps, but the right thing.

And this phone call was the right thing too.

"Priscilla, I hope you haven't placed an international phone call for the sole purpose of breathing heavily into my ear."

"No," she croaked. She cleared her throat. "No, sorry. It's a bit harder to say what I need to than I thought."

"That's a start, I suppose." Evelyn waited, but there were no sounds of impatience, no coughing, no tapping, no annoyed *hmm*, which she remembered once had driven her absolutely to the brink of madness in how it irritated her.

"I need to say that I am so deeply sorry for leaving you in that way. It should have been a conversation at a different time. I should have talked to you about it far earlier."

"I was furious with you, you know. For months. I swore if you ever contacted me, I'd give you a piece of my mind."

"You'd be within your rights to do that still."

Evelyn sighed. "I know. But now that I'm a bit more removed from it, I still think you've got shit timing and the social graces of a bull in a china shop, but perhaps you weren't wrong."

"Evie," she began, and this part hurt. "Evie, I did love you."

"I know. And I, you." Evie sighed loudly over the phone. "I didn't get it at first, but I get it now."

Priscilla needed to say it anyway. "If love were enough to change a person's mind about their hopes and dreams, I would have changed for you. But the thing is, my mind wasn't going to change. I didn't want what you wanted, and I didn't want you to give up on a thing you wanted."

"It was . . ." Evelyn started. She stopped and coughed daintily. "It was presumptuous of me to think that you would change your mind. I convinced myself you were just young, that we were just young, and that you'd want children eventually. You do seem to like children."

"Liking them fine and wanting to have them is different. And it wouldn't have been fair to you, or to any future children of yours." And it did hurt a little to say it that way, of *yours* and not of *ours*, but there was a relief in the hurt of it, a sensation that she was releasing a burden that she had been carrying around. A commitment to maybe knuckle through for the duration of her life, to bend and accommodate Evelyn's dreams, and in doing so, make herself miserable.

She hadn't wanted to turn out one of those horrible, screaming parents, the sort that had never wanted to have children. Or worse, the sort that simply wasn't suited to parenthood.

"You might have been an excellent mother, had you wanted it," said Evelyn.

"I think the wanting it is an important part of excelling in that particular field."

"Yes," said Evelyn finally. "I know. Perhaps in the future, you might be clearer." She paused. "And perhaps, in the future, I might listen to the next woman more carefully when she tells me whether that is something she wants or not."

There would be a next woman, and that was reassuring. She'd broken something in Evelyn, and Evelyn in her, but not irreparably. Not as broken as it would have been to go through with it, to stay calm and carry on and have a baby or two or even three just to please someone else. She hadn't broken up a family, was the thing. It was one thing to break a person a little; a person could heal. A family was an inexcusable thing to break.

"I wish you all the love in the world, Evie," she said. "Do you ever think about coming back? Not to me, obviously. But to the US."

"No, not to you, and not to Hallowcross. Not even to the States. It's so much easier here, with my mother, and . . ." She cleared her throat. "I've started seeing someone. It's new. I'm going slow with it for obvious reasons, but it's nice."

"Oh, Evelyn," she said. "I'm so happy to hear it." And Priscilla meant it with all her heart. "The Council will miss you."

"The European Council would probably say the same if I left." That did make sense. She had heard that Evelyn had been quick to fill a seat vacated by a retiring ECoW witch. "How are things going with Constance Witherspoon?"

Right. Evie had been here for that.

"Honestly? A little better, but only after Lex meddled and suggested she needs to treat her powers like things that should be exercised."

Evelyn hummed into the phone.

"What?"

"Well, it figures that he would think of that, and not you. Witches learn to do that, to channel their powers so they don't explode. You know that."

"I just didn't think of it that way because she's an adult, and we come into our powers when we come into our witch families."

"It would appear that you need to think outside of how you've been thinking if she's still struggling." Evelyn had a point there.

"The outbursts—they work when she's doing paranormal readings, but they're still so potent. If the wrong mundane sees her like that, or the wrong mundanes—"

"It could be a problem."

"Exactly."

"Have you thought about helping her find balance outside of magic? I know that's never been your strong suit, but it might be what she needs."

Priscilla sucked in a sharp breath. There it was, the teeny barb, the sort of sadness and anger that probably would always linger between them. There was something about breaking what had once been whole that left room for stingers that never worked themselves all the way out. She and Evelyn might be cooperating, but they would never be friends. And that was okay, because Evelyn *was* helping her. Because, fuck. She had not thought of that, and wasn't it the simplest solution in the world.

"I've got to tell Agatha. The president, I mean."

Evelyn snorted. "I do, of course, know who Agatha Vanderbilt Voisin is." She paused, as though she were going to say something, for a few extra beats, and then, anticlimactically, finished. "You do that. I've got to run."

"Be well, Evie."

The click of the phone felt final, as though the last reverberation of their former love echoed across the Atlantic.

CHAPTER 19

Agatha

Agatha had woken up to the best sort of dream, the one where someone was holding her, her body sluggish and throbbing with wanting. In the dream, she'd been writhing, close. Her eyes had fluttered open, and she'd felt it, the heavy weight of an arm twined with her own, the brush of fingers through the thin cloth of her pajamas. A carefully manicured hand, nails painted a deadly shade of red, just below where she wanted those fingers. She shut her eyes again, breathing carefully. She had told herself if she didn't move, Priscilla wouldn't, either, and she concentrated so hard on pretending to be asleep that she had drifted, probably aided by the beginning of a terrific hangover, back out of consciousness.

She awoke a second time, the sunlight brighter through her window, and she was alone.

Rolling over, she sat up, eyes catching on a neatly folded letter propped next to a fancy water bottle. It was the color of cornflowers, a light, purplish blue, one of those brand-name things. When she unscrewed the top, there was still a slight bit of Priscilla's lipstick around the mouth of it.

Goddess, that made her so hot, thinking about those lips. And about the thoughtful gesture of refilling it. She took a sip. It was cold, and so perfect. Had Priscilla gone through the trouble to put ice in it so she would wake up to a cool bottle of water?

Somehow, this little thing twisted in her chest, threatening to forget that what lay between them had ever been fake.

Agatha knew it was sleazy to shut her eyes for a moment and picture the moment before she was fully awake, when Priscilla's hand had been on her. If only she'd been bolder and grabbed that hand, dragging it down. Or up. If only she'd been brave enough to roll over and look Priscilla in the eye, tell her everything she wanted in the cold sober light of day. If only.

But instead, she'd faked sleep, fallen back asleep, and woken up alone.

At least the extra hour or so had done something to make her feel less of the impact of drinking. She downed two Advil and the water, stumbled out of bed to refill the bottle, set it back down, and pee, and committed to getting back into bed for an hour or so, until she felt less like death.

Well. Horny death.

There was one thing she could think of. One thing that would certainly take the edge off a hangover. One didn't get to be thirty-seven years old without noticing the inherent benefits of an orgasm in alleviating the misery of the morning after drinking.

It was dirty, but she wanted to do it thinking about Priscilla, those red lips that begged to have hers on top of them, those long nails and how they might scrape across her skin. How Priscilla would have to be so careful touching her with them in highly sensitive areas.

Or maybe, and this thought nearly destroyed her, maybe she wouldn't be careful at all. Maybe the firm acrylic edges of them would dig in, tracing patterns on her breasts, around her nipples. Maybe she would leave little indentations, crescent-shaped reminders of the two of them writhing and scraping deliciously against each other.

Agatha moved both hands up and under her shirt, chasing

the thought, squeezing her nipples and then pinching, hard enough to make herself squirm under the covers.

Priscilla seemed like the teasing type, and she could picture it, her lush mouth making a mess of Agatha's favorite pajamas, working her through the fabric, soaking it with her tongue. Agatha pulled her hands out of her shirt and resumed rubbing herself through it, which was much more frustrating, and yet . . .

The slip of the smooth fabric paired with the relentlessly tight pull of her fingers made her roll her body in anticipation.

She lowered her arm and reached a hand into her shorts, slipping it over her panties, tracing along the edges, drawing circles around her center, figure eights, in an elegant rhythm as close to what she imagined Priscilla's fingers being like as she could.

Priscilla wouldn't be soft, though, she thought, and she reached down and pinched, moaning loudly enough at the action, surprisingly hot, edged with pain and yet also with something more, something that she hadn't ever chased before, not really, or at least not that she could remember.

Agatha released herself, pulling her panties to the side and running her fingers down where she could feel every prickle of sensation.

She wanted to dip her fingers in, but she forced herself to skate around her entrance, to slide up the right instead, legs shaking a little as she circled herself again.

It was not enough to do this quietly and under covers. It was not enough to simulate the silent orgasm of stolen moments in bathrooms after a boyfriend hadn't done it right.

It was not enough to just lie here, touching herself and thinking about Priscilla.

Agatha threw the covers off and got on all fours, reaching a hand back, shoving aside her underwear, and rubbing her clit with an insistent motion, leaning into her own hand and then rocking back, teasing herself with the other hand.

She remembered what Priscilla had said.

I can make sure you have both the boat and the motion you need.

She wanted it to be Priscilla's hand, not hers, thrusting a finger in, and then another. She sat up, on her knees, hoping that she could spear into herself from this angle in a way that made her feel satisfied, in a way that matched the fantasy of how Priscilla would do it in her head.

As big as you need.

She had meant for this to be a quick finger-fuck, but now she was sweating, needy, the hangover long forgotten. She had a vibrator—carefully selected to be slightly smaller than Jonathan, with the knowledge that anything else would send him over a metaphorical edge of rage, and not the good kind.

She wondered what Priscilla would do, what kind of toys she played with.

About what her bed would be like in that decadent haunted manor. About what secrets those walls could whisper, so different from the cheery wallpaper here, patterned with yellow roses.

She withdrew her fingers and reached for the bedside drawer, and the trusty vibrator. When she tried to flick it on, it sputtered and refused.

Fuck, she hadn't charged it. And there was no way she was stopping to wait for that.

What the hell. If a broken escalator was a set of stairs, an uncharged vibrator was basically a dildo. Even if she did picture a dildo as something that would be bigger than two of her own fingers, the approximate width of this one.

She grabbed a pillow and straddled it, propping the vibrator on it and easing down, slowly at first, and then fucking it harder, rolling her breasts under her hands, then sliding a hand between her legs, rubbing, chasing, unable to quite get what she wanted in depth, slamming her eyes shut and thinking of what Priscilla's fingers would feel like, wondering if it would be like in the porn she'd watched, the one where two girls fucked each other on an enormous double-sided purple dildo. Back then, she had been embarrassed to be searching for things like strap-ons and girl-on-girl, unwilling to examine what it meant that the idea of a woman hovering over top of another woman was much more arousing than anything Jonathan had ever done to her.

She sank down on the too-still vibrator, rocking back and forth, spreading her legs out in front of her so that she was sitting, taking it as deep as she could, both hands working furiously, one circling with infuriating figure eights, the other playing gently, and then more forcefully, around the edge of where she was attempting to fill a void that screamed for crimson nails and a wicked, wicked mouth.

I can go as big as you want me to, Priscilla had said.

Her eyes flickered to the nightstand, to the water bottle. It was the sturdy kind, sleek and thin, and yet still the size of three thick fingers wide. And Priscilla's mouth had been on it, the faint lipstick stains reminded her.

Agatha was desperate to taste her.

Without allowing herself time to think better of it, she reached for the bottle, rocking down on the too-thin vibrator. Her filthy mind was unable to stop running Priscilla's words over with her tongue.

She brought the bottle close, licking the place where Priscilla's mouth had left its mark. Overwhelmed by the lipstick stain, the dirtiness of it all, she set it back down on the nightstand, trying to satiate herself with knowing her mouth, her tongue, had been where Priscilla's had been too.

She sank down onto the too-still vibrator, Priscilla's words echoing in her ear. Her breath caught, and she rocked downward.

It was so good, fucking herself, thinking of Prissy.

She shut her eyes, and thought of the black dress, and that slit up Priscilla's thigh. Priscilla, all raven hair and brown eyes flecked with gold, and the way she looked when she raised an eyebrow and curved her lips into that half smile.

Priscilla, Priscilla, Priscilla.

She came almost as soon as her fingers hit her most sensitive spot, her body seizing, moaning loudly.

And then, because it felt like the right thing to do, she brought her own fingers to her mouth and licked them, throwing herself onto her back, gently removing the object of her temporary affection, and wondering what the fuck had gotten into her.

CHAPTER 20

Agatha

A shower and a fresh pantsuit—pale peach, this time—helped her put aside the momentary solo indiscretion.

"Morning," said Xiomara, who was refilling a water bottle at the cooler as Agatha walked in. Her face blushed hot now at the concept of hydration in general, and it was possible that she wouldn't be able to look at anyone drinking water without getting a little bit turned on. Her own fault, really, and also entirely worth it.

The Council members had been united in their kindness recently, whether because of the threats on her life or the efficacy of her fake relationship, she wasn't sure, but she was glad that things were running more smoothly around here.

"Agatha!" Kevin exclaimed, jumping up and holding up a cup of coffee and a bag from Hopelessly Teavoted. "I picked up muffins when I got your text that you were running late."

"And a latte?" she asked, peering hopefully at the drink in his left hand.

"I'll put it on your desk. Honeycomb. Large. Hot."

"Thank you. Can you rearrange my morning schedule? I need to go down to the vaults."

"Absolutely," he said, moving toward the door to her office. She noticed that the room was missing a particular red-lipsticked councilwoman.

"Where's Councilwoman Hart?" She forced herself to sound normal, and not like she'd fucked her hand thinking about that very same question.

"She got in early to catch up on paperwork," he said. "Whatever trouble *that* means." Agatha frowned at him, but he continued, "And then she had a meeting with Constance Witherspoon, said it was urgent."

She didn't want to admit it, but Agatha felt a keen disappointment in that. They'd been doing so well visiting Connie together. But it was no matter.

Her thoughts were derailed, though, when Kevin opened the door to her office and was immediately ensconced in something red, thick, and gelatinous.

His face reddened, and he moved slowly through the Jell-O to clutch at his throat. Xiomara was the quickest to snap, and the Jell-O vanished from him into a puddle of red liquid on the floor.

Kevin coughed.

"Oh, shit," breathed Xiomara. "She took it too far this time."

"That," said Kevin, sputtering, "is the last straw. I have been working my ass off, and I value my life too much to be choked by Jell-O. I only have one life, and I intend for it to be a long and glorious one. I don't have time for this shit."

"Please, Kevin. I'm sure she didn't mean . . ." Agatha fumbled at the words. What had Priscilla meant, though? Pranking her now? Goddess, she was an idiot for thinking they were doing something. Maybe it had all been another trick, and now poor Kevin, who was wearing her coffee, which must have splattered as the hex hit, was seething, dripping in strawberry red.

"I'm taking a vacation. Paid. Two weeks." He huffed, tapping the fingers on both his hands together, and drying himself, though the shirt remained red, and she had to imagine he was sticky.

"Of course," she said, hoping her voice was placating.

Right, Kevin's magic wasn't particularly strong, which was why he needed two hands and couldn't fully handle the mess.

The prank would have been cruel to Agatha, but clearly it was even more so to Kevin, who was unable to fully remove the stain.

She rubbed her fingers across her hands, and the red goop disappeared.

Kevin turned, his expression morphing into something twisted and serious. "I don't need you to jump in and save me. Just because I don't have all-powerful witch magic doesn't mean I'm not clever enough to make my own. I am my own witch and my own person. I deserve more right now than this fiasco."

She recoiled. She couldn't ever remember seeing Kevin this angry, and there was something ominous about it, but then again, perhaps a witch had a right to be angry when he'd just been coated in a low-calorie dessert food.

He stormed out without another word, and she rubbed her fingers together again, cleaning the last of the mess.

This was a fucking disaster, and she steeled herself, breathing for a moment, and remembering that Panamanian golden frogs are considered both lucky and an indicator species that signal the conditions of the environment they live in.

Amphibian facts or not, she needed a moment alone, and she did not want to talk to anyone here about this.

"I'm headed for the vault," she announced to the room, and she made a beeline for the stairway, forcing herself not to jump at each clack of her sensible low heels.

By the time she got down the stairs, she heaved a breath of relief. She could have heard a pin drop in that Council office, but here in the stairway to the vault, the hum of the backup generator was comforting.

Keying in the code on the outer door from memory, she made her way into the chamber and pressed the button to sterilize her clothes so that any fragile artifacts wouldn't be damaged by accident.

The second chamber was harder; she concentrated with all her might and willed the chamber to know who she was until it opened into the small room that led to the different collections.

The initial analysis on the elixir from the Hildebrand von Auden estate was that it could very well be authentic, and something about it had been bothering her since the incident with the chainsaws, something she couldn't put her finger on until this morning, after the best orgasm of her life had cleared her mind completely.

The odd, rectangular canister with the screw lid was an outer chamber. They had been examining it without opening it, but she had read somewhere that the Fountain of Youth ran so magical that its glow could be seen through a container.

She had finally found that and confirmed. They had been analyzing the outer chamber, and opening the ornate obsidian container would not be actually opening the elixir. When the weight changed from one examination to the next, she knew it had been stolen, but she hadn't dared open the container yet for fear of compromising some yet-to-be-discovered evidence of who was responsible.

Hoping she wasn't about to ruin decades of scientific research on longevity and the elixir if she was wrong, she opened the container.

As she suspected, nestled in a soft slot was a delicate glass bottle, the size of a perfume bottle, with a narrow metal stopper.

As carefully as she could, she lifted the thing, holding it by the filigreed bottom point.

She frowned. All the initial magical analysis had indicated that there were precisely 4.2 ounces of liquid contained in the canister, and that every ounce of it did indeed appear to contain the sort of magical compounds that could cause a person, if they consumed it in full, to live forever. When she had analyzed it last, it had weighed precisely 4.2 ounces less, so she had assumed it had been stolen.

The research suggested it would take precisely 3.8 ounces to render an adult witch immortal.

"Oh, fuck," she breathed softly. She had been correct. The very last existing elixir of the Fountain of Youth had indeed been stolen. There was a small droplet of a bright, glowing pink potion in the bottom of the bottle, but other than that, it was entirely empty.

Whoever had stolen the elixir, the last drops of the Fountain of Youth, had presumably used a sprinkle of it to enchant the chainsaws and distract them from a much bigger problem.

There was a witch, and it had to be a Council witch to get through the doors to the vaults, who was now entirely immortal. A witch who was essentially unstoppable.

Even if they were taken apart into a million pieces, they could never die.

Agatha was screwed, and not in the way she'd hoped to be this morning.

CHAPTER 21

Priscilla

When she pulled up to the shop that now once again said Madam Cleopatra's in large, mystic lettering, the sign on the door warned that there was a reading in progress. She dawdled, killing time by scrolling through her email in the Packard, and then rifling through the glove compartment to see if Azrael had left anything good.

Her brother drove the car to work that morning, but a brief text exchange during his planning period that involved far too many questions about where she had slept last night had ended in him agreeing to let her bicycle over to Hallowcross High and leave the bike for him to take home after work. She could have magicked the bike carefully, of course, but it felt better to do the task. Benedict Hart rules were that summoning the thing was fine, but doing the work, whether it be cleaning a mess or getting from point A to point B, was an important part of being alive.

Biking, and then driving to visit Connie, had cleared her mind.

She wanted to revisit the conversation from Free Spirits with Agatha, but she needed closure first. Mending things with Evie and helping Connie find stability would put an old chapter of her life to bed and let her move forward into something new.

Whatever reading was going on in there seemed to be taking a while. Priscilla got out of the car and, grateful that she'd followed a nostalgic whim and opted for combat boots instead of heels today, started off around the pond.

Moose Pond was almost large enough to be a lake, but she was grateful that it wasn't one. This way, it was a delightful small vacation spot. The bigger and more popular lakes tended to get crowded and overrun by tourists. She'd always wanted to rent one of the houses here for a getaway. How had she forgotten that dream, paired with Agatha's own visions of glamping? How had she not seen the way Agatha would slot so nicely into her hopes for the future? How they could grow and intertwine together, winding into something more beautiful and stronger than either of them could be on their own?

She thought of what Agatha had admitted in the bar. Wanting a cozy cabin. A fireplace to fuck in front of. Agatha Vanderbilt Voisin was built to destroy her. If Priscilla was indeed a monster, Agatha was the hunter who held the arrow tipped in silver, the only poison, the revealing slice of sunlight, whatever it was that would be her undoing.

And maybe, just maybe, Priscilla wanted to be destroyed. Would it be so bad, really, to be at the mercy of a beautiful, commanding woman?

She stopped in front of the lake house set farthest from the water. Would it have a charming bathtub? She wanted to have a place where she could make Agatha moan her name in all the ways that would teach her, gradually, how very real this was all becoming for Priscilla.

Swearing, she headed back for the trailer, and by the time she reached it, a broody-looking tall blond man was slinking out. He gave her a tentative wave and a half smile that revealed a sharp set of incisors.

Good. The plan to push paranormal sales as a magical release valve was going strong. Connie had been doing a reading for a vampire.

She knocked on the door.

"Madam Cleopatra will see you," the woman said. And then, when Priscilla walked in, "Ah, I knew it was you. How are you, dear?"

Priscilla slumped down on the faded jacquard of the bench seat.

"I'm well." She wasn't.

Connie narrowed her eyes. "Don't lie to a seer. It's a waste of breath."

"Fine, things are complicated." Priscilla blew a shock of hair that had escaped from her side braid out of her eye.

"Hmm," said Connie, giving her a long look, cocking her head, and then nodding. "Yes. The cards will tell this time, I think."

"I'm not here for a reading," Priscilla added quickly.

"Humor me." She was clearing the crystal ball from the table, smoothing the tablecloth, and producing a pack of tarot cards from goddess only knew where on her person. "You can tell me what you came here to tell me while I shuffle." She pulled the cards out of their pack and deftly flipped them, fanning, cutting, rearranging, like second nature.

"Fine," said Priscilla, leaning forward. "I think the trick is to find hobbies."

"Hobbies?" Connie broke the deck, slowing down and shuffling vertically, letting the cards flutter gently against one another. "Like what, knitting?"

"Sure, yes, knitting. Reading, baking. Scuba diving. Collecting fancy spoons. Anything, really. I think what we have been missing is balance in all things, not just in your new magic."

"That's the most reasonable thing you've ever said to me, Ms. Hart."

"Please."

Connie smiled. "Priscilla."

"My friends call me Prissy."

Connie smiled even wider. "Are we friends now? That's nice. Now, be quiet and concentrate on what you need."

Priscilla was tempted to blow it off, to act as though it was silly or beneath her, but she didn't want to damage her fragile new friendship with Connie now that she was finally improving. She liked her work for the Council, and she absolutely adored the feeling of success here. She might be a mistress of the dark who enjoyed a fair bit of pain, but truth be told, she did enjoy praise too.

She inhaled and thought of Agatha. The Council. Her house. Everything she loved.

Fuck. Everything she *loved*.

Connie gave her a funny look, eyes shifting gray and misty for a moment, and then back to normal.

She pulled a card, and then another, and then a third.

"A basic three-card spread," she explained, peering down at them and nodding sagely, like the ornate little things held the key to the universe.

She pointed at the first. "The Magician." A sweeping gold figure eight made of a snake eating its own tail circled the illustration of a curly-haired mage in a cape, pretty in the face, androgynous, and holding a magic wand. A pentacle sat in the upper right corner and a goblet in the upper left, and lining the sides were flowers—peonies, maybe.

"Ah," said Connie. "You're the master of the elements. Successful, confident, and already possessing all the tools you need for your trade." She paused, cocking her head, eyes fading gray again for a moment. "Just remember, dearie: as above, so below." Priscilla shivered. That felt a little bit ominous.

She pointed at the next card. "Five of Swords." Her eyebrows rose. "Betrayal, selfishness, entitlement." A boy sat on a mountain, head in hand, five blades splayed out beside him.

"I ran for the presidency fair and square, and I didn't betray anyone," Priscilla muttered.

"The cards aren't always so literal. Not necessarily you, of course. Someone close to you." She frowned. She was absolutely certain that Agatha wouldn't betray her. Unless the realness of the feelings was too one-sided. That would be a sort of betrayal.

"Let's get it over with," Priscilla said, not liking the chill to the air that reminded her that there was real, actual magic afoot here.

"The last card. The Hanged Man." The golden edges once again flourished, and hanging from the ceiling was a blond woman, a rope around one foot, the other curled welcomingly by her thigh. She held the rope in her own hands, staring up at it, hand behind her back.

She looked familiar, but Priscilla reminded herself that people often saw what they were looking for in this sort of reading.

"Well, that can't be good." A hanging never was; witches would know.

"Things are rarely as simple as just what they are. The Hanged Man means it's time for change. Time to throttle the old ways, and let in the new. Is there something, maybe someone, that you feel the urge to give yourself over to? Surrender, if so." Connie squinted at the card. "That's funny," she mused. "I never noticed it about this card before, but does she look a bit like your Council president to you?"

"Oh no," said Priscilla. "It's time for me to go," and then the ringing of her phone startled her. She jumped and pulled out the phone.

Agatha's name was glaringly large on the screen, and she refused to look at Connie. Oracles could be so fucking smug sometimes.

She held up a hand to Connie. "It really is an emergency. Sorry! I'll be in touch," she said.

Connie smirked and waved her off, and she slid out of the bench seat and opened the door, answering the phone once she was close enough to the car to assume Constance Witherspoon was not listening in.

"Hello?"

"Priscilla." Agatha sounded relieved. "Something's come up at the Council. You need to get down here."

Fear gathered in her stomach. "Are you all right?"

"Yes. But I checked the vaults. The elixir is gone. Someone *did* break in. I knew they had, but seeing it reminded me how urgent this is. We have to find the thief."

"Only a Council witch could do that." The realization chilled her. She'd considered this, but it was more awful to have it confirmed.

"Exactly," said Agatha, her voice barely above a whisper. "And the only person I'm sure it isn't is you, but I think whoever did it wants to set you up."

"What makes you say that?"

"Well, they can't get into the vaults unless they work here. But right before I came down here, Kevin was on the receiving end of a prank that seemed like one of yours."

Something warm rose to Priscilla's chest, and she tried not to examine it too closely.

"You don't think it was me?"

"Well, I'm fairly certain that you would never prank someone with something so pedestrian as Jell-O."

"Jell-O? Really?" She tapped the steering wheel. The idea of it was ludicrous.

"My point exactly."

"So, someone stole something and tried to frame me."

"Exactly."

"How bad is it?" Priscilla needed to think about how someone might possibly be able to pin this on her.

"Bad. The elixir is rare. The rarest." Agatha paused and heaved a sigh that Priscilla could hear over the line. "It's gone. Someone took it, and if anyone finds out now, well, with the timing of the prank, it looks like it's you. I know it's not, but the optics, Priscilla."

"Dammit, Agatha, just say it." It had to be bad if the trust of the Witchery Council president wasn't enough to at least cast a shadow of reasonable doubt.

"The elixir from the Fountain of Youth. It's all gone. Not just enough for the chainsaws. Someone must have drunk it."

Realization hit her over the head, and she cursed herself,

again, for not seeing what was right in front of her. "The chainsaws were a test."

"They must have been sprinkled with it, but it's *all* gone. Someone is immortal."

"It's not me." Priscilla was aghast. She'd read *Tuck Everlasting* as a child; she wouldn't ever want to be immortal. Foolish business, truly. Clearly, Hildebrand von Auden had known that well enough to die with the cursed thing in his collection. Though he could have stood to secure it and warn inheritors of his estate a bit better.

"I know that," said Agatha softly. "But the only way to really prove it . . ."

"Oh, fuck, it's going to be a modern witch trial. Dead if she sinks and a witch if she swims. You could prove it by killing me and watching me actually die."

"Yeah, so, obviously we won't be doing that."

"Pray tell, then, what will we be doing?"

"Not telling anyone about the theft until we can prove it wasn't you."

It was the most logical thing, hiding it, but she didn't like it. The idea that the perpetrator could be the same one who was trying to kill Agatha. The idea that someone had set her up.

The even worse idea that whoever had set her up thought so little of her as to believe that she would ever in a million years prank someone with Jell-O.

"What do you need from me?" Priscilla ran a hand over her braid, racking her mind for ways to prove she was mortal without demonstrating the full extent of her mortality.

"We need to talk, and we need to do it somewhere private."

Priscilla eyed the rental office across the paved street from Connie's. "Can I call you back in five minutes?"

CHAPTER 22

Agatha

Of all the things she'd thought could have happened on this day, the day she woke up hungover, fucked herself senseless, and headed to work anyway, she had not suspected that she would discover an immortality plot, and then find herself in a hastily rented rustic cabin with Priscilla Hart.

"I know it's not exactly what you pictured, and they do have more glamorously outfitted options, but this was the only one that was available right away," Prissy said, ushering her in. "Honey, we're home," she said, smirking.

It was a one-room affair with a wood-burning stove and two sets of bunk beds against the wall, but there was a hard wooden table with drawers and chairs on either side of it, built into the wall of the cabin like the bunks, none of it movable.

"Guess they were dedicated to this specific floor plan," she said, nodding to the attached furniture and pulling back the chair to sit down. Priscilla took the chair next to her. She had shut the door and snapped to lock it securely, ensuring they were completely alone.

"We need to figure it out quickly, before someone formally accuses you. Even without the news of the missing elixir, tensions are running high, and it's coming. I think this"—Agatha gestured between the two of them—"will stop people from jumping in right away, but it's coming. And if we wait too long, we also run the risk of people thinking we are working together to bring down the whole Council."

"Shit," said Priscilla, and as though to emphasize the point, the sound of shattering glass made her jump as several clear, sharp panes flew through the window, and then began to assemble themselves together. The enormous translucent shards formed into something taller and wider than she was.

"The Loculus," Priscilla breathed, and Agatha reached for her, without thinking, pulling her out of the chair as the giant glass coffin began to solidify and thicken.

"It will take you in." Agatha's eyes were wide with terror.

"Priscilla Guinevere Hart," said a voice—Otho's, maybe. She wasn't sure if they'd used him for the enchantment or not; the glass coffin prison hadn't been called out in years—decades even, maybe. "You are being summoned for questioning in the attempted murder of one President Agatha Vanderbilt Voisin, as well as the destruction of numerous Witchery Council properties."

"I'm the president," Agatha said indignantly, but it was no use, the Loculus was not spelled for conversation, just capture. She hugged Priscilla tightly, rubbing her fingers together in a haphazard magical spell that shackled them together, and to the thick trunk that made up one of the legs of the table.

"This way, it won't be able to take you."

Priscilla's eyes darted as the gray wisps of magic surrounded them, the glass pieces locking them together in a full-sized, impenetrable coffin. Agatha had only ever studied the Loculus in theory. She had certainly never authorized its use.

Which meant that someone must have made a report to the International Council of Witchery. Her only option was to use the top secret security spells, designed to protect the president and stop her from being taken without her consent. They were tedious and took months to set up. Using them now would be leaving herself vulnerable until they could be rewoven, but there was no other way.

She swallowed, muttering them anyway and rubbing her thumb across her fingers. It was worth it to protect Priscilla.

"Fuck. If the ICoW is involved, I can't do anything to stop them, other than protest it."

Priscilla spun in Agatha's arms, as though looking for a way out. "Okay, so there's no emergency exit on this," she said weakly. "But it's fine. It won't run out of air, and someone will come for it eventually if it doesn't arrive where it's been summoned."

"How could you possibly be certain?" Agatha would have put her hands on her hips, but there was barely any room as it was, so instead she squeezed them gently, before remembering that her hands were on Priscilla's hips.

Priscilla looked down at her, and something flared in her eyes. Hunger, or maybe anger. Possibly both.

"I know," she said, through gritted teeth, "because this happened to my parents once, when they were young. They used to tell it as a bedtime story: the time they got trapped in a Loculus and had to fake an engagement so that my dad could clear my mom's name."

"Wait, you mean to tell me that Benedict and Persephone Hart, *the* Harts, met by faking a relationship to avoid legal consequences?"

Priscilla's cheeks flushed. "Well, when you put it like that, it obviously sounds much more similar to our situation, but it really was not. They were rival professors. There was some amount of green face paint pertaining to the Wicked Witch of the West, and a sexy Gandalf costume involved. It's nothing like this, honey."

The nickname slipped out so easily between them, and fuck if that didn't do something to her heart. Agatha stared at her for a moment, a long one, and then the insanity of the entire situation, the parallels to the Harts, widely known to be one of the witching world's greatest love stories, the absurdity of someone out there being immortal and trying to kill Agatha, all of it drove her right over the edge of control.

She hesitated, the feeling building between them, every breath sounding too loud, the air around them heated, and then she surrendered to it, leaning forward.

She crashed her lips against Priscilla's, and for a brief, terrible moment, she thought maybe she'd misread the other woman's heaving chest and dilated pupils.

Until Priscilla Hart kissed her back, lips against lips, parting them with her tongue, moaning into her mouth and running a hand so gently up Agatha's neck that she sagged backward, bolstered by both the cuff on her ankle and the glass prison that enclosed them.

Damn, she had been right to use up that protection spell.

"I think," said Agatha, when they finally broke apart, "that when we get out of this, you and I need to have a long talk about what we're doing. And then right after, I'm going to put in a petition to stop the use of the Loculus permanently, because I don't know about this as a humane punishment."

Priscilla raised her eyebrows.

"I could think of worse prisons than one that involves being shackled to a beautiful woman who just mauled me."

"It was much less a mauling and much more a deeply romantic kiss, thank you very much. And the shackle is my fault. I wanted to make sure the Loculus stayed put, and that they didn't bring you in before I was ready to defend your honor." It was true, too, that she didn't hate being so close to Prissy.

"Oh?" Prissy pushed her back against the edge of the coffin, tracing the edge of her jaw with a long fingernail, running it back down her neck.

"Yeah," she bit out. "Why, do you want me to propose?"

Priscilla shook her head, stepping back the inch that their prison allowed. "I don't want to do that again unless I mean it. No fake engagements." Her face was serious, the arousal of a moment before wiped away.

"That makes sense. Given the whole Evelyn situation."

"Evelyn!" Priscilla exclaimed. "Evelyn."

She pulled out her phone.

"You think now is the time to call your ex?"

"No," said Priscilla. "I think now is the time to call my brother and see if he can get in touch with Evelyn and the Council. Find out what's happening here and there."

"Isn't he at work?"

"High school gets out at two thirty."

"That can't be true. What time does he go to work?"

"You don't want to know."

Agatha tried to give her some semblance of privacy, but there simply wasn't any room for it. A step backward and she was pressed against the glass.

"Az?"

"Priss, you okay? Is it the car?" Agatha was horrified to learn that this close to Priscilla, she could hear every word he was saying.

"No, not the car. I'm in a bit of a situation."

"What, did your hot boss realize you have real feelings?" Agatha's face flamed. Was he joking? Teasing her? A traitorous part of her leapt at the thought of it. Azrael was pretty honest. Did Priscilla have real feelings?

"I'm stuck in a Loculus with her, actually, and she can hear every word you're saying, so thanks for that." Priscilla bit her lip, avoiding Agatha's gaze.

"A *Loculus*? Like—"

Prissy interrupted him, "DO NOT say it."

"Fine, fine. What did you do?"

"She didn't do anything. Hi, Azrael. Agatha Vanderbilt Voisin here. Your sister was just in the wrong place at the wrong time, and my attempt to stop the thing from taking her sort of worked, but also sort of backfired. I need you to bring someone who might be able to get us out of this."

She racked her brain. Kevin was on vacation.

"Nancy. Call Otho's niece, Nancy Ashbrooke," Prissy finished for her. Agatha nodded. That was a surprisingly good idea.

"Someone to get you out of it. Got it. And then the International Council of Witchery. Any leads on who?"

Priscilla's eyes darted to Agatha, her mouth set. "Call Evelyn."

"Are you sure about that, Priss?"

"I talked to her this morning. We cleared this up, agreed that everything turned out as it should in the end. I think she'll be amenable to helping." She cleared her throat. "Though we won't exactly ever be best friends after all of it, so I do think it's better if you call." The thought of Prissy talking to her ex *this morning*, possibly while Agatha was fucking herself and thinking of Priscilla, was deeply uncomfortable.

"What's the backup plan if the Loculus magic takes you elsewhere? To the International Council?" Azrael's voice broke through the water bottle–related reverie.

Priscilla's brow furrowed.

Agatha sighed. She really didn't want to reveal this. She cleared her throat.

"Hi, Azrael. Agatha here. I used my fail-safe against Council president kidnapping to stop the thing from taking us now that we're chained together."

"Chained together," Azrael repeated, and she swore she heard a hint of a chuckle. A snort maybe. He cleared his throat. "Good. That's good. Doesn't that take like thirteen witches and a full moon to cast?"

"And three months to set, but it was worth it."

"Az," Prissy cut in, "just make the calls."

"On it. Text me where you are and I'll see what I can do about busting you out."

"You don't have to worry about me. I have the car, remember."

"I'm sure Vickie will drive me, if only to see you trapped in a giant glass container with a woman you're definitely into."

"She's standing right here, Azrael. You *just* spoke to her." Priscilla shut her eyes for a moment, rubbing the bridge of her nose. The movement of her arm brushed against Agatha's on the way up, and she felt it, that magical connection that flared between them.

"Hi again, Agatha. She is definitely into you."

"Goodbye and thank you and I hate you," Priscilla said, hanging up the phone, and typing in the address to hit send.

"Into me, huh?" Agatha knew she was smirking but didn't bother to tamp down her smugness. "I sort of got that from the kissing me back, but it's always nice to hear."

"Listen, it's not a big deal. We've been spending so much time together, and you must be aware of how beautiful you are," she began. Those pouty little lips were begging to be kissed, and the words spilling from Priscilla's mouth were breathtakingly sweet.

Agatha had never had her beauty professed like this, not just in an enclosed space, but with the kind of fervent urgency that lined Priscilla's voice. She bit her lip, forcing herself not to look away. Priscilla was looking at her now, turning her full attention on Agatha, and she thought she might drown in the golden-brown depths of Prissy's eyes.

She wanted to tell Priscilla how pretty *she* was, and not only that, to make it absolutely clear that she thought they would be so pretty together, so pretty and so, so good.

But it was cramped in this thing, and she couldn't bring herself to find any sort of words that wouldn't make her crazy. What was she supposed to do, tell Priscilla that she thought she might be falling, deeply and irreparably? That she had fantasized about her so much and to such great length that she'd had, by herself, the most satisfying sexual experience of her life?

It was too much, and so she delayed it again, with her mouth, pressing her lips to Priscilla's. She pushed Priscilla back against the side of the glass prison, cupping her face with a hand, and trailing the other down past her waist, gripping firmly. When she kissed Prissy harder, and felt her fingers dig into that spot just past her hip bone, she almost apologized, but Priscilla moaned into her mouth.

"Do you like that?"

"Yes," Prissy breathed against her mouth. "Get a little rough with me."

Agatha flushed all over. It wasn't that she didn't want to, it was that she feared she didn't know how. She wondered if she should fake it until she made it, run her hands along Priscilla's thighs, test out the pressure, figure out the difference between just enough and too much.

Except, was she supposed to know it already?

She wanted to keep touching Priscilla, but instead, she pulled back, uncertain if there was some unwritten handbook or order of operations, something other people knew about being with a woman that she simply did not. Goddess, what if she was too weird? She flushed, thinking about the way Prissy's voice made her insides curl and do something funny.

"Too much?" Priscilla's pupils were still wide, and there was no avoiding her, not in a glass coffin. That was precisely it. Agatha was worried *she* was too much.

"No," Agatha lied, "not at all. It's just . . ." She scrambled for a lie, blushing. "I really need to pee."

"Oh no," said Prissy, but she sounded relieved. Agatha relaxed a teeny bit, but as the moment evaporated, she worried that she actually did have to pee.

"What I wouldn't give for a coffee cup," said Priscilla, "or a water bottle. That could help you."

Agatha let out a strangled moan, pulling her hand over her face.

"It's fine," she managed. "I can hold it. New bucket list item: manage to get through my life without ever peeing in a cup again."

"You've done that before?"

She nodded, slumping against the glass. There. She could trade honesty about one experience for unwillingness to admit the myriad ways she was lacking in another.

This was, somehow, more intimate, but she wanted to tell Priscilla.

"I got pregnant once." She said it matter-of-factly.

Priscilla's eyes widened. "Not with horrible Jonathan."

She shook her head. "No. In my early twenties. We both

agreed children were not in our plans. That's just never been something I wanted."

The other woman looked at her. "What did you do?"

Agatha exhaled. This was always the bit that gave people the opportunity to show their true colors, and surprisingly enough, even horrible Jonathan had agreed that it was, in fact, her body and her choice, and had never had a problem with this particular bit of Agatha's past.

"I had an abortion," she said. "And then I got an IUD, and I've never looked back. I thought about tying my tubes, but I have pretty bad PPMD, and the IUD really reduced gory periods and made that better, so I stuck with it."

She waited, agonizingly long seconds, for a response.

"Thank you," said Priscilla, raising a hand to Agatha's shoulder. "Thank you for trusting me." Realization dawned on her face. "That's why you didn't mind finding out what went wrong between me and Evie."

Agatha nodded. "It's a cruel thing to force anyone who doesn't want to have a child to do it. Most of all for the child."

Priscilla's face was soft now. "I talked to her this morning."

"You said so. How did that go?" They were laying themselves bare here, pressed up against each other, somewhat hiding from the law.

"It was good. She's seeing someone else. She's happy."

"Good," Agatha said, a tension she didn't know she was carrying in her shoulders uncoiling. "That's good."

"It is," Priscilla agreed. She paused. "Can I ask a personal question?"

"Of course," said Agatha softly. And she would tell this woman anything in this moment of tenderness and truth. Anything she asked, even if it was about her total and utter lack of sexual prowess with the fairer sex.

"Do you ever regret it?"

She shook her head. "Not a day in my life. The staff were friendly and helpful, it was safe, and it was best for everyone involved." She smiled. "We're lucky to live in a time where reproductive health care is legal, and between a person with a uterus and their doctor."

"Agatha," said Priscilla. "You're beautiful. All of you. Inside and out. I see you now. I didn't before, but I see you now."

"You say that to all the girls trapped with you in the Loculus, I'm sure." She had to tease; it was so much emotion.

"I . . ." Priscilla started, but a cloud of purple smoke materialized, and she recognized that smell, the ginger and bergamot.

A tall, dark-haired devil stepped forward, smirking insouciantly.

"Lex," said Priscilla, sounding relieved. Next to him stood Victoria Starnberger.

"Az said to bring someone who could get you two out of this." She winked and gestured to the devil. Vickie was inexplicably dressed in a long-sleeved, billowy, white cropped button-down shirt and a pair of jean shorts cut so high that both globes of her ass were visible.

"What the devil are you wearing?" Priscilla started.

"I beg your pardon," Lex interjected. "But that's exceedingly rude, cursing the name of the very creature here to break you out, jailbird." He waggled his eyebrows. "Or do you not want my help, Dirty Bertie?"

"I told you not to call me that," said Priscilla through gritted teeth. Agatha did her best to ignore how adorable Priscilla was when enraged.

"Fine, fine. Give me a minute to examine this and determine the best way to defeat it."

"Az is on his way," Vickie offered, and then, gesturing to her outfit, "I was trying on things for Sultry Sunday. That boy is corrupt, and all. It's the day in Hopelessly Teavoted where we all dress up like a pop culture reference, old or new, slutty if you want. This is my 'Manchild' ensemble."

"You nailed that, you cheeky thing, you," muttered Priscilla, and Agatha thought perhaps she ought to be put off, but it was the sort of jesting that told her Vickie had been like a sister to her for almost as long as Az had been her brother.

"Thank you. I do enjoy how my ass looks in this," she said, leaning back to try to look. Lex did likewise, smiling wickedly.

The door opened, and Azrael barged in. "What did I miss?" His eyes darted from the glass coffin, where Agatha was pressed against his sister, to Lex, who had begun tapping gently on a seemingly invisible spot on one pane of the thick glass, and then to Vickie, where his eyes stopped.

"Fuck me sideways, sweetheart, did you have to wear those to a rescue?" It was almost comical, all of them trying to look at Vickie's cheeks peeking out of the bottom of cutoff denim.

Vickie turned and sauntered up to him, tugging on the bow at the front of her shirt a little.

"What do you think?"

"I think," he said, reaching around, and squeezing a handful of his girlfriend in each palm, "nothing appropriate for company."

Agatha blinked. She wasn't entirely sure if she was imagining it, but had the devil magically scooted closer to the two of them? He winked at her, and suddenly he was right back next to the Loculus.

"Pity, you two could have had it all," said Lex to the distracted couple behind him. "Aha! There it is." He thumped at the coffin once again, and then reached into his incredibly tight pockets and pulled out a thin wire-framed pair of glasses, which absolutely should have been crushed by the force of leather against those thighs. Azrael Hart made a choked noise and muttered something about slutty little glasses, but if Lex heard it, he didn't respond. Spectacles on, he examined it again, rummaged in the other pocket, and pulled out an iron nail and a small hammer.

"That's remarkable magic," Agatha couldn't help but tell him. It was the fucking glasses. "What else are you hiding in there?"

He smiled, a crooked half thing that heated her blood.

"I can fit quite a lot in these pants. You'd be surprised."

"Maybe focus on the breakout," Priscilla said, glaring at him.

Lex shrugged. "If I must." He pressed the nail to the spot

he'd been tapping, and hit out a pattern that sounded oddly familiar, like a tune she could almost remember, but not quite.

The glass shattered completely, and then crumbled to dust. Lex flicked a wrist, and the dust, and her cuffs, were gone.

"That is truly impressive," she said, making a mental note to research devils more thoroughly.

"Well, you get to be more than three thousand years old, and you learn a few tricks. Everything, everyone, has a button you can push hard enough to break." He winked at Agatha, and though she no longer had to, Priscilla pushed closer.

Azrael cleared his throat.

"I have good news, which is that Evie is, at this very moment, clearing your name with the Council. It seems the illegitimate magical threat—a nasty explosion that would have demolished Agatha's apartment—was not traced entirely, but they were able to identify a time stamp, and she was able to provide an alibi along with phone records and GPS that pinpointed that at the time someone attempted to kill President Vanderbilt Voisin, you were in the middle of the forest on the phone with your ex-fiancée."

Agatha did not want to admit, even to herself, how glad she was that Priscilla had been on the phone during the attempted murder, and not at the precise moment she'd been training herself not to moan Priscilla's name in her bedroom.

"Well, when you put it that way, I sound like a bit of a nutjob," Priscilla griped, bringing Agatha back to reality.

"Better than a murderer," said Agatha. She shivered. "I hate that they did this at my home."

Priscilla grabbed her hand. "Come stay with us. We can set up wards around your place to try to catch the perp, and the house will keep you safe."

Agatha hesitated, and her uncertainty must have been visible, because Priscilla added, "We have a guest bedroom, and I have zero expectations. Though there is Emily, and Hart Manor is, well, eccentric."

"Who," she bit out, hoping the jealousy in her voice wasn't evident, "is Emily?"

Prissy's eyebrows raised. "You met her. Emily Lickinson? Azrael's cat?"

"Oh," she said, blushing. "I'd love to." The words slipped out before she could overthink them, and damn if a big part of her didn't want to offer to stay in Priscilla's bedroom.

It didn't seem like the thing to do in front of family and a literal devil, though. So instead she rubbed her hands and looked around.

"This place doesn't have a bathroom."

"Well, it's no cup," Prissy said, smile snaking up her face, "but there's a porta potty out back."

"When I said it was my dream to go glamping, this wasn't quite what I had in mind," said Agatha.

Priscilla smiled, a soft, secret thing, full of meaning. "One day, honey. One day."

CHAPTER 23

Priscilla

Council investigations took a long time, and Priscilla was certain her responsibilities as a Council member included looking out for the president.

It just so happened that looking out for Agatha Vanderbilt Voisin, in this instance, meant making sure she stayed out of her apartment until the Council could be absolutely sure that she was safe. In the absence of a clear villain, the hunt for the murderous prankster had slowed as the Council turned to more pressing matters. Nothing had tripped the wards around Agatha's apartment, but Priscilla insisted that it was better to be safe than sorry.

And if that safety meant hosting her at Hart Manor, well, there was nothing Priscilla could do about that. They had the space, and Hart Manor had the sentience to keep Agatha safer than any place else could.

For instance, the Council president was exceedingly safe sitting at the dining room table, a grand mahogany thing set for two. Priscilla finished a cup of coffee, and as Agatha spread cream cheese on a fresh bagel, the French press floated at her elbow, waiting to top off her mug.

She smiled, and then frowned at the table when she found herself almost touching Agatha's other elbow. Damn this matchmaking table and its shrinking ways.

"I never knew you were a bagel kind of gal. I, for some reason, thought muffin."

"I do love muffins too," said Agatha. "If it's a carb, it's for me."

Prissy smiled. She loved learning more about Agatha like this. Not just her breakfast preferences, but the time she spent organizing and planning and preparing to juggle the Council business smoothly. The more she knew, the less Priscilla felt that she knew, and the more suspicion nagged at her mind that perhaps Agatha did make a good president.

Perhaps she did deserve the position she had won.

Prissy had spent so long telling herself that she'd only lost because of the vitriol she'd faced after leaving Evelyn, because of the assumption some people made, out loud, even, that she had purposefully broken the woman's heart to drive her back to England and try to snag her job.

That wasn't why she'd broken things off with Evelyn. And she wasn't falling for Agatha for the presidency. Prissy simply enjoyed two things: being a powerful woman and fucking one.

She'd misjudged Agatha. Prissy had thought that she was weak because of her kindness and sunshiny demeanor and enthusiasm. But the truth of the matter was, she was beginning to see that Agatha's kindness *was* a strength. That Agatha's ability to remain optimistic was a skill well suited to her office. That perhaps politicians who fantasized about cruelty and doing harm were not what the world needed. That people like Agatha, people who looked at the world and saw the beauty of its bones, were people worth knowing. Worth cherishing.

She wanted to tell Agatha, one day, what a damn fine president she made.

But in the long line of things she needed to admit, that was low priority, because what was really pressing on her mind and on her body was how she felt about Agatha Vanderbilt Voisin, the woman, not the job.

She knocked on the guest room door. When Agatha didn't answer right away, she thought about leaving, but the thing was, she didn't *want* to leave. Not unless Agatha wanted her to.

"Agatha? I can come back later if this isn't a good time."

Priscilla wasn't proud of it, but she pressed her ear against the door, and, in true Hart Manor fashion, she swore it got easier to hear through.

She heard water running. Agatha was in the shower.

As soon as Agatha had walked into the guest room, the house had sprouted a full adjoining bathroom, which was *not* something she'd ever seen it do, though it had once grown a new bathtub in Azrael's bathroom for Vickie, but this was a full room, tub, shower, and toilet, with a gorgeous marble-topped double sink framed by vanity lights that could have fit right into old Hollywood.

Hart Manor liked Agatha, liked her in a way that it had only ever loved the Harts and Victoria, and Priscilla had been turning that over in her mind the last two weeks that Agatha had lived here—stayed here, she reminded herself—trying to make sense of what it did to her heart.

Could your house tell you when you'd met your soul's match, the one person it would be willing to grow around, that you ought to be willing to grow around too?

The thought was a lot, and today wasn't about her, so she leaned once more, and knocked.

"I need your help with something," she began, but Hart Manor wasn't satisfied to simply grow Agatha a new room.

The door shifted, vanishing for a moment, retreating into a pocket in the wall that had not been there a moment earlier, and Priscilla landed on the floor with an ungraceful thump. She was fortunate that the house had also grown Agatha a lush pastel pink carpet to go with a sunrise mural behind her bed.

It was like waking up at dawn in there, she thought, until she heard Agatha scream.

"Are you all right?" Priscilla sat up and Agatha darted out of the bathroom, clad only in a large towel clutched closed but inching toward blowing Priscilla's entire mind.

"How did you get in here?" Agatha sounded breathless, cheeks flushed. What had she been doing in the shower? Any possible answer made lust burrow sharply in Priscilla's stomach, creeping lower, throbbing, threatening to undo her.

"The house is fucking with me," Priscilla muttered. "There was a door, then there wasn't a door."

Agatha looked from Priscilla to the now-totally-normal door, eyebrows raised, and the carpet swayed, as though the house was laughing at her.

"If you wanted to come in my room, you could just say so, *chérie*," said Agatha. Her voice was low, and her eyes were wide, that shocking blue temporarily short-circuiting Prissy's ability to think.

"It was the house," she managed. "It has opinions."

The other woman smiled, shaking her head, as though she didn't believe it.

She took a step toward Priscilla, mouth opening to say something, but the bathroom door slammed shut behind her, catching the towel firmly, and for a split second, she stood in all her naked glory, too startled to even attempt to cover herself.

Priscilla knew she should look away, but she wasn't made of stone, and she *couldn't* look away immediately. Good goddess, Agatha was fucking beautiful, a Renaissance painting, like Venus rising from the clamshell, except her breasts could put even Botticelli's masterpiece to shame. She was all curves of flesh that Priscilla needed to dig her fingers into, from the thick slope of her thigh to the soft expanse of her stomach and her lush, full breasts, areolas big enough that fitting them in her mouth would be laughable, like trying to swallow an orange. Her nipples were tight, and Prissy wanted to roll them between her fingers, to work her mouth around them, to bury her face between Agatha's tits and her hand between her legs like she was some sort of horny teenager again, searching the internet for soft-core porn.

Fuck, she's beautiful is what Priscilla thought, and what she should have said, but she found her mouth smirking instead.

"Blame that on the house?"

Agatha flushed bright red, and then Priscilla really did have to look away finally; the blush extended down her neck and chest, and she thought she might lose her grip on reality entirely if she let her gaze drop lower again.

She turned around, because she could be classy.

At least somewhat.

"Sorry," said Agatha, and Prissy wanted to tell her that she had nothing to apologize for, that the house had clearly been meddling again, riffling through too many romance novels in the library and getting ideas. "What did you say you needed?"

The reminder grounded her, crushing any lingering desire.

"Right. Azrael needs our help with something." Since Vickie had moved out of the apartment above Hopelessly Teavoted and rented it out, she'd moved right into Hart Manor, which made Azrael setting up his master plan slightly more difficult. Which is where she and Agatha came in.

"Give me just a moment." There was the sound of rustling, a zipper, and drawers shutting. "There," said Agatha. "You can turn around now."

Agatha was dressed, but even in flowy pants and a black-and-white striped shirt that zipped up in the back, Priscilla could now imagine exactly what lay beneath.

She blinked, focusing on the task. Right. Her annoying brother, who needed their help.

"Is everything all right with Azrael?" Agatha fiddled with her earrings, adjusting them in the mirror to be even.

"Yes, but he needs a favor."

"The man did break us out of a glass prison; it's the least we could do after he managed to procure a devil who could break a Loculus and produce an alibi for you."

"I know. I said you'd probably be willing to help, even though it's personal in nature."

"Oh?"

"He needs us to distract Vickie. Take her out for an hour, and make sure she gets back here precisely at noon."

"Oh my gosh." Agatha stopped, and looked at the door, which was most definitely closed. "Is this . . . ?"

Priscilla nodded. "It *is*. My sad sap of a falls-in-love-with-everyone brother has actually been in love with Victoria for going on decades now, and he's going to ask her to marry him, proper."

"I love that." Agatha's eyes sparkled. "What can we do?"

"We take a trip to the bookstore. I'll say we need the one up near Havenwall. That way we can certainly get lost in the stacks for long enough, and if she loses interest, we'll be far enough from Hallowcross to give Az warning."

"Brilliant. How do you want to ask her in a non-suspicious way?"

"I hope you don't mind that I already have."

"What did you tell her?" Agatha brushed her hair, gazing at Prissy curiously.

Priscilla blushed. What she had said was that she was starting to really fall for Agatha, and she wanted a second opinion on the thing they had going on, a neutral third party to observe.

"Just that I needed something from Wyrds, Wyrds, Wyrds and that I wanted her to spend a bit of time with you too." Vickie had been so eager to get to know Agatha that Priscilla very much doubted there was even a hint of suspicion in her mind.

"Genius. Shall we?"

"I told her we'd meet her in the foyer in a few minutes."

The drive to Wyrds, Wyrds, Wyrds, the independent bookstore just outside of the college town of Havenwall, was pleasant. Vickie had been trying out a new recipe for strawberry rugelach, and had brought the test batch, as well as a thermos of honeycomb latte, which Priscilla knew was specifically for Agatha. It was eleven by the time they finished shopping, and Agatha made a helpful announcement that she really did need to get back to work.

As she excused herself, presumably to the bathroom, but really to text Azrael their ETA, Priscilla couldn't help but think that she and Agatha made a good team. She tried not to make too much of it. They had agreed that this relationship had an expiration date, and it wouldn't do to get all caught up in mushy romantic feelings just because her brother was about to propose to the love of his life.

"Azrael wants me to meet him in the conservatory," Vickie remarked, stuffing her cell phone in her bag. She was sitting in the back of the car, looking conspiratorially between Prissy and Agatha, and Priscilla tried not to notice her back-seat scheming.

She also tried not to interrupt said scheming, because it was a great distraction from the proposal she was determined to help her brother get right.

"Do you want to take bets on whether he's got some nerdy plant allusion in a book that he wants you to help him with?"

Vickie huffed a laugh. "It wouldn't be the first time! I tried telling him that death powers really don't help in plant craft or any sort of magic, but he says that when I'm around him, it helps him focus and tap into his magic." She got a goofy sort of smile at this last part, and Prissy snuck a glance at Agatha, who grinned.

"That sounds like him. Down bad, one hundred and ten percent of the time." Priscilla joked, but it wasn't far from the truth. If people were fates and destiny, Azrael was the Norns; Vickie was his past, present, and future, his what had been and what was and what was always going to be.

It would have made her parents proud.

"So, I was thinking," said Priscilla. "Maybe you can stay with us at the manor a little longer, if you want. You don't have to, obviously, if you feel safe to return and you'd like to have your own space. But the house likes you."

"I'd love to stay a little longer," said Agatha softly.

Not for the first time, Priscilla wondered what her parents would have said if they were here. She thought they would love Agatha. Her mother had always stressed the importance of not shaping herself into a box to fit anyone else; her father had been willing to commit fierce shadow-craft hexes if anyone so much as raised a voice against who she was and who she loved. They wanted her to be herself, fully, and wouldn't it be honoring them, really, if she explored this thing with the Council president?

Perhaps she would find that once she'd had Agatha, it would be easier to move forward when the fake relationship drew to an end. Perhaps bubbling up between them was too much lust, like a champagne bottle that they had been shaking for months, that just needed to be unstoppered to let the friction run its course, have a nice toast, and toss the thing into the recycling respectfully.

She didn't want to think of herself as a used wine bottle, but it was better than this thick longing, this oppressively hot desire.

"I'll catch you later," said Vickie, making for the conservatory.

"Come on. They'll be in there for hours, I'm sure. I want to take you to my secret spot in the library."

Agatha's eyes lit up, and Priscilla hoped she wouldn't take offense if that turned out to be a euphemism for something much more naked than a room full of books.

CHAPTER 24

Agatha

The door to the library slammed shut behind her and locked itself with a definitive slide and click. Agatha looked up at the enormous room in front of her, bigger than her entire apartment put together.

She supposed she should feel bad that she hadn't been back to said apartment in going on two weeks, but all she felt was fortunate to be standing in this beautiful room once again. She'd visited it daily since Priscilla showed it to her, but the sight still left her breathless. It was a bookish girl's dream. If someone had told a thirteen-year-old Agatha that she'd one day be able to stand in a personal library that looked as though it had been magicked straight out of a fairy tale, she would have thought there wasn't enough magic in the witching world.

Even her beloved Council library didn't have the warm touches of Hart Manor, with generations of the family and the house itself to perfect it.

She took it in again, the sweeping shelves, the kind of ladders she'd dreamed of swinging off of as a little girl.

"Oh," she said softly. "Oh, every time it's still so breathtakingly beautiful."

Priscilla hesitated. "Do you want to see more?"

Agatha paused, trying to figure out what she meant. Priscilla had given her a house tour, but if there was *more* library, she certainly would not say no. "I would love to," she said.

"I have a secret spot on the second level." Priscilla pointed next to the full wall of books that ran all the way to the extra-tall ceiling. Along the right wall was a second floor and a spiraling staircase, the banister of which extended along the edge of the thing. "This was always my favorite when I was younger."

Priscilla snapped her fingers and lit the fireplace, which she had explained was enchanted not to get too hot. Agatha ran her hands along the high-back velvet chairs, took in the enormous, beautifully woven rug, the hardwood floor that glistened underneath. A suit of armor stood proudly in the corner, and beside it, two leather armchairs so wide that they could have easily accommodated two people each.

"Can you show me your secret upstairs?" She hadn't meant for it to come out quite so throaty, but she also didn't *not* mean for it to be tinted with possibility. The promise of the unknown stretched between them, and Prissy's lips parted, and then curled into a satisfied half smile.

"I can, honey. I really can." Her eyes darkened for a moment before she pointed to the staircase.

Agatha wanted to climb the ladders, to reach the tallest shelves, but more than that, she wanted to see the place that Priscilla had loved. She might not want to admit her feelings in full, but she did want to know everything about Priscilla Hart, even if it hurt her all the more when she left according to their bargain later on.

The agreed-upon ending of their fake relationship loomed; just as soon as they caught the would-be killer, that would be the death of this too.

She didn't want it to die, but after all, it was just physical. A crush at most.

Wasn't it? Surely she wasn't such a fool as to think she could have a real future with her fake girlfriend.

"Come on." Priscilla took her hand and pulled her toward the stairs and then up them. There was more room back here than she had realized, and the second floor went back farther than the room on the first. "I want to show you my reading room."

They stopped at a carved wooden wall with an intricate depiction of Artemis and her huntresses running through the woods, bows pulled taut, fierce, imposing, and powerful. She was as gloomy and unknowable as Agatha had once thought Priscilla, all sharp angles and poised arrows ready to strike. Agatha thought that Priscilla Hart might belong carved onto a marble relief. Beautiful enough to be immortalized in art. She ran a hand along the bow, the wood smooth and cool against her finger.

"Not quite there," said Priscilla, nudging her hand over.

Priscilla pressed a finger on top of hers, and she felt that sensation down to her bones. When the other woman moved her hand over, to one of Artemis's curls, Agatha didn't even bother to ignore the fire igniting within her. She shifted, pressing her legs together and preparing to haul Priscilla against the carving and get her fill of the time they had left, but the wall flipped, revealing a small antechamber, lined with busts and paintings, and an additional spiraling staircase.

"Up there," Priscilla whispered, and Agatha had a feeling they were entering someplace sacred. It was possible that the solemnity was about the raging desire she had to kiss Prissy, and maybe do more, but whatever the cause, she was speechless.

"I don't usually bring people up here," Priscilla continued. "It's the rare collection, where the grimoire usually hides. Technically, it lives wherever it wants in the library, but I know it prefers up here."

When she wound her way up the staircase, Agatha followed, hardly daring to breathe. They reached the top, which had ornately carved wooden shelves lining one wall, full of books so old she'd hardly dare to touch them. A long, expensive-looking chaise lounge stretched out next to the wall of books, and a sturdy oak desk, polished and fancy enough that it would have looked at home in Oxford, sat in the corner next to a leather couch.

"I used to come here and read poetry," Priscilla said, rubbing one arm of her sweater.

"You liked poetry?" There was something so fucking lovely about that, it almost killed her to know it. Too much of Priscilla was exquisite, and Agatha wasn't sure if she could bear it.

Priscilla blinked. "Yes, I like poetry."

"Tell me," said Agatha, "Tell me about poets you like."

A white cat yowled in the corner, slinking over to Priscilla and rubbing her leg until she petted it.

"Emily Dickinson, namesake of my beloved Emily Lickinson," she said, and the cat darted down the stairs and vanished, presumably into the library main room or the house. "But Emily Dickinson is more my brother's favorite. I do love her, obviously—I'm queer and bookish, so that's a given. But if I had to name my favorites? Goddess, I got lost in Elizabeth Bishop. Mary Oliver. Audre Lorde. The kind of words that wrap around your soul, that consume you, and that beg to be consumed, over and over again. Words that are like a lover." She paused, swallowing, as though maybe she'd said too much.

It was the most vulnerable Agatha had ever seen Priscilla, and she got a sense that there were few people who saw such softness in the woman.

Agatha could feel herself flush, and she walked the room, pausing at the desk and turning, hands braced on the edge of it. "Words like a lover sound decadent." Priscilla's brow furrowed, so she quickly added, "Decadent in a good way. I'd like that, I think."

"Would you?" Priscilla stepped closer to her.

"Yes." It was a whisper. A confession, and truly, her whole soul.

Priscilla leaned forward, hands on either side of the desk. "You understand that I'm not just asking you to read poetry?"

"I do," Agatha breathed. "Though you can read poetry to me if you like. I just . . ." She paused, flustered. "You distract me."

Priscilla ran a thumb along Agatha's bottom lip. "The feeling is mutual," she purred.

"What if we—" Agatha started.

"If we just—" Priscilla bit, and then laughed at the simultaneous misfire of words. "You go first."

"I was going to say . . ." Agatha could smell her, that lemon, the edge of mint. Madness. This was madness. Her brain was addled by wanting, that was all. She was starting to admit how much she liked Priscilla, but it was of course because her feelings were muddled by lust.

"What if we fucked?" she blurted, before she could talk herself out of it.

Priscilla sucked in a sharp breath, and Agatha went on, hurried, frantic to play it cool enough, to keep composure. "What if we did it once, just to get it out of our systems?"

"Yes," whispered Priscilla, pressing a kiss to the side of her face, just next to her mouth. "A thousand times yes."

Agatha leaned in, and their mouths collided, sweet, hot, and yearning. She lost herself in it, felt Priscilla press her against the desk.

"It doesn't have to mean anything," Agatha whispered, her voice coming out all wrong. Breathy. Strangled.

"All right," said Priscilla, and her mouth was moving, harder, her tongue parting Agatha's lips, her hands skating Agatha's waist, hips, thighs. She moaned, hands moving through Priscilla's hair, and then lower.

It was so perfect, and she didn't want to ruin it, but all the facts in the world couldn't distract her from this particular set of anxious thoughts. What if she was terrible at sex with women? What if years of mediocre men had worn her down to something unusable, unworthy of love, or even sex, that felt good?

Her body tensed up, and she willed it to relax, willed herself to calm down, and not to ruin this one wild, beautiful chance.

Priscilla stopped, pulling back, eyebrows furrowed.

"Hey. What's wrong?"

Agatha chewed her lip. She could distract with something else, like she had in the Loculus. She could lie and say that it was nothing, but she suspected that Priscilla wouldn't let it go so easily. Her only option was truth.

"I don't know what I'm doing," she admitted. "I want to, but I haven't. I don't know. I'm worried it's too late to know, and that there's no way I'll ever catch up."

Goddess, this was mortifying.

Priscilla cupped her face with both hands. "You are enough," she said. "And it's not too late. But if you want to stop here and think about it, or wait until you're more comfortable, you always can." Her face was so open, so earnest, that Agatha wanted to be honest too. She could lie and pretend it wasn't a big deal, but it was a big deal. It meant something to her, and there was no way to change that, to make it not mean something.

She did not want to stop; everything in her was wound so tight, and she felt certain that she couldn't possibly go on without doing something more. "I want this," she said, her voice shaky. "I just don't know how. I mean, I know, like I've seen, but I don't *know* know." Her cheeks were burning, half agony of embarrassment, half hope of desire.

"I can show you," said Priscilla, looking right into her eyes and pushing a strand of hair behind her ear. "If you want."

"Y-yes," Agatha breathed. "I'd like that."

"Take your pants off."

Agatha nodded, unbuttoned, and unzipped, letting them fall around her feet, and then stepping out.

Priscilla reached around her, fingers skating under her shirt, and pulled it slowly, agonizingly upward, the edges of her hands just barely skimming Agatha's skin.

She shivered and reached.

"I want to see you too," she whispered, and Priscilla nodded, shrugging off her sweater. Agatha reached for her pants, but she shook her head.

"Let me teach you what you should expect. From any partner." Her eyes narrowed. "Of any gender. I can't help but think no one has ever taken care of you the way you deserve."

"I—" Agatha started, but Priscilla was kissing her again, walking her back toward the desk, and gently pushing her toward it, helping her slide up it.

She squeezed Agatha's thighs, one in each hand, high enough up that it made Agatha whimper a little bit. When her thumbs started to circle, firm against the flesh of her thighs, Priscilla let out a moan that Agatha wanted—no, needed—to capture. She leaned in, kissing Priscilla harder, swallowing the sound of it, fucking her mouth with her tongue.

"You like being worshiped," Prissy murmured, "and I know well enough by now to know that when I see a goddess, the correct position is on my knees."

But she didn't move downward; instead she pulled back, looking at Agatha's breasts.

Agatha had always felt a shade insecure about them: the heft of them, the stretch marks on the sides, and the areolas that she'd feared were too large ever since some guy in her freshman algebra class had loudly exclaimed that he was grossed out by a pair of tits he saw with areolas bigger than half dollars.

Hers were twice that, at least. She needed to get out of her head.

"What are you thinking?" asked Priscilla, and again, she thought about brushing it off, about bringing her lips to cut off the question, changing the subject with her tongue, her hands.

But she wanted to do this, to really do it. "I've always been a little nervous about my breasts. About them not being svelte or dainty. Neat."

"Fuck," breathed Priscilla. "I'm obsessed with every single thing about your tits. I haven't stopped thinking of them since the house stole your towel and left me breathless and horny. I'd go to war for these tits."

"Oh," said Agatha, and then, "*Oh*," as Priscilla ran a finger down the curve of one, and then the other, and then reached with both hands, pulling the sheer fabric of her bra down so that she was almost fully exposed, the underwire of it pushing them up and together.

"I want to touch you everywhere," said Prissy softly. "I want to show you what it is to love this body the way I love this body."

Love. The word hit with too much impact, but there was a difference between loving a body and loving a person, and she forced herself to remember.

"Touch me," she breathed. "Show me. Ruin me."

Priscilla's eyes were dark. "All right," she said silkily. "You don't have to tell me twice."

And then her mouth was on Agatha's neck, kissing, licking, lapping against her collarbone, laving a path down her breasts, tongue twirling, slick and wet, on each nipple. She bit down gently, and then, when Agatha mewled, writhing, she bit down harder, and continued the ministrations with each hand, moving back up to kiss her mouth, fingers rolling slowly, agonizingly.

"I need," she whispered, voice reedy.

"I'll give you what you need," said Prissy, and she pinched, applying pressure. Agatha felt it low in her stomach, igniting like a flame. She was all heartbeat and breath and longing, nothing else.

"I want to show you what it is to ache, to burn, and then, when you think you can't take it anymore, when you're at the absolute edge of your patience, to give you what you need."

"Fuck," Agatha bit out. "Fuuuck."

"Yes," said Priscilla, grinning wide. Her pupils were blown, her brown eyes dark, her tongue licking across her lips in a way that made Agatha press her thighs back together.

Prissy made a disapproving noise with her tongue.

"No, honey, spread those for me."

And when she dropped to her knees, Agatha was glad for the firm support of the desk she was sitting on, because surely her legs would have given out. Priscilla pressed a kiss to the inside of her calf, one and then the other, moving up gradually, agonizingly slow, kissing, and then following the path of her lips with her thumbs, rubbing little concentric circles higher and higher on each of Agatha's thighs until her face was so close on each press of her lips that her nose grazed Agatha's panties.

She'd worn a nice pair, silky and light blue, and they were soaked now, the evidence of the teasing clear, but Agatha was too gone to be embarrassed.

Prissy looked up at her, all dark eyes and glossy raven hair and heavy desire.

"You're so wet," she said, running her mouth up the crux of Agatha's legs, where her thigh met her hip. An inch over and Priscilla's mouth would be on her, but for now, only her words were, Prissy's hot breath hitting her so close to where she wanted the other woman to be.

"I'm sorry," she breathed.

Priscilla bit her sharply on the thigh, and she keened.

"No being sorry. I'm going to show you how to do this the way you deserve to do it. Without reservation or apology."

"Okay," she said. "I'm not sorry."

"That's right." Priscilla looked smug. "And because you've been a good girl, getting so wet for me, and not being at all sorry, I'm going to reward you."

She wasn't sure that the sound that came out of her was entirely human when Prissy pressed her tongue to her center, licking her through her panties.

"Oh god." Her hands scrabbled, for the desk, for her breasts, and then down again.

Priscilla's eyes snapped up to hers.

"Do you want to play with your tits while I lick you senseless?"

Agatha whimpered, nodding.

"Then fucking do it." Priscilla dropped her head down, breath hot against Agatha's center.

She trembled, hands rising and then gripping. Palming, rolling. She pinched her nipples, hard, harder than Priscilla had, and she could feel herself go even more slick.

"That's it, baby," Priscilla cooed, and fuck, this was already seared into her mind like a brand. Hart lowered her face, licking over the fabric once more, before reaching with a finger, dragging the panties to the side, and licking again.

Agatha groaned, unable to resist the urge to rock forward, fucking herself onto Prissy's face. Prissy responded by pushing her thighs open wider, pinning them with surprising strength, and licking her carefully on each side, top to bottom, and then again, before circling her tongue around Agatha's clit. Agatha tried to rock, to move closer, to increase the pressure, but Priscilla had her pinned.

"Not so fast. I promised to show you, and I'm sure as hell not going to show you anything other than my best work."

Agatha panted, nodding. Sweat ran down her back, and she wanted to apologize again, but she remembered not to.

"This next part is important. Are you ready for my best trick?"

"Fuck yes."

Priscilla winked. "It's simple. Keep talking to me. Tell me what you want."

Agatha froze. "What if I ask for something you don't want?"

"Then we'll talk through it."

"What if I ask for something weird?"

"There's no weird, there's just sex, and what you're comfortable with and what I'm comfortable with. As long as you keep talking, it won't be weird. I promise. Can you do that?" She pressed kisses to the inside of each of Agatha's thighs.

Agatha blushed. "Yes."

"Good. Now, what do you want?"

Agatha shut her eyes. "I want," she began, taking a deep breath, and then exhaling. "I want you to keep licking me. I want you to fuck me with your fingers. Fill me up. Let me ride them until I can't stand it."

"That's so hot," said Priscilla. "Do you like these?" She rubbed two fingers against Agatha, a shallow dip over her panties that was everything and yet not even close to what she needed.

"Yes. I guess."

"If you guess, I'm not doing it right. Give me a minute and I'll show you more."

Priscilla returned her tongue to Agatha's cunt, licking from bottom to top, and then dipping her tongue in.

"You taste," she said, licking her clit for a few long, dragging seconds, "so fucking good. Sorry about these."

She tore through the delicate silk panties, tossing them aside.

"I'll buy you new ones. I just needed to see something." Prissy licked her again. "Fuck yes, that makes you even more turned on, doesn't it?" She smacked lightly at Agatha's thigh, gripping her ass when the impact of it made Agatha buck forward onto her face, and for a few long minutes, she stayed there, until Agatha was concerned that she wouldn't be able to breathe.

She was so close, reaching for that peak, and Prissy pulled back, raising a hand.

"I'm going to fuck you with my hand today, and next time, I'm going to fuck you with whatever you want. I know we joked about size, but I mean it. I can be whatever you want in that department." She waggled her eyebrows. "By silicone, magic, or both, you can have whatever you like."

She didn't wait for Agatha to respond, sliding one long finger in, and then a second, curling and pumping, but not touching the sensitive bud that Agatha so desperately wanted her to touch.

Impatiently, Agatha snaked her hand between her thighs, but Priscilla swiped it away, removing her fingers, leaving Agatha horrifyingly empty.

"Stay focused and take care of those tits for me," she growled, and Agatha whimpered, following her directions.

"Good girl," Priscilla said, face smug again, and slid her fingers back in. "Do you know what good girls get?" She muttered it against Agatha's pussy, licking one side, then the other, fingers drawing in and out, and in and out, urgently, and then more urgently.

"What?" Agatha asked, forcing herself to look at Priscilla, on her knees, finger-fucking her with abandon.

"Exactly what they need," said Priscilla, licking her lips and then diving back in, circling Agatha's clit, pumping her fingers harder, and curling, moaning a little into her skin, the vibration of it sending Agatha closer and closer. Her tongue moved expertly, and just when the circling was almost there, she pulled back and sucked, slowing the rhythm of her hand ever so slightly, and then picking it back up, the fucking and the circling.

Agatha screamed when she came, so hard that her eyes watered.

Priscilla kept pumping her hand, in and out, riding out the tremors, and Agatha gasped for breath, trying to get ahold of herself. When she had, she tugged on Priscilla's shoulders, pulling her up to standing and kissing her deeply. She could taste herself on Pricilla's tongue and something about that made her desperate to do it all again.

"Can I?" she said, reaching for Prissy's pants.

Priscilla's hands covered her own, breath rising and falling, rickety.

"Next time," she said, squeezing Agatha's hands. "This time was to show you, and I know you, Agatha, you like to be prepared. Take the time you need, and when you're ready, all you have to do is ask."

"Oh," said Agatha, and it was then that she realized she was both incredibly satisfied and incredibly stupid.

There was not a shot in hell that it would be just one time. There was no getting it out of her system; Priscilla Hart *was* the entire system for her now.

CHAPTER 25

Priscilla

Priscilla pushed the door to Hopelessly Teavoted, hoping that an Americano and a Peelin' Good chocolate chip banana muffin could help her sort through the quagmire of the past week. She'd spent most of it avoiding Agatha, telling herself it was fine to focus on congratulating her brother and Vickie on their engagement. And between checking in on Connie and catching up on Council paperwork, she did actually have her hands full with work.

It was supposed to be just once, just to get it out of their systems, and yet she had found herself whispering sweet nothings and meaning them, found herself coaxing Agatha into coming, so beautifully, around her fingers.

It had *not* meant nothing. In fact, for Priscilla, it had meant the polar opposite of nothing.

The shop was fairly empty, and she recognized Hazel at the register again.

"Priscilla Hart!" The girl's eyes lit up, smile reaching wide. She looked around, thoughtful for a moment in that way that could only mean she was about to serve some sort of sharp teenage insight. "Hey, whatever happened to that hot British woman you used to come in with?"

And there it was. People never gave kids enough credit for how observant they could be.

It had been ages since anyone had seen her and not known that she was a runaway bride. Small towns were good for that. But she had forgotten to consider that teenagers don't necessarily care to keep track of adult drama. Azrael told her that some of them still stared openly in shock to see a teacher out and about around town, and that speculating about staff members was about as far as their interest in adult gossip went. Other adults in the town were just unknown olds.

That was refreshing.

"That ended a while ago," she said, managing a smile. It was like running a tongue past a place where a tooth had fallen out; she knew something was gone, in this case someone she loved, and she could feel the spot of emptiness. But it didn't hurt anymore.

It was okay, because she'd gotten out of it before it was too late. It had been bad timing, but she hadn't gone along with a family, and it wasn't like they had been married for years and years. The sharpness of the remaining pain now was the possibility, how close she'd come to signing up for a life that could only shatter other people into pieces in the end.

"Rough," said the girl, wincing.

"Hazel," said the other kid at the counter, with the name tag that said Cole and had their pronouns on it. They looked a little older. College-aged, maybe. "It's not polite to comment on other people's breakups unless they ask for your advice."

"No, it's okay this time. I think it's okay to ask after people," said Priscilla, and for some reason, she went on. "It was tough for a while there, but I'm out the other end now. I'm thinking of seeing someone new."

"Hot," said Hazel, and that made Priscilla laugh, because it *was* hot, and it was just like Hazel to put it bluntly.

"Yeah, she is." She tried not to think of Agatha and just exactly how hot she was in this particular moment; that kind of daydreaming never led to a focused day of accomplishments.

"This is great," Hazel began. "I want to hear all about what happened with the *Bridgerton*-ass lady, and then about whatever new hot lady you've got in your pocket too."

Priscilla suddenly regretted the specific word choice of *okay*. Hazel was nice, but she absolutely did not want to spill her guts to her teenaged barista.

Cole elbowed Hazel again, but she ignored them. "So, it's like if someone is going off to a different college, right, they might be a good fit while you're in high school, but then the best thing to do is break up so you can both have the college experience you need." Hazel smiled, proud of herself and her advice. Priscilla heaved a sigh of relief; there had been no question in that, and maybe she could move this conversation along.

"That's an overshare, Haze," said Cole. But then they paused and shrugged, flicking at their eyebrow ring. "But it's not wrong. Hey, do you want Vickie? She's in the office."

The look of gratitude Priscilla shot Cole was straight from her heart, because Hazel turned and started arguing about the efficacy of promposals in a modern artistic high school scene, and dropped the whole Evelyn issue.

She hadn't come here with the express intention of visiting her brother's fiancée, but now that it was an option, she found herself needing an outside opinion.

"I might see if Vickie has a minute."

"Head on back!" Hazel winked, and the two returned to the business of gossiping and occasionally refilling sugar packets.

She walked past the kitchen she knew so well, and the storage area. The door to the office was a few inches open, but she knocked anyway.

"Come in!" Vickie's voice was cheery. Priscilla loved hearing her happy, loved knowing that not only was the shop really still in the family, but it had also given her old friend a sense of purpose that she had so long sought out.

Pushing open the door, she gave a weird little half wave with the hand holding a muffin.

"Mind if I sit for a little?" she asked, knowing the answer, but wanting to check in anyway. For most people, she would have barged right in, steamrolled through. But for Vickie, who had grown up next to her, an odd not-so-mundane girl with the power to summon the dead, she would ask nicely. Vickie wasn't just the love of her brother's life; she was Priscilla's trusted confidante too. Together they had defeated a mega-church run by an evil man who had bargained with the king of devils last year, and that, on top of surviving their teenage years together, essentially made them bonded forever. It was a friendship worth pausing for.

"Please," said Vickie, gesturing to the chair across from her desk and moving a stack of papers so that Priscilla could set down her cup and her muffin. "Those Peelin' Good muffins are some of my best work, especially since I accidentally summoned a vintage baking ghost off an estate sale set of teacups. She gave me the best trick for moist muffins before I sent her along to whatever comes next. What's going on?" She looked concerned, eyes taking in Priscilla's face and her stance, a little more hunched than usual. Prissy straightened up, but Vickie had seen it. The uncertainty. The wondering. She sat back, resting her hands on the desk, waiting for Priscilla to tell her what the matter was.

"Did I ever tell you why I want so badly to be Witchery Council president? All jokes about my type in women aside, why I wanted it?" Her voice sounded small to her, but it was quiet in here, and maybe it was all right to take a break from booming loudly in this instant.

Vickie shook her head.

"I wanted to build something for myself, the way that my father did. On the Council." Priscilla dragged a hand down her face. Building something was enough. She didn't know how she'd gotten it so twisted as to pursue power at the expense of her reputation.

"That makes sense." Vickie gestured around her. "Like the shop for me. I get that. My parents wanted something else for me, so it's a little bit different, but in a way, thwarting their wishes, getting disowned, pursuing my own thing, was also because of them. Benedict and Persephone were so lovely you wanted to make them proud; mine were so shitty I wanted the opposite. But I still get that drive. That need."

She sighed, leaning forward, and then back again. This was the part that was harder to say. "Lately I've been thinking about, like, why president?" Priscilla hadn't wanted to admit it to herself, but the thing was, she couldn't seem to figure out why it had actually been so important to her. It had loomed large in her mind for so long that she couldn't trace the origin point, that she thought maybe there wasn't one. That maybe what she'd thought she wanted, desperately, was close to, but not actually, what she wanted at all.

"And?" Vickie looked at her like she knew the answer, and like she'd listen until Priscilla got there. Fuck, Azrael's whole English teacher mojo must be rubbing off on her. She had that stares-inquisitively-until-the-person-bares-their-soul look down.

"Because it's what I always said I wanted, and I am Priscilla fucking Hart, and I seize the world and take what I want." She didn't want it, though. She knew that now, and if she was honest, she supposed she had sort of known for a while. It was just hard to give up on a dream, even if the other dreams didn't go away with the release of the one.

"What is it that you want about it?" Vickie cocked her head, voice gentle, not looking away, even when Priscilla screwed her eyes shut to think. When she opened them, her friend sat there, waiting patiently.

"The work, I guess."

"You're not satisfied with the work you're doing as a Council member?"

She paused. Priscilla loved what she did, and she also didn't particularly want more work. "No, I guess I am," she admitted. And it was true. She'd seen the role of president intimately, at Evelyn's side, and now at Agatha's. She didn't want that intense responsibility. She didn't even think she'd be good at that much multitasking.

"Would you even want the job, or is it just the title?" And there was Victoria, senses perhaps sharpened by her ability to summon the dead by touching an object they had loved in life, dealing her plain old mundane logic unsparingly. There was brutal honesty in that question.

Priscilla thought for a moment of the things that would summon Agatha if she were dead. Her favorite pens, and that prized pothos she kept in her office. Probably her planner. All the things Agatha cherished most were Council-related. She *loved* the job in a way that Prissy didn't.

And that was all right, to like a job and want to do it but not love it. Priscilla couldn't have been bothered to be summoned by any office-related objects if she were dead. Hers would be the earrings she'd inherited from her grandmother, the simple hoop ones. Maybe her favorite book of poetry. Definitely the chaise lounge in her hidden reading spot.

"Fuck," she muttered. "Fuck. I have been chasing a title, not an actual dream." It was shitty, but again, it would have been shittier to get it and not want it, so she supposed that it was tantamount to running from Evie at their would-be wedding.

"Well, there's your answer. It's never too late to go in a different direction." Vickie smiled. "I did. It was scary at first. But worth it in the end."

"Right. It doesn't take away from my dad's legacy to go my own way." There was so much relief in saying it out loud. Benedict Hart would be proud of her, actually, for reassessing, and for focusing on what she really wanted.

"Exactly." Vickie folded her hands.

Priscilla smiled. "You're a gem." She paused. "Hey, you wouldn't happen to know anything about immortality, would you?"

Vickie eyed her appraisingly. "Because I have death powers?"

"Yeah, but not eternal immortality. Corporeal immortality, the Fountain of Youth sort."

"I don't have any experience with that," said Vickie thoughtfully. "But I can speak to being the last soul someone has interacted with, when I touch their object and it burns. In those five minutes, the people who would want to live forever, anyone who is actively trying to cling to the world instead of moving on, that's never a person who was trying to do much good in the first place."

"So not altruistic, got it." Priscilla frowned. That didn't narrow it down too much.

"Not just that," said Vickie. "It's a selfishness but also a deep insecurity, usually masked by egregious over confidence. People trying to live forever are either afraid they'll never amount to anything extraordinary, overly entitled, or both."

Priscilla nodded. She felt like that did narrow it down, but she still wasn't sure who she'd want to slap that awful description onto.

"Thanks, Vickie," she said.

"Glad to have a reason to take a break from the mayhem of sorting out the scheduling calendar," she said, tapping at the giant calendar on her desk.

"I'll leave you to it." Vickie loved this job, and Priscilla was awfully glad she'd wanted the shop. Speaking of careers Priscilla had no interest in, scheduling calendars were not for her.

"Enjoy the muffin." Vickie waved, picking up a gel pen and tapping it against the page in thought.

"Oh, and Vickie?" She'd made it too much about her, and she didn't want to leave without a note of reciprocity.

"Yes?"

"Congratulations again. You've always been family, you know." She smiled.

"Thanks, Prissy. I'm so happy." Vickie waggled her fingers, the light glancing off a beautiful antique ring that had once belonged to their grandmother. Az had had it refitted for the proposal.

“Between this and the office he built me in your dad’s old shed, I got pretty lucky.”

“You both did,” said Prissy softly, and Vickie blushed, turning back to her schedule.

When Prissy shut the door, she decided.

It was time to finally talk to Agatha about her feelings.

CHAPTER 26

Agatha

After days of back-and-forth with the International Council, she'd finally persuaded them to let her have a shot at reprogramming the Loculus. And they had agreed to let Priscilla help her in her quest to reform the outdated glass prison, though she'd been careful not to emphasize Hart's involvement too strongly.

If she could just go through the research one more time, she almost had the perfect spell to overwrite the old automated deployment magic and reset it so that the Council could give it individual wishes and instructions. She was so close, and after many late nights and magnification spells to decipher notes and records addled by time, elements, and in a few instances, magical interference, she knew what she needed to do. If she was correct, it would take her plant craft and Priscilla's shadow craft to get it just right, and the significance of their powers pairing together so well was not lost on her.

Still, it would be tricky. She rubbed her temples, trying to clear her head with sea turtle facts.

Olive ridley turtles were, in her opinion, the cutest type of sea turtle, though leatherbacks were also majestic and ancient-looking. Both turtles migrated yearly from where they hatched and laid eggs in Indonesia to California, which meant that turtles swam about ten thousand miles a year.

Agatha could do about ten laps in the twenty-five-yard lane at the local Y twice a week. At five hundred yards a week, and fifty-two weeks a year, give or take a few she skipped, she figured she swam twenty-five thousand yards a year. It took her a few minutes to figure out about how many miles that was; by her calculations, it was about fourteen. If a sea turtle could swim over seven hundred times the number of miles she could, that was an oddly comforting fact in the universe. No matter what she did, there would always be creatures swimming longer or faster. All she could do was her best.

And her best in Witchery Council business was no small task. She breathed and focused on the issue at hand.

The Loculus had been enchanted ages ago, with the help of witches from both sides of the Atlantic, and there were decades of finicky residual spell work to untangle. She needed to check one more thing before she could be sure it wouldn't do something awful, like freeze them all in time, or implode the entire building, or something.

She pressed the button on the intercom in her office. "Kevin, can you bring me the 1966 repair report documents, please?" The Loculus had been overhauled sixty years ago, so the records had been specially preserved and mailed delicately from the International Council archives to avoid damage.

Kevin had returned, albeit reluctantly, and she'd been walking on eggshells around him just to try to make sure that he didn't quit on her entirely after the pranking fiasco.

His organization system alone would be nearly impossible to replicate.

"Here you are." He deposited them on her desk, tone not exactly frosty, but not what it once was either.

Agatha sighed. She had work to do to repair their relationship, like she had work to do on the Loculus, and she had to figure out how to talk to Priscilla about her more than friendly feelings. Her emotional to-do list was creeping close to matching her work list.

Kevin opened the door to leave, and as though summoned

by the power of Agatha's gaze, Priscilla looked up, locking eyes with her. Goddess, Agatha saw those gold-rimmed brown orbs in her dreams, the beautiful and the dirty alike.

Determination flickered across Priscilla's face. She stood up and caught the door from Kevin, ignoring his side-eye as he passed and pulling it shut behind her.

"Hi," she said, a smile inching up her face.

"Hi," said Agatha. Her chest was doing something weird and warm and fluttery.

A few awkward seconds stretched, and Agatha cleared her throat. "Do you want to give this paperwork a second glance? I think that if we can figure out how to untangle a patch from the sixties, that would clear things up to reroute the original spell from the bit they were fixing."

Priscilla's eyes lit up. "I'd love to help. And then maybe we can also talk after work?"

"I'd like that." Agatha's cheeks heated as she thought about the way Priscilla had looked up at her, a few strands of hair falling across her forehead as she rewired Agatha's entire brain from between her legs. She blushed. There would be time for that later.

"I think that with the correct bioorganic compound, a simple tracing spell could illuminate where the patch was, and then we can use a counterspell to undo the patch and work our way in."

Priscilla studied the papers, playing with her long black braid. "Your plant craft would definitely help," she mused.

"I see what you mean. I think I have everything I need to put this together, and I can brew it in the conference room if you give me about an hour." She paused. "We will need a third witch. Someone trustworthy and very powerful."

Agatha nodded. "I can ask Otho and move the Loculus in carefully enough not to trigger it in the meantime." She looked at Priscilla. "Can you bond it? With shadow craft?" Priscilla closed her eyes, concentrating, and snapped her fingers. A wooden braid, about two inches long, appeared in her hand.

She opened her eyes. "One of the last few I carved with my dad. It's strong enough to hold."

Shadow-craft witches could carve tokens and use them to harness shadows, a brand of magic mercurial and mysterious, bound by the act of creating art. Priscilla, like her father before her, carved her own tokens in wood, though Agatha hadn't missed that she didn't do it much.

"I don't take it lightly," said Priscilla softly. "My dad taught me shadow craft takes decades to master. We had a rule. Only when absolutely necessary, and only when already prepared. No crafting things that we didn't already have. No summoning shadows we hadn't already studied and observed."

"Thank you for doing this," said Agatha. "I hope it works."

"We've got this, honey." Priscilla winked at her.

It was the first time Priscilla had called her that since . . . and it did something to her. A funny, twisting something, born in part from desire and in part from gratitude. She'd beaten Priscilla Hart for this job, and for some time, she'd been so certain the beautiful witch would never forgive her for it, and so certain that she could never forgive Priscilla for catalyzing the dramatic fall of Jonathan.

But she was beginning to believe in second chances. In starting over, and in the beautiful possibilities that in a wide world full of wonder and beauty, a person you liked, or even loved, might find it in their heart to forgive you. To move forward.

Hope burrowed in Agatha Vanderbilt Voisin's heart, and it had been so long since that hope had been romantic and real. There had never been any real hope for Jonathan, she knew that, but the loneliness caused her to keep going, just in case. Even if it wasn't ever real.

She had known people to have a real thing, a beautiful, breathtaking kind of love, the kind to grow old with, and to lose it. She had known people to let it slip through their fingers, to fumble and drop it when times got rough. To make mistakes so consequential they couldn't be undone.

But Agatha was not going to be like that. She was not going to die with regrets one day. She was going to go wholeheartedly into this, to tell Priscilla how she felt, and to know that even if it crashed and burned, or never took off to begin with, she had given it her all. People said that it was better to love and lose than to never love at all, and Agatha felt that with her entire foolish, delusional heart.

Because what if the person she loved *was* willing to love her back? To take a chance? To run toward the sunset and never look back? She had to know.

But first she was going to solve the problem of this fucking Loculus, because after the forced entrapment in it, she was certain that it had gone too long operating on its own strange impulses and needed the oversight of the magical committee of the ICoW.

Otho was grumpy about it, but of course agreed to help her. Together they wove the careful web of magic that held the Loculus precariously in the air, swaddled by invisible, stabilizing ropes, as they moved it carefully from her office to the conference room table.

Priscilla was already there setting up.

"I need about thirty more minutes, and then I need both of you. Agatha, I'll need you to administer the spell after I brew it; Otho, to stabilize it during the process. I will rewrite its directions."

"Fine," sighed Otho. "I'll tell Nancy to cancel my one o'clock with the head of the ski lodge; I'm sure he'll be overjoyed to hear that his Yeti problem is going to have to wait."

"The Yeti will still be there in the morning," said Priscilla.

"If he's not caused any major damage yet, he probably won't." Agatha winked.

Otho clutched at his ascot. "My goddess, was that a pun?"

"Indeed."

"Terrible, absolutely terrible! But also quite funny. I might have Nancy use that when she talks to dear old Pete. He's the sort to get a kick out of it, and it's not as though I could solve a

Yeti overnight. The relocation search alone will probably take weeks, at best."

He bustled out.

"I love this new side of you," Priscilla said, smirking.

"So do I. Just wait until you see the rest." She could *do* this, not just fake dating, but real flirting, real chemistry, and goddess, did it feel good. Priscilla's eyebrows lifted, and Agatha winked and headed back to her office. She was going to fix this blasted Loculus; that would be the last time it imprisoned someone unfairly without waiting for more deliberations than an initial suspicion.

By the time she'd caught up on some of her email—not all of it, of course; that would be a gargantuan task—it was already time to meet Prissy and Otho in the conference room.

It smelled nice in the conference room, and not just Prissy's typical lemon-mint scent; whatever Priscilla had brewed was bubbling softly.

"What is that?" Agatha inhaled, letting it calm her mind from the stress of both the giant glass coffin and the declaration of feelings she had planned.

"Rosemary, for clarity. Rue, for protection. An assortment of base spell-work blends from my mother's recipes, and iodine for contrast."

"Brilliant," said Otho, puffing up. "Absolutely brilliant, Priscilla. A Hart through and through."

Priscilla's pleased expression was enough to melt Agatha's heart, and Otho was right. It was a clever potion.

This had to be the turning point. It had to be downhill from here. She was solving one of her greatest magical problems with a beautiful, smart woman.

Otho waved his hands, clapping them together twice. "It's stable."

Priscilla snapped, and the potion wove through the air, violet with a grayish shimmer, weaving in a flourishing column of liquid. She took the wooden braid in her hand, murmured something, and held it out. Shadows poured from it until it disintegrated into nothing and the smokelike strands wove their way into the suspended potion, tinting it darker. More magical, more foreboding, and infinitely more powerful.

"Exquisite," pronounced Otho, nodding.

"It is," she agreed, reaching toward it. "Ready?"

"Yes."

The liquid pulsed, and Priscilla shut her eyes, concentrated, and snapped again. It congealed near the top of the Loculus in, unsurprisingly, the place Lex had fiddled with it to disintegrate.

No one knew the exact origin of the Loculus, though it had been recorded as in use since the 1600s. Whenever it had been dismissed, disintegrated, or even taken into pieces, it always came back together. It was seemingly indestructible, said to be forged in the same Fountain of Youth that the elixir was.

So it was true that Agatha did have an ulterior motive. She hoped to discover who was truly familiar with the elixir, and if they had anything to do with the overly eager Loculus, which according to Council records, had been acting strangely for a few years now.

Priscilla's potion made it easy to see the strands of magic, and Agatha rubbed her fingers together to peel away the first few, discarding them in the cauldron. She paused where they grew more complex, overlapped with clear spaces that must hold other magic. Here she would go one by one, pulling each thread out gently with magic, rather than the motion of removing that thatched first layer of magic that was all lit up by the spell.

It was careful work, but she enjoyed it; spell diffusing had always been a strong suit. The tangled web of spell work reminded her of an intricate root system, and her plant craft called to it, as though it were a hundred-year-old tree or a mycelial network buried deep beneath the ground. When she got to a difficult bit, she recited facts to ground herself. Scientists estimated that at least 30 percent of the soil beneath them all was mycelial, and that was reassuring. She liked to think of the world, however seemingly disconnected, as actually intertwined by secret, hidden fungi, like invisible strings tying humanity together. She got through a particularly difficult knot of magic and let out a sigh of relief.

There. She stepped back, rubbing the sweat from her brow. Priscilla snapped, and an elegant, black lace–edged handkerchief appeared in front of her.

"Thank you," said Agatha. "That was more difficult than I expected, but it's done."

Priscilla pulled a vial from the pocket of her dark green blazer and held it up. "If you would both step back, just in case, I'm going to tint the original programming that was patched here, and respell it to capture my command. Then we can command it to return to ICoW headquarters to be activated by official judiciary proceedings after they have reached a verdict."

She paused at the sound of a knock on the door, and Agatha turned.

"I brought you all some water," said Kevin, smiling. A peace offering. He set three bottles, glistening with cool condensation, on the table.

Her assistant was starting to forgive her for getting caught in the crosshairs; the object of her affection was currently doing a great deal for her competence kink; and she was on a roll with achieving the items on today's to-do list. Agatha felt like she could carve this moment into destiny as one of her greats.

"Thank you, Kevin. We should be done here soon, and then I'll go over the minutes with you and we can log the records."

"Sounds good!" Kevin bobbed his head and ducked out.

Priscilla took a quick drink, set down the bottle, and bent over the Loculus with the vial. She poured it carefully, and this time the liquid was orange, spreading across an intricate pattern of woven magic, more delicate than the patch Agatha had removed.

There was a gaping, ripped hole the size of a fist, the edges of it ragged where the magic had frayed.

Agatha watched as Priscilla snapped a few times, pressed

her ear close to it, listening, and examined it from several angles until she seemed satisfied, then snapped a few times.

The edges wove together, mending the sides of the hole with ragged bits and strands of gold magic that reminded Agatha of the little flecks of gold in Priscilla's eyes.

"Benedict Hart would be so proud," murmured Otho, and Agatha was so proud to be watching it, so she supposed he would have been, indeed.

When the magic had knit together completely, Priscilla leaned over again, snapped, and whispered to the Loculus. She snapped once more, and the dye drained from the strands, returning to the cauldron and then dissipating into the air.

"There," she said, sounding pleased. "A solid programming if I do say so. It should do exactly what I say now."

She snapped her fingers, and Agatha wanted to turn to congratulate her, but when she stepped forward, her hands ran into the firm glass side of the Loculus. It was, instead of where it should be, around Agatha now.

It had inexplicably imprisoned her, and without the normal lag time to form and reform. She was going to raise her hand and bang against it—she wanted to say something, to ask for help, to get them to summon Lex again, but a splitting pain in her head gave her pause.

Otho turned to Priscilla, horror and apprehension on his face, pointing, but before Agatha could hear what he had to say, the world went black.

CHAPTER 27

Priscilla

The International Council of Witchery triumvirate stood before her, grim and terrifying. Priscilla knew that it was serious, because it meant the portal restrictions had been granted an emergency override, for use in only the direst situations.

Council rules were clear with individual nations and in international magical law: portaling was almost exclusively shut down. The rules specified that it was absolutely not to be used except in the event of clear and present danger of preventable mass casualty or cases of potentially destabilizing political crime.

So she was halfway to becoming an international war criminal, it turned out.

Priscilla slammed her eyes shut. This was not how she had imagined her afternoon going; she was going to show off her skill with the Loculus spell and woo Agatha in earnest afterward. She was going to reveal her hidden feelings, to finally tell Agatha that they were real, and that they weren't going to be together just once, just to get it out of their systems.

Instead, she was here, set up in the Council courtroom, which had been temporarily taken over by the three witches looming on the bench before her. Unlike most modern witches, who dressed in mundane clothing, the triumvirate wore robes, similar to those of mundane judges, but shimmering with rich magical history passed down through generations of the most revered judicial body in the witchery community.

A witching courtroom was almost exactly like a mundane one, with the exception, of course, of the magical projection box that displayed evidence interactively projected for the jury. Because it was only a preliminary hearing, Priscilla stood in front of them, and not on the stand. Juries were not called for this sort of hearing, only immediate witnesses and the judges.

The eldest judge, Horatio Thistlewinch, raised a hand.

"Priscilla Guinevere Hart, you stand accused of the kidnapping and attempted assassination of North American Council of Witchery president Agatha Vanderbilt Voisin. How do you plead?"

"Not guilty," she said, eyes bouncing from the judges to Otho, to Kevin and Nancy. Azrael sat next to Otho, face drawn and serious. Only the prohibition of nonwitches not specifically summoned could have stopped Vickie, Priscilla told herself. It was nice that her brother was here, even though there was no way in heaven the judges would let him testify.

Probably for the best, as under oath he might have to reveal some of her more nefarious at-home pranks against him. Not that any of them came close to what she stood accused of now.

Judge Thistlewinch nodded. Next to him, Esmerelda Clay raised a hand. "Would the first witness, Nancy Ashbrooke, agree to give testimony?"

"Yes," said Nancy, voice a little shaky.

"Nancy Ashbrooke, what did you see of the kidnapping of Agatha Vanderbilt Voisin and the theft of the Loculus?"

"Very little," said Nancy, wringing her hands. "I was outside of her office, at my uncle's desk, logging the travel plans for the month, and there was a boom, and then a blur of motion, and the Loculus whipped out of the conference room so fast I couldn't even see who was in it. It was all in a weird cloud of shimmery red, and it knocked into Kevin."

As though feeling it all over again, Kevin rubbed a purple bump spreading underneath a bandage on his forehead.

"Thank you," said Judge Clay.

"Mr. Kevin Cross, would you agree to give testimony?" Judge Thistlewinch asked once again, in a way that made it very much clear that this was not actually a question but a command.

"Yes," said Kevin, his voice cracking a little. He cleared his throat and went on. "I was at my desk. I stood up when I heard a boom from the conference room where Priscilla was working the spell, and then I felt the impact, and that stunned me for a moment, and the next thing I knew, the president had been kidnapped, and Otho was yelling, asking Priscilla what she had done, and Priscilla was just standing there, looking guilty."

It was an unfair assumption, and she wanted to say so, but there was no use talking until it was her turn; it wouldn't help her case to interrupt. She knew as well as anyone the etiquette expectations for such a hearing. Still, she wanted to shake Kevin, for calling her guilty just because she'd been practicing magic on a powerful artifact that happened to have been involved in the crime. And most of all, she wanted to shake the guilt she felt over being the reason Agatha's anti-kidnapping spell work was not available to her at the time of the attack.

By using it to protect Priscilla from the Loculus the first time, she'd left herself vulnerable until a full coven could recast it. It did make Priscilla look guilty, precipitating that use at just the right time.

"Otho Ashbrooke, do you agree to give your account?" Ashanti Antonov, the third judge, peered over horn-rimmed glasses at him.

"Certainly," said Otho, looking at Priscilla, brows furrowing.

"Your magnanimous Honors," he began, a pedant as always, "I have known Priscilla Hart for her entire life, and I want to start by noting that I do not believe her to be an arsonist, a kidnapper, or a murderer. I believe her to be an upstanding citizen and a fine member of the North American Council of Witchery."

"Very well, Councilman Ashbrooke, noted. Now please try

and give us an honest and straightforward answer about what you saw."

He nodded, looking at Priscilla apologetically.

"Well, we were working on the Loculus. Priscilla had prepped the potions and Agatha and I had stabilized the Loculus and brought it into the room. I stabilized it again, Priscilla spelled an older patch with her potion, and then Agatha worked the magic to remove it. After that, Priscilla applied a second potion, and this time, she worked a spell to repatch the Loculus, and then did the work to reprogram it. She stood up, said it should do exactly as she commanded, and snapped her fingers. And then, most unfortunately, it snapped into place around Agatha, and poof! Flew off in a burst of shiny red magic."

"Did you hear her give the command?"

Otho shook his head. "No. It's delicate spell work, so much so that it's the sort of thing to be whispered quite intimately. The Loculus *is* over four hundred years old; it requires a careful touch. But I'm certain Priscilla told it to return to its proper place, and not to kidnap anyone."

"Otho Ashbrooke, please confirm. Did you or did you not hear her issue the order?" asked Judge Thistlewinch.

"I did not," said Otho, squirming.

"Is there any other relevant situational information we should know about this incident before we question the accused?"

Priscilla winced at that word. She was accused, it was true, but she was innocent. She schooled her face to be impassive and waited her turn.

Kevin raised his hand.

"This is not a classroom, Mr. Cross. Speak." Judge Antonov looked cross.

"I brought them all water, and I think that there was something weird going on."

"What makes you say that?" Thistlewinch's eyes narrowed.

"Well, Priscilla kept looking at Agatha."

"Looking?" Judge Thistlewinch parsed the word, as though Kevin had just suggested Priscilla had engaged in stabbing someone, or stealing baby animals from their mothers.

"Like long, furtive glances," Kevin added hastily.

She *had* been looking at Agatha. But that was about all her complicated, tangled-up affections, not about plotting abduction.

"Very well," said Thistlewinch, his now-impassive face not giving anything away.

Fucking Kevin. She should have known he was bad news, the little snitch. Meddling where he had no idea what he was talking about and getting her into all sorts of trouble here.

"Priscilla Hart, do you agree to give us your account of the events?"

"Yes, your Honors." She nodded. It was best to be as brief and as factual as possible. To let her innocence do the arguing. "Thank you. It is as Otho said. I brewed the potion. Agatha removed the patch. I reworked the new patch and spelled it to return the Loculus to the Council, to follow only my command. My next step would have been to command it to the behest of this tribune, but it malfunctioned."

"It malfunctioned?"

"Correct. I whispered to it all the words to return and wait to do my bidding, and instead, it jerked through the air, cracked Agatha in the head, and then materialized around her in a flash of red smoke. It whooshed out of the room, and it took me a few moments to process what had happened. I did not tell it to attack Agatha."

The judges turned without another word, Judge Antonov snapping to create a bubble of silence as they deliberated, mouths moving so little that it was impossible to determine what they were saying.

"Priscilla, we know you're innocent," said Otho grandly.

"Well, I don't think we necessarily *know* that." Kevin eyed her, jaw set.

"*I* believe you're innocent," said Nancy, shooting Kevin a glare.

"Let's just see what the judges say." Kevin's expression was smug. In normal circumstances, Pricilla would have verbally eviscerated him, but it was bad form to mouth off violently in a courtroom while being accused of a crime.

The minutes dragged on, and Priscilla tamped down her fear for Agatha. The longer they delayed here, the longer it would be before she could hunt down the real culprit and, more importantly, *find* Agatha.

She knew what she had to do, but goddess, it was going to hurt like hell.

With a crack, the bubble of silence receded. The three regarded her soberly, and Judge Clay spoke first.

"Priscilla Hart, unless you can provide further substantive alibi in this incident, I'm afraid we will have to take you into custody until a thorough investigation can be completed."

Priscilla swallowed. She could not lose the time; who knew what sort of a maniac had kidnapped Agatha? Even a powerful witch could be outnumbered or outspelled by great evil magic, and she couldn't live with herself if she allowed that to happen.

"Per witchery laws, I would like to provide my own alibi in the traditionally accepted manner." She gritted her teeth. It would hurt, but she didn't see any other option here.

Judge Clay's eyebrows shot up, and Judge Antonov clutched her chest.

"Are you certain?" Judge Thistlewinch asked.

"I am, yes." Goddess, she was, despite the consequences.

"Very well, please be seated. As you know, this will not be a comfortable process, and we wouldn't want you to fall should you lose consciousness."

She slipped into the chair on the stand, trying to shake the feeling of guilt that came from sitting there. She was not guilty, but gravedirt could fade or be an ineffective batch; at times, witches had even been known to cultivate enough of an immunity to it to lie, as a master poisoner might do with a poison. And the guilt of Agatha being exposed to a kidnapping gnawed at her. She had to be free enough to make it right.

The only solution in this kind of an inquisition was much, much worse than gravedirt.

Judge Clay clapped her hands together, and leather cuffs braced Priscilla to the chair. "In case you pass out," she said apologetically.

Thistlewinch rustled around in his pockets and pulled out a stoppered vial of purple liquid, murmuring a quick spell to check the expiration date.

"It's been a good while since we've had case to use veronica flower extract. On account of, you know . . . the human rights objections to the terrible burning-alive feeling it induces along with the vision."

Priscilla braced herself. She did know in theory, but she had to imagine it would feel worse than her mind could predict. Still, she was willing to brave torture for that woman.

He unstoppered the bottle and held it to her lips. It tasted unpleasant, slightly sweet and rubbery, like licking candy off tire tracks, and instead of an aftertaste, a corrosive burning spread through her chest.

That was just the first part. The spell wasn't even set yet.

"*Ostende* the conference room of the North American Council of Witchery, noon to 2 p.m." He snapped, and Priscilla's body went rigid. This was going to be agony. Most magic did not take verbal spell work; the strength and intensity of this particular casting required not only one, but both participants in the spell to say it.

"*Ostende*," she repeated, gritting her teeth already, and the searing, rippling heat radiated out from her chest, down her arms, up her neck, through her torso, her legs, until it felt as though she were being burned alive.

She let out a small shriek of pain before her body adjusted to the burning, and then a louder one when the full weight of the agony set in. Time stretched out, impossible to measure while the spell tore her apart psychically, and she had been screaming for so many seconds that her voice was hoarse, and then came the slight numbness, not enough to stop the burning, but just enough for her to compose herself to answer questions.

With deadly truth.

A sheen of sweat beaded on her forehead, and she screamed in agony again as she watched. A shadow Priscilla crawled up in front of her, forming into a transparent figure over a shadow cauldron. A shade of Agatha and of Otho joined her.

"What did you tell the Loculus to do?" Thistlewinch's voice was thunderous. Shadow Priscilla leaned down and whispered softly to a gray version of the glass prison.

"To return to the Council and do my bidding." Priscilla didn't even try to stop the tears streaming down her face. The rivulets of them were a small relief from the pain.

"What did you intend it to do next?" Judge Thistlewinch peered at the shadow version of this afternoon.

"I would have transferred the command to the tribune." Goddesses, it was like dying. Like someone had poured corrosive acid in her chest and it was spreading outward, fire consuming every bit of her in pain.

"Who kidnapped Agatha Vanderbilt Voisin?" Thistlewinch glared at the shades.

The shadows whirled as the Loculus took Agatha and vanished, leaving the shadow of Otho pointing at shadow Priscilla.

"I don't know." Prissy smiled, despite the agony. "But when I find out, I'm going to make them suffer tremendously."

"Why were you looking at Agatha Vanderbilt Voisin?"

Agatha's outline reappeared, and Priscilla's turned toward it, leaning ever so slightly, feet pointed in Agatha's direction.

"Because I'm in love with her."

"Oop! Plot twist!" yelled Kevin, that asshole. Nancy elbowed him while Otho muttered something furious about his lack of decorum.

"Very well," he said, snapping his fingers. The shadows vanished. The other judges looked at him and nodded.

"You're clear to resume your role in the investigation, once that potion runs its course. Please report back to us as soon as you have any new information. Thank you all so much for your time."

Priscilla was going to say something, but the agony of the spell ran its course completely, and instead, she slumped to the side, not the first witch unconscious in the progression of today's events.

When she came to, Priscilla was in the break room, Nancy fanning at her face. Otho was bustling back in.

"Oh, thank goodness. Are you recovered?" Otho pulled at his bow tie.

Priscilla cracked her neck, stretching it from side to side. "I'll be sore, but I'll make it. We have to find the kidnapper."

Otho nodded, his face serious. "The first twenty-four hours are crucial. All available Council members will search, and the interns and assistants will hold down the fort here."

"Who will run things in Agatha's absence? If everyone is looking?"

"Kevin," said Otho, sighing. "We had no other choice." He leaned in conspiratorially. "I do fear he's too pretty to actually be able to run it."

"Uncle Otho," Nancy hissed. "We talked about this. You can't just say that."

"Very well." Otho straightened his jacket. "It's not ideal, but it should hold until we make some headway into where precisely we should be looking, since we have no trace, and the Loculus moves at something like twice the average of a high-speed train, so it could have gone very far by now."

"Agreed." Even as she said it, Priscilla had a fleeting thought that maybe they shouldn't be trusting an assistant with the oversight of the entire Council, but then again, she wanted to save Agatha as much as the next person. More.

"The other members have set off already, but I wanted to stay to tell you. We've split up directions and possible magic hot spots and other lists of places to visit, but since you and the president are so close . . ."

"Since you are in love with her," offered Nancy helpfully. Priscilla winced at the open admission of it, but she wasn't wrong.

"Right, since you are her paramour, we all agreed it best you start with places that Agatha might go, in case the assailant took her somewhere personal. Who better to know where she could be?"

Priscilla nodded grimly and sat up, aching everywhere, but not about to let that slow her down. "I'll find her, and whoever did this will rue the day," she said.

Kevin walked into the break room and gave a small double take.

"Yikes, you look worse for wear," he announced.

Fucking Kevin.

She ignored him and stomped out of the room, snapping her fingers to delay the pain of the inquisition as long as possible and making a mental list of all the places that she might check first.

CHAPTER 28

Priscilla

It had been nine hours since she'd woken up, after an evening of searching late into the night, and a final determination that she did actually need to sleep for a few hours to track Agatha effectively. Priscilla, after torture and hours of frantic, fruitless pursuit, had finally crashed, slept, and then resumed the search.

She'd been to Agatha's apartment, to all the shops on Main Street, to the grocer's down the road just in case that sparked any sliver of memory that might help.

For the past half hour, she'd tried sitting in Free Spirits, checking each bathroom, thinking back on everything that they'd talked about last time, trying not to agonize over the gripping fear that maybe she would never kiss Agatha again. Never touch her, never see her, never get another chance to discover the bits of her that made her shiver and whimper at the touch, or the jokes that made her smile despite herself.

That was the worst part, the not knowing. Was she already too late? Had Agatha already vanished completely? Would Priscilla have felt it in the universe, have known it if the woman was dead? Or what if Agatha was in mortal peril, minutes away from her fate, and a lack of trying, a lack of knowing well enough where Agatha could be, was keeping Priscilla from saving her just in time?

Not that it would necessarily help, if the abductor didn't care about any of that.

Priscilla remembered something her father had told her once. She was young, helping him with the case of a witch who had been abducted by a mundane who'd caught her off guard. The captor didn't know she was magical, but had bound her hands in a way that made her magic inaccessible. It had been scary, and Priscilla had been sad, and scared, and fretting about not finding the witch as well as what would happen if she, too, fell prey to the baser nature of humankind.

Benedict had told her, when the human police were helpless, and the Council's search seemed at a dead end, that witches were protected by a sense of magic threading through the universe. Not enough to stop bad things from happening, but enough that if they needed a little bit of luck, sometimes magic could tip the scales. He'd told her to be still, and know that better days are coming. Listen to the shadows and never be afraid.

It was why she had followed the hunch to begin with. It was why she was listing so desperately now, waiting in light and silence for even a trace of the smokelike wisps.

She'd heard her mother say it happened in love, that magic tipped the scales in a missed bus, a party someone didn't mean to attend but ended up going to anyway, one person happening to catch another person's eye in a crowded room. Someone showed up for an acquaintance's birthday on a whim, and bam, there it was, a soulmate. Someone happened to step in something awful and run late, missing the bus and waiting for the next one, and boom, a connection. Witches and mundanes alike could choose their destiny, but the universe could nudge them toward a good thing.

Or away from a bad one. Which is why Priscilla had to hope that if Agatha was abducted, if she was hidden, if she was in some way unable to practice magic, her magic would find a way to put her somewhere she could be helped. Somewhere, if not safe, then at least survivable.

And Priscilla was determined to find her.

The server circled back a third time to ask her if she was absolutely sure she didn't want to take advantage of any happy hour specials other than an appetizer she had barely touched. And there, at the edge of the menu, she saw it. Just a tiny tendril, a nudge. A shadow.

And it was then that she remembered. Hygge. A cozy cabin in the woods, with a flickering fire and all the amenities of a home, just sequestered away, tucked neatly into the corner of the forest somewhere. Endless time to read, or snuggle, or just be.

Glamping. Agatha's dream. If there was anywhere to find her, it would be in the woods. And suddenly, Priscilla felt as oblivious as a lamb walking into a slaughterhouse.

She needed to go into the woods, to see what it would be to live without the restraints of her modern life for a moment, just the way Agatha would have. She needed to trust that Agatha's magic would steer her somewhere safe, that if someone had bothered to take her rather than to try to kill her this time, the goal would not be murder, at least not right away. She needed to trust her magic and her instincts to carry her there. And if there was anyone who could point her in the right direction, it was Connie Witherspoon.

Priscilla ran out of there and back to the office so fast that she almost collided with Kevin, who was practically bouncing up the street, an impressive feat at six-foot-she-didn't-care inches tall.

"Priscilla," he said eagerly. "Any leads?"

She wasn't sure what made her do it, but she thought of her mother, who'd told her when in doubt, to hold a thing close until she was willing to say it with her whole chest. It was a whisper, a lingering memory of her mother, that made her hold tight to her suspicion. Just in case saying it out loud would curse her in some awful way.

"No, but I'm getting frantic. I have to go get in the car, maybe just start driving around randomly to see if anything looks off."

He nodded, a serious expression on his face. "Absolutely. Yeah." A sympathetic smile crept all the way up to his eyes. "It's tough when you want something and wanting it isn't enough to make it so."

Priscilla looked up, surprised. Kevin was the resident himbo. He was good at organizing, great at assisting, and terrible at common sense and human interactions. He didn't give out helpful little aphorisms.

When she cocked her head, he furrowed his eyebrows slightly, and she wanted to ask him something; she just wasn't sure what.

There would be time later.

For now, she had a fake-turned-real psychic to visit and a hearse to track down. Her habit of leaving the behemoth parked behind the tea shop was starting to come in handy, and before long, she was on the road, flying miles past the limit to make it to Madam Cleopatra's in record time. The benefit of the hearse was that other cars gave it a wide berth, for obvious reasons. No one ever fought her for a merging lane or a turn signal when she drove Uncle Larry's precious.

The door was open, and Connie stood there, waiting, face expectant. She looked at a watch with the sort of complicated dials that Prissy never understood.

"You're late," she said. "Come on in."

Priscilla followed.

Connie beckoned for her to sit, and she did, adjusting her weight on the worn bench seat.

The woman waved at the crystal ball on her table.

"I've been scrying all morning, and around noon I sensed that you would come see me. I have been waiting since then. What on earth took you so long?"

"I just figured out that it's a cabin. That Agatha is in a cabin." Priscilla's hands needed to do something; for the tenth time that day, she unspooled her braid and rebraided it nervously.

"Respectfully," said Connie, and Priscilla braced herself for it to be anything but, "of course she's in a fucking cabin. The question is which one. It's in Stowe, and I can almost see it. A-frame, brown paint, big windows like a pair of eyes on the front. Trees on either side and a stream behind it."

"So anywhere in a seventy-square-mile town. You don't have anything more than that for me to go off of?" A town name was good, better than searching all of Vermont, but that was still a large enough span of land, enough cabins and homes that she might not get to Agatha in time.

Connie shrugged. "I know it's an A-frame, and I can tell you all about the interior—crackling logs, stone hearth, very pretty—but that's it."

"Finding the right A-frame in a woodsy snow resort town with an abundance of cozy, cute cabins is going to be like finding a needle in a haystack." She yanked on her braid, lowering her hands to her lap and digging them into her pants.

"Ah well," said Connie. "At least it's not snowing!" She was already packing away the things and practically shoved Priscilla out the door.

Priscilla was not surprised at all, then, when the first few flakes fell as she made her way up the mountain, the hearse groaning at the incline. She snapped for good measure to reinforce the tires; devil damn her if those things had been replaced anytime in the past decade.

Azrael and Vickie had agreed to research vacation rentals in the area, cross-referencing together from the Hart Manor library, which Az had enchanted for optimal focus that day. He promised to text her a list of the most likely addresses as they went. And Vickie had a set of Agatha's favorite pens that she'd left at the dining room table. Without even being asked, every hour, on the hour, she touched it, and every hour she texted and reassured Priscilla that there was no ghost to summon. Her death powers would have, if they could. That group text chime was beginning to calm something in her, and it was entirely possible that she'd never be able to hear the little chirp of a message alert again without a sensation of overwhelming relief.

Agatha was alive. And Priscilla intended for her to stay that way.

The first A-frame was the third in a row on a road down a steep mountain, the last bit of it dirt alone until it turned to gravel driveways for each property. It was set between trees, beautiful and bucolic. She parked the hearse and got out.

A little dog barked, and soon enough she saw him, pressing up against the front window, paws low enough that it was just a small, fluffy snout of tan and brown hair staring out at her. As she drew closer, she could see his nose against the glass and the furious wave of his curly-haired tail, an overly eager welcome flag moving at double time.

She knocked on the door, and a tall, broad man in a ski cap and a sweater with little cartoon mice on sleds embroidered onto it opened it. He had a mustache, threaded a little with silver, and, inexplicably because his hair was dark brown, strands of red, and a-few-days-old stubble. The man didn't look like a kidnapper, but then again, who was she to say a kidnapper would look a certain way?

She was almost certain that this wasn't the cabin; behind him there was a dark-haired woman typing at a table who looked up from her laptop quizzically. Two young children shrieked and giggled over some sort of word search activity they were doing on the coffee table. One of them had, apparently, discovered BUTT, and they both thought this was funny enough to dissolve into peals of incomprehensible laughter. Priscilla thought of Evelyn, and the bittersweetness of that loss. It was better now, healing over by the determination that she could fight for the things she wanted. For the person she wanted now.

"What can I do for you?" the man asked, a cup of coffee in one hand, a half glance to the kids, and then back to her.

"I'm looking for a friend, but I think I have the wrong cabin." She was glad to see a slice of happiness in the world, but this wasn't where she would find Agatha.

"Oh," he said. "No problem. Is your friend okay?" His eyebrows were enormous; they crinkled in worry.

"I hope so," she said, cracking her knuckles and flexing her fingers. "Thanks anyway."

The woman at the laptop waved. "I hope you find your friend," she said, returning to whatever was on her screen that made her type so furiously, and then pausing to give the man a smile and a wink, which he returned.

"Butt cheek jiggle," shrieked one of the children. Priscilla was glad to live in a world where the people who found such things charming, or the very least, tolerable, had children, and then people who didn't could choose not to.

"Thank you," said Priscilla softly, stepping backward as the man closed the door to the chaos within.

The next few cabins were similar: a few clearly empty, unrented; a few with families in various states of disarray; and one with a group of college kids, alarmingly drunk for 7 p.m., but not appearing to have any intentions of going out, so she couldn't really fault them for it.

When she got to a little cabin with a sign that said THE SHIRE, she thought for sure this would be it. Other than the sign, it was not built like a hobbit hole; it looked like an A-frame that fit the description from Connie, same as the others.

A shiver of hope slipped down her spine, a hope she wanted to trust was magic, and not just the fact that there were no little dogs or any other giveaways that this was a family vacation.

She knocked on the door.

"Get that," shouted someone, sounding distressed, and Priscilla raised her fingers, poised to snap if needed.

A long-haired man with a shaggy, ill-trimmed beard answered the door. His eyes were haggard, and he was standing, arms crossed. Peeking from behind him was a brown-haired woman, eyes red from crying, still pretty in that slightly puffy, soul-crushing kind of way.

"What can I do for you?" He asked it as though the weight of the world was on his shoulders. He slouched, hunching forward, slicing a few inches off his still-imposing frame. She had interrupted something. What she saw in front of her made her glad that she hadn't swallowed her reservations and married Evelyn to save face.

It felt, once again, like coming up for water, realizing that she could trust her instincts for telling her when to run and when to dig in her heels and fight. The mixture of relief at the closure of her failed engagement and panic at the prospect that she might fail Agatha, too, if she wasn't quick enough warred in her chest.

"I'm looking for my friend," she began tentatively. This wasn't the cabin. The woman burst into tears. "Are you all right?" she offered awkwardly.

"No," said the woman, miserable. And then, to the man, "You said you wouldn't. You promised. You said you'd never." He shut his eyes.

"I didn't think I would," he said. Then, turning to Priscilla, "It's just us here."

"I'm fine," mumbled the woman. She returned to her crying, head in her hands, and the man just stood there, looking awkward.

"Good luck," she shot out nervously, turning and sprinting back to the hearse.

She was glad, once again, that she had found the courage to say what she wanted before it got to something like this. And terrified at the prospect that loving someone again, letting someone in, could potentially put her in the middle of a devastating breakup like this one day, but that fear had to be worth overcoming. She would find Agatha and take her chances.

Azrael's next suggestion was a ten-minute drive away, and as she approached it, she felt it in the air. This was it.

Her heart pounded. She rapped on the door.

"Coming," said a voice, muffled, but she knew that voice. She'd know that voice anywhere, the way it was mapped onto her brain and written in her veins now.

Agatha opened the door, wearing, of all things, jeans and a lavender plaid flannel. Priscilla froze; she'd never once in the entire time she'd known Agatha seen the woman wearing denim of any sort. The pastel was on brand, but in flannel? It was almost too much for her brain to process.

"Can I help you?" Agatha asked, just as Priscilla was about to dive in for a hug. She pivoted awkwardly, faking a stumble. There was nothing on Agatha's face to suggest she'd been kidnapped and was now found.

Her mouth dropped open, and she waited for the punch line. For Agatha to hug her. For Agatha to recognize her. For Agatha to pull her close and run her hand against the line of Priscilla's jaw. She worried for a moment that Agatha was angry with her, furious enough to stand there pretending not to know her, but the look on her face was puzzled. Quizzical.

"I'm sorry," said Agatha. "Who are you?"

Her breath caught, her brain whirring to catch up to the impossibility in front of her. Agatha did not know her at all.

They had stood in uncomfortable silence for too long, but the only thing to do, the only thing at all, was to introduce herself.

"I'm Priscilla," she offered awkwardly. Her blood ran cold. Had Agatha hit her head? Would she remember Priscilla eventually, or had Agatha been spelled to forget her entirely? What if the woman she finally knew she had all of these intense feelings for forgot everything, forgot her, just as she was about to figure her shit out? What if it was permanent?

Priscilla's chest tightened in fear, but she tried to keep her face impassive. It wouldn't help to frighten someone who didn't know her anymore, even if every cell in her body was screaming out in anguish that maybe she had flown too close to the sun. Maybe she had almost been too happy, finally figuring out what she wanted for her career and for herself. Maybe people didn't get to be happy in their jobs and in love. Maybe it was too much to ask from a universe stretched too thin.

Agatha stared at her, blue eyes unblinking for a few seconds and then narrowing, as though trying to sort through a complicated puzzle.

"I'm sorry, do I know you?" She stared, and Priscilla bit back the scream building in her throat, swallowing her emotions, the way she'd practiced for years. Agatha continued, "I have the strangest feeling that I do, but I just can't place you." Her lips curled into a smirk, eyes raking up and down Priscilla's body appreciatively. "I'll be honest. I wouldn't hate getting to know you. I don't really do this, but would you like to come in?"

CHAPTER 29

Agatha

The sound of a bird—a thrush, perhaps—had woken her halfway that morning. Gradually, she became aware of other things. A creek trickling steadily, the noise slipping through the window, which was cracked open, not too wide, just enough to let in sound.

Cool mountain air, and the soft whir of a fan above her. The feel of clean bedsheets, the pillow her face was partially buried into. The slat of sunlight streaming onto the white comforter when she opened her eyes halfway. The warm glow of the wood panels of the cabin when she opened them all the way, sat up, and yawned.

God, her head ached. Either her allergies were acting up offseason or she'd had more than the two glasses of wine she remembered drinking last night while putting the finishing touches on her research proposal.

She checked the clock. It was already past 9 a.m.

Fuck. She only had the cabin for another month, and if she didn't get this proposal done on time, there was a good chance the university wouldn't invite her back as an adjunct for the fall semester.

And if that happened, she'd be royally screwed. Subletting the room would only float her for so long. She had a few months' rent that could take her until the semester, but only if she had a job. Without that job, she'd have to take up waitressing or resort to running a foot fetish camgirl site.

She did have nice toes, so there was that at least.

She wished, not for the first time, that she could teach the sort of specialty electives she had loved so much as a student, but here she was, slogging along with her work on research, assisting the professor of Rhetorical Applications of Grammar. Which, sure, sounded like it could be fun for an English nerd like her, but ended up being a snooze fest at the hands of Dr. Ventura Calliope Hogglesbury, who apparently believed that putting undergraduate and graduate students alike to sleep was crucial to the study of grammatical argument.

It was not Agatha's favorite part of the job, but it was the only way she could get a foot in the door at the University of Havenwall.

And now, here she was, in the cabin for the rest of the month, determined to get done with this alarmingly boring research contribution. Then she could dress up her CV enough to convince them to keep her on again in the fall for as large a load as possible of English 101.

This was not how she'd seen her life going, and when she shut her eyes against the beautiful morning sunshine, she could almost imagine a life where she was powerful, successful, and going to work every day to do exciting things that she loved.

Maybe in that life, she'd have something other than a steady rotation of nice jeans and pastel flannels that at least set her apart from some of the other adjuncts in their colorful hue.

But no, in this one, here she was, in a cabin . . . somewhere.

That was odd. She'd certainly been here for what, at least a few days? And this was the cabin she always went to, wasn't it? And yet here she was, unable to think for one second about where the hell she might be.

The creek sounded familiar, and the bed felt right. The only thing uncanny was where she fit into it all. Maybe she really had hit the wine harder than she'd intended. She had a vague memory of watching TV and drinking, curled up on the couch by the fireplace, but she couldn't for the life of her remember when she'd gone to bed or what she'd been watching.

To calm herself, she remembered that leatherback turtles had survived every mass extinction, and that sea turtles had been swimming in the oceans for one hundred million years. Surely she could survive a few too many glasses of wine.

Agatha decided that this must be the work of an accidental hangover, and she reasoned that, schedule or not, she really could afford to take a few more hours of sleep. It would be nice if she had some sort of magic wand to wave, to make the feeling go away. But magic wasn't real, and she was an overworked and underpaid English professor, not a fairy princess.

Agatha shut her eyes and let the world fall away for a moment, hair against the pillowcase, lulled to sleep by the chirping of the birds and the tinkle of the stream cutting through the woods. It really was quite lovely here. Shaking herself awake, she couldn't put her finger on what she needed so badly to remember. It must be stress about her work.

So she got up, worked through breakfast and lunch with the desperation of someone who knew there was absolutely no way to catch up to her deadline completely, and yet wanted so much to try.

A knock at the front interrupted her train of thought, and she sighed, rubbing at the crease between her eyebrows and getting up to answer.

The woman at her door was an unexpected distraction, and not one she could really afford, having already let herself sleep in far too late.

But she couldn't even remember the last time she'd gotten laid. Agatha frowned. Come to think of it, she also couldn't remember the last time she'd gone out on a date. Or the name of her last boyfriend. Or girlfriend?

Goodness, this deadline was really crushing her brain.

Still, opportunity had come knocking, and who was she to turn down a tall, slender girl in a black cropped sweater that looked like it cost Agatha's monthly salary, tailored black pants that had to have been made specifically for her, and bright red nails and lips with the potential to be oh so beautiful and oh so cruel.

Agatha felt as though she knew this woman. For a moment, her brain misfired, and she almost called her Cherry, but the woman said her name was Priscilla. Perhaps that sense of trust and familiarity was just the intensity of the attraction. And perhaps that was why she threw caution to the wind and invited a complete stranger into her cabin.

"I'm Agatha. Would you like to come in?"

The woman eyed her carefully at the repeated invitation, brown eyes wide. She had a few little specks of amber—no, gold, it was gold—in her eyes, and the edges of them, just around the rims, were gold too. She'd never seen anything like that, or rather, for some reason, she felt like she *had*. Agatha blinked, trying to recall why those strange, enchanting eyes felt like home.

"Certainly," said the woman. Priscilla.

She followed Agatha in, and when Agatha went to close the door, and lean against it, Priscilla watched her, stalking back and forth across the room like some sort of dangerous, sleek jungle cat. Emotion warred on her face, and Agatha had the fleeting thought that maybe she should have asked a few more questions before letting a stranger into her personal space. Still, her body, and her intuition, said this woman was not a threat.

"You don't recognize me at all?" the woman finally said. Her features were tight with worry, her pouty mouth set in a line.

Agatha shook her head. "I feel like maybe I've seen you in passing. You do look familiar, but I can't place you, I'm sorry. The coffee shop on campus, maybe?"

Priscilla looked horrified. She tugged at her sleek black side braid. "Campus?"

"Yeah, where I work." Agatha frowned. Maybe not the coffee shop, then.

"You work . . ." Priscilla sounded as though this was incomprehensible, which was strange. A university adjunct wasn't the most glamorous job, but surely it wasn't shameful enough to provoke this kind of disbelief.

"At a college?" Agatha crossed her arms. She must really be a stranger, so it was odd that this Priscilla felt so familiar. She toyed with the idea of giving her a piece of her mind about how condescending it was to react that way to her job, but something stopped her. Maybe it was those killer cheekbones. Agatha decided she was willing to let it slide and see where this interaction could take her. For science. And research.

The other woman dragged a hand down her face, letting out a deep sigh.

"Listen," started Agatha, walking toward the woman carefully, noting the way she froze, the way her eyes tracked Agatha's movements, her body. "Maybe we could, you know. Get to know each other?" She raised her eyebrows suggestively. She was on deadline, for god's sake, and she didn't have time for a whole song and dance where she pretended she wanted anything other than to be as close to the mystery woman as possible. She couldn't explain it, but she didn't just want this woman. She trusted her implicitly. And besides, Priscilla was smoking hot.

Moving as if on instinct, which was wild, because she had literally just met this person, she reached for Priscilla's face, tracing a finger down the side of it. The other woman's skin was so soft. She couldn't *not* touch it. Priscilla caught her hand.

"Wait," she said, clutching the hand to her face, and then dropping it. "We do know each other."

Agatha frowned, then stepped back. Something familiar tugged at the edge of her mind, but she knew she would have remembered someone who made her feel like this. She might be scatterbrained at times, but it wasn't as though Agatha could forget an entire person.

"I'm sorry," she started.

The woman shook her head. "Can I just make a quick call?" She tugged miserably at her braid again.

This was odd behavior, to pace the living room and then

insist on pausing for a phone call. But upon quick analysis, Agatha determined that she could trust her feelings. Priscilla felt like home. She knew in her bones she could trust this woman. And besides, Priscilla was definitely hot enough to excuse that kind of crazy.

"Sure," she said, crossing her arms.

Priscilla pulled out a phone, tapped it, and raised it to her ear. "Az. Found her." The relief in her voice was palpable.

She couldn't hear the response from whoever Az was, but that reaction was a bit alarming. Maybe her face showed it, because Priscilla looked concerned, raised a hand, and continued. "I mean, I finally found the most beautiful woman in the world."

My brother, she mouthed.

That was definitely crazy behavior, calling her brother at this precise moment, but again. Those lips. The smooth strip of her stomach visible beneath the cropped sweater. Who was she to turn down a little bit of crazy?

Agatha bit her lip. Fine. The woman was still hot enough to allow it. She wasn't proud of that mental calculus, but there it was anyway.

"The thing is, if memory was an issue here, what kind of spell would fix it?" Priscilla spoke haltingly, as though she was choosing her words carefully.

She puzzled over that one. What could this woman possibly mean by *spell*? It couldn't be spelling and letters, and it didn't sound like she meant a fainting spell. She couldn't possibly mean a *magic* spell, unless . . .

Agatha whirled around, checking the corners. There was no one else here. No hidden cameras she could think of. She'd been renting this cabin for years, though she couldn't quite remember how many, and she'd never had any issues.

Still. Was she on some kind of reality television show, about to be punked?

Priscilla was nodding and listening, and then for a second, she looked like she was going to start snapping her fingers. She hung up the phone, stuck it in her pocket, and returned the full strength of her gaze, dizzyingly alluring, to Agatha. "Can I make some tea?"

"Sure," said Agatha. She might let this beautiful stranger do anything, foolish or not. Tea seemed pretty tame on the spectrum of possibilities.

Priscilla walked to the kitchen area, which was just around the corner, and then Agatha remembered that after a full day of work, she ought to back it all up and shut down the computer for the night. With any luck, she wouldn't want to pull the research out later. She hoped she'd be knuckles deep in a different sort of passion.

"Tea is in the cabinet, and there should be a kettle sitting on the stove," she yelled, making for the dining room table and her computer.

For a second, she didn't even recognize it, and she found herself staring at her laptop, wondering if she had the wrong one. Recognition slipped in front of her eyes, like a slide on a projector, and, probably from too many hours spent staring at the screen, her head began to ache.

She backed up the file, waiting the minute or two it took to upload to Dropbox properly, and then double-checked that she'd saved the latest version of it.

From the kitchen, she heard Priscilla bustling around, and then, inexplicably, the sound of the woman snapping, like she was performing some sort of offbeat song or had just remembered something important.

Agatha sighed. She'd always had a thing for a beautiful person who also happened to be strange and unusual. It was a real character flaw.

But Priscilla was emerging now with two steaming cups, her computer was away, and she took the cup passed to her, smiling at the fragrance of it. It smelled minty, and like something she didn't quite recognize.

"I'm sorry for being a little weird earlier," Priscilla said, smiling at her.

"That's fine. I get nervous around cute girls too." Agatha gave her what she hoped was a winning smile.

Priscilla cocked her head, an eyebrow raised. "I like your chutzpah. It's like you can't remember to be embarrassed about how you really feel. It's a good look."

Agatha grinned and took a sip of the tea. She frowned. It was inexplicably odd-tasting, and she also had the strongest sense that she absolutely had to keep drinking it.

She drained the cup, setting it down on the table.

"So," she started, but a wave of dizziness hit her, and she sat down, staring at the table, which was familiar and then not, and again up at Priscilla, familiar and then not.

And then the pain exploded, agonizing, a white-hot blinding flash of it, and the shadows fell from her eyes.

She was not a university researcher and adjunct professor.

She was not in a cabin she recognized.

And this was not an unfamiliar woman in front of her.

Shit.

This was not an unfamiliar *witch* in front of her.

The headache was awful, and suddenly she knew exactly why, in her befuddled state, she'd thought she was hungover.

Memory magic was like drinking for days, and that kind of spell, one to make her forget herself completely and think she was someone else, one well woven enough to keep her from getting too suspicious and realizing that she was all wrong, was enough to make her feel like a semitruck had slammed into her brain. She swallowed again, throat dry, and clutched at her head. Everything hurt, and she felt like she was dying.

Good goddess, she had thought she was a normie, with no magic or anything.

She looked down.

She was wearing *flannel*. If she weren't already in a chair, that alone would have been enough to get her to sit down.

"Agatha?" She looked up, and Priscilla was kneeling on the ground next to her chair, at eye level. "Do you know me, honey?"

She threw her arms around Prissy's neck, pulling her close, leaning in to press her lips against the other woman's.

"Wait," asked Priscilla. "Do you know who I am, or are you still just trying to get into my pants?"

Agatha stiffened. She blinked, the fuzzy memory of fake her going through the motions of trying to seduce Priscilla Hart.

"Oh no," she groaned. "Both, *chérie*, if I'm honest."

"It's fine," said Priscilla, smirking. "Both is good. You're cute when you've had your memory wiped and rewritten entirely. Can you tell me who you are?"

"Agatha Vanderbilt Voisin, NACoW president, old enough to feel a little bit foolish about this all, and young enough to hope that maybe you're willing to make some foolish decisions."

"There you are," said Prissy gently. "That's my girl." Her smile was slow and soft.

Agatha tried to stand, Priscilla following, but when she swayed and long arms caught her, she remembered just how agonizing coming down from the high of being spelled like that was.

The pain ached in her head, but her whole body felt wrong, like she was looking at the world through a fuzzy filter, like a camera lens that needed to be cleaned.

"It will get better with sleep," murmured Priscilla. "Come on. Let me get you in the car, and you can get some rest on the way."

"We have things to do," she protested as she climbed into the Packard, leaning into that lemon-mint scent as Prissy buckled her in anyway. "All I remember is being cracked in the head in the conference room, and I have no idea who took me, or what happened."

"Are you safe? Are you—does anything hurt?"

She shook her head. "I think I'm okay. I have no idea what happened to me, but I have a hunch that it's not about me as much as it is the Council. I think we may all be in grave danger. We should go straight to work."

"Running ragged when you're in no condition to do so won't

stop that," Priscilla said, and she did have a point. Agatha was so tired, and in so much pain, that there was no possible way she could be of any use like this.

"I guess they will be able to search based on what we know, and I can brief everyone tomorrow." She admitted it reluctantly, feeling the weight of truth like a blanket after more than twenty-four hours of deception.

"'I'll take care of it. Sleep, Agatha," said Priscilla. "We can do all the things in the morning." Priscilla's hands were in her hair, stroking gently, and then the car was in motion, the feel of it so soothing that some of the agony of the past day slipped away, lulling her toward slumber.

Usually, Agatha could never sleep with a to-do list like the one her brain was building, but goddess, she was tired. The memory magic and the curative tea were both exhausting, draining, and the little stream still trickled outside as they drove away, soothing, calming. She found herself drifting, swiftly on her way to being fast asleep.

CHAPTER 30

Agatha

She had a list of things to do immediately upon her return to the Council, and, thanks to Priscilla's incredible foresight, among other skills, she also had a planner and a set of pens in an assortment of bright colors.

But after she woke up groggy and then made a few phone calls halfway through the drive home, she hadn't been able to put pen to paper, even though it was impeccably beautiful college-ruled paper, and the pens were her favorite, the gel kind that wrote smoothly and crisply, capturing each turn of the tight cursive she preferred.

All she wanted to do was talk to Priscilla.

She looked over at Priscilla, who had one hand on the wheel and one fiddling with her long black braid, pulled over her right shoulder.

"Thanks again for the pens," she said.

"Of course," said Priscilla. "You know, Vickie has your favorite set. She was touching them every hour for me, to reassure me that she couldn't summon your ghost. So I'd know you were still alive."

"Oh, *chérie*. I'm sorry that you had to worry." Agatha had been thinking about that. "I don't think whoever captured me wanted me to die. I think they wanted me out of the way, hidden in plain sight. I think my magic helped influence where I ended up in a way that you could find me. I am beginning to suspect the spell was intended to make sure that I would have become an actual adjunct, forgotten I had powers, and drifted into mundane obscurity."

"That's terrifying," said Priscilla. "And I'm not sure what it means about the plans of whoever is behind this."

They drove in silence for a few minutes, and Agatha knew she should focus on the case, but focus was hard when she also wanted to talk about her feelings.

"I want to talk to you about us," she began.

Priscilla's eyes lit up, dancing in the Vermont starlight streaming through the windshield.

"I think we would be quite excellent," said Priscilla, waggling her eyebrows.

"Yes. Phenomenal. Mind-blowing. Literally magical." Agatha sighed, biting her lip at just the memory of the library.

"But?"

"No *but*." Agatha ran a hand through her hair, catching her fingers on a tangle, rubbing her thumb against her fingers to rectify the oversight. "No *but*. Just that I wanted to check in and make sure that's what you want."

"Don't make me pull this car over. You are exquisite," said Priscilla, emphasizing the last word lasciviously enough that Agatha squeezed her thighs together. "You're a fucking work of art, Agatha. A goddess divine. I don't just want. I need."

Heat flooded her cheeks. "You too," she managed weakly.

"Say more." Priscilla raised both hands to the wheel, steering them through a particularly sharp turn, and that made it easier, that her focus was on the road.

"I haven't done it before. With a woman. I know I can be a lot. Exacting. Overly dedicated to plans and scheduling. I know all of that about me. I just want to make sure that when we do it, if you have any feedback, you know that I take great notes. You can tell me."

"Agatha," Priscilla said softly. "The only feedback I will have is that I'd like to see you every morning for the rest of eternity.

My only notes are that I'll never go to bed alone without dreaming of you, that what I want instead is for you to be there, thinking of me too."

Agatha drew a sharp breath. "I already am. Always thinking of you."

It was big, this feeling between them, this thing that they had finally unveiled. She didn't quite have the wherewithal to talk out loud about how she felt.

She wanted to focus on what she could say.

"I think I'll have the imprint of your hands on my body for the rest of my life," she said, not quite believing that she had found the courage to say it. She had, in the past, been reserved, quiet about physical romance, not talking about it unless it was absolutely necessary for logistical purposes. Never like this. "I'd die to feel your fingers against mine, against all of me. Even looking at them now is agony, knowing what they're capable of. What you're capable of."

"Fuck, honey," said Priscilla, swerving a little, gripping the wheel with white knuckles. "You can't just say a thing like that and expect me not to pull over and make you mean it."

"We have places to be," said Agatha, grinning. "And I do mean it. You can make me show you just how much later. For now, we have a saboteur to catch. I want to rain my unbridled wrath down upon the person who has been messing with me for months." Her nostrils flared. Someone had kidnapped her and fucked with her memory. When she found out who, there would be heaven to pay.

"I love it when you talk dirty," said Priscilla.

Agatha laughed and returned to her list when they hit another set of curves.

She could get going again about the way it felt to have Priscilla Hart between her thighs, but she wanted to survive the day, and she suspected what she had to say might send them careening off the side of a mountain.

CHAPTER 31

Priscilla

She woke up next to Agatha, who she'd practically had to beg to get into bed and actually sleep. Memory spells were no joke, and only the promise of the morning could get the formidable woman to finally shut her eyes. So when the sunlight drifted through the blinds the house had conveniently opened in her room, for the first time that she could remember, she didn't find the glare of the morning so odious.

This morning, the brightness of the sun, even this early, was *beautiful*, but that might have been the spell woven by the goddess sleeping next to her, all soft blond hair mussed around her face, a slight ruffling snore fluttering adorably from her nose. Priscilla wanted to put her hands in that hair, to stroke it gently, but she also didn't want to wake her. Agatha needed the rest. Agatha needed those cute little sniffling snores sawing in and out as her chest rose and fell.

Priscilla was in so deep that even snoring seemed sexy, and that was saying something.

She really wasn't in the habit of staring at people and watching them sleep.

And yet here she was, willing and eager to watch the rise and fall of Agatha's chest beneath her velvety green comforter, which she had stayed on top of for some semblance of she didn't know what. Propriety? Consent? She wasn't sure, only that it had not seemed right at the time to climb under there with Agatha when she fell asleep. It had seemed so intimate, to lie in bed with someone under the same blanket, sharing breath and air and space, the occasional jostling of limbs a reminder that she was not alone in the universe or in bed.

The point was, Priscilla had found herself so much in her own head that she'd grabbed a crocheted blanket from the basket that Hart Manor had produced next to her bed, despite it most definitely not having been there earlier that day, and slept curled up under it.

And now here she was, staring at a beautiful woman, willing her to wake up.

Agatha blinked and looked at Prissy, gaze blurry.

"Morning," she said, groggy, a smile creeping up her face.

"Feeling better?" Priscilla would be willing to cut off another finger to make it so if she didn't.

"Mmm," said Agatha. "I do. I just have the most horrible taste in my mouth." She rubbed her thumb against her fingers. A mouth-cleaning spell. "Better," said Agatha, smiling fully now, with teeth.

Priscilla snapped, doing the same. Actually brushing teeth felt better than a magic scrub, but one of the benefits of being a witch was that she never had to choose between morning breath and getting up before she got to give her sweetheart a kiss.

"Can I kiss you?" breathed Priscilla, before she could think better of it.

"Please." Agatha looked at her with the same fierceness that she had without memory, and it twisted something in Priscilla's chest.

Her mouth was on Agatha's before she could even reach her hair with her hand, lips meeting gently and then more firm, insistent. Crushing. She wound her hand into Agatha's sleep-mussed hair, and pulled her face closer, capturing the little gasp Agatha let out, moving to suck on Agatha's bottom lip for a moment until she moaned, and Priscilla cherished that sound, wanted it emblazoned in her brain forever.

The comforter stretched between them, a barrier both chaste and obscene, moving with every roll of their hips and yet stretching, impenetrable, between them. Priscilla had loved that comforter, but she resented it now, for getting in between her and Agatha, even temporarily.

"Hi," said Agatha, pulling back. Her eyelids were heavy, her lips swollen from kissing. "I should contact the Council."

Prissy shook her head. "I already did. I spoke to Otho last night, and to Kevin this morning." She frowned, still not quite pleased with the amount of power this situation had dropped in Kevin Cross's lap.

"Kevin?" Agatha's eyebrows knitted together in confusion.

"Apparently, he did an excellent job running things smoothly while everyone searched, and was even disgruntled to give up the helm last night when people could return to take over for him." She still kind of hated that guy.

"He can be so fussy sometimes, really." Agatha rolled her eyes.

Priscilla shook her head. "Shh, honey. He doesn't exist here, not in this bed."

"No?"

"Nope." She tossed off the crocheted blanket and rolled toward the edge.

Agatha pulled the comforter up, waving it up and down gently.

"Step into my office."

She raised the blanket all the way, and Priscilla swore softly.

Agatha was wearing nothing underneath, not a stitch of clothing. Priscilla had put this woman to bed fully clothed, and here she was, unable to look away from any of it. The heavy pull of her breasts pressed together and against the mattress she lay on. She was on her side, and Priscilla could see the curly thatch of hair between her legs, the voluptuous mounds of her ass and her hips, and the soft curve of her belly. Agatha was infinitely beautiful. A study in softness, head propped up on her hand, curves that begged for her lips, her tongue, her nails.

"I fear I'm overdressed," said Priscilla wryly, and she snapped her fingers, evening the score and then slipping under the top sheet.

Agatha pulled it up above their heads, the sunlight dappling through the window.

It felt surreal, like she had woken up in a beautiful life that was not her own, and yet she was so extraordinarily lucky to be here, to be alive, and in this moment, with this person. Few people had the good sense to cherish a love like that in the time they had it, but Priscilla was determined to be one out of many.

She would never take Agatha Vanderbilt Voisin for granted. She knew better now than to assume anything, than to do anything other than be fully present in the moments that stretched between them, to live voraciously.

Agatha reached for her.

"You're beautiful," Agatha murmured quietly, and Priscilla watched her eyes wander, drinking her in. She traced a slow finger along Priscilla's collarbone, one and then the other, looking at her breasts and sucking in a breath.

"Can I touch you?" Agatha's voice was soft. Breathless.

"I will literally have to levy an official fine against you if you don't. Council policy, I'm afraid." She guided Agatha's hand to her chest, feeling her nipples tighten with expectation.

Groaning, Agatha slipped a palm around one breast, and then the other, cupping them, and then rolling her fingers gently over the nipples.

Priscilla keened a little bit, the sensation ripping through her. She could stay like this, Agatha handling her tits, for an eternity.

"I'm not sure what I'm doing," said Agatha, but she didn't stop. Her cheeks were flushed, and she rolled her fingers over and over, not dissimilarly to the way she cast her spells. There was a magic to a beautiful woman touching Priscilla, that was for sure.

"You're doing so well. Keep doing that." She dragged her

mouth back against Agatha's, throwing a leg over her thigh to pull her in closer. She felt every roll of Agatha's fingers both where they were, and between her thighs, and the sensation made her feverish with want.

"What if I do it wrong?" Agatha breathed heavy against Priscilla's ear.

"There's no wrong. And I can teach you. Remember the library? It's just like that, but we'll do it together."

"Okay," whispered Agatha, tweaking Prissy's nipple in a way that made her momentarily lose track of her ability to do any sort of explaining. "What do we do first?"

"Well," said Priscilla, skating her fingers across Agatha's tits, her stomach, the curve of her ass. "First, you tell me what you want."

"I—" Her breath hitched, color flooding her chest and cheeks.

"You can do it." Priscilla stroked her skin gently.

"I want you to put your fingers on me. In me." Agatha's cheeks flushed a deeper red, her mouth parted a little in anticipation.

"There you are," said Prissy, sweeping her fingers down the side of Agatha's leg, not quite where she had asked, but inching closer. "That wasn't so bad, was it?"

Shaking her head, Agatha whimpered. It was heating up under the blanket here, and Priscilla could feel the sweat beading lightly on her neck, but there was no breaking this moment. She needed to be here, sequestered in this room, under this comforter.

"What do you want?" whispered Agatha, her voice coming out throaty in a way that turned Priscilla's insides molten. "Tell me. Teach me."

"I want the same thing," she said, dragging Agatha's hand lower. She went gently, slowly, placing the hand on her stomach. "We can do whatever you're comfortable with. As much or as little as you like."

Agatha's blue eyes darkened, and her lips parted. "I want you to touch me the way you want me to touch you, and I want to stay here, under this blanket, with you, until I do what I've wanted to do, really, since the moment I saw you."

"Since the moment you saw me?" Priscilla paused a little in surprise, letting her hands fall still on Agatha's thighs.

"I wasn't admitting it to myself then, but yes. Since the moment I first saw you, on my first day on the Council. You were tearing into Humbert Ravenscrow for some sort of minor infraction. You were livid with him, so frigid, so sharp, practically snarling, and I just . . . some part of me wanted to take you apart, bit by bit. I want you untethered. Unleashed. Feral." Agatha's eyes were hooded, pupils blown wide with desire.

Priscilla slid her fingers between Agatha's folds, rubbing them along each side of her entrance, and then grazing them, ever so slightly, across her clit.

"I like to be teased a little, almost touched completely. Make me beg for it, Agatha." She continued the slow descent of her fingers, dipping two of them inside, just a shallow press, to feel how wet she was. She did to Agatha what she'd want done to her, and watched the other woman cant her hips, watched her blush for it. Savored it as the delicious longing, the need, crept up Agatha's face.

"Then I want you to circle." She ran her fingers around Agatha's clit, a repetitive, careful, slight pressure. "Go gentle at first, and then gradually harder, finding a rhythm." Agatha squirmed, pressing her thighs against Priscilla's hand.

"Can I," she gasped, her fingers edging closer to the parts of Priscilla most desperate for her touch.

"Fuck yes," said Priscilla, gasping a little as Agatha repeated the motion, shaky at first, and then growing more confident. It was so good to be touched like this, by her. She was teetering into it, like a baby deer on weak legs, sometimes pausing to feel what Priscilla was doing to her and mimicking it, but always enthusiastic, tongue pressed against the inside of her own cheek, gasping and moaning and doing her best to keep up. Looking at her face was enough to drive Prissy closer to release, feeling her tentative fingers grow more and more confident was enough to carve Agatha's name into her heart a thousand times over.

It was exquisite, being touched by someone trying so hard to please, to learn.

"I like to slide in shallow first," she whispered into Agatha's ear, slipping her fingers in, two of them, and Agatha moaned, hips jerking, her own fingers repeating the motion, adding a thumb at Priscilla's clit.

"Look at you adding in your own twist," she purred. "Such a good girl."

Agatha tightened around her fingers at that, and Priscilla pressed her thumb against Agatha, feeling the way she faltered, the way she was furiously finger-fucking and then she was still for a moment, still new enough to need that concentration to pause as her legs tensed, her body shook, and her eyes rolled back, pussy clenching around Priscilla's curling fingers, moaning a long-drawn-out, incomprehensible sound at the feel of it.

"That was . . ." She opened her eyes, moving her hand against Priscilla again, circling her clit slowly, and picking up speed. "That was incredible. Can I taste you?"

"Oh, fuck," said Priscilla, the words on Agatha's tongue and the feel of her nails rubbing ever so gently against Prissy's folds, enough to make her swollen and strung out with longing. "Fuck yes."

Agatha pushed her gently so that she was on her back, and crawled down.

"Can I take off the blanket so I can watch?"

Nodding, Agatha bit her lip and tossed it off herself.

She straddled Priscilla, breasts begging to be licked, and lost her focus for a moment as Priscilla gave them precisely what they were asking for.

Eventually, Priscilla watched Agatha remember her intentions. With the same fierce look of determination Priscilla knew from Council meetings, Agatha slid down Priscilla's body, pushing her legs up so they bent at the knees, and leaning down, face hovering an inch away from where Priscilla wanted her so desperately.

She was slick with desire, too desperate to think, but she didn't want Agatha to fret.

"I'll talk you through it," she managed, between gasps, but Agatha's quick fingers were already in her cunt and then around it and then her mouth hovered, breath hot, tongue swiping, tentative at first, and then more insistent, slipping in and then up, up, and around her clit.

"You can . . ." Priscilla meant to tell her she could vary it, do what she liked, go with what seemed like a good idea, but Agatha had started circling, slowly in one direction, and then swiftly, her fingers slipping in and curling, holding, until Priscilla couldn't help it: she rocked onto Agatha's hand and against her face.

"I can what?" Agatha breathed against her, the sound hitched and tortured.

"I don't remember. Just don't stop."

A smile curled up Agatha's face and she ducked back down, licking, circling for a few minutes, and then taking Priscilla's bud gently between her teeth and tugging in a move that had Priscilla so close. She backed off, sucking, and started moving her fingers slowly, and then quickly, keeping the pressure on her clit steady, and it was so good, each falter, each pause, even hotter for the knowledge that Agatha was determinedly pressing through her fear of the unknown, that she was licking her in a way that said she loved this and wanted it to last. There were a few fumbles, a few moments she reached to gently guide Agatha's hand or tug her head, each one of them filled with an almost unbearable sweetness. And then Priscilla was climbing, back arching off the bed, shuddering, and clenching against Agatha's fingers, coming against her face, relishing the look of smug satisfaction on it when she finally sat up, not removing her hand, still pumping in a shallow, torturous way, all the way through it.

"Fuck," said Priscilla, throwing her head back against the pillow.

"We did." Agatha's smile was so wide that Priscilla couldn't stand to be so far from it. She grabbed her face, pulled her back up her body, and kissed her. Hard. "You're a really good teacher," Agatha murmured before returning her lips to Priscilla's mouth.

Agatha tasted like Priscilla, and like all her wildest hopes and dreams.

By the time they'd made it into the office, grinning too enthusiastically at each other, Priscilla had practically forgotten her own name, let alone the pranks she had set up months earlier. So when the sparkler trap that she'd set months ago and completely forgotten about had gone off in the break room and singed Kevin's hair a few hours after they returned, Priscilla knew that the conversation with the Council was not going to be as easy as she had hoped.

"I know you didn't mean anything by it," said Agatha. She didn't look mad, just disappointed, and that was worse.

"I set this up months ago. I forgot it, I swear. I thought you were the only one who would touch the spare jar of orange marmalade. It's just not a great flavor." Priscilla made a face. No one in the office even liked orange marmalade other than Agatha, and how was Prissy to know that Kevin, in a fit of needing to be useful after relinquishing his temporary duties in the wake of Agatha's return, would try to deep clean and organize the break room pantry?

Kevin frowned, wiping a speck of the offending spread from his face. "I don't get paid enough to be burnt to a crisp and jammed."

"We can talk about a raise," said Agatha soothingly, and Kevin crossed his arms and sulked right out of the break room, muttering something unintelligible.

"Priscilla," Agatha started, warning in her voice.

"I forgot it was even there." Priscilla raised her hands in protest. "I swear, it has to be like six months old, maybe more."

"I know. It's fine. I get it. No more pranks, though." Agatha ran a hand over her face.

"I promise."

"Are there any others that we should know about?" Those blue eyes were sharp. Demanding.

Priscilla racked her brain. The problem was, she'd set up so many pranks, and Agatha hadn't always told her when they went off. There had been many a time over the past eight months that she didn't see it, but found out when she checked to see that the hex itself was gone.

She really didn't want to come clean about that—they had just had such a hot, beautiful morning—but she didn't think she had much of a choice.

"I'm not sure," she admitted. "I set up so many, and I didn't always know when they went off. I think you either hid or didn't notice the effects of some. Or they got someone else."

Agatha rubbed her fingers against her temple.

"We can talk about this after I debrief with Otho and Kevin. I need to loop in the mundane mayor, and then we need to talk pranks. This isn't great timing, what with an actual unknown criminal on the loose. I can't afford to have clowns popping out of closets and trip wires going off when I'm trying to solve an international magic incident."

"I would never stoop to clowns," said Priscilla, aghast. "And I'm sure it's normal pranking. Look. I'm sorry. I am. But can you honestly tell me you didn't set any pranks up for me that I haven't discovered? That you kept track of everything you set up?"

She knew as soon as she saw Agatha's frown that the answer there was yes.

Shit.

"I," said Agatha, drawing herself up to full height, "am the president of the North American Council of Witchery. I would not participate in business so messy as setting and forgetting hexes. I admit to a lack of maturity in going tit for tat when your pranks did land, but I certainly kept track of everything and was careful to make sure nothing interfered with any other Council members besides you."

Dread and guilt pooled in Priscilla's stomach. "I am sorry," she repeated.

"Just . . ." Agatha rubbed her temple again. "Just make a list of all of the pranks you've pulled, and all of the attempted arson and assassination, and see what's left that we should look out for, and if there are any patterns." Fuck. Priscilla wasn't actually sure she'd be able to remember every prank, but this seemed like a bad time to say so.

"Do you want me to come with you to talk to Mayor Khalil?"

"I do not," said Agatha, voice edged with frost. "Regardless of any other *things*, this is work."

It made Priscilla want to tear her hairs out one by one, but she returned to her desk to try to make a list of all the pranks she'd set up, growing increasingly embarrassed as the list went on, and she found herself truly unable to keep track of everything she had set into motion. And to tell the truth, when she looked at them altogether, the list was damning.

At the time, she'd thought she was just giving as good as she got, that this was a healthy, friendly, and yes, at times, flirty competition.

But she was beginning to suspect that she had, in fact, taken it too far. Especially if Agatha found out that she had been meeting with the mundane mayor on her own, well, that wouldn't be good. It was absolutely in the interest of magical-human diplomacy, and Agatha would eventually understand, she was sure.

And yet, looking at a growing list of pranks that involved light pyrotechnics, permanent markers, an ungodly quantity of baby oil, and—fine—a regrettable arrangement involving a colony of fire ants that she could not for the life of her remember where she'd rigged the hex to go off, she was beginning to feel like a petulant child.

Priscilla had been so sure that she was mature, that she was making clear decisions, that her penchant for pranking was just personality and not age.

And it wasn't exactly the pranking that was the problem; it was the impact. It was that she ought not to have taken her role in the Council for granted. She ought to have pulled her head out of her ass long enough to see that in all her fraught ambitions to be president, she wasn't even taking her job seriously enough to avoid childish antics.

She was a damn good Council member. But that was somewhat dampened by the fact that she was also acting out with a series of magical mishaps and mayhem to avoid the truth.

Sometimes, enough was enough, and the joking to avoid dealing with real feelings, particularly after breaking her engagement, might no longer be a healthy coping strategy.

Priscilla had braced herself for the kind of apology she needed to make to Agatha. She had practiced it in her head, reciting it, tweaking the words prettily until it was gracious and thoughtful, and conveyed exactly how much she had grown to appreciate Agatha, not just as a friend and lover, but as a fellow councilwoman. As the head of the Council.

The door to the conference room opened, and Priscilla's first instinct was to think that perhaps the room itself was cursed, for Agatha's face was thunderous. Kevin looked oddly smug, and Otho was wringing his hands the way he did when he was nervous.

"Priscilla." Agatha's hands were on her hips, her face stern. Her eyes were narrowed, and she swallowed, as though thinking hard on the next words out of her mouth. "Did you continue to meet with the mundane mayor in secret to talk about a potential crossover initiative to end Loculus use permanently in North America? Because I'm *certain* that you're aware that's a gross violation of what I asked you to do."

Shit. Shit. She'd forgotten about that, and she had meant to tell Agatha, because the mayor had such a good idea that would help support banning the Loculus, and pitch the concept that witches, instead of working so hard on the finicky portal magic, would overall benefit from high-speed rail lines and investment in universal infrastructure to reduce pollution and improve mass transit. The Loculus was a terrible idea based on the number of mundane sightings of it, spawning hundreds of conspiracy theories about the thing, and the portaling just didn't seem necessary when they ought to be looking toward bullet trains, community carpooling initiatives, and other options that would cut down on consumption and save the world that magical and nonmagical people alike lived in. He'd helped her put together an entire report, and the proposal for local trail revitalization and travel initiatives that would use the best of mundane technology to create jobs for witches and mundanes alike. It was going to be a surprise, but she could obviously see how it did not look good in this moment.

"Priscilla?" It was Otho this time. "Is this true?"

"Yes. But I can explain."

Otho sighed. "I'm afraid I'm going to have to recommend the president convene an emergency Council meeting. I'll need to reach through the proper channels for portaling approval, and then I will see everyone in the Council chambers in twenty minutes."

Priscilla turned to Agatha, waiting for her to shut it down.

But Agatha only nodded. "Approved. Call the meeting."

CHAPTER 32

Agatha

The tittering conversations inundated her from all sides at the Council room table, and her head ached. The past forty-eight hours had been a whirlwind of criminal activity, criminally hot activity, and now the potential criminality of her beloved. She had not even managed to say those three small words to this woman, and now she needed to formally reprimand her for undermining Council initiatives in what might actually be a fireable offense.

She was fucked.

"Order," Agatha yelled. She hadn't meant to yell, but it was fair to say that her temper was dancing a thinner line than usual. She'd had many showdowns with Priscilla Hart in these chambers, just none that had also involved her too-quickly-beating heart begging her to forget her duties as councilwoman and president and forgive the woman on account of that thing she did with her tongue.

Which was, obviously, not an option.

"I said come to order," she repeated, and whether it was the cold clip of her tone, the slight spark of unused magic flickering around her, or the flashing of her eyes, the room went so silent that she could hear the pen Kevin dropped. The monstera plant in the corner shuddered so loudly she could feel the breeze of its fronds waving.

"Oopsie daisy." He giggled, eyelashes fluttering, bending down to pick it back up. "Just getting ready to take minutes—carry on."

Agatha strongly considered magicking a portal into the floor so that she could fall onto it rather than deal with this.

She counted to ten in her head, listing facts to ground herself. Sea turtles laid about 115 eggs in each clutch, but only about one in one thousand sea turtles survived to adulthood. That meant every living sea turtle beat incredible odds, and so could Agatha.

She took another breath.

"Priscilla Guinevere Hart," she thundered.

"I see we're mad enough to use middle names," said Priscilla. At the look on Agatha's face, she added quickly, "Understandable. I would be too. If you'll only let me explain, maybe just to you."

"No. That's entirely inappropriate. Explain now. Here. In front of the entire Council. And no more ridiculous jokes or shenanigans." She frowned. This was not a time for personal affairs. This was a serious, whole-Council issue, and Priscilla needed to know it.

Priscilla's face went a little bit white, and she nodded. "I can do that. Tell me what you need from me."

Mathilda Alvarez looked over at Priscilla with her mouth hanging open slightly. They were friends, and Agatha knew in this moment that whatever she was to Priscilla, fake girlfriend in public, real lover in private, her friends were not aware of it. They had faked a relationship, and certainly Mathilda would have heard about it, but Prissy clearly hadn't talked to her about it.

This filled Agatha with a deep sense of hot shame. Priscilla's own friends did not see her as capable of bending to another person's needs. And here she was, thinking that they had real feelings.

But Priscilla *was* bending, showing her affection, her vulnerability here, in front of everyone, and Mattie's stricken expression was evidence enough of the marvel of that, and Agatha found herself wondering if it meant anything.

"Close your mouth, Councilwoman Alvarez. You look like a fish," said Otho.

She'd forgotten how prickly he could be when agitated.

"Councilman Ashbrooke, there is no need for insults. Let's keep this civil and as short as possible." She fixed him with a stare.

Otho's eyebrows knit together, but he nodded. "I promised Mayor Khalil that things will go smoothly, and they have been, just not precisely to the official plan." He shrugged, waving his hands as though it were a small inconvenience, and not a total violation of protocol.

"Be clear, Councilman: you mean that he's been meeting with Councilwoman Hart alone, and that she's been plotting with him." Agatha felt her voice go sharp again and didn't bother to hold it back.

"*Plotting* is such a strong word," Priscilla interjected, "and the connotation suggests something more sinister than the reality of the thing." Agatha shot her a glare that, surprisingly, stopped her right there.

Otho slammed a fist against the table. "We need to get to the bottom of this."

Xiomara Cohen nodded next to him, adjusting the collar of her dress. "I'd like the floor, President Vanderbilt Voisin."

Agatha nodded. "Go ahead."

"I'd like the record to show that part of the issue here is a general disrespect for the Council and its function. In addition to this gross violation, which I will get to in a moment, Councilwoman Hart has been hexing us all for her own amusement for too long. I'm very aware that it's perhaps part of whatever odd courtship the two of you have going on"—she paused, gesturing between Agatha and Priscilla—"but the fact of the matter is that you have only ever hexed Priscilla, and not in a way that has interfered with work. She's hexed all of us, and you, at times, in a way that interferes deeply. The times when an outside intruder may be behind it notwithstanding. For example, I do not particularly relish days in which visiting the archives provides me with a thousand tiny paper cuts that prick but don't bleed. That lasted for a full day, anytime I touched anything made of paper. I didn't want to make a big deal of it, but it was a big deal. It's been horrible to be in the cross fire. And none of us wanted to suffer through the time that the mini fridge was enchanted to smell like old tuna fish. This is unproductive, and distracting. Paired with the clandestine meetings with the mundane mayor, I do think we need to consider whether or not Ms. Hart is fit for this job. That's two strikes."

None of it, not a single word, was wrong. There was a reason, in the end, that she was president and Priscilla was not. She could both love Priscilla Hart and know that she wasn't the right fit for the job she'd vied for. But it shouldn't be up to her alone, and she was in charge because she was the sort of person who would put it to a vote and follow the results with fidelity, separate from her personal feelings. "Council?" She looked first at Hester Grimsby.

"I agree," said Hester softly. "We ought to give Councilwoman Hart a chance to explain herself, and to defend her actions, but it cannot be ignored. It's a pattern."

Next to her, Gemma Hexley nodded. "I do think we should take into consideration the details and motivation here. If Priscilla will tell us what she was doing with the mayor, perhaps we can come to a fair judgment about the validity of her secrecy."

"Noted," said Agatha. "Councilman Cumberbund?"

Devin startled a little from curling a blond tendril around his finger, and flashed a charming smile. "I mean, I was cross the day the bathroom enchanted the mirror to show us all on our most unflattering moment. There was significant emotional damage that day. I had to take sick leave to recover. But I am glad that unlike whoever was trying to kill the president, her hexes are at least not deadly. Points for not killing anyone.

Points off for the mirror trauma." Agatha resisted the urge to roll her eyes at Devin Cumberbund's unflappable shallowness.

Florian Akinde cleared their throat. "I didn't find the mirror prank too damaging, but the unsanctioned meetings concern me," they said. "How do we know the best interests of the magical community are being represented if our government operates in clandestine meetings? And I know we are all overworked, but I second the concern that we still have no leads on the prospective killer." It was true, but none of the traps had been triggered, and in the absence of pressing danger, the full docket of work continued.

"Councilwoman Nakayama?" Agatha turned to the old woman, who had been roused from a nap to attend.

"Hmm," said Mei, looking around. "I agree there is a pattern, and patterns give us important information." She fixed Priscilla with a stare. "I, too, should like to hear about what Priscilla Hart has been plotting with the mundane mayor before I make a decision."

"Well, Councilwoman?" Agatha turned to Priscilla. If she could only explain, maybe this could all be better. Simpler. Maybe Priscilla had good reason, and goddess willing she'd care enough to tell the truth now, after everything.

"I can't," said Priscilla faintly, pulling at the collar of the white shirt front under her black sweater. Agatha felt her heart drop to her stomach. Perhaps Prissy didn't care enough to come clean, after all, and wasn't that just a slap in the professional and personal face. "I'm sorry." Priscilla was actively looking down, maybe to ignore Albert Thistleworth adjusting his monocle and glaring at her.

"What do you mean, you can't?" Agatha thundered. This wasn't another joke, not another game. Why was Priscilla being so fucking immature? Why didn't she care enough about her job, or about Agatha, to cut it out?

"I mean," said Priscilla miserably, "I gave Mayor Khalil my word, on my honor, and on the Hart name, that I wouldn't share until we finalized. But I swear, on my same honor and name, that I am acting in the best interest of the Council. I'd like to prove myself, and ask for a week extension to wrap things up. I move that the Council reconvene at that point to determine if this is acceptable."

Agatha fixed her with a pointed stare, trying to decide if this was some sort of trap. If they could all expect to walk out of here suddenly coated in oil and goose down, or with the word *PENIS* scrawled in Sharpie across their foreheads.

She didn't think it was a prank. She shut her eyes, and thought about what she would do for any of the Council members. If it weren't Prissy. She didn't want to be too harsh or too lenient just because of her personal relationship.

Thoughtfulness. Her platform had been thoughtfulness. Other than the mudslinging, she had campaigned on the idea that she was old enough and wise enough to avoid knee-jerk reactions.

"I can approve a one-week time period, but only if the majority of Council members agree. Council, please adjourn for ten minutes to deliberate, and then return to vote." She snapped her fingers, and dividing walls went up around each of them.

She took a few minutes of the privacy to crack her knuckles and silently scream in frustration and hurt. Just because she wanted it to be fair didn't mean she didn't also want to wallop Priscilla for putting her in this position in the first place.

Priscilla knocked on the divider, the sound muted but the vibration enough to get her attention. Agatha sighed, rubbed her thumb across her fingers, and magicked the sound barrier down.

"Agatha, honey." Her voice sounded desperate, and Agatha was glad she couldn't see her clearly. Easier to stay strong.

"The time is not up." Agatha did not look up; it would be hard for Priscilla to see where she was looking through the opacity of the glass, but she didn't trust herself not to break.

"Let me talk to you," Priscilla begged. Agatha didn't dare look at the partition on her other side, where she thought maybe Eleanor Willoughby had opened her door to eavesdrop. *Let her do it*, Agatha thought. Priscilla could go ahead and get on her hands and knees in public and prostrate herself on the altar of love, and it still wouldn't change anything unless she was willing to also tell the truth—the *whole* truth.

"Later." Agatha's tone was firm enough that, though she could hear Priscilla's palm slap lightly against the divider, the other woman said nothing.

The vote was 7–6, enough to stay Priscilla's consequences for a week.

Agatha left the chamber with the awful hope that she had a good explanation, and the sinking feeling that even if it *was* a good one, it wouldn't be enough to move her to forgive the woman she loved for her betrayal.

In the elevator afterward, she found herself alone with Priscilla, possibly because the other Council members had scattered like dandelion seeds in the wind as soon as the meeting was concluded.

She didn't blame them; she wouldn't want to be caught in this cross fire anymore either.

"I have a good reason," Priscilla began.

Agatha held up a hand, shaking her head. "Please. Save it for the Council."

When the other woman looked stricken, she softened a little. "I don't want to hurt your feelings, Priscilla, but I have to be responsible. Presidential."

That might have been the worst thing to say, but if it was, Prissy's face didn't show it. Her eyebrows were still furrowed, worry written across her face.

"All right," she said quietly. "I understand. Can I ask you something, though?"

"I suppose."

"I realize I don't even know your middle name."

"That's not a question."

Priscilla stared at her, searching. "What is your middle name?"

"I don't have one," she bit out.

"Oh," said Priscilla. "Okay." She opened her mouth and then closed it again, swallowing back goddess knew what additional important secrets, but Agatha found herself too tired to press.

She didn't know what was worse, that Priscilla had lied by omission, or that she was being so responsible and mature about the consequences of it.

Agatha sighed, stabbing at the button for the lobby, and wishing she had something more than the promise of information in a week.

CHAPTER 33

Priscilla

For not the first time in her professional career, Priscilla Hart wondered whether it would be better to fall on her sword and preserve her honor or to discard the dreadfully uncomfortable thing.

She'd leaned on her honor to leave Evelyn the day of the wedding. It had been awful and embarrassing and ultimately, yes, freeing.

This was obviously not the same, but the honorable thing to do, despite Agatha's insistence that she tell, was to put a pause on everything: the romance she'd been denying for so long now, the truth about her covert activity with the mayor, and the need to tell her person all the things going on in her head. She needed to do this right, even if it took patience, and more waiting than she wanted.

Agatha, inexplicably, after months of disdain and rivalry, was her person. And, as it turned out, Priscilla wanted nothing more than to curl up next to her and tell her all her problems, have her help sort out what to do and how to do it.

But obviously that was impossible, because Agatha was the object of her affections and of all her complications. And it was true, she realized, the older she got, that just because someone was her person didn't mean that they were perfect. It didn't mean that they would never turn away, or fail to communicate something important, or hurt her without meaning to. People were complicated, and putting two of them together in any sort of relationship, even more so. She had to trust that Agatha would still be there when she had done what she needed to do. It was a risk, that trust, but then again, loving someone always was.

She looked up from the document she was typing in, lazily, at half speed, not bothering to magic off the extended acrylics she happened to be wearing for the task. She preferred it this way, selecting individual letters as needed, her speed slowed down by the clack of the crimson spears against the keyboard.

Kevin lingered outside the door to Agatha's office, leaning against the wooden frame in that manner of a man who thinks his doorway lean is enough to do something for a person.

Priscilla didn't want to eavesdrop, but she told herself that a bit of espionage was good for the soul, and made her way to the water cooler closer to the door, pretending to be very busy recalibrating the spout and straw attachment of a bottle.

"That's a very pretty dress," Kevin was saying, in a voice laced with intentions. She didn't look up to see Agatha's face, but she did note that Agatha didn't say anything, not even thank you.

Her fingers moved to snap—pants scorpions seemed so appropriate—but she remembered her promise to prove herself, which started with keeping pranking activities to recreational spaces, and not in the office. She flexed her fingers instead, and then busied them with filling the water bottle, and listening. As a little treat, she let herself look. She could always claim to have her eyes on the clock that hung above the door to the office.

"So, listen, Agatha, I'm guessing whatever weird little enemies-to-lovers fling you had with Hart is over now. I was wondering if, since I'm leaving my position as your assistant, you'd like to get a drink sometime. Or dinner." He flashed a megawatt smile. "I just respect you so much, and think we'd look cute together, is all."

Priscilla's heart dropped, and she wondered if maybe someone had pranked her, because it literally felt as though the disobedient organ had attempted to shrivel, crack, and exit her body.

"No," said Agatha coolly.

"Shucks. No to dinner? What about bowling?" Kevin's smile was lopsided and indulgent, and it took all of Priscilla's strength to prevent herself from marching over and attempting to smack it right off his stupid face. She was both proud of her newfound maturity, and infuriated by it; the sound alone would have been so satisfying.

"No, as in the weird little fling, which, by the way, is an offensive way to refer to your boss's relationship, is most certainly not over." Agatha paused. "And even if it were, I'm not interested in you for drinks, dinner, bowling, or anything else outside of official Council business."

Kevin's jaw dropped. "I saw that playing out differently in my head," he said, ruffling a hand through his hair. "Well then. Off to plan B, I suppose."

He turned, face still stunned, and walked back to his desk.

Priscilla couldn't help herself; she leaned over, just far enough to be in the line of sight of where Agatha sat at her desk, door open. She tilted her water bottle in the air, hoping that Agatha would take it as a toast to laying down the law and shutting down an arrogant himbo, but for some reason, that made Agatha blush a deep scarlet.

Agatha raised a hand to wave. She'd seen Priscilla standing there the whole time, maybe.

She waved back weakly and returned to her desk. If she couldn't catch the would-be killer, well, it was a close second best to watch Agatha shut down Kevin so thoroughly. And since there had been no evidence of additional attempts on Agatha's life, and not even so much as a trigger of any of the wards or alarms, she really couldn't make any more progress on catching the murderous and potentially immortal thief. Even Connie had hit a wall with prognostication, unable to tell them anything other than to be cautious. In the absence of any leads, it was time to sort out this business with the mundane mayor and start planning grand gestures.

Mayor Khalil rarely came into the Council building, which was disguised so that most mundanes thought it looked like a condemned building, and mundanes who might be delighted to explore such a thing thought it looked like a ritzy accountant's office.

So when he did arrive, in full mundane inquisitiveness, whirling around the place to observe it as though it didn't look very much like the inside of any typical government offices, the magical staff of the North American Council of Witchery very much gawked, some of them stopping to stare at this mundane, who looked exactly like them, only outside of the context of the places they typically interacted with the nonmagical.

Priscilla could have laughed at it all. The Witchery Council offices could have been a set for any office sitcom, and were certainly not worth gawking at. They didn't even have delivery dragons the way the international offices had, but people were strange, and sometimes even just knowing that there were things about another person they could not understand made them behave oddly.

Once he was ushered into the chambers along with the Council and staff, he seemed to relax a little.

"You know, it does look remarkably like the Council chambers for Hallowcross," he joked.

"Indeed it does," Priscilla said. "Magic and nonmagical, politicking tends to become boring and tedious. Important, though."

"Council members, please join me in welcoming Mayor Khalil of Hallowcross to the NACoW proceedings today. Mayor Khalil, we appreciate you joining us as a measure of good faith."

There was a smattering of applause at first, and then it became thunderous.

"Thank you so much for having me," said the mayor. "I wanted to thank the North American Council of Witchery for years of collaboration, particularly in my work, and my predecessor's work, with the Hart family. It has been such a comfort over the years to know that the magical world is working in tandem with my own, and to know that we share a common goal of safety, peace, and happiness here in Hallowcross and the great state of Vermont."

"Hear, hear," said Otho, tapping a champagne glass that he hadn't been holding a second ago. Across from her, Agatha shot him a disapproving look, and he made it vanish abashedly, as though he had just remembered the rule against alcoholic beverages on the Council floor.

"I think what the Council would very much like to know is what you have been working on with Councilwoman Hart, who has been very secretive about the plans." Agatha levied a stern look that made Priscilla wince a little, even though it wasn't directed at her.

"Ah yes. Thank you, President Vanderbilt Voisin. I appreciate Councilwoman Hart keeping her word to keep it all under wraps until I had it finalized. You see, I've been working with my contacts as well as our state representatives, and I just got the go-ahead for our two-pronged approach to travel and tourism initiatives."

"Go on," said Agatha, and Priscilla didn't dare look at her face. If it was still staring in stern disapproval, she'd have to simply lie down on the floor right here and die.

"So, at the state and local level, Priscilla and I have been working on an initiative to bring a high-speed railway stop to Havenwall. It's not quite in Hallowcross, but it's close enough to get to, and it makes sense to put it in by the university. It would be part of a larger Northeast Corridor railway system, and the implementation of the line would make travel smoother and more seamless than the portaling system I understand your international organization is struggling with. We'd like to pitch the recruitment of magical architects familiar with mundane construction in the development, and also request a Council grant since the rail line would benefit us all. Mundane and magical alike, I think we can agree that high-consumption travel modes like planes and traditional gasoline-powered cars simply must be replaced with more environmentally conscious alternatives."

Priscilla reminded herself to breathe as Agatha nodded along.

"A high-speed railway sounds like a lovely solution," she mused. "Obviously, it doesn't solve international travel issues, but connected with similar projects across North America, it could alleviate some of the stressors on the continent. It's something I've thought about a lot, actually."

"Priscilla mentioned that she found your notes on this when reviewing the docket on mundane-magical interactions." This was the tricky part, the part where Agatha could finally deduce what exactly Prissy had been messing with in her office the day of the horrendous pink lipstick prank.

"I didn't know you'd read them," said Agatha, and for a moment, not long enough for anyone who didn't know her and love her so thoroughly to catch, her presidential composure dropped, and Priscilla saw her. She was just Agatha, a woman Priscilla wanted to be better for.

"I read everything. I know I haven't always been what I needed to be, but I'm doing the work to be better now. I went back and caught up on everything that is interesting to you. I care about the projects." *And you*, Priscilla wanted to add, but it wasn't the time or the place. It hadn't been an evil sneak; it had been a supportive sneak. If she had to do it again, she'd ask directly, but she didn't regret the work she'd put into this initiative, not one bit.

"On to prong two," said Mayor Khalil excitedly. "The tourism and travel. Priscilla and I have been working with Constance Witherspoon, known professionally now as Madam Cleopatra, and by the way, thank you. We appreciate so much that there are no more awkward psychic outbursts to take care of. It turns out that Constance Witherspoon *loves* nature and will be spearheading a Hallowcross chapter of the Green Mountain Club, dedicated to maintaining hiking trails and cabins, organizing community volunteers, and promoting at least an occasional return to nature for both mundane and magical families alike. Starting with the campground where her psychic shop is located. She'll be rebranding as less of a caricature and more of a holistic psychic–slash–campground caretaker. It will be unusual, but we think it's the sort of crossover job that could help all parts of our community feel at ease. Priscilla?" He turned toward her, and she cleared her throat.

"Her unique perspective will help people and witches feel safe, providing a valuable service to the community," she began. "And I think this will cure the magical outbursts. It could be healing. Restorative. I think it's the kind of balance most of us could use," Priscilla finished.

Agatha smiled, and this time it reached her eyes. "Well, that sounds like you have been aligned with the Council goals after all."

"I'm happy to hear it," said Xiomara Cohen. "I was afraid you'd gone rogue."

"No," said Priscilla. "I mean, maybe, sort of, in keeping it secret. But I wanted to make sure that it could work first. And Mayor Khalil wasn't sure about the funding on the state level, and a few other approvals and red tape with the mundanes."

"In the future, we expect to be looped in," said Agatha sternly, but her eyes were relaxed. Priscilla thought that maybe she was happy about this, and hope curled, tender and tentative, in her chest. "We do need to vote as a Council, and Mayor Khalil, I apologize for any discomfort this may cause, we will each be divided into separate magical chambers for the ten-minute deliberation. Would it be all right to sequester you in one as well? It will be where you are, seated, with a table, only a barrier, sort of like a magical cubicle that is both soundproof and cannot be seen through. Light passes in, so it won't be dark. You will just be alone for ten minutes."

The mayor swallowed but nodded. "Certainly," he said.

"We meet back in ten minutes to vote." Agatha ran her thumb across her fingers, and goddess, had there ever been a mode of practicing magic so complementary to her own, but yet different enough to make it work? Priscilla was gutted by everything she loved about Agatha. Even their fingers belonged together.

But they needed to resolve the Council business first.

When they voted, it was unanimous, in favor of the initiatives and of reinstating full trust in her, with the caveat that she swore on her good name not to prank at work anymore.

CHAPTER 34

Agatha

The rest of the Council had gone home hours ago, and Priscilla was waiting for her. Before anything else, they needed to talk.

She wrapped up her notes on the minutes Kevin had taken, and she didn't need to look up to know that Prissy would be standing there.

"Hey," she said softly, raising her head.

Priscilla was staring at her, face stricken. "I need to tell you something, and I'm sorry if it's stupid." There was a bare honesty to her voice that didn't match her normally aloof exterior.

"You can tell me anything, *chérie*," she said, though her heart raced, and nerves twisted in her stomach.

"I— It's going to be sloppy. Emotional." Priscilla made a face. "But it's going to be true, so I am going to say it." She looked a little bit pale, and the anticipation was stressing Agatha to the brink of sanity.

Penguins mated for life, she reminded herself. And so did wolves, beavers, California mice, gibbons, shingleback lizards, and an odd aquatic parasite called a diplozoon paradoxum, a flatworm that literally needed to find its mate and become permanently conjoined in order to reach adulthood.

There, that steadied her nerves. She'd rather be a beaver than a worm, and there was probably a joke in there somewhere, or at least a T-shirt, but she'd be pushing up daisies before she admitted that particular thought right now.

"Whatever it is, just say it." She stood up, rubbing her palms against her red skirt.

"Agatha," Priscilla began, looking at her, gaze focused. "Honey." She paused, biting her lip and taking a breath. "I want to bend toward your love and your needs like a flower to the sun, not because I think I need to change for you, but because I know I want to grow with you, and toward you, intertwined into something that makes both of us better and stronger. Always." Her breath caught. It was beautiful. Breathtakingly so, in fact. She was certain it was the absolute most beautiful thing she'd ever heard.

Agatha leaned back against the desk. "Oh," she said, hand on her heart. *"Oh."*

"Say something other than that," said Priscilla. "Goddess, I meant to say I loved you and ask if you loved me, too, not just announce it like the daily fucking special. But it's true. I love you. I need you. I want to be with you, and around you, always. And I think you love me."

"I do." Agatha had never said anything more honest in her life. "I love you too."

"There's a lot to talk about," said Priscilla, shifting her weight from one heel to the other.

"It can wait." And suddenly, the rest of it really could. Agatha beckoned, and then Priscilla was in front of her, taking her head in her hands like it was the most precious treasure, cradling it, kissing her softly, peppering her mouth, her cheeks, and occasionally her forehead with the imprint of her lips.

It was divine.

"I don't want to rush," Agatha murmured.

Priscilla stopped kissing her, though she didn't remove her hands from Agatha's face. She drifted them down to her shoulders and around, pulling her in for a hug.

"We don't have to. We can pause the sex, and even the kissing, if you want. I'm happy to just hold your hand, or, fuck, even just sit next to you, Agatha. I'd sit quietly in the same room as you if you wanted me to. I want you to be happy. I want to give you what you need from me. I want to be me, but better. With you."

"Oh, I want to have sex," said Agatha, eyebrows raised. "Lots of it. Tons. Everywhere. What I meant was, can we go slow emotionally? I want to know what it is to love you fully in each stage. I don't want to run too fast into a thing and miss any second of what we're doing."

"My love," said Priscilla. "Goddess divine." She stroked up Agatha's arm and pushed a lock of hair behind her ear. "My sweet. I would like nothing more than that."

"Good. Now let's get out of here. I need to sleep in my own bed." It had been hard leaving Hart Manor, and part of her knew that one day, she would want to stay there for good. Another part of her, though, wanted to take this slow. To do things right. And that meant spending time on her own too.

There was no relationship that should be the sole source of Agatha's happiness. That wouldn't be fair, and it wouldn't be balanced, and if there was one thing an extremely organized Council president knew, it was that fairness and balance were crucial in everything.

"I'll walk you home and then head back to mine." Priscilla stroked her hair again, and Agatha didn't hide the way she leaned into it, the feeling of those long, dexterous fingers against her scalp.

"What if I want you to stay?" she whispered. *Forever*, she thought, but that part could wait—or it should wait, anyway. Just because she'd taken her own space didn't mean she didn't want Priscilla to sometimes be in that space too.

Priscilla kissed her forehead. "If you want me to, I'll stay for as long as you like. Forever."

"Let me just pack up."

Agatha gathered her things and switched off the light with a slip of her fingers. Priscilla snapped, and the chairs all pushed in neatly, the main office area of the Council tidy and precise.

They walked out, hands intertwined, and headed toward Agatha's apartment building.

In the sky, the sun set prettily into orange and pink, and Agatha had a feeling like her entire life had been building to this moment, if she could only be open enough to really see it for what it was, to appreciate every second and soak it up, turn it over in her mind and know that whatever came next, whatever happened, Priscilla would be there.

She could trust Priscilla, she realized. For all the pranking and animosity, they had turned something contentious into something kind, and something fake into something real. She wanted nothing more than to be grateful for every second of it, even if one day one of them died, or the planet spiraled into the sun, or some other twist of fate wrenched them apart. Any future suffering was worth the beauty of the way they loved each other right here, right now.

"I want to take an evening to think about what it means that all of this pretending has turned into something real," Agatha said softly.

Priscilla bumped her shoulder, not dropping her hand. "Anything you want. And I, uh, have a question for you too."

"Anything," Agatha echoed.

"You can say no, but I wanted to know if you'd be willing to be my date for Az and Vickie's wedding. I've been reluctant to ask because, well, obviously weddings historically have been so shitty for both of us. I'm the best woman, so it's a big ask; I have a lot of responsibility. And I know you're already on the guest list, and that you've already RSVPed, just you. I wasn't stalking you, I swear. I was helping Az with seating charts."

"It would be an honor to be stalked by you," said Agatha, grinning. "Besides, it's not stalking if you want the person to be checking up on what you're up to. Then it's just cute."

Priscilla laughed. "Is that a yes?"

"It's an *I'd love to.*" They kissed again, once, just a soft peck outside the main entrance to Agatha's building, and even in that tiny moment, there lived more affection and romance than Agatha had dared to dream of before.

CHAPTER 35

Priscilla

The two weeks leading up to her brother's wedding should have filled her with dread. She'd worried, before, that her own past would make her unable to wholly celebrate Azrael's future. After all, the last time she'd arranged such a thing, it had ended in literal flames and agony.

But Azrael and Vickie were different, the kind of destined to be together that made her believe in love. Among other things, that is, because Prissy was starting to feel that maybe she could be different too. Maybe Agatha was different. The past did define her somewhat, as it did every person, but she got to choose the future. She could choose to work, to be better, and more mature, and more honest this time around.

Some time ago, her brother's fiancée had asked her if she'd ever set a soul seal upon her heart, and do the magic spell that bound two creatures together stronger than human wedding vows might do. It had been when she was with Evelyn. And though she had loved Evie, she now knew what it was to love someone so completely that she wanted their souls to be intertwined eternally one day.

She'd said no back then. But it turned out *no* hadn't been *never*. It had just been inconceivable because she hadn't found the right person to help her conceptualize how beautiful forever could be.

So instead of panicking, she'd spent the weeks arranging flowers and arguing with Uncle Larry about the appropriateness of Jell-O shots at a formal event. She'd seen Agatha every day, either at work or at her place, or sometimes at Hart Manor. And when the day finally came, she and Agatha drove together, with Vickie, to the historic Vermont home that she and Az would be married in, outside, in front of a crowd of their closest friends and family.

Amelie and Maximillian Starnberger had declined their invitation, which Priscilla personally thought was for the best. She doubted Vickie wanted those assholes there, but she understood why she might ask them, anyway. A wedding was a perfect occasion to believe that someone, somewhere, could forgive, if they needed to. Just maybe not Victoria's snotty parents.

She carried Vickie's dress, a simple, long-sleeved lace thing, up the stairs, holding it in front of her to avoid mishap or the need for magic, which would certainly cause problems. This was a mundane venue, and though she thought she had spotted at least one shifter on the catering staff, and she knew for a fact that the events manager was a Harpy, there was a significant need to avoid magic.

Which is actually how Vickie and Az requested it to be. They had done the magic, set the soul seal, and were eternally bound. This ceremony and reception were about celebrating and commemorating that, about making it public to everyone, mundane and magical alike.

It was the beginning of a beautiful partnership.

"I can't believe we are actually doing this," said Vickie, and Prissy smiled.

"I mean, you've actually done a much more serious ceremony already." She was about to mention the soul seal but remembered herself in time.

Agatha shot her a look over the wedding coordinator's head, which was silly, because, again, Harpy. But maybe prudence was a good idea given the rest of the staff was mostly nonmagical.

"It's just really exciting." Vickie ran a finger along the banister at the top of the stairs. "And this place is so beautiful."

"You're going to make a beautiful bride," said Agatha.

"Let us know now if you're going to make a break for it, though. And maybe don't run in heels." Priscilla was serious about that one; she knew firsthand that a getaway in Louboutins was not for the faint of heart.

Vickie threw her a look and laughed. "No chance of that, but I appreciate the tip."

She held up the sparkly pair of Chuck Taylors that Priscilla had desperately tried to talk her out of. "No one will see them under the dress, and my feet will be comfortable the whole time. Plus, I like to look up at Az and remember how tall he is, and how much I'm into that." She nibbled her bottom lip.

"Gross," said Priscilla, pantomiming throwing up. "Happy for you, but that's my brother. The only use for his height from my perspective is setting up a good guillotine prank that will definitely get him and not me if we're walking together."

"Try not to decapitate my groom," said Vickie drily.

"Of course not!" Priscilla put a hand to her chest. "Always just enough off the top of his hair to piss him off about a short haircut. It's no fun pranking someone if they're already dead."

"Come along, ladies," said the wedding planner. "I have champagne set up in the changing room."

They'd gotten Vickie into the dress, and toasted to a good life and happiness for the couple, and before they knew it, Hank from the tea shop was knocking on the door, clad in a charming little cape-and-suit outfit that looked like it could have come straight off Nathan Lane in *The Birdcage*.

"Thanks for walking me, Hank," said Vickie, and Hank nodded. If she was sad that her own parents wouldn't be there, by their own choice, she didn't say so. And maybe it was better this way: Vickie choosing family who would be there for her the way the Starnbergers never had been.

"It's my pleasure." He smiled widely and gestured for Priscilla and Agatha to go ahead.

Uncle Larry had offered, too, but Priscilla thought privately that Hank was a much better choice. Less likely to hit on the bridesmaids, and that was a good thing, too, since the only bridesmaid not related to her was Agatha. Her girlfriend had been upgraded from guest to a member of the party so fast it had almost given Priscilla whiplash.

The thing about Victoria Starnberger was that she loved love, and so she had almost cried when Prissy told her that she and Agatha were serious and would be attending the wedding together. She'd half expected the woman to ask Agatha to move into Hart Manor with them all on the spot. And one day, when they were ready, she'd like that. Living in Hart Manor with her beloved and her brother and his wife, defying expectations about family units in a house. The manor itself was as much a part of her family as her brother was, and she couldn't imagine ever leaving either.

She was no Uncle Larry, after all, hell-bent on finding strange ass in a retirement community full of it. Good for him, but she'd take her house and her girlfriend.

The ceremony was a lovely, short thing, and the reception was full of delicious food and dancing, though it was all kept relatively simple. There was pie for dessert instead of cake, and it came in more varieties than Prissy could have imagined, each one more delicious than the previous. There was something equally pleasing in the simplicity of Az pressing play on a playlist for the reception instead of having a DJ or live band. Nothing like the elaborate event with hundreds of people that Evelyn had envisioned.

Priscilla sat a circular table next to Agatha, watching Az and Vickie in their first dance, and all she could think of was that this thing, this way of doing it, didn't seem half-bad.

"I think I'd get married someday," said Prissy lazily, without even thinking about the implications of saying it to the woman she was seeing. Or maybe, she thought, thinking exactly of the implications. She meant what she had said.

"Yeah," said Agatha. "Not at this moment, but one day. This

has been a beautiful day, but I'd love to have a moment to unpack my emotions for myself tonight."

"Certainly," said Priscilla. She'd learned that Agatha both enjoyed and required solitude. At first her instinct had been to demand the time and space, but that felt wrong. She had been nervous that the space meant a lack of interest, but she had reminded herself that feelings were not facts, and taken time to listen. Agatha told her that it was part of recharging, spending some time on her own. And in the end, it wasn't relieving to fixate on her anxieties. What felt better was to listen to the person she loved.

"I'll call you tomorrow," Agatha said. "But for now, would you like to dance?"

She was about to get up and show Agatha Vanderbilt Voisin what an incredibly talented dancer she was, but Priscilla paused at something out of the corner of her eye.

A puff of purple, glittery smoke.

"Lex," said Agatha, meeting Priscilla's eye. "Rain check on that dance, then. Come on, let's make sure he doesn't wreck anything."

"He was invited, believe it or not. I don't think he ever sent back in his RSVP card, though." Vickie and Az had had a heaven of a time trying to figure out how to reach him to check whether or not he'd be here.

Lex was leaning against a pillar at the outskirts of the room, making himself as nondescript as possible, typically glittering purple smoke almost clear, and only visible to a trained magical eye. Devils had this way of appearing around mundanes so that they seemed like slightly more than human, but not enough to raise suspicion. Pretty, shiny bait, setting a trap for bargains.

She walked over to him, his arms folded over the dark purple suit that matched Agatha's corset-top flutter-sleeved gown.

"Priscilla Hart, I must say, I love that color on you." He waved a hand, and a flick of purple magic flashed, there and gone again in a moment.

"Come now, Lex. You can't expect us to believe you showed up just to compliment my outfit." She eyed him suspiciously, though she was beginning to trust that he had actually turned over a new leaf in pursuit of being a better devil.

"I'm here to congratulate the happy couple, as I believe is human custom for a wedding, no?" He picked a nonexistent bit of lint off his dapper tuxedo jacket before blowing at a flop of curly hair that had fallen over his eye.

That hair was getting a bit longer, and she wondered what that was about.

"Fine," he relented, without even any further prodding. "I need to warn you about something."

"Go on," said Agatha, a glint in her eye. "Is it about the Fountain of Youth elixir?"

"Bravo! I can see why they made you president." He eyed Priscilla. "No offense intended."

"None taken," said Priscilla dryly. "She's a far better president than I would ever make."

Agatha blushed, smiling at her. And for a second, Priscilla forgot the devil and his distractions.

"Focus, ladies!" Lex frowned. "I'm trying to make amends here. And since Vickie and Azrael don't need me, I'm going to help you."

"Why would you do that?" Priscilla narrowed her eyes at him.

He sighed. "Let's just say I've made a very unusual bargain with a human who is insisting that I rethink some things. She's very persuasive. And part of what makes humans so human, I guess, is their ability to change. So I am going to be helpful." He said that last word like it pained him a little, and she had to resist the urge to laugh.

She, mouthed Agatha to Priscilla, and Lex glared.

"Help us, then."

He dragged a hand over his face. "I don't know who, but someone close to you, close to the Council, is immortal."

"Yes, we figured that."

"It's someone with magic."

"Also figured that. Do you have any information we don't know?"

"I'm not a bloody mind reader! You'd need your Madam Cleopatra for that."

"That," said Agatha, "is a really good idea."

"See?" Lex preened. "Helpful."

"It's so good an idea that we have obviously already tried it. She can't see who it is, and if she did figure it out, she'd tell us right away."

"Dammit," said Lex. "This is why I don't bother helping people. I'm sorry, but that's all I've got. Unless you'd like to know how to deal with the person once you've caught them. That I can advise on."

"What the fuck?" said Priscilla. "Obviously, we want to know that."

Lex sniffed. "If you're going to be prickly, I don't have to be helpful. I'm trying to do a good thing here, thank you very much."

"It's all right," said Agatha, patting him on the arm. "We appreciate you."

The devil examined his fingernails for a moment.

"Well, the only thing to do is to separate the body parts and store them in secure magical locations far enough apart that they can't get back together on their own."

"Separate the body parts?" Priscilla had a horrible flashback to the unfortunate incident with the chainsaw in the greenhouse, and the memory of the loss of the top of her left pinky made her shudder.

"Of course!" exclaimed Agatha. "That all makes sense now. I read an odd footnote recommending storage of immortal body parts in the *Compendium of Forbidden Magics*, volume three, chapter fourteen, and I just assumed it was some sort of weird kink, but it is actual instructions. Brilliant."

"It can be a weird kink *and* instructive," said Lex petulantly, but Priscilla ignored him.

"How do you recommend we separate them?"

He shrugged. "How should I know? I've actually never dismembered an immortal, believe it or not." He waggled his eyebrows. "Everything I do with members leaves them very much attached, I guarantee."

Prissy gagged a little.

"Focus," said Agatha. "Anything else you can tell us?"

"Well, it won't be gory. Blood isn't an issue anymore for the immortal. Frozen, you see, magically stilled. Like cutting off the head of a doll, except it will give you much more sass than any toy, even a haunted one, would manage. The sort of people seeking immortality are never terribly pleasant."

He adjusted his suit jacket, sighing. "I suppose since it's clear that Azrael and Vickie don't want me to join them, and you two have all the information I know about immortality, I'll vanish into the night, as one does."

In a flourish of perfumed smoke, he did just that.

"Well, that's all we're getting from him," she muttered, frowning.

"We can try Madam Cleopatra again another day," Agatha offered.

"Right. Tonight is for celebrating."

"Hey," said Agatha. "Tomorrow, after I've had some time, can I pick you up from your place and take you with me to the cabin?"

Agatha had rented the little cabin she'd been kidnapped to, now that she'd had time to set up the proper precautions. She said it was a Council expense, and insisted that they keep it on retainer until the perpetrator was caught. It had been warded and guarded to the fullest extent of the Council's ability, and yet nothing had been triggered since. Agatha had said she had this hunch that something about that cabin could lead them to unravel the final strand of the mystery. Plus, the cabin had a truly epic bathroom that Agatha kept sending Priscilla pictures of, and Priscilla, personally, had a hunch that she could make Agatha scream her name five different ways in that tub.

Priscilla did not hate the idea of fucking Agatha Vanderbilt

Voisin in a claw-foot tub, not one little bit. Her hair piled on top of her head, sweat gathering sweetly on her skin. Goddess, she was divine. A work of art, but one that Prissy wanted to touch, to sink her teeth into. They didn't let her do things like that at museums, and once, as a kid, she had tried.

"I'd like nothing more," she said, thinking of what she could do with candles and bubbles in a fancy glamping bathroom. "Now, put a pin in all the business, honey, and let's see about that dance."

It was nice, really, to have a moment of rest. She would take a few days away from stressing about the Council and the ominous quiet of the would-be murderer, and come back refreshed and ready to solve the case.

CHAPTER 36

Priscilla

When Agatha didn't show up at 8 p.m. sharp, Priscilla worried. Agatha loved punctuality and schedules. She told herself that perhaps she'd got caught up in something, some sort of home project. She was always doing things like deep cleaning cabinets and organizing her filing system, the sort of undertakings Priscilla largely avoided.

Agatha found it comforting, which Priscilla sort of understood. The Benedict Hart cleanup method had always been to fetch the broom by magic but do the sweeping by hand, and it was a good one. Even if Priscilla was, at times, reluctant about putting it into practice.

It was this thought that led her to the library by 8:25, when Agatha also wasn't replying to her text messages in a way that made her feel terribly reassured.

Priscilla: Are you on your way?
Agatha: Srry, at the cabin. Will call later.

She frowned. It wasn't like Agatha to skip letters, but perhaps she was lost in paperwork. She did get lost in mountains of that from time to time. Priscilla figured that she would wait a little while and then call, and to pass the time, she did something that thinking of her father and his advice made her do.

She went to the library to find the Hart family grimoire, the book imbued with the magic and wisdom of generations of Harts.

She raised her hand and snapped her fingers. Books fluttered out of the way, the sound of rustling seeping from the top floor down, and from the place where it hid, the grimoire skimmed through the air and into her waiting hands. The worn leather cover was aged, and had been handled by so many Harts, but it felt like pressing her hand against something shiny and new when she touched it. It felt like hers, and Azrael's, of course—bone magic passed through bloodlines, born and chosen, and also through grimoires.

This heavy brown tome with the anatomically correct heart with magic eyes and runes encircling it bore the magic of every Hart before her. When a witch died a death not inflicted by their heir—to prevent murders for magic—their powers slipped into a grimoire. This one held not just Benedict and Persephone, but every Hart who had come before her father, and all their partners, all their people, all the love from years and decades and centuries of Hart witches. The patterned leaves on the binding looked like they could be alive, and the heart was so vivid in her mind that she often felt it was beating.

Only a Hart witch could summon this grimoire in this library, and the pages flipped with ease. She felt her parents in these pages, and saw them too: it was tradition for Harts to leave footnotes.

When they had died, she'd felt it, like suddenly stepping out into the sun, her body imbued with extra warmth once, and then a second time. The power passing through them to her, and into this sacred book. And something, at the corner of her eye, hard to even catch, something in the shadows, beckoned, and she knew she needed to check the book. That this was important.

She found the page for spells for patience and her father's footnote underneath. The one she thought she had remembered, and knew she needed now.

When you love someone, you give them the time they need. And you tell them directly that this is what you're doing: giving them time, giving them space. You tell them to their face that you're doing it, and you don't leave room for doubt or worries to sow their seeds. There's a reason miscommunication is such a popular idea in books and movies; it's so very human. And witches, we are human too. Mostly.

Priscilla knew then what she needed to do. She did love Agatha. She'd known it for a while, but now she knew it enough to trust it. She wanted to follow that trust into the rest of her life with this woman, and now that she knew that with certainty, she wanted the rest of her life to start right away. Priscilla sent the grimoire back to wherever it hid between other books, and she strode out of the library, down the hall and the staircase, and through the foyer to grab her keys.

The entire drive there, she practiced in her head what she would do. Find Agatha. Tell her that she would give her time. Leave respectfully if Agatha wanted it, but also, if she didn't want it, take her in her arms, kiss her passionately, and carry her up the stairs. Tell her every way she could think of all the secret and not-so-secret affections and longings of her heart.

When she arrived at the cabin, the lights were on, and that made her heart hum with relief. Agatha was still here. She'd probably have a good reason for running late, and Priscilla could tell her that if space was what she needed, space was what she could have.

She snapped her fingers to unlock the door, figuring what she had to say was important, and that she wouldn't actually go anywhere private without permission, so it would be all right to walk in and make an impression.

The cabin smelled like pinewood, and a crackling fire rose out of the grate, but the coziness seemed off, somehow. She walked up to the loft carefully, rounding the corner to the second-floor landing that looked out over the first floor.

Normally, she would have been happy to see the charming nook with a desk in the corner, but the feeling was overshadowed by the sight of Agatha herself, tied to a kitchen chair, hands in fingered gloves to keep her from doing any sort of magic.

"What," said Priscilla, "the fuck." She was about to storm the rest of the house; Agatha was gagged and couldn't answer, but her eyes widened, and she tipped her head toward the hallway.

Kevin rounded the corner from the bathroom. Priscilla gasped.

She *knew* Kevin was an asshole; she just had never imagined him clever enough to be a scheming one.

"Oopsie!" He skidded to a halt. "Well, I guess you caught me. Damn. I was just about to vanish the president with one of those lovely memory spells I've grown so fond of, and take her place forever, but this certainly throws a wrench in things."

He tapped the tips of his fingers together, and the door prodded her gently, but it was like being shoved by an overeager dog: irritating but not enough to tip her over. Kevin always did have weak magic. Priscilla snapped, raising a protective barrier between Kevin and Agatha.

"Why would you tell me all of that?" She snapped again, and the gloves from Agatha's hands materialized on his, along with the bindings. "Why are villains always monologuing?"

"Oh, come now," said Kevin, wriggling, but unable to escape. "Surely the bad guy gets to have some fun lines too. I'm smart enough to pull it off, and I should get to shout it from mountaintops at least once. It's been hard work convincing you all that I'm a dumb, pretty face." He grimaced, pulling his hands to no avail. "Fucking gloves." He glared at her. "As soon as I get these off, you're toast."

"Shut the fuck up, Kevin," said Agatha, wiping her mouth with her newly freed hand. And then, turning to Priscilla, "He knocked me out from behind, and when I came to, I was in the back of his car, tied up, gloves on, and unable to magic my way out of it."

"You really ought to be more careful about who you trust," said Kevin airily. "Just because I'm such a nice guy doesn't mean I'm actually a *nice guy*. Do you know how many so-called nice guys in history did heinously clever shit? Tons!" He smiled wide, and Priscilla absolutely hated how correct he was. It was too true that people were willing to give a seemingly nice guy, even an iffy guy with faint hints of niceness, the benefit of the doubt, the sort they would never afford even a genuinely nice woman.

"Do you want me to hex him so that his breath matches his intentions, always? The worse they are, the worse it will be?"

Agatha shook her head. She stood up, rubbing her arms where they had been restrained. "I am going to knock him over the head. It's not terribly enlightened of me, but what the hell, I need a bit of tit for tat."

"Be my guest," said Priscilla, crossing her arms, snapping the barrier down and smiling evilly. "We can sort him out with magic when you're done beating the shit out of him, as he so deserves." She readied her fingers to snap just in case.

With a windup that suggested this woman was no novice at throwing a punch (which Prissy made a mental note to ask her about), Agatha's fist connected with Kevin's face so hard that the crack of it reverberated through the cabin like a cartoon. Kevin swayed from the impact, stumbled a little, still tied, and then shuffled backward, a glint in his eye.

"You bitch," he growled, turning and running. He attempted to vault off the landing, falling headfirst instead.

"Oh my god," Prissy started, but when he hit the floor below, he shattered.

Her brain took a moment to catch up with what she was seeing, and she blinked several times to make sure that it was what it looked like.

It was unbelievable, but it was also inevitable. There were always consequences for attempting to steal immortality from the universe. And right now, those were clearly on display for both Priscilla and Agatha to see.

"Motherfucker," said Kevin's head. It lay two feet away from his body, which was twisted at an odd angle, each limb separated. His torso twitched, alone and limbless. His left leg had landed, from the knee down, by the kitchen table; his right wrist had fractured off, hand on the mantel, and his left arm, shoulder down, was on the sofa. His final foot sat where it had fallen, several inches away from the welcome mat that read SHOES OFF, WITCHES.

Just as Lex had promised, there was absolutely no blood.

She blinked for a moment, taking it in. Hearing about it was one thing, but seeing it was wild.

Agatha and Priscilla stood frozen a few seconds longer on the landing, until the arms and legs began to crawl toward the torso.

"Shit," said Priscilla, rushing down the stairs and grabbing for the hand on the mantel. Most important was Kevin couldn't tap those fingers from both hands together, Mr. Burns–style, to make magic. They were lucky that he needed two hands for magic; had he been a single-handed practitioner, they might have been in real trouble here. But as it was, Kevin was comically as impotent as such terrible men often are. Priscilla snapped, and the hand was in a mitten. She snapped again, and the mitten was sewn shut. Agatha did the same for his other hand, but when she set it down, it made a grotesque finger-walking beeline to drag itself toward its partner, so she was forced to put one in a wooden box, and the other in a rather heavy storage ottoman, which she sat on promptly to prevent any mishaps.

"This feels deeply unfair," said Kevin's head. "First the arson failed, and now the elixir. I did research, and none of it, not a single account, had anything about this kind of immortality side effect."

"Everything has side effects, Kevin." Priscilla smiled smugly. "And it sounds like you overestimated your research abilities, along with so many other things."

"It was in the fine print of the *Compendium of Forbidden Magics*, volume three, chapter fourteen," said Agatha matter-of-factly, as though rattling off the precise location of arcane information was something anyone ought to be able to do off the top of their head. Agatha was so fucking smart, and it was hot as hell.

Kevin sulked. Pretty men really could be so determinedly stupid. Priscilla crossed her arms. "Consider this the side effect of your incompetence, you absolute asshat."

"That's rich coming from a woman who can't stick to a fiancée or an assistant." He smirked, which was a bold move for a disembodied head.

Agatha rubbed her fingers together, and the gag from earlier was back in Kevin's mouth.

"That's better." She straightened up. "I've found I have no remaining patience for his bullshit."

Priscilla nodded and pulled out her phone. "I'll notify Otho, and you send the emergency summons?"

"Yes," said Agatha. "I'm sure people are going to be pissed to be called in again, but when they see that we've solved the elixir problem *and* the sabotage problem, I do hope they'll forgive us."

Prissy smiled at her. "We're pretty forgivable."

"Indeed," mused Agatha. "And, *chérie*, come what may with their response, at least we have each other."

CHAPTER 37

Agatha

The Council meeting began solemnly, pieces of Kevin spread out across the table but separated by the same impenetrable temporary barriers that they used for deliberation.

Xiomara Cohen stared at the head, possibly trying to decipher the words in whatever soundless diatribe Kevin undertook behind the partition. Agatha, for one, was grateful not to hear him. She'd had just about enough of her slimy assistant, now that she knew he wasn't just a little bit gross with his asking her out, but a lot disgusting with his knocking her out, kidnapping her, tampering with her memory, and stealing from the Council. The list could go on. Men were trash sometimes.

"I've never seen a thing like it," Xiomara murmured, flexing her hands and letting out a nervous breath. "It's absolutely horrifying, to be honest. There is a reason witches don't typically seek out immortality."

Albert Thistleworth was inspecting one of the partitions with the foot in it, holding his monocle out at different distances as though this might shed light on the grotesque severed foot, startlingly dry.

It was the lack of bodily fluid that disarmed her the most, that the pieces could have shattered off so neatly, but she supposed there was a reason the Fountain of Youth had been destroyed. And right now, that reason was clearly named Kevin. She shivered a little, glad that the elixir was gone, and the perpetrator caught.

"Remarkable," said Thistleworth. "I should like to attempt a demonstration on the larger leg." The curiosity in his voice was only slightly alarming, but she hated Kevin enough to push that thought aside. It was her job, as president, to allow for the proper function of research and science, and hadn't Kevin himself tried to dupe her into thinking research her only passion and pursuit?

"I move to allow it," said Otho, nodding grimly and adjusting one of his suspenders.

"I agree," said Agatha, for they did need to know more about the situation before they determined what was best to do about it. "So long as we are all present and the hands are kept imprisoned to prevent any magical escape."

"Here," said Mei, and that was enough to bring a demonstration to the floor, so Agatha rubbed her thumb across her fingers, and the barrier around the head and each of the feet dissipated.

"Council," said Kevin, comical in the way that the head lay on its left side, tilted slightly downward so that half his mouth was covered and his face was propped on the side of his nose. "I move to release me at once. This is inhumane treatment after my years of dedicated service to not one, but two Council presidents."

"Kevin," thundered Agatha. "Given the severity of the situation, including, specifically, that the list of crimes against said Council president includes arson, kidnapping, mind meddling, and attempted murder, I am, of course, going to deny your request for immediate release and insist we use gravedirt. Priscilla?" Kevin wouldn't be strong enough, with his piddly, weak magic that took two hands, to resist gravedirt.

"I'd be happy to do the honors." Priscilla reached into her pocket, snapped for the vial that Agatha now knew she kept handy at her desk, and sprinkled it on Kevin, smiling maliciously when a few specks landed in his ridiculously long eyelashes and he had to blink them out. "There."

"Very good," said Xiomara, nodding. "May I open the line of questioning?"

"Go ahead," said Agatha. She sat back, crossed her arms, and stared at Kevin with the unwavering hatred of a person who had suffered far too much indignity at the hands of this fool.

"Kevin Cross, did you conspire to kill the Council president and undermine the authority of the Council?" Xiomara's voice was clear.

"Yes," said the head, rolling its eyes. "But when you put it that way it sounds so serious. Really I acted in the best interest of the Council; once I took that elixir, I became not only immortal but unstoppable. I can't be killed."

Xiomara prodded at the head. "Does this hurt?"

Perhaps forgetting that it was separate from the rest of him, Kevin tried to shake his head, which in turn resulted in him being face down.

"Mphg butter," he mumbled, but that couldn't be what he'd meant, so Xiomara turned the head gingerly, picking it up and setting it down so the neck was on the table, the head facing her.

"Much better. I was saying, it feels much better than before. Even the shattering is like a mild tumble—a bit disorienting, but it doesn't hurt."

"Hmm," said Xiomara, crossing her arms. "Interesting. So you also admit to breaking into the Council's most valuable chambers and stealing the elixir."

"I should think that was obvious." The head sniffed. "Yes. I did that. Again, I think I did you all a favor. Now you don't have to deal with how to secure it and keep it safe. You're welcome for that weight off your shoulders." The head smiled in what was probably meant to be sympathy, but disconnected from a body, it came across quite sinister and macabre.

"No, just the more irritating task of securing you," said Agatha. "Fortunately, we got some advice from the devil Olexandre on that point."

Agatha rubbed the bridge of her nose. How had she ever sought him out as an assistant? How had she ever failed to vet him? She supposed she'd assumed that since he'd been fine with Evelyn, he'd be fine with her, and then he'd dazzled with his capacity for Council details—a skill that now seemed much more intentionally devious—and she'd gone from there. Organized or not, even as just a head, he was infuriating.

Albert, who had been prodding away at the longer piece of leg, cleared his throat.

"If pain is not an issue, in the interest of the proceedings being fully informed by the capabilities of the separated limbs, I vote we test to see what happens if we divide this leg into three, and then place two bits together." He looked up, his face serious. It was a morbid suggestion, but it did make sense. They couldn't properly secure the criminal without knowing the precise nature of his new form.

"Now you're just fucking around with my body," said Kevin crossly.

"In our defense, Kevin, you did try to kill me, steal from the Council, manipulate us all, and frame Councilwoman Hart." Agatha's voice was dripping with disdain, and her glare must have been, too, because Kevin looked away, breaking eye contact uncomfortably.

"Potato, potahto," said the head, and Agatha turned to Albert. "Go ahead, Councilman Thistleworth."

Thistleworth produced a long silver reflex hammer, the sort a doctor might use to check a knee. He muttered something, rubbed his hands together, and tapped swiftly in two places on the leg, which separated neatly into three.

"Did that hurt?" he asked Kevin, running a hand across his jaw and squinting, as though narrowed eyes might help him see something better.

"It was a tickle," said the head.

"Good." He gingerly picked up the bit of knee, and left the lower two portions lying where they were.

For a moment they were still, and then the foot rolled, back and forth, slower and then faster, until it worked up momentum to right itself and hop. It hopped promptly to the bit of calf, threw itself back together, and the pieces knitted into one as though they'd never been separated.

"Just as I suspected," muttered Albert. "Like the chainsaws, it cannot be destroyed, only separated, and if you leave the pieces close, they will reassemble." Agatha was suddenly extremely glad she had allowed the experimenting to proceed.

He snapped, and a partition arose around the leg.

"What do you recommend?" Agatha spoke to Albert, but Kevin's head responded instead.

"Release me, call it a day, and you'll never hear from me again?" Kevin sounded hopeful, and that made her question whether or not the obliviousness had been an act, because she couldn't think of a possible situation in which anyone here would agree to that as a solution.

This time it was Priscilla who snapped her fingers, and the partition arose around the head too. "Sorry," she offered, shrugging. "I couldn't take another minute of his bullshit."

"Fair enough," said Agatha, returning her attentions to Albert.

"I suggest," began Albert, "That we divide the offender into thirteen pieces, one for each Council member, and we each take separate magical measures to make sure that the bit we are responsible for is both contained and carefully labeled for generations to come so that they understand the danger. Like nuclear waste, we must assume that generations from now, someone could find this and not even have the same language or communication system we have. The bits of Kevin Cross must be labeled as carefully as anything destructive in the course of human history. Kevin simply isn't going anywhere, and we have a responsibility to ensure he doesn't do further damage."

"This sounds like a reasonable plan," said Agatha.

"I don't relish taking a bit of Kevin home," said Priscilla, making a face, "but Hart Manor is certainly equipped to restrain a bit of him in perpetuity. And I know many others here have similarly eclectic homes that could do likewise."

She was correct, of course. And those Council members who did not have such homes still certainly had the magic to make the storage of Kevin's parts safe.

"Council, take ten minutes to deliberate, and we vote," Agatha announced.

The vote was unanimous to divide and conquer Kevin, and soon Agatha found herself taking her own piece to the Council vaults.

She brought a clipping of the pothos with her, weaving her magic with all her might to intertwine the plant craft with the layers and layers of Council spells, put in place by coven after coven specifically so only Council employees could access them. Kevin's disembodied torso, with its stilled heart, was her task to store, so she rewired the highest security vault, the one at the back of the chambers, so that only a Council president could open it.

When she was done, she returned upstairs and found Priscilla waiting, Kevin's magically gloved and guarded right hand in tow.

"Would you do me the honor of helping me do away with one hand of the fool who attempted to hurt my beloved?"

Agatha smiled, taking the hand that wasn't holding, well, a hand. "With pleasure."

The hearse sputtered and shook a bit on the way to Hart Manor, whether because Priscilla needed to have it serviced, or because the magic of Kevin's hand was dangerous cargo, Agatha wasn't entirely sure. Maybe both.

"Come on," said Priscilla when they reached the front. "We'll go in through the family graveyard entrance."

Agatha frowned. "I never noticed a graveyard on the grounds. Is it far?"

Prissy shook her head. "Not in the way you think. It's far, but not away."

"Then where?"

The smile that snuck across Priscilla Hart's face was impish and delighted, and she pointed to her feet.

"Down. This way." Priscilla hurried around the house and toward the conservatory. Agatha thought for a moment that they would go in the entrance to the old greenhouse, but Priscilla turned instead to a prickly rosebush that grew to one side of it.

She snapped, and the bush pulled back, revealing a small stone plaque that looked like a gravestone, bearing only the script lettering "We feast eternally."

Tapping the stone in each corner, she snapped and produced a few small rocks, placing them carefully on the gravestone.

"Only a Hart witch can do this," she explained, snapping once more, and the plaque slid to the side, widening and revealing a stone staircase. Another snap and sconces lit the edge of it.

"What's past that?" asked Agatha, pointing at the landing that the stairs spiraled down to.

Prissy grinned, wicked again. "The slide."

They descended the stairs together.

"Typically, we go corpse first, but this calls for extreme caution, so I'll go first with Kevin's hand." She winked and hopped onto the smooth stone slide, slipping into the darkness with a yelp of glee.

It was a sign of the trust between them for sure that Agatha paused, counted to thirty in her head to avoid collision, and jumped feetfirst down a dark chute she'd never seen before.

The trip down was a terrifying delight, the carved stone so smooth she slid as though it were a waterslide, down, twirling, past a portion lit by some magic she didn't recognize, as though living shadows on the sides of the thing brightened it. She saw here that the reason the slide was so smooth was the shadows, running up and down the walls of it, and it must have been that shadow craft, too, that slowed her descent, dumping her gently on the floor of an epic mausoleum with such care that landing on more stone didn't even hurt.

"Welcome to the resting place of every Hart witch since the manor was first built hundreds of years ago."

Agatha looked around, and it was magnificent. To the right and left of the antechamber they stood in were carved shelves in the walls with plaques describing who or what they held, and stretching down in front of them was a long hallway, lit by the same strange magic.

"What now?" she asked.

"We go to the very core of Hart Manor, for storing the most dangerous things."

Priscilla gestured, and they walked down the hall for several minutes, spiraling deeper and farther, so much so that Agatha had to wonder just how big Hart Manor was underneath. Whatever magic lay here was generational, built by bone and blood of witches, by craft upon craft, shadow, plant, maybe even rarer specialties, like dream and transmutation. They passed a few doors, and then a few final resting places, which Priscilla explained were for Harts who had good reason to be kept away from others—powerful magic gone bad, or violations of family code.

Finally, they got to a safe that looked as old as time, wrought in iron.

Priscilla snapped, and it opened. Agatha caught a glimpse of a vial that looked a deadly shade of green, a pair of handcuffs that radiated the kind of evil that suggested they would kill the wearer or something worse, and a box that made a disturbing thumping sound.

"Don't touch anything or go in it," warned Priscilla. "The consequences for non-Harts are irreversible."

Agatha listened; she did not want to find out what those might be.

Prissy snapped her fingers. A canvas bag appeared under the Council-made glass containment box, fitting around the gloved hand and then shrinking. She snapped again, and another canvas fitted the box, locking together with belts and chains. A third time, and the entire box was in a small iron safe at the back of the larger one, which Priscilla inexplicably walked over to and locked herself, pressing a palm against it, and then snapping.

"He shouldn't be able to get out of that without the help of a Hart witch, and each one of us knows better than to mess with anything in the high-security vault."

"Good riddance to bad men," said Agatha, and Priscilla smiled, running a fingernail across her cheek.

"And a good life to us, honey." She closed the big safe, snapping, and took Agatha's hand.

"Come on," she said. "Let's go live the rest of our lives without having to worry about Kevin Cross throwing knives or fire at us."

"I'm not promising I won't throw either of those, though," said Agatha, smiling and squeezing her hand. "Just not at work. We're done with the pranking at work."

"Agreed," said Priscilla, smiling. "Only pranking of a more . . . intimate nature."

Agatha bit her lip at the thought of that.

Priscilla stopped and pushed her against the cold stone wall of the hallway.

"I think I'm rubbing off on you," she whispered, skating her lips across Agatha's jawline.

"*Chérie*," Agatha murmured, "I hope you always rub off on me." She grabbed Priscilla by the lapels and pulled her in for a proper kiss.

CHAPTER 38

Agatha

Six Months Later

The decision to appoint Otho as official vice president, a role that hadn't been filled in decades after restructuring in the eighties, was approved unanimously by the Council, along with the motion that all Council members, including the Council president, take a minimum of four weeks of vacation time every year, to be scheduled and arranged as to not disrupt magical proceedings or any sort of Council matters that required a full session and vote.

And with a vice president in place, it became easier for Agatha to actually unwind, something she'd learned when she took a full week off, no Council business whatsoever, with Priscilla after they'd dealt with that dreadful Kevin business. She'd been working hard with Connie on the trails and tourism, and it had been a productive but exhausting half of a year.

It was time to take two weeks off the grid with her absolute favorite person.

"I can bring Uncle Otho the reports on the community garden," said Nancy. Since Kevin's departure, Nancy Ashbrooke had been promoted to official assistant to the president and vice president, and it turned out that she was twice as skilled as Kevin, with half the effort and none of the pesky immortality.

"Thank you," said Agatha, handing her the thick folder and then rubbing her thumb against her fingers to tweak the organization of it one last time. "I appreciate you."

A rap on the door drew her eyes, though she could have known without looking that it was Priscilla Hart who stood there, leaning against the doorway, all killer cheekbones and black satin suit.

"It's time to go, Agatha." Priscilla's smile spread crooked across her face, and she winked. "I've got a glamping cabin and a bottle of champagne with your name on it."

Agatha stood up, pushed in her desk chair, and grabbed her bag.

"There's literally nothing in the world I want more," she said.

"Nothing, honey?" Priscilla smirked.

Agatha laughed.

"Well," she said. "I can think of a few other things, I guess."

"Yes." Priscilla snaked an arm around her as they walked out together, slowly, down the hall. "I can too."

The End

Acknowledgments

This book belongs to my friends, the ones who have weathered too many phone calls, voice notes, and messages. Without you all, I don't know how I could have survived this season of my life. Thank you. This is by no means an exclusive list so if I have left you off, please take it as a sign of the chaos of my life and not any lack of love for you.

Alison, my beloved bringer of turtle facts. Your friendship is a constant I can count on at my best moments, my worst moments, and everything in between. I love you. To Kristi, bestie, not even the Atlantic has dulled our love. Our friendship is 4,000 miles strong. That would be 84,480,000 bagel thins apart. And yet here we are, still.

To my powerful girl group: Zoe, Alison, Missy, and Winnie. I just feel like our intention setting makes us Huntrix, safeguarding the Honmoon with the woven fabric of our collective magic.

To Jordan, for holding space for my worst fears and spirals and for always, always loving me through it, calling me in and out, and reminding me that even in a cruel world, there are people we can count on. You are magic on the page and in real life.

For DeAndra, my friend, I want to stay openhearted and I also want to stay fierce in my defense of people who need it most, and your balance of these two things in your writing and in your teaching gives me hope.

To Faith, my fellow teacher and author, my gosh you are a shining light in my life, and I cannot wait for the next book. You are a ray of joy, and I love you AND YOUR CHICKENS so much. Now the chickens are going to be in every acknowledgment. Your books deserve everything, and so do you. Keep writing.

To Lauren, who showed up with flowers the day of my debut,

and has been my friend through our teaching careers, our brief podcasting stint, and now at work. You're a role model.

To Megan, whose books are as beautiful as her friendship, and whose sage advice and kind words have kept me grounded. You're wonderful. Thank you for listening to way too much water bottle discussion for this book. RIP the water bottle scene, may it have a special place in your heart now that it's gone.

To Dallas, a fantastic writer and an empathetic friend. You remain as dear to me as *Empire Records*, always. I knew we were leveling up the friendship when I got into your car and *Ego Death at a Bachelorette Party* was playing. And to Mallory and Maria, whose skill knows no bounds, and whose kindness is also unlimited. I love you both and your friendship. One day we will make it to Disneyland together.

To Brigid and Kami, the best in-person writing partners, and the most loyal and unwavering friends for career and personal advice. I love you both so very much, and I appreciate your guidance and wisdom. Thank you for being there for some of the most exciting publishing moments and some of the lowest personal moments.

To the Hell chat. Thank you so much for always supporting me. To every group and Discord I am in that cheers authors on enthusiastically and lends help and consolation as needed. To every author who has encouraged me, or blurbed me, or listened when I was struggling, I appreciate you.

Thank you to my sister Abi, who has held more than her share of my stresses and sadness this year. Abi, I hope you know I can hold more than my share of yours anytime you need it. I also LOVE your determination not to let the misogynists of the sportsball world stop you from proving you're smarter, better, AND stronger than they are. Thank you to my sister Vera, who fights for her patients and who works tirelessly against a health care system designed to often fail its most vulnerable population. Your compassion is so evident in your care for your family too. To Ivana, who comes as a package deal with Vera. You're extraordinary.

To my cousin Lucy, for listening, and for existing in the world and sending me things like vacuum evaluations and all the exact right videos for my sense of humor. To my cousin Sam, across the ocean. To my grandmother, whose memory is a blessing, always. And to my grandfather. I can't get over that some graveyards bury people one over the other. That feels perfect for you both. That's the type of love we all deserve. To my Aunt Molly and Uncle Rick, for showing up for me during my childhood, and now again when things are rocky as an adult. To my cousins across the Atlantic, especially Stephanie and Lisa. I am so happy to have you in my family. To my dad, for betting me that I couldn't read *War and Peace* in the sixth grade. That spawned both a love of eclectic reading and love of doing things just to prove people wrong.

To Gail Carson Levine, who I don't know personally, but whose book *Ella Enchanted* was the very first book I bought myself from a Scholastic book fair. The whimsy and magic of that book have never left me. I hold on to it when things get tough. Thank you for that. If I listed every author I felt that way about, I'd have an entire book, so to every author whose books I have read and cherished, thank you.

To my children, sorry that picking up my first book meant realizing just how many curse words Mom writes. There is a time and a place for everything, don't curse in school, don't read the books until you're much older, and know that I support you both reading and writing and following all of your dreams, no matter what profession or hobby they might take you to. I love you both, and my home is where you are. I will catch you always, and I will be a soft place to land if you need it. You will never be too much or not enough for me, and I hope that if you look for love in your life, you remember that you deserve someone who cherishes you, and that you are more than the mistakes of those who came before you.

To my niece and nephew, I love you both, and I hope you never lose your respective fire and charm. To Matt and Liz, for the unconditional and beautiful way you love my children.

They are lucky to have you in their lives. Especially Liz, who will NEVER be nothing to me.

To Erin, and Rob, and Matt, and Annemarie, for being friends to every person in my family who needs it, always, especially the littlest ones. Your unwavering friendship to every Ruoff has saved each one of us, I am sure. I appreciate you all. To all of the children too young to have an acknowledgment by name in an adult romance book—hang on, kids! I love you all so much, and your time is coming.

Thank you to Rachel, and all the instructors whose barre classes are so tough (complimentary). I can feel them for a week, and yet exactly the thing I need when it's time to turn my brain off.

To my agent, Jess, who has helped me navigate the most difficult year of my professional (and personal) life and done so with the sharp business sense and thoughtful understanding that I need. Your keen editorial eye and your deep well of compassion are truly extraordinary. I am so grateful for you and the way you have championed my books and my career.

To Mel and Elizabeth, for the edits that made this book the best version of itself. Working with you two has been such an absolute joy. You're both made of the kind of magic I needed to bring the magic of Hallowcross alive on the page. Thank you so much for seeing Agatha and Priscilla (and Vickie and Az before them!) and guiding them, and me, to what they needed.

To my marketing and publicity team, and to my designer and to my illustrator Camila Gray, for once again creating a cover more beautiful than my wildest dreams. To copy editors and production managers and the entire team at Atria who guided this book into its final form: thank you, from the bottom of my heart.

And for you, my dear reader, particularly if you have watched your life and your faith in humanity burn down to the ground in front of you, and arisen out of the ashes, a phoenix, unwilling to give up out of sheer spite. I see you. Keep fighting. Rage and love can sustain you.

About the Author

Audrey Goldberg Ruoff is the author of *Hopelessly Teavoted* and a former high school English and journalism teacher who currently teaches middle school ELA with the enthusiasm of Valerie Frizzle, but for secondary education. She lives in a suburb of Washington, DC, with her family, a scrappy but loyal little dog, and a witchy black cat. Visit audreygoldbergwrites.com and follow her @AudreyGoldbergRuoff on Instagram.

ATRIA BOOKS, an imprint of Simon & Schuster, fosters an open environment where ideas flourish, bestselling authors soar to new heights, and tomorrow's finest voices are discovered and nurtured. Since its launch in 2002, Atria has published hundreds of bestsellers and extraordinary books, which would not have been possible without the invaluable support and expertise of its team and publishing partners. Thank you to the Atria Books colleagues who collaborated on *Vengefully Matched* as well as to the hundreds of professionals in the Simon & Schuster advertising, audio, communications, design, ebook, finance, human resources, legal, marketing, operations, production, sales, supply chain, subsidiary rights, and warehouse departments who help Atria bring great books to light.

EDITORIAL
Elizabeth Hitti Musicant
Melanie Iglesias Pérez

JACKET DESIGN
Kelli McAdams
James Iacobelli

MARKETING
Heaven Jenkins

MANAGING EDITORIAL
Paige Lytle
Shelby Pumphrey
Sofia Echeverry
Abby Borchers

PRODUCTION
Annette Pagliaro Sweeney
Allison Har-zvi
Janet Robbins Rosenberg
Esther Paradelo

PUBLICITY
Camila Araujo

PUBLISHING OFFICE
Dana Trocker
Suzanne Donahue
Abby Velasco

SUBSIDIARY RIGHTS
Nicole Bond
Sara Bowne
Rebecca Justiniano